DUSK

WARRIOR SERIES

Also by Melanie P. Smith

DUSK

Warrior Series

Book One

---

by:
Melanie P. Smith

MPSmith Publishing

Dedication:

This book is dedicated to my loving husband;

My own personal Warrior.

Without his love and encouragement,

The world would never have known this story

Chapter One

Alex stared out the side window of the taxi cab, subconsciously listening to the thump thump of the tires as they traveled across the bridge. The drizzle of rain falling as she left the airport had turned into a downpour. Somehow, that seemed appropriate. She'd been operating on autopilot, going through the motions but not really aware of her surroundings, since she got the call from her stepbrother Thomas. It was all so surreal. Her stepfather, the only father she'd ever known, was dying.

So many memories flashed through her mind. She hadn't known her biological father. She refused to refer to him as her "real" father as many did because Luke had been her father since she was seven. In every sense of the word Luke was her real father. Something had just clicked the moment they met. It was easy for her to understand why her mother fell so hard and fast for the man. Alex never felt like an unwanted addition, or a burden he had to

Dusk

carry to be with her mother. Luke accepted and loved Alex from the beginning and she loved him with all her heart. How was she going to function without him? He was her rock, the one steady aspect of her life, and he was dying. How had this happened? Thomas said he had been attacked in an alley after leaving the office. But who would attack Luke? He often worked on big, top secret projects. Had a competitor attacked him? A random mugging? Thomas had been so vague, almost secretive. He was probably just in shock. She certainly was. He was in shock and would fill her in later.

Lucius "Luke" Deveraux was a powerful man, one of the wealthiest men in the nation. So many people depended on him. He wasn't just head of Deveraux Industries, he was involved in every aspect of the company. He was intimately involved with each new project. With this power came responsibility. How many times had Luke lectured her on safety and responsibility? He wasn't a careless man. He wasn't a vulnerable man. How had he been injured in an alley of all places? It just didn't make any sense.

Alex suddenly realized the taxi was no longer moving. The driver had exited the car. She looked up to see the hospital looming in the darkness. She took a deep breath and opened the door. The driver had already retrieved her bag from the trunk and was standing under the awning next to the hospital entrance. She collected her luggage, paid the driver and walked through the automatic door. There was a group of reporters hovering at the reception desk. Alex was grateful Thomas had provided Luke's room number. The last thing she wanted to deal with was a mob of reporters. Word was obviously out about Luke Deveraux. She quickly slipped into an open elevator and closed the door. Alex was stopped by a nurse as she approached Luke's room. After providing her name and relationship, the nurse finally allowed her to enter. The woman was annoying, but Alex was grateful for the security.

The lights were dim and Luke was quiet and still. There were so many machines hooked up to him and his body was battered and bruised. Alex had never seen her father look so fragile. She quickly blinked back the tears forming in her eyes. She had to be strong. She could fall apart later. Right now, she needed this time with her father. Alex silently walked across the room to a chair positioned next to the bed. Luke hadn't even stirred. She sat down and gently picked up his hand. Again, she had to blink back tears, but she was determined to get through this without crying. She felt Luke squeeze her hand and looked up to see he was watching her. He was giving her comfort, how typical. She gave him what she knew was a pitiful smile and leaned over to kiss him softly on the cheek. Luke reached up and gently brushed her cheekbone with the tip of his thumb. "Hi princess," he whispered. "I'm glad you were able to get here. I've missed you terribly."

Alex swallowed the lump in her throat. "I've missed you, too. I thought about you and Thomas every day. I didn't think I was ready to come home yet. Now, I wish I had never left."

"You needed to get away for a while. We understood. Don't ever regret doing what you needed to do to heal. If I could have run away for a while, I would have. Unfortunately, I had to stay and run the company." Luke paused and looked out the window. "There are so many things you're going to need to know now. Things I should have talked to you about sooner, but I always thought there was plenty of time." His voice was just a whisper now. He sounded so weak.

"Don't talk," Alex whispered. "You need your rest."

Dusk

Luke looked back to Alex. "There's no time for rest. Life is going to change for you. My little princess..." He reached up and brushed a tear away. Alex hadn't realized she was crying. "I know you'll be strong and brave. You're going to have to be, your very life depends on it. Don't get too angry with Thomas. I know you think your overprotective father has rubbed off on your older brother, but we mean well. There are so many things you don't know about our lives. I'm afraid I have failed you. I haven't prepared you for what's coming."

Just then Alex noticed movement in the doorway and Thomas walked in. Over the past year, Thomas had changed a lot. Alex couldn't believe how strong and masculine he had become. He was always good looking, he was always stout, but now he was a force to be reckoned with. He was the spitting image of his father. Thomas crouched down and took her into his arms. "He's been holding on for you," he said as he leaned in and kissed her. "I don't think he has much time left." He turned to his father as he straightened. "I don't want to hear any more about failures from you. You're the last one that should be lamenting over what you did or didn't do. What you did was love and protect your family. I talked to Jake by the way. He told me the real story, filled in all the holes. He explained the things you left out. You should have let me go with you."

Luke winced. "I told him to keep his trap shut about that. Why am I not surprised? Jake never could keep anything from you kids. Thomas, we both know you have a temper. Promise me you'll keep it in check. You're going to need your wits about you. No revenge, that's what got me into trouble. Please think with your mind and heart, not with your temper." The last words were almost a croak. Luke was so weak, but he insisted on pushing himself.

4

Thomas walked to the other side of the bed and took his father's hand. "Dad, you're a great father and a great man. You've taught us well. Don't worry about me or Alex. We'll be fine. We know how to protect ourselves and we have the others. Everything is going to be okay, I promise." He reached up and brushed back his father's hair, then kissed him on the cheek. "Rest now, stop holding on for us and say hello to Marlena. I'm sure she's anxious to see you again."

At the mention of her mother's name Alex shot a look at Thomas. He studied her for a long moment, his eyes never leaving hers. He seemed to be telling her to say goodbye. Alex looked down at Luke, fragile, breathing in gasps. He too was watching her, needing her to confirm she was going to be okay. She leaned down and hugged her father tightly. "I love you so much!" She cried. So much for keeping it together until she left. Tears rolled down her cheeks one after the other. "You have always been my hero. You always will be. And just for the record you were never a failure at anything, especially a father. Thomas is right. It's time for you to rest. Tell mama I miss her. It's good to know that soon you'll have that special spark back in your eyes. The one that's been missing since mama passed away. I know you two will be together again. At least that gives me comfort."

Luke's hand tightened around hers and Thomas'. "My wonderful, special kids. You both make me proud. I pray you're strong enough to weather the coming storm. Take care of each other. I love you both so much." The last came out as a croak. Luke closed his eyes and his hands went limp. Alex fell on top of Luke's chest and wept. She looked up and saw that tears were running down Thomas' face as well. The machines started beeping and nurses quickly entered the room pushing them aside. Alex walked

Dusk

over to Thomas and collapsed into his arms. They walked out of the hospital in silence, leaning on each other for strength.

Chapter Two

As they walked through the doors of the big house, Alex struggled to keep herself together. Nothing had really changed since she'd left. The spacious foyer was as elaborate as always, sparkling marble floors led to the grand staircase. Thomas set Alex's bag on the floor and headed for the library.

"I need a drink, how about you?" he asked.

Alex wasn't up for conversation. All she wanted to do was get to her room and fall apart. "I think I'll go straight up and have a hot bath and a good cry," she replied.

Thomas stopped in the doorway to the library. He looked over his shoulder at Alex and noticed how pale and worn out she looked. He had a lot of things he needed to talk to her about, but it could wait. "Don't worry about your luggage. I'll take it to your room. Marta took care of everything. She's been looking forward to seeing you again since I told her you were coming. I'm sure everything is perfect as usual. If you don't feel up to company tonight, just go straight to bed after your bath. I'll see you in the morning." He turned back with a faint smile, walked to her and kissed her on the forehead. "Goodnight Alex. The circumstances suck, but I really am glad you're back. We've all missed you around here."

Alex nodded and sprinted up the stairs. Once in her room the tears began to fall. She walked slowly to the adjourning bathroom and began to fill the tub. As she listened to the hot water flowing, she walked around the room lighting candles. Then she locked the door and shut off the light.

Slipping slowly into the tub, she began to think of her life with Luke, Thomas and her mother. Life in this house. She really had always felt like a princess. She could admit it. She was spoiled and protected. Most of all, she was loved. Her parents, and even her brother, had made sure every day of her life was happy and carefree. She closed her eyes and let the tears flow.

Alex woke slowly the next morning. She still felt groggy and a little depressed. The thought of getting up and trying to get through the day was a bit overwhelming. She needed coffee. Plenty of caffeine and maybe she could stay busy enough to keep the depression at bay.

She slowly walked into the bathroom. One look in the mirror and Alex realized it would take more than coffee to make her look human again. She'd definitely had a rough night and it showed. Once she slipped into the hot bath, she'd stopped fighting her emotions. The more she thought about the old days, the more the tears flowed. She knew she had been lucky. She'd grown up with loving parents who had the means to give her a great life. They had all been so happy once. Nothing was ever going to be the same again. She was essentially an orphan. Her parents were gone. True, she still had Thomas and she was grateful for him. But she had lost both her parents in such a short time. She supposed that at any age that left a hole, an empty space that could never be filled. Her parents would never be there for her again.

She wasn't anxious to get married or anything, what a terrifying thought. Her and relationships did not mix well. However, last night she realized she would have no one on that special day. The thought made her depressed. No mother to fuss over her, no father to give her away. Enough Alex, she thought. Keep walking this path and you're going to be a basket case for months. You have things to do. First coffee, then a shower.

Once she felt fresh she could get to work on funeral arrangements. Luke had so many friends, employees, acquaintances as well as the media and politicians. Planning his funeral was going to be monumental. It had to be perfect. She wanted to honor the man who meant so much to so many people. Once that was done, she could focus on having Thomas bring her up to speed on company business. The key was to stay busy, little by little she would start to heal.

One thing about Luke, he always prepared for the future. All their lives her father had insisted that she and Thomas learn the company inside and out. She was a little behind after being gone the past year, but Luke had sent her regular updates on the big issues. Alex was sure she would only need a quick review. While she was getting up to speed on the company, she could arrange for a service to clean out her small apartment in Florence. She loved Italy, but this was home. She always knew she'd come back to New York eventually. For the past couple months she'd been struggling with the decision almost daily. Not coming back sooner was something she would regret for the rest of her life. If only she'd come home two months ago when she first considered it, she could have spent that time with Luke.

Alex blinked back tears and brushed her strawberry blond hair into a ponytail. That was going to have to do for now. Hopefully Marta had the coffee on. She had to smile. She was looking forward to seeing Marta again. She was only fifteen years older than Alex, but Marta had been part of the family for so long she almost felt like a second mother to her, or a favorite aunt. Alex realized she wasn't really alone. She'd been feeling lonely and isolated ever since that awful moment Luke passed away last night. She still had family, maybe not a conventional family but family just the same. She left her room and headed for the kitchen.

As she neared the bottom of the stairs, Alex heard voices coming from the library. Thomas must be up already. It was a bit early for visitors, but word must be out about her father. She wondered who would stop by this early in the morning just to give condolences. She stepped into the doorway and stopped. She had never seen the three huge men sitting around the fire with Thomas before. They were all as masculine and buff as Thomas. What was this, the steroid club for men? One of them, an extremely handsome man, was sitting in Luke's favorite chair. Seeing him there gave her heart a short stab of pain. As far as she knew no one had ever sat in that chair but Luke. How dare he come into their home and sit in her father's chair? Before she could react, she smelled coffee and her attention turned to the small table. Good, there was an empty cup. She was about to walk over and help herself when she realized all conversation had stopped. The men were focused on her.

Thomas stood up and walked over to Alex. He gave her a big hug and a kiss on the top of her head. "How are you this morning?" He cupped her chin and lifted slightly so she was looking directly into his eyes. She was so pale. Not exactly the image he wanted to present the first time she met the other warriors. They would probably think her weak, which of course was not the case. He had never met any woman as strong as Alex, with the exception of Marlena of course. She was so much like her mother. He would just have to help her convey that strength to his brothers. Their survival would depend on it.

"A little tired, but otherwise okay. Apparently we have guests. Friends of yours?" Alex asked.

"Oh, yes." Thomas replied and taking her arm he guided her toward the big man sitting in Luke's chair. "Dimitri, I would like you to meet my sister, Alex. Alex, this is Dimitri."

So, she wasn't going to get a clue who these men were from Thomas. That's okay. She could figure it out on her own. She looked into Dimitri's eyes and was startled to see…what? Resentment? Disgust? Disappointment? Why did this man, a man she had never met before, look at her with such contempt? Especially the morning after her father's death. Okay, so she wasn't looking her best - far from it. But what gave him the right to look at her like she was a step above pond scum. Anger flared in her and she went on the defensive. She didn't know this man and didn't care what he thought of her. So he didn't like her, she didn't like him either. She ignored the hand he held out to her. With a quick hello, she brushed him off and turned to the other two men in the room. "And who are these two handsome men? Thomas, it seems your taste in friends has vastly improved in my absence. With a few exceptions, that is," she said as she glanced back at Dimitri. If possible, it looked like his scowl had deepened.

One of the men smirked under his hand then smiled at her brightly. The other one looked shocked. She walked toward the two men and held out her hand. Thomas was by her side in an instant. Out of the corner of her eye, she saw him give Dimitri an exasperated look. Maybe she was over reacting, but nobody treated her that way. Certainly not in her own home. Well, sort of her home, once she moved back in. Thomas introduced the man on the right, the one with the charming smile, as Dante and the other man as Nicholas.

"It's a pleasure to meet you both," Alex said with a smile.

Each man shook her hand and said hello.

"Now, if you don't mind sharing, I'm dying for a cup of that coffee. Then, I'll leave you to discuss manly things. I have a lot to do this morning." She walked over to the table and prepared herself a cup of coffee. "Thomas?" Alex said as she glanced over her shoulder. "Do you know where Marta is? I can't wait to see her!"

She noticed this Dimitri guy was still glaring at her. What was his deal? So he didn't like her. That was no excuse for his rudeness. Thomas didn't like some of her friends either but he had never been so blatantly rude to any of them. He did get a little annoyed with Jennifer, especially when she attempted to hit on him. Alex enjoyed watching Thomas try to discourage Jennifer while at the same time play the perfect host; mothers doing of course. A gentleman was never rude to a lady. Clearly Dimitri was no gentleman.

"Later," she said casually to Thomas with a little wave as she walked out the door.

"What was that about?" Thomas demanded once he could no longer hear Alex's footsteps in the hall. He glared at Dimitri demanding an answer.

"I don't know what you're talking about," Dimitri thundered back. "As enlightening as that was, we don't have time to discuss your sister or her attitude right now. There are more pressing concerns at the moment." Dimitri was baffled and annoyed. When Alex walked into the room his worst fears had been realized. They were counting on this pale, weak woman to give the appearance of strength and solidarity? They were doomed. Yet, she stirred something inside of him. Something he had never felt before. He instantly felt attracted to her. At the same time he wanted to protect her. A spoiled, weak brat. He couldn't understand why. Yes, she was elegant and poised. Her big blue eyes were striking and so deep you could get lost in them. With a couple pounds and a little coloring in her face she'd be a knockout. But, Dimitri had met beautiful women before. Hell, he had beautiful women fall all over him constantly. So what was it about this woman that pulled at him? It was obvious she was weak, pampered and sheltered. No way could he be attracted to her. It had just been too long since he'd been with a woman, that's all. He'd focused all his time on keeping the community safe and had neglected his other needs. Any woman would have conjured these feelings - of what? Lust?

Dimitri was shocked by his initial reaction to Alex. It took him a moment to recover. When he did, he put on his poker face and attempted a friendly greeting. That's when she brushed him off like a pesky gnat and turned her attention to Dante and Nicholas. Nobody had ever treated him in such a manner. Being Luke and Marlena's daughter didn't give her the right to disrespect him. He wouldn't tolerate it. He was about to put her in her place when she said goodbye with a little wave and walked out the door. Dimitri was left to brood about the whole situation. She was weak and spoiled. She was endangering all of them. They were going to have to hide her away as long as possible. If she exhibited the same condescending, flippant attitude towards the council members...

Someone cleared their throat. "Dimitri, care to join the conversation? Or are we keeping you from something more important?" Dante asked.

Dimitri looked up, suddenly aware he had missed something. He would deal with Alex later. Right now they had to come up with a plan and it better be a good one.

* * * *

Alex walked into the kitchen in search of Marta. She found her standing in front of the kitchen sink washing breakfast dishes. She quietly walked up behind the sweet, slightly rounded woman and put her arms around her waist. "Morning Marta," Alex whispered in her ear.

Marta squealed, turned around and grabbed Alex into a big bear hug. "Alex!" Marta exclaimed. "We've all missed you so much! It's just not the same around here without you. Sit down and tell me all about Italy. Then, I'll catch you up on what's been going on around here."

Hours later, Alex sat in her old office trying to get a jump on organizing Luke's funeral. Try as she might, she couldn't keep her mind on the task. Her thoughts kept going back to Dimitri. When she first saw him, she was shocked at her instant attraction. The man was definitely hot! Even sitting down she could see what a small waist and broad shoulders he had. Then there was all that dark hair and deep chocolate eyes. She was a sucker for the tall, dark and handsome type. He put off an air of masculinity Alex had never experienced before. Seeing him in Luke's chair had thrown her, but in some ways he seemed to belong there. He had the same confidence about him that Luke always portrayed. It was hard to put a finger on it exactly. There was just something about him that demanded respect. Yet, for some reason he had such contempt for her. She couldn't help throwing his macho ego back in his face and dismissing him like he was nothing special. Yet, she had a feeling there was something special about him. The reaction from the other men when she so blatantly ignored him was telling. The other three men clearly respected Dimitri.

Maybe she had been a little rude herself. She did feel guilty about her behavior. She knew if her mother was still around she'd be disappointed. Dimitri's attitude had gotten under her skin and she reacted. But regardless of how this man treated her, he was still a guest in their home. She should have been more cordial and at least shook the man's hand when he offered it. But Alex didn't want to make physical contact with Dimitri. The thought scared her. The man was sexy and infuriating all at once. She couldn't decide if she wanted to kiss him or punch him. Oh well, chances were slim that she'd see him again. If she did it would only be in passing, right? Dimitri was Thomas' friend, but surely they didn't spend a lot of time at the house. They would meet and go clubbing or hang out over dinner or drinks or something. Alex wouldn't have to deal with the man, or the conflicting feelings she had for him. She would just avoid Dimitri as much as possible. She took a deep breath and focused once again on funeral preparations.

A few hours later, Alex walked into the library to find Thomas sitting behind Luke's old antique desk. It was strange to see him

15

there but at the same time, it seemed right. He was concentrating on some paperwork and didn't notice her until she was directly in front of him.

"You look tired," Alex said.

Thomas looked up, "No more than you, I suppose."

"What are you working on?" Alex asked.

"Just finalizing a few things that can't wait until after the funeral. I thought we'd close down for a couple days. It's going to be hard on the employees. Not as hard as it is for us, but dad had a lot of friends, the employees liked him." Thomas looked away.

"I was thinking along the same lines. I know I've been away for a year and need to be brought up to speed. But I'm almost as familiar with the company as you are. I want to help, Thomas. It's a family business. You don't have to do this alone. We're in it together."

Thomas rose and walked over to the small bar to pour himself a brandy. "Want anything?" he asked.

"Maybe a glass of wine if there's something open," Alex replied.

Thomas handed her a glass, then walked over and sat by the fire. "Alex, there are some things we need to talk about. I'm not really sure where to start."

Alex walked over and sat on the couch directly across from him. "I know. I've been putting it off, but there were some things dad said that didn't make sense to me. I'm not stupid, I gather we have a few family secrets. Why did you and dad try to shelter me from them? I'm not a fragile weakling that needs to be protected. I'd like an explanation."

Thomas took a sip of his brandy and studied her for a long moment. "Look, Alex. If I tell you what's going on, you're going to have to keep an open mind. For the record, it wasn't only me and dad that kept secrets from you. Marlena sheltered you just as much as we did, sometimes more. She was just less obvious. I know you think dad and I are just macho, chauvinistic men. Maybe we are, but we have our reasons. Can you listen to what I have to tell you with an open mind?"

Alex studied Thomas for a long moment. He looked weary of what he had to tell her. Maybe a little vulnerable and definitely apprehensive. What did he mean her mother kept secrets from her? "Okay, I'll keep an open mind, but before we get into the family stuff, who were those guys you had here this morning? Why did that Dimitri guy dislike me so much? He doesn't even know me."

Thomas took a deep breath. "I don't think Dimitri dislikes you. He's just worried and concerned about the future. Dad was the leader of an organization. Now that dad's gone, Dimitri has to take over as leader. He has some pretty big shoes to fill and there are a few complications. A big one has to do with you."

"Me? What do I have to do with some macho male organization?" Alex asked.

"Let me start with the family stuff and then we'll get into the rest, okay?" Thomas asked.

Alex was sure she wouldn't like what Thomas had to tell her, but she wasn't going to hide from anything pertaining to her family. She could keep an open mind, to a point, and see what Thomas had to say. After she heard him out, she would decide what to believe and what to question. "Go ahead," Alex said as she settled deeper into the couch. "Spill all the horrid family secrets. I can take it."

"I'm not so sure you can, especially right now. But, Marlena and dad kept putting it off and now it's too late. Neither one of them got the chance to talk to you. You need to know what's going on now. So unfortunately, I have to explain it to you."

"Thomas, stop being so melodramatic. Whatever it is, I can take it. You're acting like we're aliens sent here from mars to gather intelligence and report back to the mother ship. How bad can it be, really? Spit it out," Alex pressed.

"Okay, the first thing I have for you is sort of a diary that Marlena left you. She's much better at explaining her part in all this than I am. No matter how you feel about me or what I tell you tonight, please read the information your mother left for you. It's important!" Thomas urged.

"Mom left a diary for me? And you and Luke kept it from me after her death? How could you do that?" Alex was outraged. She'd struggled every day over the past year, trying to deal with the loss of her mother. All along Luke had a book of writings her mother left for her. He just never bothered to give them to her. She felt betrayed. She was angry at Luke, but also at Thomas for not telling her about it.

"Simmer down Alex. It's not like we planned to hide it from you. Immediately after the funeral you announced you were leaving for a while. You had already packed. You just said a quick goodbye as you walked out the door headed for Italy. When exactly was dad supposed to talk to you about anything?"

"He could have given the book to me and let me take it to Italy when I left," Alex retorted.

"No, he couldn't. The things in that book are going to shake you. It's not information to be taken lightly and certainly not something you could have dealt with on your own. You're going to have questions. You're going to be confused. You probably aren't going to believe what your mother has written for you or what I am going to tell you tonight. Dad planned on having this discussion with you once you returned home. He would have been much better at it than I am, but he didn't get the chance. Now you're stuck with me. Sorry about that. I hope I don't mess it up too bad. I didn't deal with a lot of this as well as I should have. I hope you do better than I did because we don't have much time here."

"I'm not following you. Stop talking around whatever it is you have to tell me. Just start at the beginning. If I have questions, I'll ask. There has to be a beginning, right?"

"First, here's the book from Marlena. Please promise me, before I tell you anything, that you will keep that book safe. Also, no matter what, you'll read through it before you make any judgments," Thomas pled.

"My mother left me this book. Of course I'll keep it safe and secure. And, of course I'll read it. It will be like she's talking to me again. That's something I've wished for every day during the past year. No matter what, I'll cherish the writings my mother left me."

"Okay, here we go. A really long time ago there was a community of beings."

"Beings?" Alex interrupted.

Dusk

"For now I'm calling them beings. Please just let me get through this first part. I think it's going to be the hardest part for you to accept," Thomas replied.

"Okay. Go ahead," Alex relented.

"So there was a community of beings. They originated from a species that didn't typically get along. It was unusual to have an entire community living together."

"Okay, like a tribe?" Alex asked.

"Sort of. It started with three brothers and their families. As the families grew, they stayed together. There was also this outside group of beings, a different species that hunted members of this community. They were...let's say cannibalistic," Thomas continued.

"Thomas, I'm not sure what this has to do with our family. As far as I know we aren't cannibals. You're over thinking it. Instead of trying to soften the blow for me by making up a story, just spit it out," Alex said. She was starting to get frustrated with Thomas.

"Okay, let me try again. But don't laugh, just hear me out. There was a community of beings that called themselves fae."

"Like fairies?" Alex asked.

"Yes," Thomas answered.

"Okay," she laughed.

"So the fae are vain people but they are also mighty fighters. They're just not capable of surviving in a large community for extended periods of time. Jealousy and ego get in the way. The men begin to fight over the women, the women fight with the other women and large numbers are killed in the fighting. So it was extremely rare for this family of fae to stay together, especially for several generations," he continued.

Thomas looked up and saw a slightly amused and somewhat confused look on Alex's face. He was blowing it, he knew it, but he just had to get through this and then figure out how to help her believe the impossible later. Alex raised one eyebrow and Thomas continued.

"The family stayed together mainly for protection. The second group, the ones I called Cannibals before, were actually what might be referred to as vampires."

Alex couldn't help it, she snorted out a laugh and then covered her mouth. She tried to stop smiling when Thomas gave her a dirty look. What was Thomas going to tell her? That they were in danger from a family of fairies or a bunch of vampires? Better yet, that they were vampires or fairies? She thought about it and decided she'd rather be a fairy. No drinking blood for her- no way. She didn't even like her meat rare, well done all the way! "Go ahead, continue. I'm intrigued really," she smiled. She just couldn't help it. "It's been a long time since anyone told me a bedtime story. Maybe we should wait until after dinner. What if you put me to sleep?" Alex smirked.

"Will you try to be serious please? This is hard for me and I'm doing the best I can," Thomas pled.

"Okay, go ahead. Finish your story," Alex relented.

Thomas sighed, took a deep breath and continued. "The fae's blood was like a drug to the vampires. Once they captured a fae,

21

they couldn't stop drinking their blood until the fae was completely drained. However, the fae were quicker than the vampires. In a one-on-one attack, the fae could always escape. So, the vamps started hunting in groups of three or four. One by one the fae were being killed by these vampire groups. The fae had a king that was supposed to protect them, but he was too weak and afraid to take on the vampires in battle. In response, this community, or family of fae began to experiment. They took the strongest humans they could find and injected them with a liquid formula made from part fairy blood, part vampire blood and a very rare plant indigenous to the rain forest where they lived. I've been told the rain forest has been destroyed and the plant is now extinct. Anyway, after a few failures, the serum was perfected. The fae successfully created a group of warriors specifically designed to protect their community from vampires."

"And they all lived happily ever after?" Alex interrupted, smiling. "The End."

Thomas was angry now. Wasn't this hard enough without Alex being her usual sarcastic self? He put his head in his hands in frustration. He wished his father was here explaining their history. Maybe he would know how to do this. Thomas was obviously failing, Alex was looking at him like he had lost his mind. "Forget it," Thomas said, running his fingers through his hair. "I'm not doing this right and you think it's all a joke. I give up. Take the book and read it. If you have any questions, let me know." He got up and walked out the door.

Alex sat there in stunned silence. A few seconds later she heard Thomas' car barrel down the driveway. Was he serious? What had she done to make him so angry? She was somehow supposed to take a fairytale about fae and vampires seriously?

Obviously Thomas wasn't himself. He had definitely lost it. She knew how close Thomas was to his father. Luke's death had apparently hit him harder than she originally thought. He was under too much stress and had cracked. What exactly was he trying to lead up to? Alex was confused. She hadn't gotten answers to any of her questions. She didn't understand why her father had been so stressed and anxious about leaving them. Why did he tell them they had to stick together, their lives depended on it?

Well, she still had the book her mother left her. Maybe mom provided some answers to this bizarre riddle. She walked into the kitchen and took some leftover fried chicken out of the fridge. She looked up to see Marta watching her.

"Hey, Marta. I have some reading and work to do tonight. Don't worry about dinner for me or Thomas. He just took off. I think he's mad at me. For the life of me I don't know what I did to make him so angry. Anyway, I thought I'd just grab some left overs and head up to the office to work for a while. Feel free to take off whenever you want."

"Alex," Marta said soberly.

Alex looked up.

"Thomas is under a lot of pressure right now. I know he planned to talk to you about your family tonight. I take it you were less than amenable to what he had to say. Next time he attempts to broach the subject, try to listen. I know it might sound incredible and hard to believe, but times are serious right now. Thomas needs you more than you know. Both of your very lives depend on you embracing your family legacy and working toward resolving this problem quickly. You have to work together and you're going to need to be there for each other." Marta took a deep breath. "That's all I am going to say, it's really not my place. See you in the morning," then she turned and walked out the door.

Again Alex was left perplexed. Marta knew the family secret, too. Was she the only one in this household that had been left in the dark all this time? Why? What was so important that her life and Thomas's life depended on them working together? Marta had said almost the exact same thing her father said just before he died. She and Thomas needed to be there for each other. Their lives depended on it. Was everyone just being over dramatic or was there some kind of serious danger Alex didn't know about? Luke had been attacked in an alleyway. An attack that had eventually killed him. Was her family in some sort of danger? Was Thomas in danger? If so, why had he left tonight alone? Should she be worried about his safety? Would she wake up in the morning to find that the only member of her family she had left was dead? Dead because she had made fun of his story and hadn't taken him seriously? But really, fairies and vampires? Who could possibly take that seriously?

She grabbed her plate and headed for her bedroom. She was going to skip the office and settle down in bed with dinner and her mother's book. Maybe after she read what her mother had to say she would understand this strange universe she'd returned to.

* * * *

Alex sat on her bed picking at fried chicken and potato salad. Now that she was in her room, locked away with a book written by her mother, she was nervous and apprehensive about its contents. Were the things her mother wrote really going to be life changing? Was she ready for that? She snatched up the book and after taking a deep breath, opened it and began to read.

My dearest Alex,

If you are reading this book, chances are I have failed. Failed you and failed my people. I always hoped I would have the chance to talk to you about our lineage in person when the time was right. This book contains sensitive information. If you're reading it, there are only two possible scenarios. The first one, the one I hope is the case, is that after I had a chance to explain our heritage to you, I gave you this book as a reference. The more likely scenario is that your half-brother Radek finally broke our treaty and either assassinated me or had one of his minions do it for him.

If the second scenario has played out, I am so sorry! I wanted to protect you from your destiny as long as I possibly could. I just wanted you to have a normal life. A normal childhood. Something I was never allowed to enjoy myself. I can only hope that if I have been assassinated, Luke is still available to help you through this difficult transition. I fear that is unlikely though. He is so protective of me. If I am gone, I suspect he has been killed as well. If you can, rely on Luke to help you through this. If not, Thomas will be there for you. He is the best son any mother could hope for. I love him as though he were my own. You can trust him. Yes, I know that is hard to believe right now. You're probably feeling so betrayed by all of us. Don't be angry with Luke or Thomas. This was my doing. I can't count the number of arguments Luke and I had over this issue. He wanted you to know long ago, so you would be prepared. "Information is power," he always said. "Alex will need all the power she can get." I insisted on keeping these things from you for a while longer. If you have to be angry with someone, be angry with me.

Dusk

There is no easy way to explain, so I am just going to be direct. You and I come from a special group of people, the fae. Forget all the myths and stories you have heard about fairies. Most of them are works of fiction. However, we do have some special gifts, or special powers. Typically, fae powers are not fully developed until your late twenties or early thirties. At this time, I have no idea what powers you will have. I can tell you what I know about you now. What I have seen of you throughout your childhood. You heal very quickly. More so than anyone else I have ever met, or ever heard of. All fae heal, but you heal quicker than any of us. Nobody knows why. We think you might be a healer.

I think at this point I need to tell you a little about your history and your biological father. He was a mortal man. A very good man. His name was James. I never told you much about James for two reasons. In the beginning, it was too painful. James and I were very much in love. We enjoyed a good life for several years. Then, out of the blue, your half-brother Radek murdered James. I was devastated. I knew I would lose my husband someday, but I thought it would be from old age, not a heinous murder from my own son. I have to admit I wasn't myself for quite some time. That made us an easy target for Radek.

A couple years after James' death, Radek captured us and imprisoned us for several months. Luke rescued us. Which is the second reason I have not talked to you about James. Luke and I had a special connection. After James, I thought I would never love again. Luke proved me wrong. I love him with all my heart. I also immediately saw what a special bond the two of you had. Luke was a wonderful father to you and I could see you weren't lacking in any way by not knowing your father. James, I mean. You never asked and I believe I made the right choice by not forcing his memory on you. There is a box of James' things in the safe if you are ever interested, that choice is yours. I would like you to know that James was a wonderful man. He was also a great father and loved you very much. His death was a result of our world and the evil that resides within it. It was not a reflection on James. He did nothing to deserve his awful death.

I tell you this because you need to know that you are half human, half fae. Don't think that is a detriment. Your human ancestry is very strong and pure. In addition, there are very few full-blooded fae still living. I believe our people can, and eventually will, accept you for who you are. The council will judge you based on your strength and ability, not your bloodline. I'm not worried about that either. You have both in spades. I do worry about Radek. Our capture broke the treaty before, but we decided to overlook the infraction. Radek promised he would abide by the stipulations if we gave him another chance. If he has assassinated me, he broke our treaty and war is coming. You are going to need to be strong and bring our people together. I think your human half will help you accomplish this. The fae cannot live together in communities for long. That makes it impossible for them to rally together. Humans can. Use your strengths and rely on Thomas and the other warriors. They will protect you and help you in any way they can. I just realized I have gotten ahead of myself. The other important thing you need to know, is that with my death you will become the new leader of our people. I was the Fae Queen. As my daughter, you inherit that position upon my death.

Again, I apologize for leaving you unprepared. I truly believed I still had plenty of time. Our people will need to see you. They will need to know you are a capable leader. This must be done quickly. We have many allies in the fae community, but there are some who are less loyal. I kept our heritage from you because I didn't want you to grow up under scrutiny. By doing that, I have also kept you

Dusk

*from our people. They don't know anything about you. It would be
difficult for them to trust and accept you in the best of times. If
Radek has broken the treaty and war is raging, the people are going
to be even more skeptical and afraid. They need to be introduced to
you immediately. I cannot stress this enough. Luke and Thomas
know what to do. The warriors will protect you and help you rally
and defend our people. Be careful and remember everything Luke
and I taught you.*

Alex stopped reading. She couldn't take it all in. She was a
Fairy Queen, no Fae Queen. The leader of an entire group of
people? She had to prove herself strong? They were at war? And
what in the world was she talking about an evil half-brother who
killed her father? Telling me I might have questions was the
understatement of the century Thomas, Alex thought as she put
down the book and looked at the clock. She had read to this point
three times now, but still her head was swimming. It was after one
o'clock in the morning and Thomas still wasn't home. Alex was
more anxious than before. If there was some kind of war raging and
Luke had been killed by it, Thomas was also at risk. Didn't mom
imply Thomas was one of these warriors? Thomas had talked about
warriors. Were dad and Thomas one of the warriors developed to
protect the fae from vampires? If so he was definitely in danger.

There was no way Alex could sleep until she knew Thomas
was home safe. She grabbed a robe and her mother's book and
headed for the kitchen. Maybe a cup of tea would help settle her.
Was Thomas really a warrior? If Luke had been a warrior, how had
he really died? And another thing, what was mom talking about
when she said Luke had saved them from Radek? She met Luke
when she was seven. Wouldn't she have some memory of being a

28

prisoner as a kid? Maybe she did, what was that dream she used to have over and over when she was little? Something about running through a maze, or some sort of dungeon. It was dark and humid and she was terrified, trying to keep up with her mother. Was that real? A memory she had suppressed that came out in dreams?

Alex reached the kitchen and prepared a cup of tea. She headed for the library. Maybe if she sat in front of the fire she could think. There were so many things going through her mind. What else had Thomas said? Luke had been the leader of an organization and with his death Dimitri was now the leader. And there was something to do with her as a problem or complication. Was Dimitri the leader of the warriors and she was a problem because she ran off to Italy rather than introduce herself immediately after her mother's death? Why didn't Luke force her to come home?

Alex sat her tea down on the table and added a log to the fire. Where was Thomas? She needed him right now. More importantly she needed to know he was okay. She glanced over at the book from her mother. She just couldn't read any more tonight. She had enough to digest already. She couldn't risk information overload. This was all so bizarre. She was a fairy queen. Her mother had been a pure blooded fae, probably the last of her kind. And what did she mean special powers? Vampires? What a nightmare. Maybe she would wake up, find herself back in Italy and none of this had really happened. But Alex knew better. Luke was dead. She had to accept that. And another thing, her mother died of a heart attack not an assassination by some evil half-brother. Where was Thomas? She looked at the old grandfather clock and noticed it was now two o'clock in the morning. If Thomas was okay, she was going to kill him when he got home.

Dusk

Just then she heard the door open. She stood up and saw Thomas stop in the doorway to the library. He had blood on his clothes and looked pale as death.

"Thomas!" She exclaimed as she ran to him, "Where are you hurt? Do you need a doctor? Come in and sit down."

"Stop fussing. I'm okay. Really, it's nothing." Thomas sat on the couch and propped his feet on the ottoman. "I could use a glass of brandy though."

Alex poured him a brandy and then followed his gaze to the book she had been reading. "Yes, I started reading it. It's all so bizarre, like I've entered the Twilight Zone."

"You probably have a lot of questions," Thomas said as he looked back up at her.

"Oh yeah, I have questions. I'm still trying to get things straight in my mind. But the first thing I want to know is what happened to you tonight," Alex asked again.

"There was a fight. I guess I didn't have my head straight after our talk. I think I really messed things up. I wasn't explaining it right and then I just got mad and walked out. You gotta love that Deveraux temper. Before I could call you and try to fix everything we ran into a group of vampires." Thomas looked up wearily at Alex. "Are you comfortable with me talking about vampires, yet?"

"No, but go ahead. I need to know what we're up against if I am going to be of any help to you and your friends," Alex replied.

"We were outnumbered and my head wasn't in the game. I was still worried about you and they got a couple good shots in.

Don't worry. Really, I'm fine. Just a couple scratches, by tomorrow they'll be gone."

"So as a warrior, you heal quickly too?" Alex asked.

Thomas was surprised. "I have never read that book your mom left you, but I gather she explained things better than I did? You know about the warriors then? And healing?"

"Mom explained some things but some things are still very confusing. Also, I haven't read the whole book yet. I'm not sure if she goes into more detail later on. She didn't exactly say you were a warrior, but she insinuated it. I suspect you are based on our previous conversation. I'm still trying to put everything together. I think you and Luke are both warriors and so are the three 'friends' you introduced me to this morning. You said something about Luke being the leader of an organization and now he's gone, Dimitri is the leader. I assume you're talking about this group of warriors that were created to protect the fae. I also assume that is why you and Luke have always been so overprotective of me and mom."

"So far you're doing pretty well," Thomas said. "What else did you learn from that book?"

"I learned that I am supposedly the new leader or Queen of the Fae and that I have an evil half-brother, Radek is it, that wants to kill us all. So, I guess we are at war? Mom also said that I should have been introduced to the fae community immediately after her death, which didn't happen. That probably makes things worse in some way. I haven't really figured it all out in my mind yet. Also, something about special powers, but I don't think I have any of those. How am I doing?"

Dusk

"You are actually taking this pretty well. And so far you're correct, except about the power thing. You do have some. We just aren't sure which one's or how many yet. Dad and I figure you have at least two. One is your ability to heal. We know you can heal yourself. We don't know if you can heal others. I heal quickly, but you are almost instant. You also have the ability to see at least glimpses of the future. That one we'll have to test a little, but I think that's why you are so good at fighting. You can see what your opponent is going to do before he or she does it and you counter that move." Thomas shrugged at her disbelieving look. "It's just a theory and one we'll explore, but not tonight. I've had enough fighting for one evening. I think I'm going to bed," Thomas said as he stood and headed for the door.

"Thomas?" Alex hesitated as Thomas stopped and turned back toward her. "I'm sorry."

"For what?" Thomas asked.

"For not taking you seriously. I could see you were struggling with what you had to tell me, but I didn't...couldn't believe you. It all seemed so out there, you know? The only way I knew to deal with it was to be sarcastic."

"Alex, I didn't expect you to hear what I was telling you and immediately say, hey great! I'm a Fairy Queen. Let's go celebrate!" Thomas grinned.

Alex smiled back at him. "I know, but I could have made things easier for you. I still can't believe everything I've heard and read tonight. Maybe after I sleep on it I'll be in a better position to talk it through. After reading mom's book, I was so scared that you would never come back. She was talking about war and assassinations. I still need to talk to you about that. When it got so late and you didn't come home I thought maybe you had been killed like Luke had." Alex stopped speaking, she had to clear her throat and blink back tears. She was being stupid, but she couldn't lose Thomas too. She just couldn't bare it.

Thomas walked back over and hugged Alex. "Stop it. I'm not going anywhere. Yes, what I do is dangerous. But I'm careful. And I'm good, I was trained by the best." He smiled down at her. "I have to fight, Alex. Our survival depends on it. Unfortunately, you're probably going to have to fight at some point too. Believe me, when you go out there, I'm going to be a basket case worrying about your safety. But neither one of us can hole up in the house and hide. We have a duty to our people and our family name. Luke and Marlena did prepare us for this. If you think about your childhood, you'll recognize that even though you didn't know what you were preparing for; you are prepared. Now, let's go to sleep. We can pick this up in the morning."

With a quick nod, Alex let Thomas lead her up the stairs to her bedroom. "Goodnight sis," Thomas said as he continued to his room.

"Goodnight, Thomas." Alex replied and then closed her bedroom door and went to bed.

Chapter Three

Alex awoke the next morning with a headache. She stumbled out of bed and climbed into the shower. Today was a new day. The first day of the rest of her life, or however that saying went. After climbing into bed last night she had a hard time falling asleep. So many things were going through her mind. She couldn't say she had embraced her new life but after careful thought, she wasn't intimidated by it anymore. Thomas, Luke and her mother had lived a fairly normal life as fae and warriors. She could too. As she fell asleep, she started to formulate her plan.

Prior to her mother's death, Luke had insisted on a routine. Every morning they would spar in the basement mat room. If Luke was unavailable, Thomas would take his place. Marlena had even filled in a few times. Alex was uncomfortable fighting her mother, but Marlena always had such a ball. Alex couldn't deny her mother a chance to "play" as she put it and Marlena was good. Luke told her it was good practice to fight with a variety of people because everyone had their own style. After a while Alex understood what he meant. Changing things up a little kept her on her toes. So, the first order of business was to get back into the fighting routine. She was going to talk to Thomas this morning and see if he could arrange for a sparring partner every morning at seven o'clock. If they were at war, she needed to be in shape and prepared. Exercise wasn't enough. She needed to fight.

The second part of her plan was to gather information. She needed to spend time every day reading the book her mother left her. She would also talk to Thomas and see if there were any other books or ways she could research her lineage. She also wanted to get to know her enemy. It hit her just before she fell into a deep sleep that Jake must be a warrior, too. The man she always thought of as her lovable uncle was Luke's best friend. If Luke was the leader of the warriors, Jake must be one too. Also, she vaguely remembered Thomas telling their father something about Jake spilling the beans about what really happened the night Luke was attacked. They must have been together, which meant Jake had to be a warrior. She was going to get as much information from him as she possibly could.

The final part of her plan was to talk Thomas into introducing her to some of the fae allies her mother talked about. If she could talk to other members of the fae, they could help her understand her heritage and fae culture. That part of the plan had to wait though. Mom said the council would judge her. She hadn't taken care of herself the past year and it was going to take time to get into shape. She had to prove her strength and abilities as a leader. She could lead. Hadn't Luke forced her to take control of different aspects of Deveraux Industries years ago? Like Thomas said, Luke had been preparing her for this her entire life. She wasn't fooling herself, it wouldn't be easy, but she knew she could do it.

Dusk

She popped a couple aspirin and headed downstairs for a cup of coffee. She needed to find Thomas to figure out a fighting schedule before she did anything else. The coffee helped to revive her, but Thomas was still in bed. Alex decided not to wake him. He said he was okay, but she was still worried about his wound. When he got up, she would demand he show her his injuries. Then, she would decide for herself if he needed to see a doctor.

She reached the basement and opened the mat room door. As light illuminated the room, Alex realized Thomas must still use the gym on a regular basis. Good, maybe they could coordinate their schedules. Today it was going to be a solo run. She popped in an old kick boxing video and got to work. An hour later she was sweaty, tired and in desperate need of another shower. She turned toward the door and saw Thomas. "I didn't know you'd turned into a voyeur."

"Actually, I just got here. You still have some pretty good moves sis, but I think you're a little rusty. I take it you didn't work out much in Italy," Thomas said with a smile.

"Unfortunately, no. The only exercise I got was walking. I pretty much walked everywhere I went. I guess I suffered from a mild case of depression. I just couldn't bring myself to do much of anything. I think Jennifer had about given up on me. She was begging me to come home, at least for a visit. I guess she thought your company would be good for me. It seems to be pretty good for her when she's in a mood," Alex smiled.

"Don't even go there," Thomas groaned. "We're not changing the subject. You're still in good shape, but you're going to need a lot of work. I'm sure you know, you can't take a year off from training and hope to be back in fighting condition the first time you hit the mats."

"I know. I actually wanted to talk to you about that. Last night, I decided I needed to get back into my routine. I want to get into shape and fast. I used to work out for an hour every day at seven o'clock. I know you're trying to run the company and I don't know how often you engage in those late night adventures, but can you try to schedule me in sometime?" Alex asked.

"Seven's tough for me, but I'll see what I can do. Maybe we should hire you a trainer," Thomas suggested.

"I thought about that, but for now I want to do things my way. Luke was a great trainer and I remember most of what he taught me. I just need to practice it. A new trainer would want to change my technique. I don't want to do that. Any chance I could train with some of your new found friends?" Alex asked.

Thomas laughed. "I don't think you're ready for that yet. You need to get into better shape before we invite them to take you on. They won't care that you're a girl, they'll fight to win. I'll look into setting up a few rounds with them once I think you're ready. I don't want you getting hurt. For now, we'll have to figure out something else."

"You gonna be around for a while? I need to shower, but I have a few things I want to talk to you about. Like I said last night, you don't need to run Deveraux Industries on your own. I would like to sit down and divide up the work between the two of us. I love working with D-Tech and I know how much you hate anything techno. There are a few other areas where I can take over right now. Luke kept me up to speed on the big projects." She looked at Thomas more carefully. "You still look tired, which reminds me, show me your injuries from last night. I need to make sure you're okay."

"What injuries?" Thomas smiled. "I don't have any." Thomas didn't tell her how deep the wound had actually been. If she'd seen it last night, she would have panicked. This morning, it was barely visible. By this afternoon, it would be gone completely.

"Thomas!" Alex said, exasperated. "I need to see that you're okay. Please do this one thing for me."

Thomas pulled off his shirt and showed her his shoulder. "See, not as fast as you but I still heal pretty quickly." There was a long, straight mark across the back of his left shoulder. If she hadn't known better, she would have sworn it was an old wound, something that was almost healed from weeks ago.

"Wow!" Alex looked at him, amazed. "It's one thing hearing in the abstract that you heal fast. It's entirely different to see it for myself. It's actually a little spooky. Okay, you're off the hook. Back to business. You still look tired. We have tons of funeral arrangements to make and I'm serious, I want to divide up the workload for Deveraux Industries. Let me help out here. In one breath you tell me I'm strong enough to handle this. In the next, you act like I need to be protected, like if you give me too much I might crack. I've dealt with mom's death, really. Losing Luke has been a blow sure, but it's a blow for both of us. Like dad said, we need to rely on each other. Relinquish some control brother, or I'm going to pry it away from you forcibly."

"Go shower and meet me in the library. I'm more than happy to give you D-Tech. There are a few things going on with that company that you'll need to know." They turned and headed up the stairs.

Alex walked into the library and sat down. She was trying to gather her thoughts, but didn't know how to bring up the subject. Fast, and direct she decided. She looked over at Thomas. "I need to ask you a question."

"Okay," Thomas said absently. He was studying something on his computer.

"In the book mom left, she kept saying if she was dead it was because she was assassinated by my half-brother Radek. But mom wasn't assassinated. She died of a heart attack, right? So why is the fae community so up in arms and why does it seem we are at war with the vampires? If mom died of natural causes, the treaty wasn't broken."

Thomas studied her cautiously. This was going to be difficult. "Marlena was assassinated," Thomas said reluctantly.

"What?" Alex was shocked. "The doctor's said it was a heart attack. There's no way you and Luke convinced them to lie about that and falsify her death certificate!" She was pretty sure.

"We didn't have them lie to you, Alex. And we certainly didn't have them falsify reports. That's insulting and you know it. Luke and I would never do anything illegal like that. What? You think we bribed about 15 people to make it look like your mom died naturally?" Thomas was clearly insulted.

"No, I don't think you or Luke would have done that. So explain how she died of a heart attack and she was assassinated," Alex insisted.

Thomas studied Alex for a long time. "I don't want to overload you with too much information all at once. I think you're still trying to accept the vampire, warriors, fairy stuff. Obviously mom's death, well assassination, has to do with that. Have you settled things in your mind enough that we can talk about this?"

"Yes," Alex assured him. "It's still all a little weird, like Alice when she fell down the rabbit hole, but I'm starting to get used to the idea. Tell me what happened to mom. How was she assassinated when Luke was always so protective of her? He never would have let anyone hurt her." Alex was certain of that.

"Dad was always on guard, prepared for an attack on Marlena. She was the Fae Queen. Not only did he have to protect her from a possible vampire attack, but there was always a chance another fae would try to assassinate her. There are still descendants from the former regime around that think they should be in power. Anyone who might want to take over as queen or king is also a threat. Luke seemed overprotective, but really Marlena was in a lot of danger and always a possible target. Both she and dad had to constantly be on alert, watching for trouble. It was a difficult way to live. You need to know that because you are now in the same situation Marlena was in. A hidden enemy could come out of nowhere and try to assassinate you at any moment."

Alex hadn't considered that possibility. She was overwhelmed with the knowledge she was supposed to take over as leader of the fairies and would have to demonstrate she had strength and leadership skills. She hadn't considered the danger she might be in. Mom had Luke to protect her. Alex had Thomas for now, but he couldn't spend his life guarding her. It wouldn't be fair to him. What if he fell in love and wanted to have a family of his own. Would she have to hire a bodyguard? "I guess I have more to figure out than I thought I did," Alex finally answered.

"You need to be cautious Alex, but just like dad protected mom, I'm here to protect you. Nobody will get passed me to hurt you," he assured her.

"Thomas, we both know that at some point you're going to want to have a life of your own. You'll meet someone you want to marry and start a family with. I'm not going to stand in your way. I'm also not going to be the burden that creates marital discourse, or a danger to your children."

"Whoa! Alex," Thomas interrupted. "Now you've not only gotten me married, but I have kids too? That's a long way down the road, sis. Let's not borrow trouble."

"For now this works, but one day I'm going to have to figure out how to protect myself. I appreciate your willingness to be there for me. I'm still new to this and I don't have the first clue how to shield myself from vampires or fairies. That's even more reason why I need a good training program. I need to prepare for the future, I'm going to need to fight with the warriors, but that's a problem for another day," Alex sighed. She knew this was going to be hard, she just hadn't realized how hard. "So back to mom. Tell me about the assassination."

Thomas let the subject drop. He knew Alex was right. At some point they would have to figure out how to protect Alex permanently, but not tonight. "So mom and dad were always very careful when they left the house. Dad was with her as often as he could get away, but as you know there were some times Marlena had to go out alone. Mom wasn't helpless by any means. She was a tough lady and a good fighter. Under most circumstances she could take care of herself."

Dusk

"I remember, the night mom had her attack, dad was stuck at the office. I think a meeting had run late. He called and had mom meet him so they could attend that big business dinner," Alex supplied.

"Right. Dad wasn't happy about it. If you remember, he wanted mom to wait for him to come home and pick her up. Mom refused. She said that was silly, she could ride in the limo and meet him outside the office. That way, they wouldn't be late to the party."

"I remember," Alex said solemnly.

"So John drove mom to the office. She wasn't supposed to get out of the car, but as dad approached, mom jumped from the limo and joined him on the sidewalk. She told dad she'd promised one of the ladies a catalog and wanted to take it to the party. As they turned to head back into the office, mom was shot in the arm with a dart. Dad believed it was aimed at her heart, but when she turned it missed its target and went straight into her arm. It didn't matter. It had the same effect."

"A dart? Did it have something poisonous in it?" Alex asked, shaken by this information.

"Sort of, poison for Marlena. Remember how mom always told you to stay away from the St. John's Wort at the cabin. It grew out by that rocky outcropping. Remember, the plant with the yellow flowers?" Thomas asked.

"Yeah, I remember. She said I was allergic to that plant. She tried to kill them one year and sprinkled wild flower seeds over the area, but the soil had too much clay in it and the yellow flowers bloomed again the following year," Alex recalled.

"Right!" Thomas said. "Well, St John's Wort is very dangerous to fae. If you touch it, it will cause a rash. If injected, it will make you extremely ill. But if you mix it with lemon juice..."

"Which I'm also allergic to according to mom," Alex interrupted.

"Yes," Thomas said. "If it's mixed with lemon juice and introduced into your blood stream it's lethal. Basically, once it gets to a fae's heart, the heart stops beating and you die of a heart attack," Thomas finished solemnly.

"I hope that's not common knowledge." Alex felt more vulnerable now than she ever had. She could walk out her front door, get shot with a dart from someone hidden down the road and die. How could you protect against that?

"It's not, or wasn't. And we would like to keep it that way. We're not sure how Radek found out about it, or how many he's told. Dad's theory was since Radek is half fae, he somehow got sick from lemon juice, or St John's Wort, or both and experimented. Or more to the point had Hector, his second in command, experiment. Dad extracted the dart and had it tested. The levels were far above what they needed to be in order to be effective. That's why we don't think they really knew the secret, they just happened onto it and decided to try. Also, like I said, dad thinks they were aiming for the heart, but missed. That's another indication they didn't know what effect it was going to have on mom.

Dad had an even harder time coping because he blamed himself for Marlena's death. He thought if he had left the meeting early, or somehow had tried to prepare for that sort of attack, mom would still be alive today." Alex looked like she was going to argue so Thomas hurried on. "I don't agree with dad at all. How could

Dusk

they have known anyone would use that means to attack mom? No fae could, they couldn't get close enough to the ingredients to put it together. No one knew the vampires had that knowledge. It'd been kept a secret for millennia. Even if they had known, it's not something you can really prevent, unless you stay locked up in the house forever," Thomas paused. "So how do you feel about never leaving this humble abode?" Thomas smiled.

"I admit, this information shakes me. I guess it should. I need to know the danger waiting for me out there. But, I'm not going to become a recluse and never leave the house. I'd rather die," Alex answered. She was more than a little shook by this information. "I'm going to have to think about this for a while. Vampires strike at night, right? Does that mean they can't go out in the daytime? Sunlight and all that jazz? Or is that another myth?" Alex asked.

"They can't go out in direct sunlight. They can go out on an overcast day, but they can't stay out for long. It's my experience they don't chance it. If they were outside and the sun peaked out from behind a cloud, it would kill them. It's not instant though. From what I understand it's a slow painful death. Basically, it cooks them to death. Once the sun hits them, it starts burning and doesn't stop, even if they get in out of the sunlight. It's bad enough I've never heard of one taking the chance," Thomas answered.

"Okay, then I'm pretty safe during the day. The fae can't make the formula because it's just as harmful to them as it is me. Vampires can't go out in the day, so I just have to be extra careful if I leave at night, right?" Alex questioned.

"That's basically true. I think you should be careful at all times though. Never go anywhere alone for now. Like I told you before, you have a lot to learn. Don't rush this. There's no reason to. Danger could come from anyone," Thomas pled.

"Okay. So, I think I'm safe during the day from lethal darts anyway. That means we need to get down to business." Alex pulled out a folder and started to show Thomas her ideas.

They spent the rest of the night outlining plans for the funeral, sharing information and dividing up responsibilities for the company. As soon as her head hit the pillow that night, Alex fell into a deep dreamless sleep.

* * * *

Later that week, Alex sat in the Library with Thomas, Marta and Jake. Getting through Luke's funeral had been emotionally exhausting. Everything seemed to go according to plan. That at least was a blessing. They were all so emotionally drained, none of them would have been able to handle the slightest problem. After the funeral, several of the guests had congregated at the house. Luke had touched so many lives. Alex knew they had to have an open house for those closest to him. People would need to pay their respects and honor her father. She was just glad the day was now over. Marta looked beat, too. She'd spent days preparing the house and overseeing preparations for all the food. She was priceless. After the guests left Marta declared it was time to get started on cleanup. That's where they had drawn the line. Thomas hired a professional cleaning crew to come first thing in the morning. Marta quickly objected, but both Alex and Thomas saw the relief in her eyes when they insisted.

Dusk

Thomas' friends, Dimitri, Nicholas and Dante along with three other men Alex had never met were at the funeral. It was the first time she had seen them since that morning in the library. She assumed they must all be warriors due to their build, but also because they stuck together the entire time. Alex hung back when Thomas approached them. As she watched the seven of them together, they almost seemed like brothers they had such comradery. Fighting together obviously created a tighter bond than she'd realized. She was glad, but a little jealous. Jennifer was the only real friend Alex had, and she was still in Italy. Her friend had called to give condolences but couldn't get off work to fly back to New York. It was good to know Thomas had these men by his side. Six friends that understood him, who he clearly had an unbreakable bond with. Each of them hugged Thomas before they turned and solemnly left the gravesite. Of course, they had also known Luke. He had been their leader for many years. She guessed the bond was just as tight with Luke as it appeared to be with Thomas.

Alex looked around the room at the three people who were now all that was left of her family. Funny, none of them were blood relatives but she doubted blood could bring them any closer. Thomas looked more tired and beat than she'd ever seen him. She got up and walked over to sit next to him on the couch. "Hey big bro," she said. Thomas put an arm around her and laid his head against hers. "We made it through the day."

"Barely," Thomas admitted.

"I remember feeling this way at mom's funeral. Like the world had just ended and nothing would ever be right again. Now, just a year later here we are again. I also remember that each day it got a little easier to cope. A little easier to get through the day knowing I would never see mom again. It will be like that with dad, too. This time I promise I won't run away. We'll get through it together. We don't have a choice and we still have each other," Alex vowed.

"I know. I just miss him so much. Over the past week I've realized how much I depended on dad to be here. If there were problems with the company, dad was there to talk it through. We even shared the vamp problems. It's like half of me is gone and I don't know how to get it back, like I never will," Thomas sighed.

Alex put her arms around Thomas and they just sat there in silence for a long moment. They were both lost in thoughts about Luke and the things they had taken for granted every day. Jake walked up and handed them both a glass of wine. "I think you two should try to get some sleep. You did a great job with the funeral and everything," he looked over at Marta. "With a little help from the magician over there." He gave Marta a big smile. "You're both emotionally drained and we've all had a long day. The lawyer said he'd come by tomorrow at one, so I'll be here to go over the paperwork with you. I'm sure there won't be any problems. Luke wasn't one to miss the details." He turned back to Marta. "Need a ride, beautiful?" he asked.

"I'd love one," Marta grabbed her coat and after quick hugs they were out the door.

Alex had to laugh, Marta and Jake were obviously over the moon for each other but neither one of them would try to take it to the next level. They'd been that way for years. She and Thomas had shared more than a few good laughs at their expense. What a couple of morons. They were wasting time. Both of them were obviously in love. "You think they'll ever get up the nerve to move their relationship to the next level?" Alex asked Thomas.

Dusk

"I hope so," Thomas said looking out the window at the fading taillights. "They obviously love each other and they've basically been together, as friends anyway, longer than a lot of married people. You can't try to talk to them about it though. Neither one of them will hear it. I gave up trying to meddle a long time ago. If they do, they do. If not, I guess they're both content with the way things are." Thomas turned and took Alex's hand. "Let's hit the sack. Jake's right, tomorrow's going to be another long day." They slowly ambled up to bed.

* * * *

"I'm going out," Thomas said as he stood in the doorway to Alex's office.

"Where?" she said, panic settling in her stomach.

"Dimitri has given me a break for the past few weeks because of dad, but I need to get back out there. We both knew I was going to have to start fighting again. The guys need me. I got through the funeral and even had plenty of time to work on company business. It's time."

"I know. It just scares me. Sitting here all night waiting for you to come home, or worse, worried that you're not coming home drives me insane!" Alex replied. "I've gotten a lot better in my training, maybe I could come with you."

"No way!" Thomas exclaimed.

"Double standard, huh? Make the little woman sit home while the big bad man goes out to protect the family? That philosophy went out with the dark ages," Alex argued.

"That's not it, exactly. You're not ready. Before you go out at night, I want you to practice with some of the guys. Yeah, I've practiced with you a few times, but you're used to me. Vamps are different. Plus, the others won't be easy on you. I have to constantly fight the urge to hold back because I don't want you to get hurt." Thomas smiled at the offended look on Alex's face. "I know, I overcome it pretty fast when you start kicking my butt. I'm just saying, I don't want you out there too quickly. You need to avoid going out after dark for a while longer. You're coming along really well - sooner than I anticipated. But, you're not coming with me tonight. In fact, you're not deliberately going out to fight ever! That's not your job, it's mine."

"Okay. You're partially right. I'm not quite ready. I admit it. I think I'm pretty close though. Oh before I forget, I'm going down to D-tech tomorrow morning so I probably won't be here when you get up. I want to track down that employee, Sam, dad always talked about and go over an idea I've been kicking around for the past couple days." Alex stood up and walked over to Thomas. "I'm going to try to trust that you can handle yourself. I just ask that you give me the same courtesy. When I tell you I'm ready. Please trust me to handle myself." She gave him a big hug. "Be careful and don't do anything reckless. I need you!"

Thomas gave her a quick kiss on the forehead. "I'm always careful sis, but I can't promise I won't worry about you when you go out at night. I know what it's like out there. Give it plenty of time. I realize you've been studying that book of Marlena's and, now that you're starting to accept the truly bizarre, you want to join the fight. Just be patient. We've waited over a year to introduce you, a few more weeks won't hurt. Now, I've gotta go. The guys are waiting for me."

Alex watched him leave and prayed he would be safe. This was hard for her, but she knew it was going to be even more difficult for Thomas when she insisted on going out at night. Thomas would probably want to escort her everywhere she went. That wasn't going to happen. She wasn't stupid, she knew it would be dangerous, but this was her fight too and she was going to face it head on. That day was going to be soon.

* * * *

The next morning Alex wandered through the maze of D-Tech labs. She couldn't contain her excitement. Alex always loved everything electronic. D-Tech was the branch of Deveraux Industries that dealt with technological equipment. They had a great R&D department and they had always been on the cutting edge of electronics. Their current project was the one she wanted to talk to Sam about. Alex had never met Sam. But for the last few years anytime Luke had a particularly sensitive or complicated project, he always said "I'll give it to Sam; only the best will do." So, here she was on a mission to find Sam and introduce herself.

Alex was a little nervous. Luke knew Alex had a passion for electronics, unlike Thomas who hated anything techno and wasn't shy about letting his feelings known. She and Luke had talked endlessly about D-Tech. It was decided early on that when she and Thomas took over the company, she would be taking on D-Tech. Luke assured her he had prepared his employees and contracts for that eventuality, but some of them were wary about working with a woman.   She just hoped this Sam guy could accept her. If he was as good as Luke claimed, she didn't want to lose him.

After wandering aimlessly throughout the lab area, Alex decided to stop at the next desk and ask for Sam. She came around the corner and there at the desk was a beautiful red head.   The woman looked up inquisitively as Alex approached her desk. "Hi, I'm Alex Deveraux and I'm looking for someone named Sam. Unfortunately I can't tell you much more than that other than Sam comes highly recommended by my father, Luke Deveraux. I think they worked together a lot."

The woman gave Alex a big smile, stood up and held out a hand. "I'm Sam Reed. It's a pleasure to finally meet you in person. I've probably seen a million pictures of you over the past five years. So, I guess I have an advantage. I'm really sorry about your dad. We're going to miss him around here. Sorry, I guess I'm rambling. Let me grab you a chair and get this stuff out of the way. Then you can tell me to what I owe the honor of this visit."

Alex was perplexed. Sam was a woman! Hadn't Luke said he was a man? Well, no. He hadn't actually said he was a man, but Alex was certain he never referred to her as a woman.

Sam came back with a chair and placed it in the small cubicle next to her desk. One look at Alex and she gave a little laugh. "I take it Luke never told you I was a woman," Sam stated.

"No, does it show? I'm sorry. You just took me by surprise. Thinking back Luke never said if you were a man or a woman, but the way he talked, and your name of course, I always just pictured a man." Alex was a little embarrassed to have made such an assumption.

Dusk

"Luke did that on purpose. He was always very careful with the companies we contract with. He apologized to me, but said that some of the narrow minded fools, that's the way he actually put it to me, narrow minded fools," Sam laughed. "Some of them wouldn't do business with us if they knew I was a woman. So, he was always very careful when he talked about me to only use my nick name, Sam and never let on what gender I was. I suspect it was just a habit that continued when he talked about things at home. I don't mind. Whatever gets the job done is fine with me. I know Luke valued me and my talents so that's all that ever mattered. I really am sorry about Luke. I never met a better man than your father."

"Thanks. I tend to agree, but I guess I'm a little biased. Well then, now that I've recovered from that surprise, let's get down to business. First of all, I want you to know that I will be taking over as head of D-Tech. I love electronics and my brother absolutely abhors them. I hope that's not a problem for you, to work for a woman?" Alex inquired.

"Not me. I expected as much. Like I said, I worked on a lot of things for Luke. He used to talk to me about the projects of course, but sometimes about you. He was always showing me new pictures and telling me someday I was going to work for you. He told me not to worry though. He claims you know more about electronics than he ever did. I'm holding out for proof of that before I believe him. Luke was an ace at electronics. He sure was proud of you though."

"Sounds like dad. I don't know more about electronics than Luke did, I think we just knew different things. He was easily impressed," Alex said with a smile.

"No, he really wasn't. But maybe it was different with his kids. We'll see." Sam shrugged and smiled back at Alex.

Alex liked Sam. She was easy going and obviously good at her job. A no nonsense kind of woman. All the nervousness she felt earlier was gone. It was time to get down to business, the reason for her visit. "Sam, I am actually here for a reason. Dad kept me up to speed on the new robot D-Tech has developed. It's my understanding there haven't been any more setbacks and we're ready to start selling in a couple months. Is that correct?"

Sam pulled out a brochure and spread it on her desk. "This is the current model. For now, there are only two to choose from. The female robot or droid whatever you want to call it, is basically a maid. She is fully programmable, within limits of course. The male droid is basically set up as a butler. He too can be programmed to complete different tasks." Sam smiled widely. She was clearly excited about the project and the progress they had made.

"I've seen one in action," Alex smiled back. "Dad was so excited about this project and its potential. I want to continue with the same timeline he set to reveal the droid's. We're going to get these out to the public just as originally planned. No delays." Alex was excited about this particular project, too. Luke had such enthusiasm when he originally pitched the idea to her and asked for her thoughts. They had spent hours hashing things out. Once they had a plan on paper, Luke brought it to D-Tech to get the ball rolling. She remembered how much fun they had just brainstorming possibilities. She wished he was still around to actually see his dream become a reality. "Dad always said you were the best at techno stuff. I also understand he sometimes brought you extra projects. Things that were secret and not to be shared with any other co-workers, would that be accurate?" Alex asked.

Dusk

"I would say so, yes. I was actually going to talk to you about that. I wondered if my extra work was going to continue. Not that I'm pushing or anything. If you don't want me to do that sort of thing for you, I understand. It takes a lot of trust, and this is the first time you've met me." Sam watched Alex for a reaction.

"Actually, I do want that relationship to continue if you're comfortable with me. It does take a lot of trust, but dad trusted you. That's not something he did lightly. I'm willing to continue based on his trust. Unless you do something to change my mind that is," Alex assured her.

"Oh I won't," Sam promised.

"Well then, I was thinking about the droid's that are ready for release and I had an idea I would like you to explore for me. I've always been an active exerciser. Before I moved to Italy I would spar with Thomas, Luke or my mother before she passed away. With both mom and dad gone, things are a lot busier and my schedule rarely meshes with Thomas'. So, I was thinking maybe we could work on programming a droid to be my sparring partner. You know, program it for kick boxing, karate, etc. Do you think that would be possible?" Alex asked apprehensively.

"Come with me," Sam motioned her to a door that looked like it went into an office. Alex followed, confused but curious. Sam used a key to open the locked door and then pulled a small device from her pocket. The light flashed red for a few seconds and then switched to green. Sam motioned for Alex to close the door. "This was your father's private office here at D-Tech," Sam explained. "I assume you will be taking it over as your personal office from now on." She looked at Alex in question.

"I guess. I didn't realize he had an office here. As far as I knew he did most of his work at home. Why do you have a key to his office and what was that thing you used when you walked in?" Alex asked.

"I have a key to his office because this is where Luke wanted me to work on special projects for him. He didn't always have me work in here, only when it was something sensitive he didn't want any of the other employees to know about. The sensor I used when we came in was a device Luke and I came up with to detect bugs or other electronic devices. When I turn it on, it quickly scans the entire room and once it finishes, the display turns to green if no devices are found," Sam explained.

"Why did dad feel he needed to scan his personal office for bugs or other devices when he kept it locked?" Alex wondered.

"Because I found one in here a few months ago," Sam stated with a frown.

"You what?" Alex exclaimed. "If there was a bug in dad's office, it had to be put there by someone on the inside. This facility is extremely secure. Did he know who was spying on him?"

"We think it was John Anderson," Sam admitted.

"But isn't John the Executive Director here at D-Tech?"

"Yes. When we initially began the droid project, we started hearing rumors that Corbetron was also working on a droid project. Luke has spies everywhere and he was able to get some good Intel on what was going on over there. He even got specs from somewhere. They were so close to ours, it was obvious we had a leak. Luke started taking precautions, trying to flush out the mole.

No luck. But then a few things happened that led me to suspect John was somehow involved. Luke has a detailed report on my suspicions. A while later I overheard a couple conversations that made me think I was being watched at night when I was working alone. I immediately began working on this little beauty. Actually, I'd been working on it for a while but I picked up the pace and voila. It works like a charm. Anyway, I started sweeping the office before I worked on any project that was supposed to be off the books so to speak. I've been working in Luke's office off and on for a couple years now but nobody else is supposed to have access, not even John. One day, I came in to work on a special project Luke gave me and swept the office with my little friend here. I found a bug. I immediately called Luke to tell him what I found and he came right over," Sam paused.

"He took the bug and I haven't found one since. I think John knows Luke was onto him. We haven't had any leaks or problems here since Luke took that bug. Now that Luke is gone, I'm afraid John might test the waters and see what he can get away with under your supervision. You should probably be careful and screen what you trust him with for a while. I think Luke has a file on him at home. I can't be sure, but I just got that impression from the way Luke talked. I think John was going to find himself fired in the very near future. Luke dying has been a stroke of good luck for John. Not that I think John had anything to do with his death," Sam said abruptly. "John's a weasel, but he's gutless. No way would he do anything violent like that. He's too much of a wimp if you know what I mean," Sam said sheepishly.

Alex knew there had been problems with the company and Thomas told her Corbetron had gotten a hold of some inside schematics, but she had no idea it had gone this far. "Thanks for trusting me with this information. I knew a little bit about it, but I didn't know the problem was this serious. I don't think Thomas knew about the bug either. I'm sure he would have told me if he did." Alex wondered why Luke hadn't told Thomas about the new developments.

"You might want to look through Luke's stuff. He has one of these devices, too. He was secretly working on a patent for it before we let anyone here know it existed. We signed a contract that gave me some of the rights since it was my creation. I still have my copy if you need it. I hope you'll honor the agreement Luke and I made. It's important to me."

Alex was quick to assure her. "Of course I'll honor the agreement you had with Luke. I'm sure our lawyers have a copy of the contract. If not, I'll just get a copy of it from you. I will also check on the status of the patent. Then I'll have you show me the ins and outs of that device so we can start working on marketing. I think it'll be a big seller with the CIA and other government contracts we already have. It's a lot smaller than anything else I've seen," Alex smiled. "See, you're making me look good already. Keep it up and I might think about giving you a raise."

Sam smiled back. She'd been worried she wouldn't get along with Alex. Her friendship with Luke was no guarantee she'd have the same kind of relationship with his daughter. After just one meeting, she already liked Alex and thought they would work together very well. "So, you were asking me about a droid that you could use as a sparring partner. Well, you're in luck. Luke came to me a while ago and asked for the very same thing. I have the specs in this drawer." Sam pulled out a folder and started showing the contents to Alex.

Dusk

Alex was astonished. This was exactly what she'd wanted. If she had a droid she could fight, she could get back in shape a lot faster. Alex wondered if Luke had developed the droid in anticipation of her return. She looked up with a huge smile on her face. "You must be a mind reader. I came in with all these ideas and here they are, already on paper. Any idea how soon you could get a prototype up and running?" Alex inquired.

"Actually, Luke was the mind reader. He was like a kid when he came in with this. He was so excited about his idea. He told me it was a present for someone special. I kind of thought it was for you. Just the way he talked about it, like it was Christmastime and he'd come up with the gift of your dreams. I'm going to miss that, Luke's enthusiasm for a project. I hope he passed that along to you. Anyway, I've been working on this for a while and already have the guts of the project ready. If you approve it, I can put my prototype into one of the droid bodies we already developed for the maid or the butler and you can give it a try in a day or two. Just keep in mind this is the first prototype so there are bound to be some glitches. I'll need to know about any problems immediately. If you do encounter a problem, try to get me as much info as possible on what happened. I'll need all the Intel I can get to pinpoint the flaw."

"Sam, this isn't my first rodeo. I know the drill. I can't believe you're so far along. I thought I would have to wait months before I'd have a product I could test. You could really have one ready in a few days? I absolutely approve a body for you to use, if anybody hassles you about it, have them call me. Use the male body for this one. It always makes me feel better when I can kick a man's butt." Alex handed her a business card with her cell phone number on it. "Call me as soon as it's ready and I'll be down to pick it up. So far, you're proving dad right. I think you're going to become my new best friend!"

Sam laughed as Alex walked out the door. She might be right, they just might become good friends. What a relief. Sam had been stressed about this meeting ever since she heard of Luke's passing. It was good to have it behind her. Especially since it had gone so well.

Chapter Four

Two days later, Alex was in the basement testing out her new droid. It was amazing! She could program it for karate, kick boxing, hand to hand combat or street fighting. So far, there hadn't been any glitches. Alex suspected they had worked them all out on the maid and butler prototypes. Luke was a genius. Well, so was Sam. She had to give credit where it was due. She would definitely keep Sam happy. She'd been thinking about the John Anderson problem. So far, she hadn't been able to find a file on him, but she was sure Luke had one somewhere. As soon as she found it, as long as there was enough evidence, John was going to be fired. Maybe she would talk to Sam about taking his place. She wasn't sure if Sam would be interested. It was obvious she loved her job, but would she want to take on the administrative duties as well? Alex would have to talk to her and see if she was looking for advancement in her career. If so, Alex was going to make her an offer she couldn't refuse!

An hour later, Alex shut down the droid and headed for the shower. She couldn't wait for Thomas to get home so she could show him her new toy. She wondered if dad had told him about it. Luke liked to keep things secret so he could have the dramatic big reveal. One of Luke's favorite things was surprising her and Thomas. He was so much like a little kid at times. He made such a big deal about some things you just had to laugh, his enthusiasm was contagious.

After showing Thomas her droid, they went up to dinner. They hadn't seen each other for a couple of days. Their schedules had conflicted. Alex asked him about John Anderson. Thomas knew there had been some problems, but hadn't known about the bug and he didn't know where dad would have kept a file on John. He assured her they'd look into it and figure out where Luke hid the file. Thomas knew Luke would have evidence gathered to fire John. His father was not one to forgive and forget. He demanded loyalty in his employees. There were no second chances. Thomas and Alex were in agreement, John Anderson had to be watched carefully. If they could prove he was spying for Corbetron, he would be fired immediately.

Marta had the night off, so Alex rinsed the dishes and put them in the dishwasher. She was just headed up to her room when the phone rang. "I'll get it," she called to Thomas and answered the phone. "Hello?"

"Hi, is this Alex?" a familiar voice asked.

"Yes," Alex answered.

"This is Tanya. Please don't hang up. My mom told me she saw you the other day at the grocery store with Marta. I've thought about calling you a million times, but I've chickened out every time."

"That's understandable," Alex replied.

"Okay, I know you're still mad at me, and I don't blame you. I deserve it. But please, can we just meet somewhere and talk. I want to apologize to you in person. What I did was inexcusable. I know. I can't apologize enough, but I would really like to be friends again. Adam and I never actually got together. I felt too guilty about sleeping with him before you two broke up. I told him he was a jerk and I could never trust him. He was a real ass about it. I can't believe I ruined our friendship for that moron. Will you please just meet me and have a drink? We'll drive separately if you decide you can't forgive me, you can leave. Please, just give me a chance to buy you a drink and try to make it up to you," Tanya begged.

Alex wasn't sure she wanted to forgive Tanya, but they had been friends for a long time. Adam, the jerk, was mostly to blame for what happened. Tanya had been drunk at the time, but not blameless. "Okay, one drink. When and where do you want to meet?" Alex asked.

"Really?" Tanya exclaimed. "How about the Westerner? I have to work this weekend, but maybe the next Friday night, say ten o'clock?"

"I can do Friday at ten. I'll meet you in our old booth," Alex replied.

"Oh, I am so glad you said yes. I can't wait to see you again. Friday then, goodbye!" Tanya hung up the phone.

Alex turned to see Thomas glaring at her. "Where exactly do you think you are going on Friday at ten?" he demanded.

"I'm going to the Westerner to meet Tanya on Friday at ten," Alex replied. "Don't you think it's a little rude to eavesdrop on my conversation?"

"No, not when you are making plans to leave the house after dark. That's not rude. It's my duty. You're not going," Thomas said with finality.

"Last time I checked, I don't work for you, you're not my guardian, nor are you my keeper. As an adult, if I want to go have a drink with an old friend I will. You go out all the time with the intention of chasing bad guys. I am simply going to a public place to have a drink with an old friend."

"An old friend you don't even like any more since she slept with your dirtbag of a boyfriend," Thomas quipped.

"Be that as it may, I decided to meet her and see if I've forgiven her. I think she did me a favor anyway. Under the circumstances I didn't have to come up with a lame excuse why I didn't want that gold digger, Adam, around anymore. It was hard to argue with, 'You're a cheating scumbag,' don't you think? Anyway, Tanya and I were friends for a long time. I think I've probably made her suffer enough. I'm meeting her on Friday and that's final," Alex said. Then she turned and walked up the stairs to her bedroom. She had studying to do.

So far she had made it through most of her mother's book. Sometimes it was hard to read every night. It made her miss her mom so much. Other times, she started reading and couldn't put it down. The topic was so interesting and informative. Her mom had written a lot of information. She mostly talked about the fae. Alex still wasn't sure she believed Thomas when he said she had special powers, but it was interesting to hear what some of the other fae were capable of. There were so many different things they could do. Each person was different. Some could heal, but apparently that was rare. Some could control animals and plants. Some could control the weather, fire and wind. What a trip it would be to see someone conjure fire out of nothing or create the wind. She couldn't wait to start meeting some of her people. Then there were the vampires. She still couldn't believe she had a half-brother and he was an evil vampire.

Another thing she had learned was that fae could live for thousands of years. That one took her a long time to digest. According to the information her mother left her, Marlena was 809 years old when she died. Warriors lived just as long. They thought it had to do with the fae blood in their system. Luke was 926 when he died. Funny, they didn't look a day over 40. That still wigged her out. She couldn't imagine living that many years. It explained how she could have a half-brother she didn't know though. He was supposed to be 600 years old. Alex had always been a skeptic. But once she got into the book her mom wrote, it was hard to be skeptical. Everything was so far out there she had to have an open mind, or discount everything her mom wrote. She knew her mom, so she had to believe. It was that simple. Her mom wouldn't make this stuff up. Plus, Thomas and Luke were part of it too. They were the most stable people she knew. If they were off their rocker, her whole family was. She read a little more in the book, but once again her mind wandered. She wondered what Dimitri was doing. Was he out fighting with Thomas? Were they in danger? She realized she had put them in a bind by leaving so soon after her mother's death, but she still couldn't understand why Dimitri disliked her so vehemently. Could she change his mind?

She had started thinking more and more about Dimitri. As she read the book from her mom, she often wondered how Dimitri fit into this strange world. While she was contemplating the fact that her mom was more than 800 years old and Luke was over 900, she found herself wondering how old Dimitri was. As time went on, she thought about him more frequently. It was stupid really. She hadn't seen him since the day of the funeral. She couldn't hide from her attraction to him. Even in her sorrow, she had noticed how handsome he looked in a suit. Sometimes she dreamt of him. Mostly it was when she was worried about Thomas out fighting. She would either dream he was with Dimitri, or that he got into trouble and Dimitri came to the rescue. What a silly girl she had become. She felt like she had a school girl crush on the star quarterback or something. Why did she have such complicated feelings for a man who obviously disdained her? It didn't make any sense. Apparently she was a masochist. Dimitri wouldn't give her the time of day if he ran into her on the street. Yet, she couldn't stop thinking about him, wondering what it would be like to kiss him...or more.

It was definitely time to go to bed. She turned out the lights and laid there in the dark trying not to think about Dimitri or Thomas, or if they were both safe.

* * * *

Friday night Alex was in her room trying not to let Thomas get to her. She had showered and changed into her favorite Levi's and a sexy red top. She looked good if she did say so herself. It had been a long time since she'd felt like getting dressed up to go out.

Dusk

She was just putting on her ruby earrings when Thomas knocked on her door.

"Come in Thomas, but don't think you're going to change my mind. I'm going and you're not. That's final," Alex warned. They had been arguing over this for almost two weeks.

Thomas stepped into the doorway. Alex looked good. Her color was back and she was back in shape; fit and trim. She'd been working out for over a month and it showed. She'd always been small and petite, but she didn't look fragile and weak anymore. She looked toned and if he was honest with himself, she probably was prepared. He just wasn't ready to let her go out on her own. They had gone several rounds over that. If he showed up at the Westerner tonight, Alex would have a fit. He didn't want to make her mad and he didn't want to spoil her fun. He just wanted her to be safe. "You win. I won't go to the Westerner with you. I know you want to talk to Tanya and have a good time. It closes at one, right?"

"Yeah, I think so." Alex knew Thomas had conceded the argument, but he wasn't happy about it. She really didn't want him to worry about her, just like he didn't want her worrying about him every night. He was just going to have to cope, like she did when he was fighting. "I'll come straight home afterwards, I promise. I won't be out later than one thirty, deal?"

"Deal," he said. "I'll be here when you get home so you can fill me in on your evening. I'm dying to know if Tanya's forgiven, or if you punch her out."

"I doubt there will be any punching. See you at one thirty with bells on," Alex teased as she walked passed Thomas and out the door.

The Westerner was crowded and loud, just as Alex remembered it. Once she got through the main door, she started looking for Tanya. She was surprised to see her at their booth. Tanya, Jennifer and Alex used to come here almost every weekend. They had a special booth they liked to sit in. Unfortunately, so did everyone else. They frequently had to wait for someone else to vacate before they could snag it. It was set back in the corner, which gave them a modicum of privacy but also allowed for a good view of the large room. When they were younger, they loved this booth because it was the perfect spot to scope out guys.

As Alex approached the corner, Tanya jumped up and gave her a big hug. "I ordered you the usual, I hope that's okay. I haven't been here long, but I did come a little early in hopes of getting our booth. It worked!" Tanya said with a little too much enthusiasm for Alex.

"I wondered how we got the booth so fast. I hope you haven't been waiting long," Alex said as she took a seat across from Tanya. Just then the drinks arrived.

Once the waitress left, Tanya took a deep breath. "Look, I know this is uncomfortable for both of us. I won't pretend nothing ever happened to end the friendship. I know it's my fault. I can make excuses and say he took advantage of me while I was drunk. We both know I could have said no. I was interested in Adam for a long time. It was flattering when he paid attention to me. I screwed up and it cost me our friendship. I would just like another chance. Do you think that's possible?" Tanya asked.

"I really don't know," Alex said honestly. "You both thought I didn't know about the flirting. I knew it had been going on for months prior to the party. I saw you two together and knew what was coming," Alex sighed. "To be honest Tanya, I didn't really care about Adam. It was your betrayal that upset me."

"Alex..." Tanya tried to interrupt.

"Don't. If we're going to do this, let's get it all out in the open. Adam was more interested in my dad's company than he ever was in me. He thought he could fool me into believing he loved me and eventually end up with a big piece of the pie. That never would have happened. The truth is, I planned to break up with Adam after the party that night anyway. You just gave me the good excuse I was looking for."

"Then why did you get so mad at me? I don't understand," Tanya said with a frown.

"Because it wasn't the first time you had done something like that," Alex countered.

"I never slept with any of your other boyfriends!" Tanya exclaimed. "You really never had that many."

"Tanya, I know about you and Billie," Alex replied gravely.

"What? You knew...?" Tanya looked at Alex in surprise. "You never said anything."

"What was I supposed to say? Tanya, stop making out with my boyfriend under the bleachers when you think I'm busy," Alex said a little sharper than she had intended.

"Did Jennifer tell you?" Tanya asked.

Alex looked at her, surprised. "No, I wasn't aware Jennifer knew. I guess that's something I'll be taking up with her next time I see her. It appears neither one of my friends are the people I once thought they were."

"Don't get mad at Jennifer over this. She caught us at a night game and threatened to tell you. I begged her not to and convinced her I was going to talk to you about it myself. She finally relented, but told me I only had a week. It was shortly after that when you and Billie broke up. I lied to Jennifer and told her I'd come clean. I said you were upset, but you finally forgave me and it would be better if she didn't say anything. You were so upset about the breakup that Jennifer decided to let it drop. How did you know anyway?" Tanya asked.

"I saw you," Alex answered.

Tanya put her head in her hands. "It looks like I have more than I thought to apologize for," Alex raised one eyebrow. "Of course I know what I did. I just didn't know I needed to apologize for it. We were kids. I thought it was best you didn't know. Why have you and I always been attracted to the same guys? Billie was the hottest guy in school. We both met him the same night, but he asked you out instead of me. I couldn't let it go. I pursued him. It may not seem like it from where you're sitting, but I did learn my lesson with Billie. He used me. I let him. He was never serious about me. We made out under the bleachers for a while, but at school or in a crowd he pretended like he didn't even know me. He was proud to be seen with you. I was jealous. I'm sorry," Tanya finished.

Alex realized that she and Tanya would never be close again. Maybe they could be casual friends, but Alex would never trust her. Tanya admitted she was attracted to the same men Alex was and thought that was excuse enough for her behavior. Next time Alex started dating someone, would Tanya's competitiveness kick in? Alex thought it would. She would never be sure Tanya wasn't trying to undermine any relationship Alex had. If there was no trust, they couldn't really be friends. "I do forgive you, Tanya. But I'm not sure what it is you want from me," Alex admitted. "The old days are over. Jennifer is in Italy. She has a good job and she loves it there. I doubt she's ever coming back. I have a lot of responsibilities now that my parents have passed away. I'm never going to be the party girl I was before."

Tanya sighed. "I was afraid of that. I guess I've just been feeling lonely lately and started thinking about the old days. We used to have so much fun and then mom said you were back." Tanya looked away. "I thought..." She stopped abruptly. "Do you know those two men over there? They keep looking over at us. At first I thought they were checking us out, but it's more like they're keeping an eye on us. They're hot, but I've never seen them before."

Alex followed Tanya's gaze and saw Dimitri and one of the other warriors she hadn't met yet. Thomas was in so much trouble!

"You do know them!" Tanya exclaimed. "And as usual you have a thing for the tall, dark and sexy one. Some things never change," Tanya said with a sigh. She had caught the quick gleam in Alex's eye when she looked at the dark-haired man and then quickly looked away.

"I don't exactly know them. They're some of Thomas' friends. I've met one of them before, but I've never met the blond." Alex glanced back over at the two men. Dimitri was laughing at something the other man said. Alex was taken by surprise. She had never seen Dimitri smile, let alone laugh. Of course, she had only seen him twice before, but still, he had seemed so serious. Tonight he was relaxed and man did he look sexy when he laughed. She was still watching him when he glanced over at her. Their eyes locked for just a moment before Alex quickly looked away. Dimitri was a dangerous man. She definitely needed to avoid him. "I need to hit the restroom. I'll be back in a minute." She jumped to her feet and headed for the women's room.

Alex took a couple deep breaths as she left the bathroom. Dimitri had gotten to her. Why was she so taken by a man that despised her? She just didn't get it. As she came around the corner, she spotted Tanya standing by Dimitri's table. Apparently in her absence, Tanya decided to get to know the new hot men in the club. They really were hot. She couldn't get the picture of Dimitri sitting there all casual, laughing and having a good time out of her head. She stopped a little out of their view and watched as Tanya laughed at something Dimitri said. She leaned in closer toward him, brushing his arm as she said something. Alex had seen this act before, Tanya knew how to be flirtatious and seductive. Alex had lost count of the men that had fallen for it in the past. Why not, Tanya was gorgeous. What man wouldn't be flattered by her attention?

She continued to watch as Tanya took the cherry from one of the glasses on the table and slowly slid it between her teeth, guiding it with her tongue. The men seemed captivated. She had their full attention. Alex was surprised at how much watching this all play out hurt. She was jealous of the attention Dimitri was giving Tanya. He was friendly and flirtatious. The way Alex had fantasized he might be with her one day. In mere seconds, her hopes had been dashed. She was left feeling devastated and rejected somehow. "What's wrong with me?" she asked herself. "Why did the man of her dreams have such disdain for her? It doesn't matter why, that's just the way it is. You don't have a chance with him. Accept it. If he's interested in Tanya, you should be happy for her. Didn't Tanya just tell you she was lonely? Maybe they're right for each other." But inside, her mind kept screaming, "No, he's right for me." Somehow she had to get this man out of her mind, but first she had to get out of this club. She was tempted to sneak away without saying a word, but decided she wasn't that big a coward.

She closed her eyes, fighting back tears that threatened to fall. Then, she took a deep breath and walked toward the table. She had to get this over with before she chickened out. As she headed their way, all three of them looked over at her. She plastered a smile on her face and kept walking. She could do this. A quick goodbye and she'd be outta here. The warrior she'd never met spoke first as she stopped beside the table. "So, I finally meet the illustrious Alex. It's a pleasure," he held out his hand and smiled brightly. She took it and shook lightly. "My name's Ty and I hear you've already met Dimitri here," He nodded to his fellow warrior.

"Hey," Alex said looking at Dimitri. She quickly turned back to Ty, the pain in her heart was unbearable. "It's nice to meet you," she turned to Tanya. "Why don't you hang here for a while with these guys? I've gotta run. It's getting late and I have an early morning. Thanks for the drink," she turned and headed for the door before anyone could stop her. She had to get out of here. She had a lump in her throat and was having a hard time breathing.

Tanya caught up to her before she made it to the door. "Hey Alex," she yelled. "Are we okay? I mean, I didn't step on any toes or anything did I?" she asked.

"What? Oh, with them?" she said with a little tip of her head. "No, I told you I barely know them. I'm just tired. It's been a long day and like I said I have an early start in the morning. Give me a call. Maybe we can do this again sometime," she turned and continued toward the exit.

"I'm a little tired myself. I think I'll leave with you." She turned and gave the men a little wave and a seductive smile then followed Alex out the door.

Alex continued toward the parking lot, but Tanya turned and headed in the opposite direction. As much as Alex wanted to get away from this place, away from Tanya and away from Dimitri and Ty, she felt uncomfortable letting Tanya wander off by herself. "You didn't park in the lot?" she asked.

"No, I used my usual spot down the alley," Tanya replied. "Don't worry. I do it all the time. Nobody bothers me down there. See you later," she hesitated. "Alex, I really hope you meant it when you said we could do this again. I'd really like that."

"Sure I did, give me a call sometime." She watched as Tanya turned and headed toward the alley. She started in the other direction, but a noise caught her attention. She looked back toward Tanya and saw movement in the alley. She couldn't see Tanya, but she was sure she saw a man just inside the entrance. Just then she heard Tanya scream. Alex took off in a sprint.

As she entered the dark opening, she could see Tanya lying on the ground. She looked unconscious and three men were standing over her body. Alex set her purse down in a darkened doorway, hopefully it would still be there when she came back for it. Then, she quietly walked toward the men. One of them must have heard her because he quickly jumped up and tried to grab her. She pivoted and he missed. She glanced at Tanya and saw blood. Were these vampires? She had to get them away from Tanya and focused on her. She ducked to avoid a swing from the first guy, but apparently the other two realized they weren't alone now. They stood up and the three of them walked toward her. Good. She started to back away, thinking this would get them far from Tanya and give the impression she was afraid. She kept her eye on all three men as she slowly moved backwards. When one of them jumped for her, she was ready. She twisted to the side and kicked him in the back as he went by. Then, the fight was on.

They were good, strong and fast. She was able to dodge the second guy, but the third one came at her from the side. He got in one good kick to the back of her knee. She started to go down and saw another one coming at her from behind. She let herself fall to the ground and then using her hands, she kicked back and caught him square in the chest. The fight continued. They were coming at her too fast to think about each move. She was working on pure instinct, blocking, kicking and turning as needed. The three men just kept coming at her. No matter how hard she hit, or how many times she knocked them down, they just kept coming back for more. She'd kick, turn, block and then hit, but they just kept coming. She was beginning to wonder how long they could keep this up when two more men exited a door into the alley and joined the fight. Alex knew she was in trouble, but when one of the men pulled a knife, she was sure she was going to die.

Dimitri and Ty watched as the two women left the club. It took a few minutes to take care of the tab and follow them outside. Once they were headed toward the parking lot Ty asked, "Where are they? I can't see 'em anywhere. It didn't take us that long. They should still be in the parking lot. Isn't that Alex's car?"

Dimitri heard a noise coming from the alley and his heart stopped. He looked at Ty and the two of them sprinted for the opening. As they approached, Dimitri was silently chastising himself. He never should have let Alex leave the club on her own. Were they too late? He would never forgive himself if Alex was hurt. They came around the corner and both men froze. Alex was fighting off three vampires. Tanya was lying on the ground. They couldn't tell how bad she was injured. She looked unconscious, or dead. Dimitri couldn't believe what he was seeing. Alex was good, really good. Her moves were graceful and smooth. It looked more like a dance than a back alley street fight. She was beautiful as she glided to the side, turned and kicked, then flipped and blocked. Was this the same woman he'd met a month ago? Man had he misjudged her. He stood there, frozen, admiring her moves. She had such beauty and grace. She was magnificent…amazing! There was no other word for it. This was a woman that could instantly win over her people. All they needed to do was see her fight.

He saw two more vampires step out of a door and into the alley. They immediately joined the fight. That was enough to snap him out of his shock. Five against one was too many for anyone to handle. Ty must have had the same thought because they both started moving forward at the same time. One of the new vampires pulled a knife. As Alex swung out to punch one of the original vampires, the guy with the knife got her right in the ribs. Alex went down. "No!" Dimitri yelled and lunged forward.

Alex was shocked. She blocked a kick and turned to swing at another of the men, then suddenly there was a sharp pain in her side. She went down hard. Suddenly they were all on top of her and she was certain this was it. She was going to die. Then, one by one they were pulled off her and thrown across the alley. She slid backwards and tried to pull herself up to lean against the wall. That's when she saw him. Dimitri had come to her rescue. Her side was killing her, maybe literally, but she couldn't help admiring the force and strength this man had. Ty was there too. They were both strong, but Dimitri was truly a warrior in the most basic sense of the word, majestic. No wonder the men respected him. He had such power. A look and presence about him that you'd have to be a fool to unleash. Between the two of them they took care of the five men almost instantly. When Dimitri pulled out a stake and shoved it into the first man's chest, Alex let out a gasp. The guy vanished into dust. So they were vampires. She figured as much. They were too strong and quick for common men. Once all five of the men, or vampires that is, were taken care of Alex leaned her head back against the wall and closed her eyes. Her side didn't hurt much anymore. Was that a good sign, or did it mean she was dying and had lost all feeling in her body?

Dimitri stopped in front of her. He crouched down until they were face to face. "Are you okay?" he asked, his jaw was set and he was obviously upset.

"I'm not sure," she answered honestly. "I think that guy stabbed me. I had a shooting pain in my side and almost passed out for a minute. I don't hurt much anymore, but I feel a little nauseous. Either I'm dying, or my body has already started to heal. I can't tell which one. Can you help me up? I need to see if Tanya's okay."

She tried to press her weight against the wall to stand up, but she felt dizzy and fell back down.

Dimitri grabbed her around the waist and pulled her to her feet. "I need to see your wound," he said.

"Not now, get me over to Tanya. I need to make sure she's still alive," Alex insisted.

Dimitri grumbled something under his breath, but led Alex over to the lifeless body. Alex crouched down next to Tanya's body and tried to find a pulse. She finally found one, but it was so weak. She pulled at Tanya's shirt trying to find a wound. Finally, she located the puncture mark on the back of her neck. It was deep and still bleeding. She located another one on Tanya's upper arm. There was a third one on her left leg. Alex assumed Tanya was weak because she had lost too much blood. She tried to put pressure on the wound on the back of her neck, but it continued to bleed. She was frantic. She looked up at Dimitri. "What can we do? They won't stop bleeding." Dimitri gave her a sorrowful look. "Nothing," he said. "They didn't seal the wound. She needs a doctor."

Alex wasn't willing to give up. In desperation, she grabbed Tanya's arm and pressed her hands to the wound as hard as she could. Maybe with enough pressure the bleeding would stop. "Stop bleeding," she thought over and over to herself. Suddenly, her hands felt warm and she saw a slight glow coming from her palm. It shocked her at first, but then she remembered what Thomas had said. "You heal quickly. We're not sure if you can heal others, or only yourself." Was she healing Tanya? She was willing to try anything. She wouldn't let Tanya die. She moved her hand and saw the bleeding had stopped. She quickly moved to Tanya's neck. Once the bleeding had stopped there, she moved to the wound on her leg. Alex checked once again and found Tanya's pulse was stronger. She was relieved, but as she tried to stand she felt extremely weak.

Dimitri, impatient now, pulled her to her feet. "We've gotta go. Now! The police will take care of her."

"I won't just leave her here in the alley all alone and hope the police show up to take her to the hospital. Give me my cell phone,

I'm calling the police and then waiting for them to get here before I go."

"That's not possible," Dimitri grumbled.

"Look, you don't have to stay if you don't want to. I'm staying," Alex was adamant.

"Okay," Dimitri said sarcastically. "What are you going to tell them?" he raised an eyebrow and waited for her to answer.

"I'll tell them we were attacked by a group of men and when they heard you and Ty running our way, they fled," Alex declared.

Just then, a police officer entered the alley. "What's going on here?" he demanded.

Alex pushed Dimitri out of the way, if she used the wall for support she should be able to stand. "Officer, I need your help!" Alex exclaimed. "My friend and I were leaving the club when a group of men attacked us. She needs help. I think she needs to go to the hospital."

The officer noticed Tanya lying on the ground. He subconsciously rested his right hand on the butt of his gun. "Who are you?" he turned to Dimitri.

Alex answered before Dimitri could say anything. "This is a friend of my brothers. We were late getting home, so my brother Thomas sent him to try and find us. I'm lucky he did. Once the men heard these two coming, they forgot about us and ran out of the alley." She lowered her voice a little. "My friend Tanya really needs medical assistance. I wonder if you could get her to the hospital. If you need to talk to me, maybe you could come to the house for a statement."

"I really need to question you here, ma'am," the officer demanded.

"I know that's probably protocol, but I was hoping you could bend the rules a little tonight. Pretty soon the media will show up. My name is Alex Deveraux. My father was Luke Deveraux. I'm sure you can imagine what a media circus this will be if I'm caught, after an attack in an alley, so soon after my father was killed in such a similar fashion. To be honest, I'm a little shook up about it. I would really appreciate it if you'd let these gentlemen take me home. Like I said, you can stop by the house anytime if you need a statement." She looked into the officer's eyes and gave him a weak smile.

"I'm sorry ma'am. I didn't realize. I'm sure this has been traumatic for you. I suppose it wouldn't hurt to let you go," he turned to Dimitri. "You, get this woman out of here quickly and make sure she gets home safely. I'll hold you personally responsible if anything happens to her," then he turned and walked toward Tanya.

"Are you satisfied now?" Dimitri asked.

"Yes, but I really do feel weak. Can you hold onto my arm while we walk out of the alley? I don't want to fall down and draw attention to myself," Alex asked.

Dimitri frowned. He put an arm around her waist to hold her up on one side, Ty supported her from the other as they exited the alley. Once they were out of sight of the officer, Dimitri picked Alex up in his arms and walked toward the parking lot.

Dusk

"You don't have to carry me. I can walk," Alex protested but her heart wasn't in it. It felt so nice to be held by her protector. She wrapped her arms around his neck, laid her head against his shoulder and slid into darkness.

* * * *

"She's passed out," Dimitri said to Ty. "We'll take her home in your truck and Thomas can arrange for someone to transport her car later."

"What do you think is wrong with her? Is it the knife wound?" Ty was worried. "Do you think he hit something vital?"

"I don't know. Once we get her in the car I can try to check it out. I think it's more likely she passed out from exertion. I don't know how long she'd been fighting before we got there. Then, that asshole stabbed her. You know how much the healing process takes out of us, especially if we don't have blood readily available. Then, she healed Tanya's wounds too. I've never known a healer before. I don't know how much that takes out of her. I don't even know how it works." Dimitri glanced down, worried that Alex hadn't even stirred.

"How cool was that? When I came around the corner and saw her in action I couldn't move for an instant. I was mesmerized, she was so graceful and fluid as she battled the vamps." Ty glanced at Dimitri. "All those naysayers are going to be surprised when they get a load of our new Queen. Marlena was good, but she's got nothing on Alex!" Ty exclaimed excitedly.

They had reached the truck and Dimitri balanced Alex against him as he reached for the door. Ty was right. Alex had talent and skill. She still needed practice and experience. But for someone as young as Alex to have that kind of poise and those moves was amazing. Watching her fight, he recognized a few of Luke's best maneuvers. He realized Luke had been preparing Alex for a very long time. Dimitri had never met anyone who could fight like Luke, maybe Thomas. Luke was a natural. Some of his moves were original. Many warriors had tried to copy him, but few had ever mastered the complicated maneuvers Luke had honed over the centuries. Alex was lucky, she'd been taught by the best. Dimitri only hoped one day he could be half the man Luke Deveraux had been. He settled into the truck and gently cradled Alex across his lap, making sure her head continued to rest on his shoulder.

Ty started the truck and pulled out of the parking lot onto the highway. Dimitri ran his hand through Alex's hair. He told himself he was only searching for head wounds, a reason she was still unconscious. But her hair was so shiny and soft he found himself lingering for just a moment longer. For an instant he imagined it flowing over his silk pillow case as he... "Stop it!" He told himself, now is not the time for erotic fantasies. He gently moved his hand over her rib cage. He couldn't feel anything broken. He slid her shirt up until he could see the wound. He was shocked to see it was almost healed. He gently brushed a finger over the slight line that crossed two of her ribs. Alex stirred and let out a quiet moan. Dimitri looked up, but she was still unconscious. He looked back down at her rib cage. Then his eyes moved across her perfect abs and slowly rose to her breasts. If he moved her shirt up just a little more...

Dimitri chastised himself. Here he was fantasizing about a wounded, unconscious woman. What was wrong with him? He stared out the side window and took a couple deep breaths. If he couldn't stop thinking about Alex in that way, he was going to embarrass himself. Why did she have such an impact on his emotions? She was just a woman. Okay, so that wasn't true. What other woman could defend herself against three hungry vampires then keep their wits about them when it was all over. She hadn't fallen apart or panicked throughout the entire ordeal. He wanted to cut and run. To avoid answering complicated questions by the police, but not Alex. No, she wouldn't hear of it. She continued to put herself in danger to protect her human friend. Did that come from her royal blood? An instinct to protect? He didn't know. He just knew he was proud of his queen tonight. He was honored to serve her. He was also disappointed in himself for his previous judgments. He really hadn't been fair. So she had looked weak when he first met her. Wasn't that to be expected after your father had just been murdered? It wasn't like him to jump to conclusions like that. He didn't want to examine his reasons too deeply. He was afraid of the feelings he had for this woman. Afraid of what it all meant. Better to ignore them and hope they would pass.

Thomas looked up as he heard a vehicle approaching. As it passed the window, he recognized Ty's truck. He didn't hear another vehicle. Where was Alex? They promised him they wouldn't come back until she was home. What was going on? He quickly stood and headed toward the entryway. Just as he reached the foyer, the front door swung open and Dimitri walked in with Alex in his arms.

Thomas panicked. He ran to Alex and realized she was unconscious. "What happened?" he demanded. "What's wrong with her?"

Dimitri kept walking, headed for the second floor. "You're going to need to direct me to her room. I have no idea where to go once I reach the top of these stairs." The look he gave Thomas left no room for discussion.

Thomas took the steps two at a time and was behind Dimitri in an instant. "There, to the right. The third door," he looked back down at Ty. "Ty, can you go to the kitchen and get Marta. I'm going to need her help," then he disappeared down the hallway and into Alex's bedroom.

The room was dark, so Thomas quickly moved around Dimitri and turned on the bedside lamp. "Dimitri, I need to know what happened. I'm going out of my mind here."

"I know, just let me get her settled. We'll go into the library and I'll fill you in on everything, I promise." He glanced at Thomas and saw the worry in his eyes. "She's okay. I swear. She had a wound, but it's already healed. You know her history, does the healing normally wipe her out like this? Is there something we should give her to get her strength back? We drink blood to expedite and counteract our healing process, but the fae don't need blood to heal. I'm not very knowledgeable in this area. I've never cared for a fae before. Mom wasn't active in the fighting so I never really paid much attention to her habits."

Thomas tried to think back to the few times Alex had been hurt growing up. He couldn't think of any serious injuries she had as a child. The one time she fell and broke her arm, she had gone straight to bed. His mother had made her drink some kind of hot tea or something. "I don't know. The only serious injury I can think of was a broken arm and mom gave her something hot to drink. Something Marlena made special for her. Do you know anyone in the fae community we can ask? Someone who might be willing to come here to help us with this?"

Dusk

"I might. Let's give her a couple hours. If she doesn't improve, I'll call Ariel. I'm sure if I ask her to, she'll come right over." Marta had entered the room, went straight to the bed and started to fuss. Dimitri took one last glance at Alex and then left the room. She was in good hands with Marta. He walked into the library and sat in the big chair facing the fireplace. Thomas walked in behind him. Ty was already sitting on the couch.

"You guys want brandy?" Thomas asked.

"Sure," Ty answered. "But you sit down, I'll get it." He got up and walked over to the small bar situated in the corner of the room. "You want one?" he asked as he looked over at Dimitri.

"I'll take the bottle," Dimitri smiled as he glanced up at Ty.

"No can do, brother. You have to share. I need one of these as much as you do. That silent drive here was nerve racking as hell." Ty handed Thomas and Dimitri a glass and settled onto the couch. "I have to say Thomas, your sister's one heck of a lady! Is she alright?"

Thomas smiled a little. He knew once these guys got to know Alex they would change their opinion of her, but right now he was dying to know what had happened and why his only family was lying comatose upstairs in her bed. "I hope so," he said looking at Ty. "Now, Dimitri, tell me what happened tonight."

* * * *

Dimitri filled Thomas in on the night's events. Ty kept interrupting. Thomas was grateful they got through before Dimitri

84

pummeled him. Thomas had forgotten what a sight it was to see Alex fight for the first time. They'd been fighting each other since they were kids, but he remembered Jake's reaction the first time he watched one of their matches. It was good that Dimitri and Ty had seen what she could do. That they had seen her strength and skill. Maybe the tides were turning. If word got out about Alex, some of the fae who had been sitting on the fence might throw in their support. He just wished she hadn't been injured in the process.

Thomas was a good fighter and he knew it. Alex was almost his equal. Luke had taught them both all he knew. When Thomas was finally old enough to join the warriors, he expected to be the weakest link. Not so. From the minute he was introduced to the other warriors, he was one of their best fighters. That had surprised Thomas. He later realized he owed it all to Luke. Since he was a small child, his father had been preparing him for his destiny. Once Luke and Marlena got together, Luke insisted the sparring become a family event. Marlena agreed. She had been a good fighter, too. And with her history, she wanted to make sure Alex could protect herself. Marlena didn't use her skills very often but when she did, she was hard to beat. Thomas could eventually hold his own against his father. He was proud of that. Every time he went out to fight, he felt like he was honoring his father's memory by using a skill his dad had taught him. Luke also taught Alex. From a young age she was a firecracker. Thomas needed to remember that. Tonight had been difficult. He fretted the whole time she was out and then when Dimitri walked in the door, carrying her limp body he was sure he was going to lose her.

Thomas' thoughts drifted to Alex. Fighting her was a challenge. He loved to take her on. She was so competitive. He especially liked it when he won. She didn't take losing well. That made the victory even sweeter. Thomas took a deep breath. "I'm going to check on Alex again."

As soon as he heard about the knife wound he had jumped up and ran into Alex's room. She was wearing an extra-large t-shirt, Marta's doing Thomas was certain. It made it easy to examine her ribs, but there was no wound. After carefully checking both sides - twice, he went back down to the library. Dimitri had been patient with Thomas. When he came back, he just picked up the story where he'd left off. Now, Thomas was anxious to check on her again. She still wasn't awake and that worried him. "If there's no change would you mind calling Ariel, Dimitri? I'd feel a lot better if someone that knew what they were doing checked her out."

"I was just thinking the same thing. I'll feel a lot better after Ariel tells me there's nothing to worry about." He took out his phone and started to make a call.

Thomas entered Alex's bedroom. He didn't think she had moved an inch. Marta was sitting in the chair in the corner of the room silently keeping watch. Her eyes followed Thomas as he walked to the bed and sat down beside Alex. Thomas picked up Alex's hand before he glanced back at Marta. He recognized the worried expression on her face. He just didn't know what to say to comfort her. Like him, she was reliving the horror of losing Luke and before that, Marlena. He looked back at Alex. He wasn't going to lose her. This wasn't the same. He just had to keep reminding himself of that. Alex was breathing and appeared perfectly fine. Her body had just taken a blow and needed to recover. She'd be fine in the morning.

He looked back over at Marta and saw a tear run down her cheek. He stood up and walked over to her. "Come on," he said holding out his hand. Marta took it hesitantly. Thomas pulled her to her feet and guided her out of the room. Once in the hallway, he pulled her into his arms. "Marta, she's going to be okay. I promise. This isn't the same as before. You know Marlena went almost instantly and dad had too many internal injuries. His body couldn't fight them off. Alex had one injury and her body is just trying to recuperate. I don't know what to do for her, so Dimitri is calling his friend Ariel. Once she gets here, we can all relax. I was thinking of calling Jake unless you want to," he looked at her questioningly.

"I already did, just a few minutes ago. He's on his way. He's worried too. But like you, he's confident she'll be alright with time. It was hard with Luke and Marlena, I loved them like they were family. But you two are like my kids, Thomas. I just can't stand to see my kids in pain," Marta said a little embarrassed.

Thomas smiled at her. He turned her to face the bedroom so she had a good view of Alex. "Now, look at her. Does she look like she's in pain to you?"

"Well, no. I guess she doesn't," Marta admitted.

"Right you are. I think we're in more pain than she is. She's probably dreaming about your pumpkin pie, or what she's going to do with the garden in the spring. Let's go downstairs and wait for Jake. He should be here any minute," Thomas guided her toward the stairs.

Just as they entered the library, the door opened and in walked the rest of the gang. Jake was first, then Nicholas, Dante, Victor and Bastian. That was just like the warriors. They didn't care that it was now two in the morning. They were all here to give him moral support because they knew he might need it. Jake went straight to Marta and wrapped her in his big arms. She seemed to collapse into him and then started weeping. He silently escorted her out of the room. Thomas knew Jake would take care of Marta. That was one less thing he had to worry about. He suspected they wouldn't see Jake or Marta for the rest of the night.

"So, we heard there was a paa-rty going on here at the maan-sion and decided to stop by and see if we could weasel a drink," Dante broke the silence.

Thomas smiled. Leave it to Dante to try to lighten the mood. "Help yourself. There should be plenty to choose from at the bar," he walked over to Dimitri. "Any luck with Ariel?" he asked.

"She should be here any minute. I told you Ariel's solid. I knew if I told her it was important and I needed her help, she wouldn't hesitate." They all heard a car pulling into the driveway. "I'm sure that's her now, she lives close by."

Bastian looked over at Dimitri. "Who's Ariel? You've never mentioned her before. Your new flavor of the century?" he joked. "Judging from your charming disposition lately I'd guess it's been about a century since you got laid? I think you're due!"

"Very funny," Dimitri quipped. "Ariel is a close family friend. I think you'll like her. Keep in mind, she won't take shit from any of you. Any of you guys get in trouble with her, you're on your own. I won't be coming to the rescue." Dimitri walked to the door and opened it before Ariel could ring the bell.

Ariel was tall for a woman. She stood about five-eight. Her blond hair stopped just below her shoulders. She looked at Dimitri with a serious expression. "Where's my patient?" she asked.

Dimitri guided her toward the stairs. He planned on introducing her to the gang, but that could wait until later. She was here for Alex. Obviously she was anxious to see for herself what was going on.

Victor had been standing next to the window, casually leaning against the wall. As Dimitri walked passed the doorway, he couldn't help but notice the sexy blond he was leading up the stairs. She was tall and fit. As she glided up the stairs, he noticed her tight little butt and those gorgeous long legs. He was surprised at himself. He usually didn't have this reaction to a woman. After 547 years, a woman was just another woman. But Ariel, that was one woman he wouldn't mind getting to know better. Well, in the biblical sense anyway. He reminded himself that looks weren't everything. He'd have to see if she had a personality before he let himself get too excited. He had become picky in his old age, not that he was going to let anyone in on that little secret. She must have felt him watching her because she casually looked over her shoulder. Their eyes met for half a second, then she winked at him and disappeared down the hallway at the top of the stairs. Victor gave a little laugh, then walked over to get himself another drink.

Chapter Five

Alex slowly opened her eyes. It was mostly dark, but she could see a dim light in the corner and a figure sitting in the chair next to the lamp. She was still a little foggy and couldn't remember where she was. She blinked, trying to bring the figure into focus. She blinked again, it looked like Dimitri and was he reading the paper? Where was she? Slowly her head began to clear and she realized she was in her bedroom. Why was Dimitri in her bedroom? Just then a woman appeared at the side of her bed. Now there was a stranger in her room. She must be having one of her bizarre dreams. Maybe if she closed her eyes, she would wake up and everything would be back to normal. Whatever normal was. She didn't really know anymore.

Alex opened her eyes again. The woman was still there. She tried to sit up, but her head was killing her. She immediately laid back down with a moan. The woman picked up a mug from the night stand and handed it to her. "Bad headache?" she asked.

Alex started to nod, but decided that wasn't such a good idea. "Yeah, got any aspirin?" Alex asked.

"No, but if you drink the contents of that mug, I promise you'll feel a lot better. I'm Ariel by the way. I'm a friend of Dimitri's."

Alex glanced to her right. Of course this gorgeous blond who could be a runway model was a friend of Dimitri. That's when she noticed that Dimitri had walked over to the side of her bed. He watched her for a few minutes and then turned toward the door. "I'm going to go tell Thomas you're awake. Need anything?" he hesitated for a second, but when neither woman replied he walked out the door.

"That man watched over you all night and all day. It's a good thing you woke up. I was on the verge of strangling him. I've never seen him like that. He must really care for you." Ariel said as she took the mug and set it back on the night stand.

"Dimitri?" Alex snorted. "He doesn't even like me. I'm sure he's only worried about his rep. Probably won't be good for his record if I died on his first babysitting excursion," Alex answered.

"If you say so," Ariel smiled as she turned to the doorway. "Come on in Thomas, she's all yours." Ariel patted Thomas' shoulder as she walked out of the room.

"Um, hi Thomas. Try to be nice. I have a killer headache," Alex winced. "How much trouble am I in, anyway?" Alex was beginning to remember the events that landed her in bed. Just then she remembered her friend. "How's Tanya? Has anyone checked on her?" Alex asked, concerned.

Dusk

"Tanya is fine. She'll live to steal another boyfriend." Thomas smiled as he sat down on the edge of the bed. "I checked on her this morning. She was taken to the hospital last night with a few bruises. She hit her head pretty hard. They say she had a concussion. Lucky for us the doctors think that's what knocked her out. They kept her overnight and then released her first thing this morning. I sent flowers and our get well wishes and everything," he rolled his eyes.

"This morning? What time is it?" Alex tried to look around to find something that would indicate the time but the slightest movement made her head hurt.

"It's eight o'clock at night. You've been out for about twenty hours," Thomas said with a frown. "How are you feeling? You gave us all quite a scare."

Alex closed her eyes. Twenty hours? She could only imagine what was going through their minds, especially so soon after dad. "Other than the headache, I feel fine. Oh, I told a police officer he could come to the house and I'd give him a statement. Have you seen him?" Alex asked.

"A detective stopped by this morning. He was a little suspicious when I told him you were resting. He wanted to come up and make sure you weren't injured. I lied. I told him you were so emotional after your attack, especially after what happened to dad, that I gave you a sleeping pill and sent you straight to bed. I said it would probably knock you out for most of the day. That satisfied him. He left his card and said to have you call him in the next day or two. Apparently nobody got a very good description of the men who attacked you, which means they don't have any good leads to follow up on. He was hoping you could tell him something that would help. I suggest you don't tell him Dimitri put a stake in their heart and they vanished into thin air. He might lock you up in the looney bin," Thomas smiled.

"You don't seem mad at me," Alex said, confused. "I thought I was going to get a lecture on why I shouldn't have gone out and how you told me it wasn't safe and I should have been more careful. Then I'd have to hear how I'm never leaving the house again and if I do, you're going to be stuck on me like glue. On and on and on..."

"I'd say that about covers it," Thomas answered. "Alex, I told you I was going to worry when you went out the first time. Even I didn't realize how hard that was going to be. Yes, you got injured, but you healed. We don't think that's what knocked you out, anyway. We think it was all that healing you did for Tanya. I assume that's the first time you've healed anyone," Thomas asked.

"I'd forgotten about that!" Alex said in surprise. "You were right. I guess I do have special powers. Yes, of course that's the first time. Don't you think I would have said something if I'd done that before?" Alex answered exasperated. "This is big! I can heal people."

"Yeah, and then you're down for the count for twenty hours afterwards. I think if I were you I'd be a little more selective when I decided to save someone. You know, make sure they deserve it and all," Thomas teased.

Alex sobered. "Tanya did deserve it. No, I don't trust her but I don't want her to die." Alex looked toward the window, not speaking for a minute. "Thomas, I can't have friends anymore, can I? Did Tanya get attacked because she was there with me?" Alex looked back, sadness settling on her face. "Did they smell me, go crazy and attack Tanya?"

Dusk

"No. From what Dimitri said, I don't think they even knew you were fae until one of them stuck you in the ribs with that knife," Thomas looked at her solemnly. "Then they went nuts. You should have seen me when Dimitri told me you'd been knifed. I panicked, ran upstairs and fumbled around to find your wound. Of course, there wasn't one. By that time you were completely healed. From what I heard, it was a pretty nasty wound but it was mostly gone by the time Ty and Dimitri got you here. What happened to Tanya wasn't your fault. In this instance, she was lucky to have you as a friend and close enough to come to her rescue. But you're right. It's dangerous to have human friends. They can't protect themselves and if you protect them, you'll give away our secret. Why do you think I don't hang out with Brad anymore?" Thomas frowned.

Alex hadn't really thought about Brad since she'd been back. There was so much going on and Thomas had the warriors. Brad had completely slipped her mind. "To be honest I haven't really thought about Brad. Sorry, I know he was important to you." Alex reached for Thomas' hand. "What happened? I know you wouldn't have stopped hanging with him unless there was a good reason."

"There was. We had gone out for a drink one night and were leaving the club. Brad and I were walking down the sidewalk when I smelled a vampire."

"What!" Alex interrupted. "You can actually smell them?"

Thomas looked confused. "Yeah, didn't I tell you that? It's how we hunt them. We think that because we have some vampire blood in us, it enables us to smell them. We've had a lot of debates over how that works and if vampires can smell each other. I think they can but none of us know for sure. It's just a theory and if I'm right that means they may be able to smell us, too. Not a very pleasant thought. Anyway, Brad and I were walking down the sidewalk and I smelled a vamp. I almost took off after him, but then I remembered I was with Brad. I was struggling with how I could protect Brad, keep our secret, but at the same time follow the vampire. Then, Nick came around the corner. He stopped to make sure I made eye contact and then followed the vamp trail. I knew he was trying to tell me it was okay, stay with Brad he had it covered. I felt guilty, but didn't know what else to do.

I stayed with Brad. As we approached his car, another vampire jumped us. Brad was hurt pretty bad. It was hard for me to fight like a guy, not a warrior. As soon as I could get Brad to the hospital, I hurried back to where I'd last seen Nick. It took me a while to track him, but I finally did. He had some serious injuries. I was afraid he wasn't going to make it. It turns out it wasn't a single vampire. He was headed back to his coven. Nick walked right into a pack of wild vampires. Lucky for him this particular coven was fairly small. After the fight, they just left him there to die. That's when I found him. I was able to get him back to the house and tell dad what happened. He knew a fae by the name of Tianna. She cared for Nick while the rest of us tracked down the coven and took care of them. After that night I realized I couldn't hang with Brad anymore. Not in public anyway. We tried to keep up the friendship, but he didn't understand why I wouldn't go to parties or clubs with him anymore. Slowly we just lost touch. I spent all my time with the warriors and he found other friends," Thomas frowned. "I check up on him every once in a while. Just because we can't hang out, doesn't mean I don't care anymore."

Alex was silent. She was thinking of Jennifer. When she left Italy, she knew their friendship was going to change. Jennifer was happy in Florence. She had a great job and had already been

Dusk

promoted once. Jennifer knew Italy was where she wanted to be. Alex knew she wouldn't leave New York again. They had experienced the same kind of separation Thomas and Brad had gone through. Alex realized maybe it was for the best. She wouldn't put Jennifer in danger. They would continue to stay in touch by email and phone calls, but Alex would probably never see Jennifer again.

The door opened and the woman, Ariel, walked back in. "Sorry to interrupt, but I need to make sure Alex drinks another mug of tea. She's pretty weak and the more of this we can get down her, the faster she's going to get back to normal." Ariel handed Alex another mug of hot liquid.

"So, Ariel, how do you know what's going to make me get back to normal. And, what's in this tea?" Alex asked.

"Oh," Thomas answered. "I forgot to tell you. Ariel is fae. None of us knew what we were supposed to do and I remembered mom giving you tea when you broke your arm. So, Dimitri called Ariel. Thanks again Ariel for all your help."

"No problem. I taught Marta how to make the tea. You should keep some on hand at all times. You never know when you're going to need it," Ariel smiled at Thomas. "Alex is lucky to have so many people that care about her."

Thomas smiled back. "I'm going to let you two talk. I need to warn you, Alex has been bugging me for weeks to find a fae who can answer all her questions. I hope you can get out of here before midnight," Thomas laughed as he silently closed the door.

"You're fae?" Alex was excited. "I don't know anything about the fae. Well, that's not exactly true. My mom left me a book with some information but she left so much out and you can't ask a book questions. Thomas is right, you better run now if you want to escape. Otherwise, I am going to keep you occupied for hours!"

Ariel pulled up a chair. "Ask away. I don't have anywhere to be tonight. I'm more than happy to stay and visit for as long as you like."

* * * *

For the first time in days Alex was down in the gym with her droid. She was just getting ready to start her workout when Thomas walked in. "Hey," Alex exclaimed. "Do you have time for a match? Human competition is always better than mechanical droids."

"Can't, I need to get to the office. I noticed you have two droids in the closet. When did you get the second one?" Thomas asked.

"Oh, I forgot to tell you about that. Once I got started with the droid, I remembered you telling me about the fae blood and vampires hunting in groups. So I called Sam and had her make me up a second droid. Just so you know, I told her it was for you. I thought it would sound kind of fishy if I said I wanted to fight two droids at once. Anyway, I had been working with both of them for a couple weeks before I went out to the club with Tanya. I'm grateful I did. The first couple of days with two droids was depressing. I thought I'd never get the knack of fighting multiple enemies. It helped me a lot when I was trapped in the alley with three of them," Alex looked over at Thomas. "I thought I'd start with one today, but then work my way back up to fighting them both. I'm not wasting away in the house all my life so I'm anxious to get back into fighting condition."

Dusk

Thomas groaned. "You're going to be the death of me little sister. But you'll have to find an excuse for Sam because I want my own droid. I have certain criteria I want followed very carefully. It has to be female. I want it to have gorgeous brown hair and big boobs. I've already acquired my own outfit. I want to dress my special droid in tight leather pants and a skimpy leather tank to match," Thomas smiled. "You getting all this down? If it's not to my specifications, I'm going to have to send her back."

"Send me a memo. I'll be sure to submit your request for a skank droid as soon as I get it in writing." Alex lowered her eyes at him. "I'm not making you a sex droid. That's just sick!"

"I don't want her for sex! I just like my competition to be sexy. If I have to train, I might as well have a good time doing it," Thomas countered. "See you at dinner. I have a lot on my plate today. I might be late. Oh, did you remember we have that charity event next week?"

"No," Alex groaned. "You know how much I hate those. Can't you just handle it?" Alex whined.

"We both have to be there. It's the first event since dad's death. We need to be there to show our support. But more important, we need to show solidarity in the company. Here's the problem. Obviously it will be nighttime when we leave the ball. And, obviously you will need to wear a dinner gown. Not the best attire in the event you run into trouble. I was thinking maybe one of the warriors could escort you. That way if anything happened to or from, you would have backup." Thomas tried to give her an innocent smile.

"Thomas! I keep telling you I don't need a babysitter," Alex argued.

"Not a babysitter, an escort. Think back to the alley. How would you have handled that if you were wearing an elegant evening gown?" Thomas countered.

"Okay, fine. I'll go with one of your warriors, but you have to arrange it. It's not a date! It's just a bodyguard." Alex yelled as Thomas walked out the door. She went back to the droid and got to work.

* * * *

Saturday night, Alex walked into the library. She was wearing her favorite black evening gown with medium high heels. Evening wear was not her favorite attire. Give her a sweatshirt and a comfortable pair of jeans any day. Thomas still hadn't told her which warrior was going to be her escort. Whenever she asked, he just said whoever's available. As she scanned the library, she was shocked to see Dimitri lounging comfortably in Luke's chair in a tux. Thomas had his back to her as he rinsed out brandy glasses. Alex's heart skipped a beat. Dimitri was stunning. The tux was obviously tailored to fit, not one of those rent-a-tuxes. She realized at that moment she didn't know much about Dimitri. Did he have a job? Was his job leader of the warriors? Did that pay? She had no idea. She really didn't know anything about the man. It was hard to get to know someone you'd never had a conversation with because he hated you.

Thomas turned back and spotted Alex. "You look great, sis. Are you ready to go?" Thomas put down the glass he was cleaning. "I'd like to get there by seven. There are a couple of guys I need to talk with tonight. Dinners at eight, so that should give me plenty

Dusk

of time to corner them before the meal," he turned to Dimitri, "You ready?"

"Whenever you are," he smiled at Alex.

Had she entered a parallel universe? One where Dimitri was actually nice to her? She didn't know. So far this evening was starting out pretty bizarre.

Dimitri stood up and took Alex's shawl. "Here, let me help you with that," he said as he wrapped it around her shoulders. "You look stunning," he whispered.

Alex turned, shocked by his compliment. This man was a puzzle. Prior to her injury, he had shown nothing but disdain for her. After the attack, nothing. She saw him that one evening in her bedroom when she woke up and then he was gone. She hadn't seen him again until tonight. Now here he was, acting like the perfect gentleman. Had he volunteered for this, or was he the only warrior that wasn't busy tonight? What did this all mean? Don't get your hopes up, Alex thought to herself. Just because he's escorting you, it doesn't mean anything. Remember, you told Thomas it wasn't a date just a bodyguard. What better bodyguard than Dimitri? You saw him fight. Thomas just asked for the best and Dimitri agreed. It's a big night, there are going to be a lot of people and Thomas wanted the best so he didn't have to worry. The three of them walked out and got into the waiting limo.

The party was at one of Deveraux Industries finest hotels. The hotel itself was glamorous and had the most elegant ballroom in town. When they arrived, the room was already packed. She looked around but didn't see anyone she wanted to talk to. Thomas immediately excused himself saying one of the men he needed to do business with was already there. With a wave, he hurried off.

"How about a glass of champagne?" Dimitri asked taking her arm and leading her toward the side of the room.

"Sure," Alex replied. "That would be great. You don't need to go to the bar though. If you wait about two seconds one of the servers will come by with a tray. Whether you're drinking or not, it's best to grab one. Otherwise you'll have a million people ask you what you want to drink." Alex ventured a sideways glance at him. Her biggest challenge tonight was going to be keeping her eyes off Dimitri and her imagination in check. Oh, the things she would love to do to that man. Apparently most of the women in the room were having the same thoughts. The double takes as they walked through the crowd told it all. Too bad this wasn't a date. Alex had the best looking guy at the ball. For one night she could pretend, couldn't she? Usually, the only way she got through these things was by getting a little drunk. Not tonight. If she got drunk, she would certainly make a fool of herself with Dimitri. Tonight, she needed her wits about her. One glass of champagne was going to have to last the entire evening. Maybe a glass of wine at dinner, but that was her limit!

Calista Ainsley, one of Alex's least favorite people and the town busy body, walked into the room. Calista was from the south and came from "old money." She thought that still gave her status in the community. Maybe down in the south but in New York, nobody cared. She made a beeline for Alex and Dimitri. "Here we go," Alex mumbled under her breath. She saw Dimitri give her a questioning look, but didn't have time to explain.

"Alex!" Calista said as she grabbed Alex's hands and gave her a quick kiss on the cheek. "I'm so glad you made it, tonight." She slid a little closer to Dimitri, invading his space. "And who is this handsome young man you have with you?" She looked up at Dimitri and gave him a big smile.

"Calista, this is Dimitri. Dimitri, Calista Ainsley." Alex said as she looked around for an excuse to run.

"I'm an old friend of the family, but I don't recognize you. Dimitri...?" Calista let his name fade, ending with a question, clearly expecting Dimitri to give her his last name. He didn't. "Are you from around here?" Calista asked as she lightly laid her fingers across Dimitri's hand and admired him openly.

Dimitri looked down at his hand and then raised his eyebrow at Calista, she quickly removed her hand and looped an arm through Alex's arm instead. "Not originally, no. But I have lived here for several years," Dimitri answered.

"Oh, really? Did you know Luke Deveraux then?" Calista inquired.

"Yes," Dimitri answered.

Calista looked at Dimitri inquisitively, obviously wishing he would elaborate. He didn't. Calista continued clearly frustrated. "I'm surprised Luke never mentioned you. We go way back, you know. Luke and I were close friends for a very long time. I was devastated when I heard about the attack. Just devastated. I cried for days, truth be known. I'm not ashamed to say it. When you were as close as Luke and I were, it's only to be expected. I don't know if Alex told you, but Luke and I were engaged for a while. Unfortunately things just didn't work out, but we always remained dear friends." Calista looked over at Thomas. "Your brother is looking well tonight. I see he didn't bring a date, again. He's still the most eligible bachelor in town. I was sure he would have settled down by now. Why in the world is he talking to that dreadful man? Don't tell me Deveraux Industries plans to do business with the likes of Randy Brinckley. I do hope you and Thomas uphold Luke's professional ethics. Deveraux Industries will be a disaster if you start to undermine Luke's policies and forget his moral character."

"Well, never mind that," Calista said with the wave of her hand. "I suppose you think all that business is old fashioned. Only time will tell. Alex, aren't you in your late twenties already. You know once you hit thirty chances are pretty slim you'll find a suitable husband. I guess you don't have to worry about that though. Now that you inherited all that money from your step-father," she glanced back at Dimitri and took a sip of her champagne. "Of course, I come from old money," she told him. "One of the few elite left in this town."

Alex looked over at Dimitri, he was scowling again. At least he didn't like Calista Ainsley any more than she did.

"So Dimitri, what do you do for a living?" Calista asked.

"I date rich women," Dimitri answered. "I'm sorry, would you excuse us. I just spotted someone I need to talk to." Dimitri took Alex's hand and pulled her away from Calista. "Any reason you let that old bat slam you like that?" Dimitri asked.

Alex glanced at him. He was still scowling as he pulled her into the crowd. "Calista's a gossip and a snob. She's one of the elite, a simple socialite left over from the old days. She has to get her little jabs in whenever she can because she's jealous. She chased after Luke for years, but he wasn't interested. Apparently she told all her friends Luke planned to marry her right about the time he met Marlena and the rest as they say, is history. She got egg on her face. She can't stand the fact she didn't get the guy and now the girls'

103

daughter inherits a fortune. Don't believe that crap about her and Luke being close. He couldn't stand the woman any more than I can. We just tolerate her because she's such a troublemaker. If you piss her off, she does her best to make your life miserable. I don't care what she says about me. I just don't have the patience to defend myself every time I turn the corner. So I tolerate her insults, bite my tongue and avoid the old hag as much as I can." Alex was still walking, but Dimitri reached out and grabbed her arm. She stopped and looked back at him. "What?" she asked.

"How much trouble did I just make for you with my dating rich women crack?" Dimitri asked.

"Not much for me," Alex smiled. "I'm afraid you did just paint a target on your own forehead though. Calista is going to stay up nights trying to find dirt on you. If she can't find any, she'll just make it up. Before the end of the night everyone in this room is going to know you don't have a job, you're just a gold digger out to woo the rich man's daughter. And poor pitiful me, I'm not bright enough to see you for what you really are. Luke will soon be turning over in his grave!" Alex laughed.

Dimitri hated these things. That's why he stopped attending this type of function a couple hundred years ago. It seemed nothing ever changed. There was always a town busy body eager to spread gossip. Business men who thought they were important, but were really too insecure to stay home for fear they would miss something. A movement caught his eye and interrupted his thoughts. He looked over Alex's shoulder and saw a man heading right for them. "Incoming, at eleven o'clock," Dimitri said. Alex turned to look and let out a long sigh. "Another one of your favorite people I gather," Dimitri inquired. "Need help?"

"No, this will be very short." Alex replied just as a handsome man in his mid to late thirties stopped in front of them.

"Alex, I need to talk to you in private," the man said briskly.

"Sorry, Adam. I'm busy counting how many men Arianna hits on before she goes home with one, it might take me all night. Hey, maybe you should go talk to her. You might get lucky again," Alex turned to leave. "Isn't hooking up at parties your specialty?"

Adam reached out and grabbed her arm. Dimitri stiffened and moved toward him. "Get your hand off my date," Dimitri grumbled. He wasn't sure who this guy was, but he didn't like him. He also sensed there was a history here with Alex. She was clearly upset, but trying to act nonchalant.

Alex looked over at Dimitri in shock. His date? Surely that was just for show. He didn't really consider this a date, did he? She laid a hand on Dimitri's arm. "It's okay. Adam was just about to tell us why he's man handling me in public. Weren't you Adam?"

Adam looked at Dimitri, then gave Alex a pleading look. "Alex, I really need to talk to you in private. Could we just go into the other room for a moment? I promise it won't take long."

"No. Anything you have to say to me, can be said in front of Dimitri." She knew she was pushing it but she reached over and slid her hand into Dimitri's, wrapping her fingers around his tightly.

Dimitri froze. Her hand was so soft and delicate. Her touch sent a warm tingle rocketing through his body. He was about to pull away when he glanced over and realized she needed moral support to get through this encounter. He tried to ignore the sensations her touch had awakened in him. He gave her hand a little squeeze in comfort, then glared at this Adam clown.

Adam frowned and let out a little sigh. "Fine, I guess we can talk here. Well first, I wanted to give you my condolences for your father. I was sorry to hear about his death, especially so soon after your mother's condition. I know you were close to both of them and it must have been a devastating shock." He glanced nervously at Dimitri then back to Alex. "If there's anything I can do for you, I hope you'll give me a call. Anything at all, you know I'm a good listener." He smiled at her and tried to move in closer. "We had such a special relationship once. I think you know how much I loved you, Alex. I still do. I always hoped one day you'd agree to be my wife. I know we had a slight misunderstanding, but if you'd let me explain I think we could still work things out." Adam paused and looked at Dimitri. "Please just call me. Or better yet, come by the house sometime," he added quickly. "If we could just talk in private I know you'd agree, we're perfect for each other."

Alex felt the atmosphere grow cold. She was afraid Dimitri was going to throw Adam across the room. As pleasing as that thought was, she needed to stop this nonsense. "I just want to make sure I'm clear," Alex stated coldly. "When I walked into that bedroom at the Griffith's party two years ago and caught you naked on the bed with one of my best friends, tongue down her throat and I won't mention where your poor excuse for a penis was, that was just a little misunderstanding. You really loved me. You still love me and you want to marry me. This unconditional love has nothing to do with the fact that my wealthy father has just passed away and you think you can get your grimy little hands on my fortune. Does that about cover it?" Alex asked.

Adam turned bright red, clearly angry. He quickly glanced around to make sure nobody had overheard her. Alex was relieved to see they were essentially alone in the corner. Nobody could hear anything. Dimitri had shifted slightly and was shielding them from the crowd.

"I'll take that as a yes." Alex continued when Adam didn't respond. "I'd tell you where to shove your condolences, but I'm too much of a lady. Don't bother me again, Adam. You were a manipulative gold digger when I met you. You were a cheating dirtbag when I dumped you. And now you're just an opportunistic fool trying to capitalize on the death of a great man. It didn't work before and it's not going to work now. Leave me alone. Otherwise, I'll be forced to use my new power and wealth to gain a little support from the local police department."

She turned to walk away, but was abruptly stopped. She realized she was still holding Dimitri's hand and he hadn't budged. He was standing there, big and daunting, his massive body looming over Adam. She looked at his face and froze. "One more thing," Dimitri said. His voice was so low it was almost a whisper. Somehow that made the words even more threatening. "Alex won't need to contact the police. She has me. So, let me make sure you are crystal clear. You will not contact Alex again. You will not call her, you will not email her, you will not send a message by carrier pigeon. You will not mention her name, not even to your closest friends. If you even think about contacting Alex in the future, you will answer to me. Got it?" Dimitri asked.

Adam didn't respond. He just stood there, frozen, staring at Dimitri.

Dusk

"Are we clear?" Dimitri demanded his voice a little louder now.

"Yes," Adam croaked. Then he turned and scurried away.

"I need air," Alex whispered. Dimitri led her toward the open French doors and out into the courtyard. They continued along the path to the gardens. She stood there, slowly breathing in and out until she felt she had her emotions in check. It was then she realized she was still holding Dimitri's hand. "Oh sorry," she said as she dropped it quickly. "I wasn't thinking," she finally looked into Dimitri's eyes. "You're a scary man," she said flatly.

"I think you handled that well." He said casually as he looked into her eyes, trying to read her. How had that weasel convinced Alex to go out with him in the first place? He couldn't imagine her accepting one date with the fool. He didn't want to think about it. When Dimitri realized Adam was an old boyfriend he immediately felt a jolt of jealousy, then contempt for the man. He had held Alex. Kissed Alex. Probably made love to Alex. Dimitri couldn't even go there, the thought of that weasels grimy hands touching her was enough to drive him insane. Then when he heard she had caught him in bed with one of her friends, he wanted to kill the guy. The idea this low life had caused her one minute of pain infuriated him. She handled herself well, he had to give her that. She was still angry but as he studied her, he could tell she was beginning to calm down. "Do you want to talk about it?" he asked.

"I don't know. Probably not. I'm sure you think I'm a complete moron dating that guy for one minute." She looked away in shame. She knew she had lost any chance with Dimitri after that little scene. Gain an inch, then get catapulted back a mile. She should have known better. When it came to men, Alex was a horrid train wreck waiting to happen. Start to care about someone and wham, derailed!

Dimitri reached over, lifted her chin with one finger and looked directly into her eyes. "I think that guy's a fool. He didn't deserve you. And, I think you're right, he's a simple gold digger. I'm sure he showed up tonight knowing you would be here, thinking he could sweet talk you back into his life. You were his ticket to easy street. He doesn't know you very well does he?" Dimitri asked.

Alex was surprised. Not the reaction she anticipated from Dimitri of all people. "I'm sorry. I guess I owe you a little background on Adam since you had to witness that scene back there," Alex hesitated. "Don't worry. I won't hold you to the threat. It was a good bluff. I'm sure it worked. Adam is a weasel, but underneath it all I think he's just a coward. He won't bother me again. He won't want the confrontation with you."

"I don't bluff," Dimitri stated simply. "And I think I caught the high points, or low points, already. But if you want to talk I've got plenty of time," he said.

Alex walked over to a bench and sat down. Dimitri followed. He sat next to her and picked up her hand again in support. "When I met Adam, he was charming. I guess he grew on me. I didn't fall head over hills for him or anything. There was something about him I never trusted. But, we had a good time and little by little I developed feelings for him. After a while, I started to see the real Adam. I didn't like it and tried to pull back, but he wouldn't allow that. Then he started hinting that I should talk to my dad, get him a promotion. He loved me. Didn't I want him to have a respectable job and so on? When I didn't talk to my dad immediately, he started to get more forceful. He never hit me or injured me in any way." She said quickly as she felt Dimitri stiffen.

"He just tried to intimidate me, which didn't work. Next he started to nag. Our relationship would be better if he had a more respectable position at the company, stuff like that. I'd finally had enough and decided to end things for good. I was trying to figure out how to get out of our relationship without a big scene. One night we went to a party. I knew I couldn't just break up with him. He wouldn't accept it. I had tried that before. He just kept calling and apologizing until he wore me down and I gave him another chance. I needed a good reason but couldn't think of one. Halfway through the party Adam was nowhere to be seen, so I went upstairs. I wanted to go somewhere quiet and formulate a plan. I walked into the master bedroom and that's when I found Adam and Tanya on the bed. I no longer needed a plan, he cheated, the relationship was over."

"Tanya?" Dimitri asked in surprise. "From the club? And you still talk to her? The two of you are still friends?" he said incredulously.

"Yes, Tanya. And no, we're not still friends. That night at the club was the first time I've spoken to her since the party. She called and wanted to buy me a drink. I hadn't been out since before mom died and it seemed like a good idea at the time. I realized a couple things that night. First, I wasn't upset at Tanya anymore but I could never trust her. I'd always wonder about her and anyone I dated or wanted to date. Then, after the attack, I realized it's not safe for Tanya to be my friend. Knowing me puts her in danger. So, yes I have finally forgiven Tanya. For one thing she was drunk that night and Adam was stone cold sober. I blame him more than her. For another, I'd known what Tanya was for a long time and decided to keep her as a friend anyway. I can't hate her now for simply being who she is."

"That makes sense in a strange sort of way," Dimitri paused. "You okay now?"

"Better I guess," Alex answered.

Music drifted from the open doorway of the ballroom. "Well, if you're going to drag me to a charity ball, do I at least get a dance before we eat?" Dimitri asked with a smile.

Alex laughed. "Sure, that's the least I can do. I did drag you here, force you to tolerate Calista Ainsley and Adam Chastaine, then if that wasn't enough I drug you out to the garden to air my dirty laundry." She stood up and walked toward the open patio door. "Thanks for listening and not jumping on the opportunity to make me feel stupid about my sordid past."

"Anytime," Dimitri smiled. He pulled her onto the dance floor and into his arms.

Considering how the night began, Alex was actually enjoying herself. Once they re-entered the ballroom things drastically improved. Dimitri was an excellent dancer. Being in his arms made her forget all her troubles, it also stirred passions deep inside that were hard to ignore. It took an enormous amount of self-control not to grab this gorgeous specimen and kiss him blind. What was it about this man that brought out such desire in her? Thank goodness the music stopped and they were directed to the dining hall for dinner.

Dusk

* * * *

Dinner went well. They were surrounded by friends and Dimitri was good at socializing with new people. She was still amazed this was the same man she'd first met in the library. He'd been charming and understanding all evening. She couldn't help wondering if this was like Cinderella, at the stroke of midnight the fairytale ends.

Alex was standing in a group of people finishing off a glass of champagne when she realized she was starting to feel a little too good. She'd forgotten her promise to only have one drink. How many had she had? A glass of wine with dinner and two, no three glasses of champagne. Or was it four? No three, she thought, well maybe four. Whatever the count, it was obviously one too many. Good thing Dimitri was all the way across the room with Thomas. She wasn't going to make a fool of herself tonight. No more alcohol or she might jump on the man and try to have her way with him. Alex smiled, that was certainly a pleasant thought.

A few hours later, Alex exited the women's room and went in search of Dimitri. She was getting tired and wanted to go home. As she scanned the ballroom, she spotted him lounging in a chair, head back against the wall with his eyes closed. So, he was tired too. The party raged around him as he slept quietly in that uncomfortable chair. Alex stopped a minute to admire him. He looked so cute in a rugged and sexy sort of way. She'd never wanted a chance with anyone in her life as much as she wanted one with him. They seemed to be getting along pretty well tonight. Did she dare hope for more? Just then, he lazily opened his eyes, looked at her and smiled. She smiled back and continued across the room.

112

"I'm ready to head home, how about you?" Alex asked, silently wishing the night didn't have to end.

"Sorry, you caught me catnapping. I was out pretty late last night and had an early morning. You could fire me for sleeping on the job, but since I'm a volunteer what's the point?" His mouth curved into a slow smile.

Alex wondered if he had really volunteered. Was it possible he had wanted to spend an evening with her? No. He was just joking around. But what if...? "Maybe you could make it up to me some other time," Alex said coyly. The words were out before she could stop them or consider the consequences; must be that champagne.

"Oh, yeah?" Dimitri raised one eyebrow, intrigued. "How's that?"

"Well," Alex hesitated. Keep it light, she told herself. "I need a sparring partner. I've been training with my robots, but human competition would be nice. I'd love a chance to kick your butt in a fight."

Dimitri laughed. "Not exactly humble are you? What makes you think you could kick my butt? I'm bigger, stronger and of course more experienced."

"Willing to put your money where your macho ego is?" Alex teased. "Fifty bucks says I can beat you."

"I have a better idea. The loser buys dinner," Dimitri countered. He wanted to spend more time with Alex. Time alone, getting to know her better. He decided not to tell her he'd been keeping an eye on her from a distance. But he was never far behind when she went out alone during the day. Thomas said she was learning about their lives pretty quickly, but he didn't know if she was aware she was in danger. He wouldn't scare her but now that he was the leader of the warriors, he couldn't let Alex get hurt either. He worried he was falling in love with this woman. The more he watched her and interacted with her, the more he was drawn to her. He'd never met anyone like her before. He was tired of fighting his feelings and trying to pretend they would just go away. But was acting on them smart, especially now? Before he could take back the offer, Alex answered.

"You're on, it's a bet." She held out her hand to shake on it.

Dimitri shook her hand, but didn't let go. "Help me up. Let's go home."

They started across the ballroom, both deep in thought. "You up for a short walk to the parking garage, or do you want me to call John and have him bring the limo to the front door?" she asked.

"Maybe a walk. The weather's nice outside and the walk might feel good." What? Now he was talking about the weather? What an idiot, Dimitri thought. You are so desperate to extend your time with Alex, you're talking about the weather. He had to get a grip! He was entirely too caught up in this woman. He thought about her all the time during the day and fantasized about her at night. Right now, all he wanted to do was push her up against the wall and kiss her, slowly and passionately. What was he going to do? Being so close to her was distracting. If there was trouble, would he be too distracted to do his job? When Thomas asked for volunteers to take Alex to this ball, most of the guys said they'd be happy to go. He told himself it'd be best to stay away from her. Let someone else do it. But, the thought of someone else spending so much time with

Alex gnawed at him until he finally couldn't stand it. He told Thomas as the leader, it was his responsibility. He wouldn't pull one of the warriors off the street for an entire evening to attend a party. He wondered if Thomas had seen through his lame excuse, but to Thomas' credit he didn't say a word.

They exited the front door and continued down the sidewalk. There was a slight breeze that added to the atmosphere of the evening. Most of the businesses were closed down for the night. The security windows were pulled, doors locked and the doorways were dark. Dimitri turned. Alex thought he was going to say something but realized he was trying to move her out of the way, to shield her. Suddenly, a man jumped from the shadow of a doorway. Before she knew what was happening, Dimitri was lying on the ground, bleeding from his head. Was he okay? It looked like he may have been knocked out. She turned to see the man holding a metal pipe, but she didn't think it was a man. She was pretty sure it was a vampire. He was charging toward her, pipe raised. She was mentally preparing to fight, cursing her long dress when Dimitri shifted and kicked the vampire's legs out from under him. The vampire went down hard and the pipe clattered away.

They were on the ground, wrestling. Dimitri was bleeding profusely. She knew he was hurt pretty bad and the vampire kept hitting Dimitri's head against the pavement. Dimitri was holding his own, but how long could he last with that wound? She had to help, but how? She needed a weapon, something to use to stake the vampire. She remembered the pipe, that might work. Where was it? She was frantically looking around on the ground. It had to be here somewhere. She glanced back at the two fighting men. She saw Dimitri reach into his boot and pull out a stake. He quickly thrust it into the vampire's chest. She felt instant relief until she saw

Dusk

Dimitri slump back to the ground. He wasn't moving, he just laid there motionless.

Alex ran over to him and rolled him onto his back. She needed to help him up and get him to the garage. They needed to get home. Thomas would know what to do. Dimitri groaned. He started to push himself up, but fell back down again. He had so much blood oozing from his head. But that didn't stop him, he tried to get up again. Alex moved in behind him. She linked her arms through his and pulled him backwards. She got him as close to the building as she could, then moved in front of him to help him sit up.

"Thanks," Dimitri said. Lifting his hand to cover the gash on his head.

"Your head's still bleeding. What can I do to help?" she said, a little panicked now.

"I'm okay," Dimitri could hear the concern in her voice and needed to calm her down. "I just need to sit here a minute and catch my breath. We need to get out of here. They'll smell the blood and I'm not up for another fight yet." He glanced over when he felt her sit down beside him.

"I couldn't find the pipe," Alex said, her voice a little shaky. She closed her eyes in an attempt to hold back the tears that were starting to form. "I knew you needed help, but instead of jumping in, pulling him off you or coming to your aid, I started looking for that stupid pipe and I couldn't find it."

"Hey," Dimitri said as he put an arm around her. "I'm okay. Look at me." All he wanted to do was comfort her, but they needed to get out of here. Alex finally looked up, straight into Dimitri's eyes.

"I'm okay. I was here to protect you, not the other way around. I do this all the time. The scent was just a little off and I thought he was further away than he really was. If he hadn't been on top of us so quickly I wouldn't have been injured at all. This was my fault, not yours. It's just a flesh wound. The important thing is he didn't get to you. Maybe you should call the limo and have it pick us up here though. I'm not sure I can walk and we really do need to get out of here as soon as possible." Dimitri gave her the best smile he could muster.

Alex took the phone Dimitri offered, called John and then handed it back. A trickle of blood was running down his temple. Alex reached up with a finger and brushed it away. She had left her purse at home, so she didn't have anything to press on the wound to stop the bleeding. She brushed her thumb across his cheek to wipe away another trickle of blood. Dimitri was just sitting there so still, looking at her with those beautiful chocolate eyes and that dashing smile. Without thinking, Alex leaned in and gently pressed her mouth to his.

As soon as she realized what she'd done, she quickly moved away. "Sorry. I'm so sorry. I didn't mean..." She stopped when Dimitri grabbed her hand. He slowly raised it to his mouth and kissed her palm.

"Don't," he said as he glanced over her shoulder. "Our ride's here. Can you help me up? Or maybe John..." his voice trailed off and he didn't finish. John was by her side in an instant. He helped her lift Dimitri to his feet. Together they were able to guide him to the limo. Once inside, Dimitri slumped across the back seat and passed out.

Dusk

Alex sat in silence watching Dimitri as they approached her house. She was so worried, the bleeding still hadn't stopped. She kept thinking of Luke as he lay there, battered and dying in the hospital. Thomas would know what to do. She called him to warn him she was bringing Dimitri home and he had a head injury. As they pulled down the drive, she saw the door open and Thomas and Nicholas stepped out.

As soon as the limo stopped, Thomas yanked the door open and peered inside. He quickly surveyed the interior of the car. Alex knew he was checking her out to make sure she wasn't injured too. "Stop wasting time on me, Thomas. Get Dimitri into the house and take care of him. I'm not injured. He protected me." She jumped out of the car and hurried inside.

They took Dimitri up the elevator and into the spare bedroom. It was a simple room next to the one Alex occupied. Her mother had decorated it in neutral colors. She wanted any guest to feel comfortable whether they were male or female. For that reason, she hadn't put anything too frilly or masculine around to decorate. Alex didn't really like it, she thought it was too impersonal. The first thing she noticed when she walked into the room was several bags of blood. She looked at Thomas in shock. "Do you think he's lost so much blood he needs a transfusion?" she asked.

Nick smiled as they laid Dimitri on the bed. Thomas glanced over at her. "No," he answered. "Take off his boots while I take care of this," he ordered as he moved to an IV rack. Nick abruptly left the room. Alex wondered where he was going, but was too captivated by what Thomas was doing to pay much attention. He hung the blood bag on the rack and then pulled a needle out of a small hard case. It looked like a medical kit. Alex stood there, watching Thomas as he prepared Dimitri's arm for the needle. Thomas looked up at her. "Boots!" He demanded.

"Oh!" Alex jumped. She went to the bed and pulled off his boots. Then she started to pull the sheet over Dimitri's body.

"Wait," Thomas ordered. "We need to get him undressed. This is going to take a while and he should be comfortable. He can't sleep in those clothes."

Alex looked at Thomas in shock. Did he expect her to undress Dimitri? She looked down at the bed and saw that Dimitri's head wasn't getting any better. "Thomas, his head won't stop bleeding. What should we do?"

"Give it a minute. Once I get this bag hooked up I can look at the wound," Thomas answered absently. "I'm going to need your help with this, you're not going to pass out or anything are you?"

"No, but don't you think it's more important to stop the bleeding? What if he has brain damage?" Alex questioned.

"No, I think it's more important that I handle things my way and you try to get that tux and shirt off him," Thomas countered. "I'm the one that knows what I'm doing here. Have you ever cared for a wounded warrior before?" Thomas challenged.

"No." Alex could tell Thomas was getting impatient with her, but she didn't care. He was annoying her too. She stepped back to the bed and tried to gently remove Dimitri's jacket. Once she finally got that off, she started to undo his shirt. There was so much blood on it. Maybe it looked worse than it was because it was white. But

Dusk

Alex knew better. She'd seen his head bleeding. She was worried he'd cracked his skull and had serious damage. Once she got the shirt off, she looked back at Thomas. He'd just finished hanging the IV. She gathered up the clothes and took them into the bathroom. She came back with a wash cloth and started to clean up the blood. She couldn't help but notice how wonderful and masculine his chest was. She wished she could lie down next to him and run her fingers through all that dark, perfect chest hair.

She immediately cut that thought, she didn't need to go there right now no matter how hot he looked lying there shirtless. She gently washed the blood off his face and started to move toward his head when she noticed Thomas was by her side. "I need you to hold his arm perfectly still. He can't move while I insert the needle, then I can handle it from there." Thomas seemed to know what he was doing. Alex wondered just how many warriors he had patched up like this in the past.

Once Thomas got the needle in, Alex let go of Dimitri's arm. She stepped back and was going to go back to washing his face when Thomas suddenly looked up at her. "Get the pants off too and I'll look at his head." She noticed the IV was all hooked up and blood was running into Dimitri's arm. She thought she saw a slight smile on Thomas' face before he turned his head but she wasn't sure.

"I really don't think Dimitri would appreciate knowing while he was helpless and unconscious, a woman he barely knows undressed him down to his underwear," Alex argued.

"Of course he would. He's a guy and you're a beautiful woman. He'd be happy to know you undressed him. He'd be unhappy that he was unconscious and couldn't enjoy it," Thomas laughed.

"Not funny Thomas," Alex quipped.

"Look, I have to see what I can do about this head wound. He can't heal until it stops bleeding. Head wounds bleed a lot, but this one is pretty serious. I have to put pressure on the wound until the bleeding stops. The blood from the IV should help. So, you have to undress him and make him as comfortable as you can. We're all adults here, Alex. What's the big deal? What's gotten into you anyway? I've never known you to be shy," Thomas questioned.

I'm not shy with anyone but Dimitri, Alex thought but she didn't say anything. "Fine," she conceded. "I'll finish the job, but if he's angry or uncomfortable when he wakes up, he's gonna have to take it up with you." Alex pulled down the sheet and started to unbutton Dimitri's pants. She held her breath. She could do this. Her heart was beating so fast. It was bad enough controlling her desperate urge to hold and caress him while he was just lying there helpless without a shirt, but now she had to remove his pants. What if her hand accidentally touched his privates? She'd be mortified. His long legs were so masculine and firm. Thomas was in the room. She could control herself. She'd seen men in their underwear before. This was nothing different. Just a guy, lying on the bed in his underwear. Yeah, right! She decided her apprehension wasn't only because of her feelings for him. It was also about his feelings toward her. The problem was, she didn't know what those feelings were. Before, she was positive he disliked her intensely. But now, she wasn't so sure. He didn't freak out over that kiss - she closed her eyes, what had she been thinking! But he was so sweet when she freaked and didn't seem to mind at all. She'd like to say he enjoyed it but that was the problem, she just didn't know. There hadn't been enough time.

She took a deep breath and started to pull down his pants. As she pushed them lower, her eyes hesitated on the large bulge under his briefs. She closed her eyes and with a quick pull, his pants were down around his ankles. She lifted one leg at a time. Don't look up, Alex. Don't look up and you won't spontaneously combust. She finally got the pants off and stole one long gaze up that gorgeous body. Then, she realized his socks were still on. That seemed weird, so she focused on removing his socks then quickly pulled the sheet over his body. Well, she thought, that's over. At least I'll have good dreams tonight!

She looked up and saw Thomas watching her, amused. "What?" she demanded.

"Nothing. I just didn't realize until this moment that you had the hots for Dimitri," he said, humor obvious in his voice.

Alex glared at him, then turned and disappeared into the bathroom with Dimitri's pants. She walked back out with a clean wash cloth. "Are you finished with his head so I can clean up the blood?" she wasn't amused at Thomas. She certainly wasn't going to respond to his obvious interest in her feelings for Dimitri. She was going to deny, deny, deny until she knew where things stood. She would not reveal the depth of her feelings for this man to anyone, not even her brother. She didn't know how much of that Thomas had witnessed and realized her cheeks were growing hot. She was not going to be embarrassed. It was perfectly natural for a woman to admire a sexy man lying on a bed in his underwear. A woman would have to be dead to be unaffected by that body!

"I'm finished," Thomas answered. "Now, he just needs rest and plenty of blood. I'll come check on him in an hour or so to change the bag. You can go to bed if you want, you look beat."

"I think I'll stay with him until he wakes up. I hear he did that for me when I was injured. I guess this is payback. Thomas, before you go, explain the blood through the IV for me. I'd really like to know what's going on." She looked up at him and he could see the worry in her eyes.

"Oh that," Thomas replied. "Sorry, I keep forgetting you don't know all this stuff. Like you, our bodies heal by themselves. Remember you saw my shoulder wound, but the next day it was almost completely healed?"

"I remember," Alex answered.

"Well, with a serious wound like the one Dimitri got tonight, especially a head wound because they bleed so severely for so long, we need extra blood to replenish us after the healing process. That wasn't very clear. When we get a serious wound, our body sends extra blood to the wound to help it heal quickly. The healing somehow depletes the blood. That leaves the rest of our body short, I guess. So, we need blood to replenish the blood used up to heal the wound. Or in Dimitri's case what he lost because of the wound. Does that make sense?" Thomas asked.

"I think so," Alex was silent for a moment. "Do you always take it through an IV?" she inquired. "I've never seen you or dad go through this."

"It doesn't have to be taken through the IV. We can also drink it. However, most of us aren't thrilled with the taste or texture so we prefer an IV. I'm not sure if it has to do with the vamp blood in us or what. If that's the case, you would think we'd like to drink blood. I can't stand it. Most of us feel the same way. Dad hated it too. However, drinking is the quickest way to get large amounts back into the system. If Dimitri was awake, I'd make him drink at least one bag. Then I'd let him get the rest intravenously. He's using up a lot to heal the head wound, and on top of that he lost a lot before we got the bleeding to stop. I brought up three bags, but we'll probably end up giving him four just to be safe. Also, you never saw this because it was one of the thing's mom hid from you. Plus, dad and I didn't get injured very often. I credit all the training dad insisted on. We fought well together. It was like second nature and easy to cover each other's back." Thomas was watching Alex for a reaction.

"What? Did you expect me to run out of the room screaming?" Alex laughed. "It's not anymore bizarre than the other stuff I've learned over the past month and a half. Why are you looking at me with such nervous anticipation?"

"I don't know. It's not every day you hear your brother and your father drank blood." Thomas sighed with relief. "I just thought you might be a little freaked out by it, that's all."

"No more than anything else. Getting it through an IV seems sort of scientific anyway, not creepy like vampires sucking your blood. I don't know, maybe it's a little weird, but I'm not that creeped out about it. I might be if I saw you pour yourself a glass and guzzle it like Pepsi or something." Alex looked back at the bed. "While he's out, I'm gonna go change. I watched you pretty close. I think I can change the bag myself if you want to go to bed. I'll take care of him tonight. If I need anything, I can come get you."

"Okay, if you're sure. I'm pretty beat. I was out late last night. We were looking for a particular group of vampires. They've been very active lately and they're starting to be more vicious in their attacks. None of us wanted to break the trail and go home, we want those guys bad. Then, I had those staff meetings early this morning," Thomas yawned. "On top of that, there was the charity event. Once I got home, I planned to hook up with Nick and Dante to help out for a couple hours, but then you called. I had to pull Nicholas back here to help with Dimitri, which left Dante on his own. We don't like to do that, it's too dangerous. That's why Nick couldn't stick around to help out here. I'm glad I had you, trying to handle that all myself would have been tricky. Sometimes if we're unconscious, the body jerks when we insert the needle. That's why I needed your help to hold him still," he glanced back at Dimitri. "You're sure you can handle this?" Thomas inquired.

"Yeah, I can handle it. I'm not that tired, I think I'll read for a while. Go to bed. You look beat!" Alex left the room and headed in to change.

Dusk

Chapter Six

Dimitri had slept well, or he was unconscious all night. Thomas had brought a fourth bag of blood into the room, placed all of them into a small cooler and then went to bed. The fourth bag was almost depleted now. It was early in the morning. Alex was watching the sunrise through the window. Dimitri still hadn't stirred a bit. She pulled the blinds shut tight to keep most of the sunlight from entering the room. Then, she walked over to the bed and very gently sat on the edge. Leaning over Dimitri, she used the dim light to examine his head wound. Surprisingly, it looked good. It wasn't completely healed like Thomas' shoulder had been the day following his injury, but it was well on its way. Alex suspected this wound had been more serious and would take longer to heal. She reached over and gently pushed his hair aside. She wanted to make sure the entire gash was healing.

Dimitri woke and felt someone playing with his hair. No, they weren't playing, they were touching lightly on his head. Then he smelled her, that wonderful flowery fragrance that he had become so accustomed to. It was Alex. What was she doing? Then he started to recall the events of last night, all the events of last night. Well, he thought it was last night. The grand finale was her kiss, so soft and gentle. Too bad he had been injured. Well, actually that was probably the reason for that kiss in the first place. So, maybe he was glad he was injured. And maybe he was sick! He slowly opened his eyes and watched her.

She was examining his head. She must be checking on his wound. He realized he was in a strange bed. It must be one of the Deveraux guest rooms. He also realized he was in his underwear. For a fleeting moment he wondered what had happened to his clothes. Forget the clothes, the way Alex was leaning over him gave him a great view of those perfect breasts. If he sat up just a little, he could lean forward and press his mouth against that tight t-shirt and...bad idea Dimitri. Now you woke up junior. How are you going to hide that, lying here in your underwear covered by a thin sheet? Good going. Think of something else, quick. But how? Alex was so close, her smell was intoxicating. He just wanted to pull her on top of him and...

"Good morning." Alex felt Dimitri stir and realized he was awake. She sat back and studied his face. "How do you feel? I think you were hurt pretty seriously last night."

So he'd only been out for one night. Good. He smiled up at her. "Did you take care of me?" That's when he noticed the IV pole and the empty bag of blood. He looked back, searching for some sign of discomfort.

Alex noticed his eyes go to the bag and then back to her. "Not exactly. Thomas hooked you up and got things started." She deliberately looked over at the blood bag. "I just changed the bags as needed."

Dimitri was still studying her face and noticed the fatigue. She must have been up all night taking care of him. He reached up and brushed a finger over her cheekbone. "You look exhausted." He moved backwards to make room for Alex. Then, he gently pulled her down on the bed next to him. "I'm still a little tired, yet. Why don't you lay down here with me and we can both take a little nap?"

Alex resisted at first, but what was she thinking. If Dimitri wanted her next to him, she was more than happy to comply and she was so tired. She lifted her legs onto the bed and Dimitri covered her with the sheet. Then he put one arm around her and pulled her close. They were cuddled, spoon style and her heart was pounding a mile a minute. She shifted slightly to settle in closer and felt the large bulge pressing against her. She smiled. Good, he wasn't in complete control of himself either. She was so exhausted, she couldn't keep her eyes open. As soon as they closed, she was fast asleep.

Dimitri lifted himself up on one arm. He laid there next to Alex, watching her for a long while. She had been so exhausted. Once her head hit the pillow she was out. His hand was resting casually on her slim waist. He reached up and brushed her hair away from her face. She had such beautiful features. Those big blue eyes, of course he couldn't see them right now but when he looked into those eyes it was like getting lost at sea. Sometimes during a raging tempest. He smiled, then leaned down and kissed her temple. He loved her perfect little nose and those tiny lips. What he wouldn't give right now to kiss those lips. He couldn't deny his feelings for her any longer. He had fallen in love with this woman. The question was, what should he do about it? Their lives were so complicated and dangerous. Was it really fair to act on his emotions when he knew he had to leave her almost every night to fight a war with the vampires? He didn't know the answer. He wasn't sure he could stop himself from acting on his feelings much longer though. He rested his arm around her waist, laid back down and slowly drifted off to sleep.

Alex heard something clang and woke up abruptly. She opened her eyes to see Thomas taking things from a tray and arranging them around the small table by the window. She panicked and started to get up, but was held in place when Dimitri's arm locked around her. She struggled, but stopped fighting when she felt his lips brush her ear and he whispered, "Relax, you're not going anywhere. It's just Thomas."

Thomas turned around. "Good, you're awake," he said.

Alex was surprised he didn't have the slightest reaction to the scene he walked in on. Like it was perfectly normal for his sister to be lying next to his almost naked friend in the guest bed. She was so embarrassed. She wanted to run to her room and hide, but Dimitri wasn't letting go of his death grip.

"Morning Thomas," Dimitri said cheerfully. "Sorry about last night. I appreciate your family taking me in and seeing to my recovery."

Thomas glanced down at Alex. She was obviously embarrassed. He wanted to laugh out loud. Better to pretend everything was perfectly normal. He didn't think Dimitri would forgive him if Alex over reacted and bolted. "Alex did most of the work. I think she stayed up all night checking on you and changing your blood bags. You surprise me sis," Thomas said casually. "I thought dealing with this for the first time would freak you out. But you handled it like a pro." He smiled at Dimitri. "I bet you're hungry. I know I'm always famished the morning after..." Thomas hesitated and his smile widened "...an injury," he finished.

Alex narrowed her eyes at him. She wasn't amused with his innuendo. Thomas was going to be in big trouble!

Dimitri laughed.

Apparently he was amused, Alex thought.

"Yeah, me too," Dimitri said casually. "Did you bring enough for two?" He had sat up in the bed, but somehow was still maintaining that death grip so she couldn't escape. Just then her stomach growled softly. Dimitri smiled down at her. "I think Alex is starving too."

"Plenty," Thomas answered. "I've gotta bolt. I have things to do at one of the offices. Oh Alex, I think I may have figured out where dad might have put that file we've been looking for. I'll check on it while I'm out and about today. See you at dinner." And with that Thomas turned and walked out the door.

Alex rolled over on her back, put her hands on her face and groaned.

"What's wrong?" Dimitri asked, trying to sound concerned but she could hear the smile in his voice.

She opened her eyes and peaked through her fingers at him. "You know, don't be coy." She sat up intending to get out of bed.

He grabbed her and quickly slid her underneath his body. "Is it so bad, getting caught in bed with me, that is?" he asked. He was serious now. Clearly searching for an honest answer.

"No," Alex admitted. "But why did it have to be Thomas? I'm never going to live this down. The sly innuendos have already started and I haven't even done anything. At least he wasn't upset about it."

"Why would he be?" Dimitri asked. "We're both healthy adults. This is natural." He leaned down and gently kissed her neck just below her earlobe. "I've been meaning to talk to you about that, the haven't done anything yet part I mean." He gently kissed her temple.

Alex's heart was racing. She was shocked at how his words and actions were affecting her. She wanted him to kiss her, hard and deep. She wanted him to ravish her. Was this really happening? Was Dimitri really this attracted to her too? Or was he just looking for a quickie? Alex didn't do quickies. Maybe she should make that clear, right now. She was about to speak when Dimitri pressed his lips against hers. It started out gentle, but quickly deepened into a hard and hot kiss.

Dimitri slowly moved back. He was still hovering over her. They were both breathing hard. "I want you, Alex. And unless I've completely lost my senses, I think you want me too." He was looking down at her, his eyes were smoldering with desire. But there was patience there too if that was possible. He was waiting for her permission to continue.

Oh, what the heck. She did want him. She'd deal with the consequences later. She reached up, put her hand behind his neck and in answer pulled him in for another kiss. This time she was in control. She went to work on his mouth with wild abandon. If she was going to be reckless, it was going to be memorable.

Dusk

It was memorable alright. The things that man could do in bed. She knew she was inexperienced, but none of the men she'd dated were anywhere near that talented. They had finally managed to pull themselves out of bed and inhale the food Thomas left for them. Cold eggs had never tasted so good. When they were finished, Alex started to clean up the dishes. She really needed to get the day started, but Dimitri had so expertly maneuvered her back into bed. He said he wasn't finished. What could she say, you only live once. She hadn't protested, not even a little.

* * * *

A few days later Alex relaxed, naked under her thin sheet next to Dimitri. Her head was resting on his big shoulder. She was slowly moving her finger over his chest, playing with that gorgeous dark hair. His head was propped against the headboard, his hand resting on her hip. "Do you mind if I ask you something?" Alex asked hesitantly.

He looked down at her. He sensed something in her voice, a hesitance maybe. "No, ask me anything." He wanted her to be at ease with him. "I don't have any secrets." They'd been together every day since the night of the party. Dimitri finally felt like Alex was starting to get comfortable with him. Some days their schedules would only allow them to meet for lunch. Other days, they spent hours together. He looked forward to the time they shared, but it always left him longing for more.

Alex laughed. "You have more secrets than anyone I know," she countered. "Maybe that's just because this is so new. We're just starting to get to know each other. I was just wondering how old you are.   If that question is too personal, or if it makes you uncomfortable..."

"Alex," Dimitri interrupted.   "After what we've just experienced with each other, I don't think anything is too personal. No, it doesn't make me uncomfortable to share that information with you. I know I can trust you. It might make you uncomfortable though," Dimitri hesitated.

"So you're really old then," she replied. "Well, for an old man you still have some pretty good moves," Alex teased. She quickly sobered. "Tell me, I can take it. I don't know if Thomas told you, but before mom died she wrote some things down for me. So I know fae and warriors can live for a very long time. Mom was more than 800 years old when she died and Luke was over 900 years old. I kind of figured you'd have to be pretty old to take over as leader of the warriors when dad died. I don't think you could be over 900 though, because then dad probably wouldn't have been the leader. So, how old are you?" she inquired.

"Four hundred and sixty-three," Dimitri said soberly.   He guided her to a sitting position so he could look her in the eyes. "Does that bother you?"

"Honestly?" she asked.

"Of course," he said, his heart dropping. Of all things, his age was going to cause them problems.

"Yes and no," she said flatly.

"Explain please," he said.

Dusk

"Well," Alex paused trying to gather her thoughts. "If I had to guess, I'd say you look like you're in your mid-thirties. Maybe a couple years older than Thomas. So it's not like I would ever look at you and say, 'Hey old guy.' In that way it doesn't bother me at all. That night at the ball, my date was the most desired guy there. I'd say that's pretty cool."

"Not true. Thomas was the most desired guy at the ball. I'm just the free loader remember," he paused. "But?" Dimitri pressed.

"But, that's a huge advantage," Alex answered.

"I don't follow you," Dimitri admitted.

"You have the advantage. You have over 400 years of knowledge. I can't even imagine the things you have lived through and experienced. The things you know firsthand. What it was like to use electricity for the first time, drive a car the first time. You are more than 400 years old. You've had so many experiences, gained so much knowledge. I'm a mere twenty-eight. How boring does that have to be for you? How could I possibly keep your interest? If we were just talking about the human stuff, I would still be extremely ignorant," Alex sighed.

"So, you think you are going to bore me because you didn't ride in buggies and use oil lamps?" Dimitri questioned.

"I'm being serious," Alex said, exasperated.

"I can see that. I just don't get why you think all that stuff matters," Dimitri countered truly baffled.

"Let me try it this way. In the past, relationships for me have always ended badly. Because of that, I have to admit, I really haven't had that many," she looked away from him. This was too hard to admit. "It just started to seem inevitable that if I cared for a guy, I would get hurt. So, I stopped allowing myself to care. Problem solved, I wouldn't get hurt. Then you came along. I don't want to scare you away, but I need you to know that I care for you a lot. I don't do shallow flings. It's not in me. But it's probably routine for someone your age. When you walk out that door and go back to your life, it's going to hurt me. I just think you have the advantage," she paused.

Dimitri spoke up. "When!" He had been frustrated and a little confused. Now he was angry and insulted.

She heard the resentment in his voice. "I didn't mean to..."

"Do you honestly believe we could have just shared those passionate moments so completely, so intimately, if we didn't care for each other? If the feeling wasn't mutual? I know we haven't had a lot of time together, but I didn't realize your opinion of me was so low." He yanked the sheet off and started to get up.

"Dimitri stop. Please!" Alex begged.

This woman was going to be the death of him yet. He swung back around but stopped when he saw tears forming in her eyes. Seeing her vulnerable like this broke his heart. She was trying so hard to hold back the tears. It made him want to pull her close and protect her, but she was so infuriating. What was all this nonsense? He leaned back against the headboard and watched her try to regain her composure. Just then a thought struck him. Had all of Alex's relationships been as bad as the one with that moron Adam? If she'd never had a man truly love her, if they had all used her and discarded her because of Luke's power and wealth, how could she trust the feelings they were sharing? Had her experiences made her insecure and untrusting of true relationships? She couldn't know he loved her, he'd just figured that out for himself. Maybe he did have an advantage. After 400 years of meaningless relationships, Dimitri knew without a doubt he was in love with Alex. He knew he wanted to spend the rest of his life with her. He couldn't imagine life without her. He didn't know if she loved him. But she was right, his experience told him without a doubt that she did care for him.

Alex had pulled her legs up and was resting her forehead on her knees. Dimitri turned and positioned himself so he was facing her. He gently cupped his hand underneath her chin and forced her to look up at him. "Sometimes I'm slow, but I think I'm beginning to understand." He leaned down and kissed away a tear. "From what I gather the men in your life have all been less than noble, to put it mildly. Has anyone ever loved you, Alex? Just loved you, for you?"

Ever so slightly Alex shook her head no. Now the tears were falling more quickly. He closed his eyes and silently wanted to kill every man that had ever hurt this wonderful, special woman. "Come here," he pulled her into his arms. "Maybe this will help," he said as he gently brushed a hand over her hair. "I don't want a meaningless fling with you. I want to spend every free moment I have getting to know you better. I don't know if I can make you happy, but I'd like the chance to try. I think that maybe we have a shot at something good here if you're game. I'd like the chance to explore it, see where it leads. Maybe living more than 400 years gives me an advantage, but it can also be a disadvantage. Look how it shattered the mood in five seconds flat," Dimitri tried for humor.

"I shattered the mood, not your age," Alex was embarrassed. Why had she brought up her insecurities? Why had she ruined the wonderful mood? No wonder the men in her life had all fled, or cheated. Was she incapable of having a normal relationship? This all started when she began to imagine the numerous women Dimitri must have had in over 400 years. Probably beautiful, sophisticated women who knew how to please a man. She was inexperienced and apprehensive in bed. There were so many things she wanted to try with Dimitri, but she'd held back because she was afraid she would embarrass herself. He had stolen her heart the first day she met him and she was terrified. He had disliked her so much in the beginning, what if he realized his first impression was correct. She didn't know if she could stand it. She realized Dimitri was waiting for a response. Did she want to explore this to see where it led? Yes! She wanted to scream. But she needed to know why he had disliked her so intensely in the beginning. How was she going to ask that question?

Dimitri was still looking at her. "There's more," he finally concluded. "There's something else that's bothering you." He had just put his heart on the line, threw his feelings out there, and she hadn't said a word. Not responded in any way. If she was that troubled, that insecure - which of course was ludicrous, he would just have to show her how much she meant to him. He'd have to allow himself to be vulnerable, risk his heart completely and hope she didn't crush it like a bug.

Alex closed her eyes and took a deep breath. "Yes, Dimitri, I want to spend more time with you. I would like to explore this and see where it leads. I've been happier over the last few days than I've been in a long time."

"Why do I hear another but coming?" Dimitri inquired.

Dusk

"Because I guess there is one. Well, not actually a but. I do need to know something though. Before we agree to take this any further," Alex looked at him shyly.

She was so adorable, he couldn't help it. He crushed his mouth to hers and tried to gather strength from the kiss. Maybe his passion, his strong emotion for her would help them get through this. He pulled back and smiled. "Thanks, I needed that. Now, you were saying?" He raised his eyebrows at her in question.

Alex was a little shaken by that kiss. There was something different about it, a feeling of desperation maybe. For the first time, she wondered if she had underestimated Dimitri's feelings for her. Was it possible that he was feeling just as on edge as she was? That he really did care for her as much as she cared for him. Did he feel vulnerable and terrified too? Maybe that was another advantage he had because of his age. The possibility of rejection wasn't so terrifying. She wondered how many women he had loved. Four hundred years was a really long time. That was one question she was not going to ask. At least not yet.

She looked over at him, then looked away. He had moved back to her side and was leaning against the headboard again.

"Alex, what is it you need to know?" What was troubling her, Dimitri wondered. "I told you, ask me anything."

"Well, I was just wondering why you hated me so intensely when we first met." She couldn't look at him. She needed to know, but at the same time did she really want to? Too late, it was out there now. She tried to mentally prepare herself for his response.

Dimitri was floored. Hated her? Why would she think he hated her? He thought back to that first meeting. He remembered being stressed. They'd lost Hector again, Luke was dead and the council was demanding a meeting with Alex, immediately. They were angry that Luke had kept her hidden away for so long after Marlena's death. Things had been so volatile at the time. The council wasn't helping. They basically dumped it back on him and expected everything to be fixed in a few days. When Alex walked in the door and he realized who she was, he was surprised. He was finally going to meet their new queen. Part of him had wondered if she really existed. Then to top it all off, there was the instant attraction.

"Dimitri?" Alex asked apprehensively.

He realized she was anxiously waiting for his answer and he hadn't said a word. He had been too stunned by her question. "I didn't hate you Alex," he answered, perplexed. "In fact, I was shocked at the instant attraction I felt for you. I do remember you looked weak and that was a serious disappointment. I hadn't met you before. Luke refused demands by the council to bring you in for an introduction. I saw the pressure they put on him and wondered why he wouldn't relent. Why he was willing to make them angry to protect you. Then you walked in looking so beautiful, but weak. I remember thinking my job had just gotten a lot more difficult. I couldn't introduce you to the council. If they saw you, the way you looked, we would all be doomed. I immediately assumed that was the reason Luke had been hiding you.

The night before, we located Hector, only to lose him again after being ambushed by a large group of vampires. The first day I met you, I was frustrated with the Hector situation and the council, devastated by Luke's death, but mostly I think I was just exhausted and overwhelmed. For the life of me, I can't think of what I did to make you think I hated you. In fact, I got the distinct impression you disliked me. Actually..." he broke off. How could he tell her he thought she was a spoiled brat?

"Actually, what?" Alex asked.

"Actually, after the way you acted when I tried to shake your hand, I sort of thought you were a pampered, spoiled rich kid. Which made me even more hesitant to introduce you to the council," he cringed and looked over at her. She just sat there silently watching him. Dimitri looked at her sheepishly. "Sorry. I didn't know you, shotgun reaction. Will it get me out of trouble if I tell you once I got to know you a little, I knew my first impressions were way off? I was sorry for them and felt guilty for judging you."

Now Alex was thinking. Could the look in Dimitri's eyes that first day have been disappointment and exhaustion? When she thought back, she had wondered at the time if it was disappointment or resentment. She had decided it was resentment and hatred. But Thomas also said Dimitri didn't dislike her. Maybe it could have been disappointment. She did look awful that morning. So based on the pressure he was under, she could understand why her appearance would not have been a welcome sight. She saw Dimitri was still watching her. "I think we both made snap judgments that day because of the emotional baggage we were experiencing at the time. We may have lashed out at each other. When I walked in the room and saw you in Luke's favorite chair, it threw me. I don't think I really gave you a chance after that. Then when Thomas introduced us, I thought I saw disdain or resentment in your eyes. But now I think maybe it was disappointment," Alex paused.

"You don't need to apologize for that, I probably did look weak," Alex continued. "I can't explain why dad thwarted the council. I've actually wondered that myself. I didn't know he had gone to that extent. But why didn't he stop me from leaving after mom's funeral? Or at least ask me to come home when things got sticky? I suspect he was just trying to protect me. He was so devastated after losing mom. I think he really should have gone away for a while. He couldn't or wouldn't, so he wanted to make sure I could. He was always so protective of mom and me. I never understood why until after his death. Now that I've learned about all this, I admire him even more. We were under constant threat and he was our shield. Our hero." Alex stopped for a minute. It was still so hard to talk about dad and realize he was gone forever.

Dimitri took her hand. He knew how much Luke had loved this woman, obviously that bond went both ways. He now understood why Luke adamantly rejected the council's demands. He would do the same thing if necessary. He would do anything to protect Alex.

"Anyway, I'm sorry about the way I acted that first day. Later on, I regretted my rude behavior but I was so flabbergasted at the thought someone I had just met disliked me so intently. I guess it's probably clouded my judgment ever since. I think the first time I actually saw the real you was that night at the charity ball. I'm glad Thomas arranged for you to be my escort," Alex smiled at him. "Bygones?"

Dimitri pulled her on top of him. "Bygones." He cupped her face in his hands and looked her straight in the eyes. "Alexandria Deveraux you are the most beautiful, intriguing and exasperating woman I have ever met. Not to mention sexy as hell." He smiled and gave her a quick kiss. "Promise me you won't ever let a misunderstanding come between us. I hate knowing you thought I disliked you all that time. I wish you would have said something sooner. You can talk to me about anything. I want you to ask me questions. I want you to get to know me. Just like I want to get to know you. I promise I will never hurt you, not on purpose. You're too important to me," then he kissed her passionately.

Hesitantly Alex pulled back. "We're not going there again. Look at the time. Thomas will be home soon. I need a shower, and I certainly need to get dressed before he gets here." She frowned, she just remembered she had one more question.

"What now?" Dimitri asked. She almost laughed, he looked so exasperated.

"I was just wondering who Hector is. You mentioned he's been a problem and you were trying to catch him, but he kept eluding you. He must be important to cause you that much grief. I just wondered who he was, that's all." Alex inquired as she sat back against the headboard.

"Thomas hasn't talked to you about Hector yet?" Dimitri asked in surprise.

"No, I don't think so. However the name does ring a dim bell, I just can't put my finger on who he is. I've learned so many new things over the past couple months, it's hard to keep it all straight. Now you really have my attention." Alex sensed Hector was someone important and she wasn't going to like what Dimitri had to say.

"Hector is Radek's First Lieutenant. I assume you know who Radek is?" Dimitri asked.

"Oh, now I remember. Yes, I know. Radek is my evil half-brother. He is also half vampire and I think he's their ruler or king or whatever. I've been reading the book my mom left me. I did want to talk to someone about a few things she wrote. I realize that since you're just a measly four hundred and some odd years old and Radek is six hundred, it all happened before your time. But could we talk about my mom's history one of these days? I have some questions and maybe you know the answers."

"Sure, why don't we talk about it when you buy me dinner after I obliterate you in our sparring match?" Dimitri teased.

"Maybe. I'm not sure I want to wait that long. You're not completely healed yet. That was a pretty big bump on your head. I'm not fighting you until you're in top shape. When I beat you, I don't want to hear any excuses," Alex smiled. "Now, back to Hector. I have a feeling there is more I should know about him. Let me think, it was something about mom's death. Oh yeah, Thomas said mom was assassinated and they believed Hector was the one experimenting with the poison because it would have most likely made Radek sick. Is that correct?" Alex asked.

"Yes, we are sure that Hector is the one that murdered your mother." He studied her for a moment. "I am so sorry about that, Alex. You have lost so much in such a short period of time. I wish I could take all the pain away." He tucked her hair behind her ear. "Anyway, Hector is the one that murdered your mother. Being the coward that he is, he immediately went into hiding. We, the warriors, have been trying to track him ever since," he paused. "Alex?"

She looked up. He had something bad to tell her, she could hear it in his voice. "What?"

"Once we knew for sure it was Hector that killed your mother, Luke became obsessed. He was on a mission to find and kill Hector at any cost," he paused again.

Dusk

Alex closed her eyes, she was afraid she knew what was coming. Thomas still hadn't given her any details about Luke's death. Obviously Hector was responsible for the loss of both her parents. "Go ahead."

"Luke was good. He tracked Hector to a farm house, but somehow Hector got word we were coming and was gone when we arrived. There was evidence to show someone had recently been there. We knew we just barely missed him. Luke was relentless. He'd find him, but we'd miss him somehow. Thomas started hunting without Luke, trying to track down Hector on his own. He thought your dad was becoming a little reckless and was going to get hurt. We all did, actually. Luke couldn't be reasoned with. His top priority was to make Hector pay for Marlena's death. Don't get me wrong, I understood his need for revenge. So did Thomas. But he thought if he could get rid of Hector himself, your dad could focus on healing instead of vengeance.

Thomas, Nick and Dante got information one night that seemed like good Intel on Hector. Rather than relay their plans to Luke, they struck out on their own. The vamps were having what could only be described as a wild party. They had captured some humans and were taking turns feeding on them. The humans were apparently drunk. If vampires drink the blood of someone who is drunk or high, they get drunk or high. So anyway Thomas, Nick and Dante show up at this party. They realize Hector isn't there, but they can't just leave and let the vampires kill the humans.

At that point, they called Luke and requested help. We all went to back them up. When we got there, the scene was horrific. They had managed to save a couple of the humans, but three of them were dead. Torn to pieces by the vamps, blood was everywhere. Dante told me they had killed about twenty vampires before we arrived. Thomas, Dante and Nick had pushed the two remaining humans up against a barn and they were standing in front of them creating a shield.

There were more than thirty vamps still there. I have no idea how many were at the party to begin with. Some of them always flee when the fighting starts. The three warriors were desperately trying to fight for their lives and the humans. Once we stepped in, it was easy to dispatch the remaining vampires. That's when we noticed how seriously the three warriors had been injured. Thomas was the worst. Nick told me Thomas kept stepping in, trying to protect him and Dante as well as the humans. Your brother is a brave man. He's also the best fighter we have now that Luke is gone. I know you worry about him when he's out working. He's never alone and he really can take on the best and walk away without a scratch."

Alex interrupted Dimitri. "I know Thomas is good, but I've seen you fight too. I think you could give Thomas a run for his money," she smiled at him. "That's why I want to take you on. If I defeat the best first, that might pose a challenge for the rest of the guys and I will have sparring partners any time I want. They couldn't resist outdoing the master."

"The Master?" Dimitri laughed. "I guess your plan has merit, but don't think I'm going to let you win. Flattery might get you sexual favors, but not leniency in the ring," Dimitri was grinning. "Anyway, I just don't want you to worry too much about Thomas. He really is good at what he does."

"I know. But I can't help but worry. In the last couple months I've been injured, so have you. That's after my mother and my father were killed. There's no guarantee any of us are safe."

Dusk

"True, but for the most part we are usually better prepared than our enemy," Dimitri countered.

"For the most part?" Alex asked.

"Yes. That brings me back to my story. Thomas was hurt pretty severely. I think that's what brought Luke back. He realized he was putting us all in danger. He had been taking risks, which made Thomas take risks. He was furious at Thomas for taking on that many vamps with so few warriors. He also realized why Thomas had gone there without him. He told me we were still going to focus on Hector but he wouldn't sacrifice his son, not even to avenge Marlena.

The night Luke was attacked, it wasn't in an alley. He had gotten some Intel on Hector. He called me and a few of the other warriors and outlined his plan. He knew it was going to be extremely dangerous, and he was afraid it was a trap. We all decided, trap or not, we had to act on the information we had. Luke decided to leave Thomas, Nicholas and Dante out of the op. He told the rest of us it could be a suicide mission and let us decide for ourselves if we would go. We all went of course. Hector has to be stopped."

Alex interrupted Dimitri. "Why did dad think it was a trap? Why did he think it had the potential to be a suicide mission?"

"The information had come from an informant that had given us bad information in the past. The problem was, sometimes he gave us good information and we were able to take out the target without any problem. We weren't sure whose side he was on. We couldn't decide if he was giving bad information on purpose, if the vamps were feeding him bad information, or if he was completely innocent and we just got unlucky sometimes," Dimitri paused.

"Okay, that makes sense. Continue." Alex was grateful Dimitri was telling her this story. She didn't feel like he was holding anything back. She knew Thomas would have. He still tried to protect her from everything.

"So, we were suspicious of the information but felt we needed to act on it anyway. We had to promise not to tip off Thomas, Nick or Dante. If any of them found out, it would have been impossible to keep them from the fight. Basically, your father was trying to protect Thomas. I know he's still pissed about that, I would be too. But I understand your father's motives. Thomas wasn't completely 100% at the time of your father's attack. Luke didn't want to put him in danger so soon.

Long story short, we got to the cabin where Hector was supposedly staying. He was long gone. I'm not sure he was ever there at all. We were ambushed by an army of vampires. Your father was hurt the worst. All of us were injured pretty badly. Jake was trying to get Luke to his office where he could set him up with blood and hide him when he was stopped by a police officer. They saw how bad Luke was hurt and almost arrested Jake. He had to do some pretty fast talking. Jake told them he was on his way to pick Luke up and had found him lying in the alley, beaten. They rushed him to the hospital, which of course didn't do him any good. We had to sneak blood in to try to save him. The injuries were too severe. We couldn't help him. He kept telling us over and over, find Thomas and get my Alex back here. I need to see my kids. Once we got Thomas there, we all went home. I think the nurses were getting suspicious. Like I said, we were all in pretty bad shape."

Alex was silent for a long moment. Finally, she looked up at him with tears in her eyes and simply said, "thank you."

Dusk

Dimitri reached over and held her close. They sat there in silence for a long time, each deep in their own memories. Finally, Alex sat up. "I'm going to shower and order a couple pizzas for dinner, do you want to stay? Thomas should be here any minute. We have plenty of hot water in this house, so feel free to jump in the shower yourself if you want to. I'll use the guest room."

"I can't stay tonight, but I'll take you up on that shower." He climbed out of bed and walked toward the adjoining bathroom. Then he suddenly stopped, turned around and walked back. He took Alex in his arms and kissed her gently. "I really am sorry for your loss. All of them. Luke was a good man, we all miss him desperately. Probably me more than the others, I know I can never truly fill his shoes." He glanced around Alex's room. "Now, where did you put my pants?"

Alex smiled. "You could always stay in your birthday suit. That's my favorite outfit you own."

He flashed that sexy grin and disappeared into the bathroom. "You're welcome to join me," Dimitri yelled through the closed door.

Alex slowly walked into the guestroom to shower. She had learned so much tonight. It had been an emotionally exhausting day, but a very productive one. She still worried about her relationship with Dimitri. She hoped he wouldn't break her heart. Standing there under the hot shower, she admitted to herself for the first time she was in love with Dimitri. She realized she had been for a while. Could things work out for her this time? She was confident Dimitri wouldn't cheat on her. That was something at least. She trusted him. It was a new experience. Honestly, she had never trusted a man before in her life. Well, except Thomas and Luke of course but they didn't count.

She was still contemplating the things Dimitri told her as she dried off and got dressed. It bothered her that Dimitri had thought her weak. She understood why and wasn't upset with him for it, but she was determined to make sure he never viewed her as weak again. No matter what. She was also going to start fighting this war. Hector was responsible for the death of both her parents. He was going to pay. She wasn't seeking revenge, she was seeking justice.

She would need to talk to Dimitri about the council. He said they were putting pressure on him right after Luke's death to meet her, but he didn't say if he was still under pressure. Why hadn't he taken her to the council? She wasn't weak now. Was he still worried about their reaction? Did he think they'd find her lacking and reject her? Could they do that? She still had some things to talk to Dimitri about. For now, she was going to have a hot meal and then she might go to bed early.

* * * *

Alex got home on time for a change. It had been an early morning. She'd headed out first thing to deal with a couple problems that needed her immediate attention. That meant she'd missed her morning workout. Now she was home and in the mood for a good hard fight. Maybe she'd get the droids out today. She changed her clothes and started down to the gym. Just as she reached the foyer, the doorbell rang.

Dusk

Marta was on her day off so Alex answered the door. Dimitri stood there, smiling. "Did we have plans?" Alex asked hesitantly.

"No," his smile widened. "And if we did," he let his eyes travel slowly down her body. "It looks like I'd be outta luck."

"Come in," she shut the door behind him. "I didn't have time for my morning workout so I was headed down to catch up. If you're ready to lose that bet, you're welcome to join me. I'm sure you can find some sweats and a t-shirt if you want to change." She glanced at his clothes. He was wearing black Levi's, a black Harley Davidson t-shirt and a leather coat. "It looks like you're dressed to fight, is something up?" Alex became instantly worried.

Dimitri lightly brushed a finger down the scowl on her forehead. It immediately disappeared. "No, nothing is wrong. I thought I'd find a beautiful blond, take her to dinner and maybe spend a relaxing evening in front of the fire before I have to go out tonight. If you're not available, I can keep looking," he smiled.

"Very funny," Alex retorted.

"How about I change so you can lose that bet, then we can head out to dinner," Dimitri suggested. "I planned on buying, but I'm a liberated man. I don't mind if you pick up the tab, just this once. I hear you're a poor loser though. You're not going to pout are you?" Dimitri laughed.

"Come on, Ace. We'll see who the poor loser is." Then she turned and headed down the stairs, Dimitri on her heals.

She was sitting on the mat stretching when he walked into the gym. He was wearing a pair of sweats and a tight t-shirt. He walked over and held out his hand. She took it and he pulled her up hard, knocking her off balance and into his chest. Dimitri laughed, leaned down and kissed her. "Before we start do you need any rules? We don't normally have any since there aren't any on the street, but since you're a girl and all I thought I'd ask." He looked at her in challenge.

"No rules. This isn't my first match, you know. I used to fight Luke and Thomas all the time. Let's get started." She stepped back and before he knew it was coming, she punched him in the stomach. He was taken by surprise, but no way was he going to let Alex know she'd gotten in a good shot. She had jumped back, so they were now circling the mat, each reading their opponent, watching for the slightest indication they were about to pounce. Dimitri moved first. He faked a movement to the right, knowing she would sense it and then lunged to the left. He grabbed her around the waist. She kicked out and they both went down.

They were wrestling around vying for position. At first Alex had been on top but Dimitri quickly flipped her over and straddled her. She wiggled, scissored her legs and then knocked him back with a quick shove to his chest. He fell back and she jumped to her feet. He was up in an instant and the game was on again. Alex came at him with force. She swung, he blocked. She kicked, but he pivoted. Dimitri was having fun, but he thought Alex was taking this too seriously. He watched her as she came at him time after time. She was good, there was no doubt about it but he had more experience. This had gone on long enough. He had hoped this would be fun for Alex, too. She was way too serious. Obviously there was something going on here he didn't understand.

As Alex threw another punch, Dimitri blocked it, but wrapped an arm around her waist and tumbled them both to the floor. She was an amazing woman and she definitely had talent. But he didn't want to fight anymore. He wanted to kiss her. He let Alex push her way on top of him, but was instantly sorry. She pushed her knee into his groin. A little further and he was going to be in agony. She smiled down at him. "Give up?" she asked.

"Nope," he countered.

"I could make you scream like a girl in about half a second. You sure you don't want to give up?" She asked again with a cocky smile.

She was surprised when he grabbed her head and pulled her mouth to his. The kiss started out hard and fast but soon became deeper, more passionate. Dimitri slowly moved his hands up her sides and back down, never letting up on the kiss. Alex shifted. In an instant she was on her back. Dimitri straddled her, holding her arms above her head as he pinned her body to the mat. "I never give up," he said with a smile. "How about you?" he countered.

Alex was furious. He wasn't playing fair. Okay they said no rules and she'd fallen for his trick, but she wasn't giving in yet. She tried to force him off her. She twisted and wiggled, but no use. She was stuck. She knew she couldn't use his trick, he wouldn't fall for it. After stubbornly lying there for a few minutes she finally conceded. "You win. Now get off me," she angrily demanded.

"No way!" He kissed her again. She wasn't giving in that easy. She bit him.

"Ouch!" He yelled. "What'd you do that for?" He sat up and pressed a finger to his lip. "You're mad at me because I won?" he said incredulously. "You are a poor loser."

Alex got up and started walking toward the showers. She knew he'd follow.

Dimitri quickly jumped to his feet and grabbed her by the waist. "Stop right there," he demanded as he turned her around to face him. He was surprised when he saw her smiling.

"I'm going to take a shower," Alex replied casually. "Care to join me?" she teased.

Dimitri smiled. "There is this water game I've been wanting to teach you." They both laughed as they sprinted for the shower.

Hours later they were in the library in front of the fire. Dimitri was sprawled across the couch leaning against one arm with Alex nestled in front of him. He was massaging her neck and back when he focused on her shoulder blade. "You have a huge knot right here. Why so much tension? Are you stressed about something?" Dimitri asked. "You've been unusually quiet all evening."

"Umm, that feels good. Maybe you could just stay here and do that all night," She moaned.

Dimitri moved her hair aside, leaned down and kissed her neck. "Spill it, what's got you worried?" Dimitri persisted.

"Oh, all right." Alex sighed and leaned back against Dimitri's chest. He wrapped his arms around her and waited. "There are several things. The first is just the usual. It's almost time for you to go out and fight. Having both you and Thomas out there while I'm stuck in here always makes me tense."

"Alex, we've talked about this," Dimitri started.

"I know," Alex cut him off. "I've had this argument a million times. Both you and Thomas frequently remind me how dangerous it is out there. But that's the point. You tell me how dangerous it is for me, but want to pretend it's not dangerous for you. We all know better. I'll cope. I do every night, don't I?" Alex took a sip of her wine. "It's not worth going into again. We've been over it all before and we're simply not going to agree. You asked and I told you, that's all. It's not a big deal."

"I know it is a big deal. I wish you wouldn't worry about us, but I also know it's inevitable. I could come back tonight. Do you feel up to a house guest later on?" Dimitri asked.

"You would do that? Don't you have things to do in the morning?" Alex liked this idea. Even after she heard Thomas stumble into bed every night, she still worried about Dimitri. If he came back here, she'd know he was safe and unharmed.

"Yes, but so do you. I'll have to leave first thing in the morning, but I assume you'll be going to work anyway. This will give me something to look forward to all night. It'll be nice to slip into a warm bed next to a beautiful woman after a long night's work." He kissed her head again. "So what else is on your mind?" Dimitri inquired as he lifted her shirt slightly and started to rub her stomach.

"I've been thinking a lot about the things you told me the other day," Alex paused.

"You're going to have to be more specific. We talked about a lot of things the other day," Dimitri inquired.

"All of them, I guess. But more specifically, I've been thinking about the situation mom and dad created with the council.

Well I guess not just the council, the whole fae community. Mom's heart was in the right place, but I'm not sure she did the right thing. She kept me from our people all that time. Then, dad did the same thing after mom's death. It made me look weak. You told me that was your first impression. I think it's because the seed was already planted. The whole community is probably wondering what is so bad or undesirable about me that mom and then dad kept me a secret," Alex finished. Why did she always end up talking about such difficult things with Dimitri?

"That's not true," Dimitri insisted. But he wondered if she had a point.

Alex smiled at him. "Stop trying to protect me and not hurt my feelings."

"I will always protect you, but I admit I might hurt your feelings unintentionally on occasion. I do try very hard not too though." Dimitri leaned down and kissed the top of her head.

"What I'm saying is they probably all think I'm the Hunchback of Notre Dame or something. Everyone keeps me hidden, why wouldn't they think the worst?" Alex took a deep breath. "Even you are keeping me hidden. Do you still think I'm a disappointment? Or that the council will reject me? Am I still a problem for you? Are you ashamed of me because you still think I'm weak?" Alex finished.

Dimitri sat up so fast Alex thought he was going to dump her on the floor. He set her on the couch and then stood up and started to pace in front of the fireplace. He was taking slow, deep breaths. She was worried what he was about to say or do. He turned back and crouched in front of her, taking her hands into his. "Sometimes Alex, you make me so angry I could scream!" He seemed calmer now, at least he wasn't yelling at her. "How can you not know how proud I am of you? After all this time, you still think you're a disappointment to me? What do I have to say or do to make you understand how wonderful I think you are?" He seemed exasperated.

"Then why have you not introduced me to the council? I don't understand. You told me how much pressure they were putting on you immediately after dad's death. It's been months since dad died and you still haven't let them meet me. What am I supposed to think? You have to be in trouble with them now too, just like dad was. Yet with you it's different. I'm here and you still don't want them to see me." Alex looked at him, pleading for an explanation.

Dimitri climbed onto the couch next to Alex. "I'm not hiding you exactly," he started.

"But..." Alex started to interrupt.

"Just hear me out, okay?" Dimitri took her hand again. "I guess I am sort of hiding you. But not because I'm disappointed or ashamed of you in any way. That's just ridiculous," he looked at her intently. Alex stopped breathing, was that love she saw in his eyes. No, he'd never told her he loved her. But it was compassion. For now that was enough. Somehow she believed him. He wasn't ashamed of her. She felt such a feeling of relief. He continued. "I want to reveal you at just the right moment. The moment that will have the biggest impact. I don't want there ever to be any doubt about your abilities or your leadership skills. Yes, the fact that you're an unknown has probably been a problem in the past for Marlena and Luke but not for me anymore."

Alex looked confused.

"I'm not in trouble with the council. They've been satisfied for a long time now," Dimitri stated flatly.

"But how?" Alex asked, now she was truly confused.

Dimitri didn't say anything for a long time. "You and Ariel have been spending quite a bit of time together lately, haven't you?" Dimitri asked.

Alex was taken by surprise at the sudden change of subject. "Yes," she answered hesitantly.

"Ariel really likes you a lot. It's been a long time since she's had a good female friend other than Breena. She confided in me the other day that she's missed that. She's grateful the two of you have hit it off so well. I know it's none of my business, but can you tell me if the feeling is mutual?" Dimitri asked.

"Why are you changing the subject, Dimitri?" Alex wanted to know.

"A couple of reasons. I think you're having such a hard time with things because you are lonely. We spend as much time together as we can but when I'm not with you, I spend time with the other warriors. I'm with them every night. I have six good men, good friends to talk things out with. You left your only real friend in Italy. I know you miss Jennifer. I'm wondering if you and Ariel might become good friends," Dimitri said simply. "I think having a good friend you can confide in will help you through this. I also think Ariel will help you get your self-confidence back."

"Okay. I feel the same as Ariel. I think we have already become good friends," Alex admitted.

Dusk

"Good. You remember she's fae, right?" Dimitri asked.

Alex was still confused. Where was this leading? Dimitri wasn't giving anything away. "Yes, that was kind of the point in the beginning," Alex answered. "I wanted to learn more about my people and Ariel was willing to help me."

"I promised her I wouldn't do anything to hurt your friendship. I hope I can keep my promise to her," Dimitri hesitated. "I initially brought Ariel here for two reasons. First, I was just as worried about you as Thomas was. You had been unconscious for a long time and neither one of us knew what to do. I needed to bring in someone from the fae community to help. Someone I knew I could trust completely," Dimitri looked over at Alex.

"I understand. You told me she was a close family friend. Naturally you would trust her if the friendship had lasted for centuries," Alex answered.

"True. As you have probably learned by now, Ariel is her own person. She won't be controlled or manipulated by anyone. I would trust her with anything," Dimitri smiled.

"Yes, I know that too," Alex grinned. "I think that's one reason I like her so much."

"It's important that you remember her independence. Her refusal to comply with the rules has certainly been a challenge for her parents over the years. She chooses her friends very carefully and is always loyal to them. Sometimes to her own detriment. You're lucky to have her in your corner. You need to know that. You can trust Ariel, with anything. Even if you talk to her about me, she won't break your confidence. I will never know anything you tell her unless you tell me yourself. Do you understand?" Dimitri asked.

"Yes, I understand. Really, Dimitri I know Ariel is a great person. It's nice to know you trust her so explicitly, but I think I have already gotten there on my own. I do trust Ariel." Alex was still a little confused.

"Good. The second reason I picked Ariel to come here that night was because her father is on the council." Dimitri was watching Alex for a reaction.

"The council? So, let me guess. You brought her here to meet me then had her go back to her father and report. He believed her because it was his daughter. You used her to get yourself out of hot water?" Alex wasn't sure how to feel about this. "Was Ariel okay with your plan, or did she even know?"

"Ariel knew. I told you, no one manipulates Ariel. Even if I could have, I wouldn't. Remember, she's also my friend Alex. I wouldn't use a friend. I didn't use Ariel. The plan wasn't just my plan, we came up with it together. Her father, Oberon, isn't just on the council he's the council leader. Like I said, Ariel doesn't always follow the rules and she's caused more than a little trouble for Oberon throughout the years. She's even had to come before the council herself. The last time was because they felt she was withholding information about a friend."

"What happened?" Alex asked.

"They couldn't prove she knew anything, so she was set free," Dimitri explained.

"Did she?" Alex wondered. "Hold back information I mean."

Dusk

"Of course!" Dimitri laughed. "And she got a kick out of having to stand before the council. Her father was furious. Anyway Oberon is an intimidating man to everyone I think, except his daughter. We thought if we could convince him you are worthy to be queen, but we need to keep you a secret, he could help convince the other council members. Oberon is like a second father to me, our families have been very close for years. He was pressuring me like the others, but also trying to protect me from the rest of the council members. He wants me to succeed," Dimitri paused. When Alex didn't say anything, he continued.

"I explained to Ariel what had happened that night in the alley and told her I needed her help. She hadn't met you, but I had talked to her before about you. She was also sensitive to the situation I was in with the council. She was more than happy to come over and help that night. I think she sensed I had feelings for you too. Although I hadn't told her yet. She was anxious to help me, but also curious to meet you. You won her over immediately. She went back to her father and sang your praises for days afterwards. It was part of our plan for her to give you a plug or two, but she wouldn't have been as convincing if she didn't like you as well as she does. After she'd gone on about you for a couple days, I made a surprise visit to Oberon. He was primed and ready for my pitch. Once I convinced him it was better to keep you from the community for a while, my job was done. Oberon took care of the rest. The council hasn't bothered me since." Dimitri was watching Alex now. He really wanted to know what she was thinking.

"I still don't get why you want me to be kept a secret," Alex confessed.

"Because I think we need to introduce you in a big way. By keeping you a secret, Marlena put you at a disadvantage. Basically,

160

we need to have time to market you. To demonstrate your strengths before the big reveal. Face it Alex, you don't exactly come across as intimidating at first glance. I know what you can do because I've seen it. But standing in front of the council, or a big crowd, you'd just look like another woman. A beautiful sexy woman, but not someone to be respected and loved. Do you understand?" Dimitri asked.

"I guess I do. I know I'm small and petite. But I can still hold my own," Alex said defensively.

"I know you can, babe. I just want everyone else to know that too before they meet you. I want them to be so afraid of you nobody will ever want to take you on. They'll give you their support, not see an opportunity for power," Dimitri explained.

"How does hiding me accomplish that?" Alex asked.

"Eventually you are going to have to prove yourself to your people. You should have to. But I guess what you don't know is that you are already well on your way. You impressed the hell out of Ty. He hasn't shut up about the night you fought off three vampires all on your own. Sure you got hurt, but not until you were outnumbered five to one and the vamp brought a knife into the fight," he smiled at her.

"Really? Ty is telling people about that? Doesn't it make me look weak though? The fact that I got injured and passed out?" Alex asked.

"Not at all. The way Ty tells it, you were courageous and brave. You risked your own life to save the life of one of your people. Sure Tanya was human, but she was still yours. Then while you're in the middle of fighting off three vamps, and winning..."

Alex interrupted. "I'm not sure anyone can claim I was winning that fight."

"Well, Ty makes that claim all the time. You weren't losing, who knows what would have happened if those other two hadn't jumped in and the guy hadn't stabbed you. You just might have won that match. Anyway, you were holding your own five to one when the cowardly vamp pulled a knife and stabbed you. Then, injured and weak, you went over and healed Tanya. It's the stuff legends are made of. He usually stops the story there, you know kind of forgets to mention the whole passing out and in bed for days part." He leaned down and kissed her lightly. "Don't worry about impressing your people, Alex. No one could see you in action and not be impressed."

She wasn't sure she was comfortable with Ty's over exaggeration of the events that night, but if that's the way he told the story, she did sound really good. She smiled over at Dimitri. "Ty's version makes me sound pretty awesome. So...how do you tell it? Am I as big a heroine when they hear it from you?" Alex asked with a sly grin.

"I'm the quiet, silent type. I usually don't tell the story, I just agree during all the important parts and I ensure everyone in the room walks out in awe of my queen."

She snorted. "No one could possibly be in awe of a queen they've never even met. But, I guess it helps that people are actually hearing good things about me. Now I just hope I can live up to their expectations."

Dimitri smiled and pushed her down on the couch. "You exceed mine every day." He slid his hand up her shirt and kissed her passionately.

* * * *

Alex sat in her car outside Ariel's house. She was early for their appointment. She took a deep breath, trying to calm her nerves. She'd been nervous about this meeting all day. She had to do it just right. If she presented it wrong, Ariel would feel like she had to choose between Alex and Dimitri. There was no doubt, Ariel would choose Dimitri. She checked the clock again, ten more minutes and she could go up. She tried to go over what she wanted to say one more time in her mind.

Alex rang the doorbell and tried to look casual. She felt anything but right now. So much was riding on Ariel agreeing to help her. Ariel opened the door and smiled at Alex. "Come in, I just want to grab my jacket. Are we taking your car or mine?" Ariel shot a glance over her shoulder. She noticed Alex looked nervous. Now she was even more curious about this meeting.

"I can drive. I know where we're going, so that's probably easier," Alex replied.

Ariel stopped at the door. "Lead the way," she said. "I have to admit I am intrigued. I can't wait to hear what it is you have to show me."

"It's not that big a deal. I just needed to talk to you alone and thought showing you what I had in mind would be better than trying to explain it." They had reached the car and Alex unlocked the doors. "Get in, we can talk on the way."

They rode in silence for quite a while. Ariel decided to stay silent until Alex was ready to talk. She wasn't about to guess what all this cloak and dagger stuff was about. She was afraid she wasn't going to like it though.

"So I had this idea and I need your help," Alex began. "Before I get into the specifics, I need to ask a favor though."

Here we go, Ariel thought. "Go ahead," she said reluctantly.

Alex sensed the hesitation, so she hurried on. "I need to know that whether you agree to help or not, you won't say anything to anyone about it. That includes Dimitri. I'm not trying to hide anything from him," she continued quickly. "I just want to talk to him about it myself when the time is right. Can you do that?" Alex asked.

Ariel looked at Alex for a long time. She didn't have enough information to agree to keep secrets from Dimitri. "Alex, Dimitri and I go way back. He basically saved my life once. I can't promise to keep something from him if I believe strongly he should know about it. You can't ask me to do that. If I kept something important from him, it would ruin our friendship. Especially if it was something that put you in danger. Are you going to ask me to do something that will put you in danger?" Ariel asked.

"I guess it could, how about a compromise. I don't want you to do anything that will cause problems with Dimitri. I really don't. I also promise you, I intend to fill him in completely on my plan. I swear, I'm not keeping secrets from him. I just want to wait until after I have taken all the precautions I need to. When I talk to him about this, I need to be able to ensure him I will be safe," Alex paused. "I just need some time. If you aren't willing to help, I will need to find someone else that will help me. Again, that's going to take time." Alex looked over at Ariel. She hadn't lost her yet. "All

I'm asking is that you give me that time. If I don't tell him, you can. Do we have a deal?" Alex asked hesitantly.

"Why don't we do this? I promise to hear you out and tell you if I can help you. I also promise I won't tell Dimitri anything unless I truly feel he needs to know. If I decide I have to tell him, I'll let you know beforehand. That will give you a chance to tell him first. Then if you don't, I will. Does that sound fair?" Ariel asked.

"I think I can live with that," Alex agreed hesitantly.

"So what's this grand plan you have?" Ariel asked.

"We've been spending time together for a while now and it's really helped me a lot. But, at this point just talking about special powers and theories isn't helping me figure out what mine are. Thomas has told me for a while that he thinks I'm a healer, but I was only able to heal Tanya that once. I'm worried I don't really have that gift," Alex glanced at Ariel. "I wonder if it was just a fluke. Do all fae have powers? What does it mean if I don't have any?"

"Not possible. Either you can or you can't. If you healed someone, you can. It's that simple. What makes you think it was a fluke?" Ariel asked.

Alex took a deep breath. "Because when Dimitri got hurt that night at the ball, I couldn't heal him. I tried in the limo all the way to my house. I was desperate to help him but I couldn't. I tried everything I could think of, but nothing. I was so scared when Tanya got hurt. I knew she needed help or she would die. The problem is, I don't know how I healed her. I don't know what I did to make my powers work. That's why I think it was a fluke. I was just as scared for Dimitri, maybe even more scared, but I couldn't do anything to help him." Alex was silent for a minute. "I haven't told anyone else about this. I'm so ashamed I failed," Alex sighed.

Ariel looked at Alex and saw she truly was upset about this. "Alex, this is all new to you. I don't know what you did to help Tanya or why your powers worked that night and they didn't work on Dimitri. Maybe your emotions got in the way with Dimitri, you couldn't think straight because you care about him so much. I don't know. What I do know is that you have healing powers. We just need to find the trigger. We also need to figure out how to control them so you have the power when you need it, but you don't wipe out all your energy in the process. I admit, I have never met a healer before. They are extremely rare. I am willing to help you figure it out though. A lot of our powers work the same way. It took me awhile to figure out how to conjure fire."

Alex interrupted. "You never told me you could conjure fire. That is so cool! Will you show me sometime?"

"Sure. It is pretty cool, and it comes in handy in a fight. I also agree with you, I think we've talked about it enough and we need to start acting. We need to figure out what you can do and how to call it at will."

They pulled off the main highway and onto a gravel road, well it was more like an overgrown driveway. It was clear nobody had used this road for a very long time. It was still light outside, but it was starting to get late. Ariel was getting a little nervous. She didn't want to be out in the middle of nowhere after dark. Alex had been secretive about this meeting so Ariel was sure she hadn't told anyone where they were going. The two of them wouldn't be enough to fight off a group of vampires. They pulled up beside a large cabin. There were weeds growing around the front porch and it looked vacant.

"What's this?" Ariel inquired.

"We're here," Alex said with a smile. "I know, it looks deserted. We used to come here all the time but after Thomas and I grew up, we were too busy with our friends to bother. Our family eventually stopped coming here. It needs a little work, but it's still inhabitable. Come on in, I think you'll like it." Alex pulled out a key and opened the door. It was a spacious cabin and very well furnished. Alex was right, Ariel loved it. With a little work, it would be a great getaway. Alex put her purse on the table. "I want to show you something before it gets too late. I don't want to be walking around out here alone after dark." Ariel was glad to hear it. Maybe Alex was safety conscious after all.

They walked out behind the cabin. There was a small garden set on a hill. Beyond the garden was a large meadow. Beyond the meadow was a large outcropping of rocks. Ariel walked over to the rocks and looked down. There was a steep drop off. She was beginning to understand why Alex brought her here. The meadow was a perfect place to practice powers and even have fighting matches. They wouldn't need to worry about protection as much because the only approach would be from the house or the forest. If anyone came, the gravel would give them away. The forest would be the only vulnerable angle. "Let me guess, you want to come here to learn your powers and practice fighting." Ariel said as she looked back at Alex.

Alex smiled. "Exactly! I think it's the perfect place. We should be well protected. I can't learn at the house. What if the neighbors saw something? Plus the warriors are always coming and going. I would be too self-conscious to learn anything there. But, I thought the cabin would be perfect. I'm also planning on installing a new security system. That way if we somehow got stuck out here at night, we could hunker down knowing the cabin was secure and leave first thing in the morning. That's the part that is problematic. Sometimes I work late. I want to have a regular schedule to practice. Sometimes we might be here after dark. I thought maybe once we got set up, I could see if Dimitri would come out and stay with us once he finished hunting for the night. I know I'd feel a lot better about being this isolated if he was with us. What do you think?" Alex asked.

"I think it's perfect. I'd have to think about the overnight thing though. That's one part of the plan I won't do unless you clear it with Dimitri. Even then, it's going to make me nervous. I might consider it if he could come out and stay with us though. We're pretty isolated out here. If the vamps found out and planned a big attack, the two of us would be doomed. Do cell phones work in this area?" Ariel asked.

"No, that's why we have the land line. Pick it up, it still works," Alex countered.

"We'll decide about the overnighters once we get settled and talk to Dimitri. That's one condition I'm not budging on. If we are here after dark I insist Dimitri knows we're here. Can you live with that?" Ariel asked.

"I can live with that," Alex answered enthusiastically. "Does that mean you'll help me?" she asked.

"Is this the totality of your plan? Come out here and learn to fight and develop your powers, or is there something I'm missing?" Ariel asked.

"No, that's it. It has to be a secret for now from Thomas. Like I said, I don't plan to keep secrets from Dimitri. Thomas is just so overprotective of me. If he knows I'm out here, he's going to feel like he needs to be here with me, day or night. I appreciate how much he cares but if he feels like he has to follow me around all the time, he can't have his own life. He has things of his own he needs to get done. He can't babysit me forever," Alex confessed.

"Okay, I get the secret from Thomas. So, tell me why you plan to keep this from Dimitri for a while. I don't understand," Ariel admitted.

"Not for long. I just want to clean up the cabin, make the garden presentable and get rid of all these weeds. I also need to fix the driveway and add more gravel. Right now it looks like a dive. I just want to fix things up and like I said, arrange for security on the cabin. Then I plan to bring Dimitri out here and explain my plan to him."

"Do you think he'll judge you if he sees it like this?" Ariel was confused.

Alex took a deep breath. Apparently she was going to have to bear her soul before Ariel would agree to help her. "Maybe. I guess so. I guess I want to impress him, show him that I can handle myself."

"You already have. Don't you realize that, Alex?" Ariel laughed.

"What do you mean?" Alex asked.

Ariel looked at Alex for a long moment. She was amazed this strong, independent woman was so insecure when it came to

Dimitri. It was obvious he was head over heels in love with her. Couldn't she see that? "I didn't plan to talk to you about Dimitri, but I'm beginning to think maybe I should," Ariel admitted. "I don't think you realize the effect you have on that man."

"Wait," Alex interrupted. "I don't think it's a good idea to talk to you about Dimitri. I know I'm insecure when it comes to him and I'm trying to work on that. However, knowing my own insecurities, if we start talking about Dimitri, I'm afraid I'm going to ask you some things that I'm dying to know. Things I have no right to ask. It wouldn't be fair to ask you and I'm afraid it would change our friendship if I did. So, before I embarrass myself, I think we should just stop here." Alex took a deep breath.

"So don't ask. I'm going to tell you. I am three hundred and seventy-six years old. I've known Dimitri all my life. His father and my father were best friends, like brothers. When Dimitri's father died, my father took him under his wing. Dimitri was grown by then. He didn't really need my father, but dad's always had a soft spot for Dimitri. He's always thought of him as family, like his own son. That's why dad protects Dimitri from the council to the extent it has caused him grief. Sort of the same way he does with me. I just cause dad a lot more grief than Dimitri ever did," Ariel laughed.

"I didn't know Dimitri's father had died. He never told me that. He's been so good to me about my father's death. He's so supportive. I never thought to ask him about his dad. Another example of what a moron I can be sometimes," Alex groaned.

"You're certainly being a moron right now," Ariel agreed. "Anyway, because of our history, Dimitri is like a brother to me. I can only talk about my lifetime because he's a very private person. He doesn't talk about his relationships, not to anyone. So, I don't know about the time before I was alive. What I do know, is that Dimitri has never cared about any woman in my entire lifetime the way he cares about you. I can see it. He's happier than I've ever seen him. That man's in love with you and you sit here thinking you have to pull a few weeds to impress him. I don't get it," Ariel took a breath. "If you took him to a dilapidated shack, he'd be thrilled because you included him in your plans."

"You think he's in love with me?" Alex asked.

"You are a moron, I know he's in love with you. Just like I know you're in love with him. If the two of you are too stupid to tell each other, you deserve the agony you're going through. I know Dimitri's been around for a long time. Yes, he's been with other women. Hello, he's a guy and four hundred years old! But none of them have meant anything to him. Yeah he's cared about a few of them, but he's never been in love with any of them. He's putting his heart on the line with you, Alex. I'm going to give you fair warning, I promise if you hurt him, you're going to have to answer to me." Ariel watched Alex for a long moment. She hoped her message sunk in.

"Oh," Alex paused. "Will you throw fire at me?" Alex asked with a grin.

"Girl, I'll do worse than that. I don't care who you are. Just be good to Dimitri or your royal butt is mine. He really does love you. Personally, I think you're good for each other. My suggestion to you is bring him out here now, as soon as possible. Tell him what you're planning. He's not stupid, he's going to see the value in your plan and he can help. If there's a vulnerable spot, he'll find it and he'll have the perfect solution. I'd also feel a lot better working out here alone if Dimitri was in on the ground floor of the security system," Ariel admitted. "Now, it's getting late, let's get out of here before it gets dark."

* * * *

Hector stood in front of the majestic antique desk biting his tongue. Radek was in a mood today. He'd been ranting for what seemed like hours. In reality it had probably only been a few minutes. Hector was growing weary of the theatrics. He was pissed! Radek was responsible for the mess he was in. The warriors had been chasing him for over a year now. He told Radek they needed to be more secretive about the assassination. But no, Radek wouldn't hear of it. He wanted to make a statement. It's easy to make a statement when you're heads not the one on the line. Now, he was summoned to this ridiculous cave Radek called his headquarters to give another damn report.

There was no getting through to him. Radek loved this cave. Apparently it resembled his fathers and it was the place he had taken Marlena after he abducted her. That was the problem. Kidnaping was apparently the family pastime. How hard was it to understand that after you kidnap the Fae Queen, your headquarters is no longer a secret? You need to move. Obviously it's poor tactics for the enemy to know the location of your headquarters. Radek's ego and sentimentality toward his father wouldn't let him admit it was a problem. Maybe not for Radek, but it was a big problem for Hector. Especially if Radek was going to continue to summon him to give his reports in person. He sent a messenger daily, wasn't that enough?

Now here he was after a long night of trying to capture yet another fae without success, to give a report to his boss. Dawn was already approaching. He was going to have to stay here all day and hope he could elude the spies the warriors had watching the cave at dusk. He wished he could just disappear and leave all this nonsense to Radek. Maybe if Radek was the one putting his life on the line, he'd be a little less reckless with his demands. Unfortunately, the one person he'd like to escape was the one vampire that could find him anywhere. As his sire, Radek could track Hector to the ends of the earth. He could never hide from this lunatic.

"Have you located the names of the council members yet?" Radek demanded.

"Like I told you before," Hector answered with all the patience he could muster. "It's complicated. The warriors are still tracking me. I have to be very careful or I will be caught and killed by one of them. That makes it more difficult to find and capture a fae I can question," Hector inwardly sighed. How many times did he have to go over this?

"Excuses!" Radek thundered. "I sent you more vampires. Now I want those councilmen."

"I realize that," Hector sighed. "But the vampires you sent me are too young. It's true, they have located a couple of fae. Then they promptly sucked them dry. It's a little difficult to question a dead body." Hector was getting impatient now. He knew he had to tread carefully. When Radek got this way he was unpredictable.

Radek slammed his fist down on the desk. A large crack crept across the surface. He glowered at Hector. "I want results, no more excuses," he demanded. "If you don't have the names of those council members for me in one week, I'm moving on to plan B."

"Plan B, being to kidnap the new queen?" Hector said flatly.

Dusk

"Precisely! You know all about plan B, don't act as if this is new to you. We've discussed it all before." Radek sat down in the big chair.

"Yes, we've discussed it before and my position hasn't changed. Kidnaping the new queen is still a mistake. Look, you insisted I had to be the one to assassinate Marlena. You knew the warriors would come after me, but you still insisted it had to be me. Even I am surprised at how long this has lasted. I thought they would accept the fact that she is gone and move on. So far, they haven't. With the treaty broken, the vampires have become active again. They can't focus on me forever. But until they give up, I have to be careful. Finding the council is going to take more time. You do understand that, don't you?" Hector asked.

"Yes, I know. But I want my kingdom!" He glowered. "It's been over a year. I tried to wait for that woman who gave birth to me to die on her own. She just wouldn't. I didn't have a choice. Now I want my kingdom. I deserve it. It's my right!" Radek pouted.

"And we are working towards getting you that kingdom. But you have to be patient. I need at least two months to find the names of the council members and capture them. Once we have them here, they can denounce Alexandria as the queen then bestow the kingdom upon you. You know it's the best plan. Capturing Alexandria will only complicate things. The warriors will come at us with a vengeance. They will infiltrate your headquarters again. You remember the mess they left last time don't you? I'm afraid this time could be worse."

"That woman Alexandria," he said the name with contempt. "She has no right to try to step in and rule my kingdom. I'm the first born child. My father understood that and left his kingdom to me. These fae will not deprive me of my rights! They are weak. They need me!"

"Of course," Hector tried to cajole Radek. He was never going to get out of this room if the man didn't calm down.

"I will give you one month. If you don't at least have the names by then, I'm doing things my way," Radek said. "Now, I'm hungry. I want one of the diabetics. Their blood is always so sweet. I've had a rough day and I deserve a special treat." He looked straight into Hector's eyes. "You pick one and bring it to me. I also want Lilith. Make sure she doesn't make me wait."

"I'll have one of the diabetics brought up. Sammael will get word to Lilith. I'm sure she'll come quickly, she knows you dislike it when you have to wait." Hector began to retreat.

"No!" Radek bellowed. "I said I want YOU to bring me dinner and summon Lilith. Do it yourself. I'm also going to need another desk. This one is broken. That won't do." Then, with a flick of his hand Hector was dismissed.

The petulant tyrant. He wanted Hector to do it. He wanted Hector to do everything. Get my dinner, get the council, get my kingdom, get my girlfriend. I'm just going to sit in my disgusting cave and pretend like I'm a mighty king. One of these days Hector was going to have enough. He'd been trying to come up with a plan to escape, but how? There was no escaping as long as Radek was alive. Could he somehow set Radek up? Make sure he was killed by the warriors? Then Hector could step in as king. He was running the kingdom anyway. Losing Radek would be good for the vampires. So far, he hadn't figured out a plan. If Radek kept this up, he was going to start focusing all his energy on finding one.

Dusk

"Everything okay?" Sammael asked eagerly as Hector quietly shut the door to Radek's private office.

"I need a diabetic. Radek is in the mood for something sweet," he said sourly. "But don't take it into him. He insisted I had to be the one to bring him dinner. He's in a mood, so make sure you wait. I need to find Lilith." He turned toward the living quarters.

"She's in the war room practicing. I can tell her to come up when I get the diabetic," Sammael offered.

"No, I'll do it. Radek doesn't want to wait." He turned and headed in the opposite direction. Maybe it was the fae blood in Radek that made him so unstable. Sure, vampires weren't known for their level heads but Radek was off the charts. He was neurotic. Then there was Lilith. Radek would freak if he knew about Hector and Lilith. He'd definitely kill them both if he ever found out. But vampires didn't have one lover. Lilith needed variety. Hector didn't need Lilith, but appeasing her had its advantages. Sammael had followed Hector down the hallway. Hector turned. "Did you get the triplets I asked you for?"

"Yes, of course," Sammael said enthusiastically. "They are already in your room."

At least he'd have a release tonight from all his frustration. And if he died in the morning, he'd die a happy man.

Chapter Seven

Alex had been thinking about what Ariel said all the way home. Could she be right? Did Dimitri really love her? She'd been so off her game for the last while. Yes, she'd had a large shock when her mother died. Then, just as she was finally getting back to normal, her father was killed. Then the big whammy; all the fae, vampire, warrior stuff. Her world had been turned upside down and she was feeling insecure. She hadn't really had confidence in anything, let alone her relationship with Dimitri. Part of it was probably the rocky start, but still. She had not been herself. That was part of the reason she was so anxious to start working with Ariel. She thought if she really did have some powers maybe that would help her gain some confidence. Maybe then, she would feel like she was worthy to be part of this war. Worthy to be the fae Queen. Worthy of Dimitri's love?

At least she was running her part of the business successfully. The only major problem was the stuff with John Anderson. Thomas had found the file dad started on him, but there wasn't any hard proof. She was also a little concerned that they couldn't find dad's bug finder. Oh, Alex was confident John was involved in the leak. It was just a matter of finding enough evidence to fire him. She hadn't really had the time to give that situation justice. Sam was still on alert though. Alex was confident they would eventually have enough to fire John. Hopefully, Sam would step into that position and things would be better at D-Tech.

She walked in the door and immediately went in search of Marta. She was going to need her help.

Marta was in the kitchen finishing up dinner. "Hey Marta," Alex said as she walked in and started to set the table.

"Oh Alex," Marta looked up. "Thanks, I was just about to get to that myself."

"That's okay. I'll take care of it," Alex replied. She glanced back at Marta over her shoulder. "I was wondering if you are swamped tomorrow, or if there's any way you could help me with something. It will probably take most of the day though, so if you're busy I understand."

"Tomorrow should be okay. What do you need help with?" she asked curiously.

"Well, I thought I would clean up the old cabin. I know we haven't been there for a while, that's how I know it's going to take all day. I thought we could make it useable again. We'd need to clean out all the dust, change the sheets and all that, but I don't think it would take more than a day to get it back in useable condition. Especially if we both worked on it." Alex tried to keep her tone casual.

Marta was a little curious about this request. Alex had always liked the cabin, but around high school she had stopped wanting to go on the weekend trips. As an adult she'd never shown any interest in spending time out there. "What brought this on?" Marta asked curiously.

"I don't know, nostalgia I guess," Alex answered absently. "I had some good times there with the family and I always liked it when I was younger. I thought if I fixed it up, maybe Dimitri and I could go there occasionally to get away from everything." Alex looked up at her. "So are you game?"

Marta smiled. She liked Dimitri. She thought he and Alex were good for each other. They seemed to have gotten off to a slow start, but now they both seemed really happy. "I'm game. I'll gather up the cleaning supplies we'll need and load them in the car tonight. That way everything will be ready to go in the morning. We should probably take the SUV. The road might be bad and we'll have plenty of room to carry all the supplies. I'll also pack a lunch so we won't need to worry about leaving to find something. I don't dare take anything that has to be cooked. I don't know what condition the stove or oven is in. Are sandwiches okay?" she asked.

"Sandwiches will be perfect," Alex said. "Thank you, Marta. I know this is going to interrupt your schedule. If there's anything I can do to help you get back on track, let me know. Oh, did Thomas get home?"

"Yes, he's working in the library. Will you go tell him dinner's ready while I get the food on the table?" Marta asked.

"Absolutely. You staying for dinner tonight or heading out?" Alex stopped in the doorway to ask.

Dusk

"I'm meeting Jake. He said there's something he needs help with. Good thing I'm a miracle worker. By the time Jake asks for help, he's usually made a mess of whatever it is he's working on. Now scoot before your dinner gets cold. I'll see you at eight." Marta grinned as she gathered up her things.

* * * *

Thomas was still asleep when Alex and Marta left for the cabin. Good, Alex thought. Now I don't have to come up with an excuse for why I'm going there. Thomas would probably insist on joining them anyway. He was too busy with everything going on to take an entire day to hang out at the cabin while she and Marta cleaned. She'd make sure they got home before dark and Thomas would never know. If they got everything done today, she could bring Dimitri out and pitch her plan. She was starting to get excited now. Things were falling into place. No more waiting around, she was taking action. If she didn't have any special powers or fae talents, she would at least have a place to learn some new fighting techniques. The meadow was going to be perfect!

Alex and Marta had been working for hours. The downstairs was sparkling clean and they were just finishing up with the bedrooms. To their surprise, they didn't have any major repairs to make. The appliances all still worked. Marta had set the refrigerators' temperature so in about a day, it would be ready to use. The oven was still in great shape. There were a couple windows that wouldn't open, Alex thought they might be rusted shut. She would leave that for the security guys to deal with. At least they were closed instead of open. They could still secure the house, so it wasn't a priority. She looked over at Marta. "Can I ask you a personal question?" Alex said hesitantly.

"You can ask. If it's personal, I always reserve the right to decline to answer," Marta said with a smile.

"Well, I was just wondering about you and Jake." Alex was watching Marta. Her back stiffened and Alex thought she was going to refuse to talk about this topic.

"What do you want to know?" Marta asked.

"It's obvious you two care for each other. You spend a lot of time together and you both seem so happy. So, I was just wondering why you never hooked up." Alex said trying to ease into the conversation.

"Jake and I are good friends. We're comfortable with each other. There's nothing more to it than that," Marta answered.

"Do you love him?" Alex asked.

"Alex!" Marta exclaimed. "What kind of question is that?"

"Actually, I think it's a straight forward one," Alex retorted. "It should be a simple yes or no. Do you love Jake?" Alex persisted.

Marta looked torn. Alex knew she was walking on thin ice here. Marta usually wouldn't tolerate her or Thomas bringing up the subject of Jake in this way. "Yes," Marta confessed. It was almost a whisper. Alex barely heard her.

Alex kept watching Marta. "You know he loves you, too. Right?"

Dusk

Marta looked up sharply. "No, I don't know that he loves me too. We are friends. He's comfortable with me because he's known me for so long, that's all. He depends on me to help him out, just like Luke and Marlena did."

Alex laughed. "I'm going to tell you the same thing a friend told me yesterday. You're a moron!"

Marta was shocked. Alex had never spoken to her that way before. What was going on here?

"Yeah, you heard me right. You are a moron. Jake has been in love with you for years. Just like you have been in love with him for years. I feel bad for both of you. If you weren't both such cowards, you could have been experiencing love, experiencing living for the last decade or so. Instead, you both cling to the ridiculous notion that being friends is fulfilling enough. You accept less, because asking for more would make you vulnerable for about a half a second. You know you love Jake, why haven't you ever tried for more with him?" Alex pressed.

Marta started to cry. Alex felt bad. This was not the reaction she was expecting. She didn't mean to make Marta unhappy. She thought she was doing her a favor. Alex quickly moved to the other side of the bed and pushed Marta down to sit on the edge. She sat down and wrapped her arms around her. "Marta, I am so sorry!" Alex exclaimed. "Forget what I said, I should have kept my big trap shut."

Marta sniffed. "No, I'm glad you said it. I do want more with Jake. I've had these feelings for so long, been friends with him for so long, I'm terrified to hope for more. He is such a great man. He's successful and strong, what would he want with a house maid like me?"

"Marta!" Alex exclaimed. "If you are holding back because you think your job is not important enough, you're fired!"

Marta looked up at Alex in shock. "What?"

"I will fire you right now. I'm serious. You are more than a house maid and you know it. You are family. Sure, you keep the house but so what. You are also there for me and Thomas when we need you emotionally, physically, whatever. You're more like a close aunt than an employee. Since moms been gone you've been like a second mother. Most mothers clean their own houses and cook their own dinners. Does that make them less? Of course it doesn't. Jake loves you for who you are. He also depends on you. I've noticed the two of you have been spending more and more time together lately. I think that's because the little amount of time the two of you have allowed yourselves in the past just isn't enough. You both want more and keep coming up with excuses to see each other. Yet, you don't put yourself out there. I know you are special and I won't have you demeaning yourself. Jake knows how special you are, too. Believe me Marta, he loves you. Even if you don't take my advice and put your heart out there, I hope you will at least think about it. I'm going to with Dimitri. If I can, so can you," Alex sighed.

"What do you mean?" Marta asked.

"Well, I'm in love with Dimitri. It seems so weird to actually say that out loud, but I am. I've known it for a while now. I also know he cares about me. I don't know if he loves me. So I've been content to just sit back and enjoy things the way they are, it's safe. But what if he does really love me? What if we both just sit here, happy to let things ride? Eventually we could slowly drift apart because we both want more, but neither one of us is willing to take the chance. Think of all the amazing times we could miss out on because we were both too scared to put ourselves out there. Believe me Marta, I know how you feel. Compared to Dimitri, I feel inadequate. I am terrified. But if there's the slightest possibility that Dimitri loves me too, I want to know. I want it all. If I put my heart out there and find out he loves me too, then the moment of vulnerability I have to go through to find out is worth it. For Dimitri, the risk is worth it." Alex looked back over at Marta. "Jake is worth it too. I know he loves you, but you have to decide for yourself if he's worth the risk. Not that there's much of a risk there. I know he loves you even if you don't."

Marta didn't know what to say. What if Alex was right? What if Jake did love her and this whole time both of them were just being stupid and cowardly? If that was true, they had already lost so much time. Marta was definitely going to think about it. She looked toward the window and realized it was getting late. She jumped up. "Alex, look at the time! We've got to go, now!"

Alex looked at her watch and panicked. They still had to load up the car and stop to get something for dinner. They would be cutting it close. She had to be home before dark. "Help me load up the cleaning supplies. We've got to get out of here."

"Leave them. I'll throw them in the closet and we can buy more for the house. If I don't get you home before dark, Thomas will never forgive me," Marta said anxiously.

They quickly threw the cleaning supplies into the pantry, locked the cabin and hurried to the car. They stopped at KFC and grabbed a bucket of chicken from the drive-thru and pulled into the house just at twilight. Alex noticed there were several cars in the driveway. Some of the warriors must be here, she decided. She helped Marta carry the food into the house and hurried up to her room. She was in desperate need of a shower. Her clothes felt so dirty and grimy.

After her shower, Alex pulled on a robe. She'd just throw on comfortable clothes for the rest of the evening. As she exited the bathroom, she stopped. Dimitri was sitting on her bed. He looked so angry. Her heart dropped, was he mad at her? She'd just remain casual and pretend she didn't notice. "Dimitri, what's up?" Alex asked.

He was off the bed in half a second. "Where have you been all day?" he demanded. "I've been worried sick about you. I called your cell, no answer. I called here at the house, no answer. I came by, but Marta wasn't here either. I've left you at least a dozen messages and you couldn't even call me back to tell me you were okay? After about the third message you should have known I was worried."

Alex hurried over to her purse. She didn't get phone service at the cabin, so she had turned her phone off. They were in such a rush to get home when they left, she'd forgotten to turn it back on. She quickly checked the display and saw there were fifteen messages. "Fifteen," she looked back at Dimitri and grimaced. "Are they all from you?"

"Probably," he said flatly. "Alex, I've been going out of my mind all day. When I couldn't reach you, I told myself you were just in meetings or something, but when you never called me back I panicked. I started showing up at all of your businesses I could remember. I probably made a nuisance of myself. I'm not sure some of those employees will ever let me back through the door. I couldn't help it. I had to find you. I was so worried. I thought you had been kidnaped by Radek, or worse that you were injured…or dead." He had moved to the window and was looking out into the darkness.

Alex walked over and stood between him and the window. "I'm sorry. I truly am. I never thought you would try to reach me before I got home." She wrapped her arms around him and laid her head on his chest. "Please, Dimitri will you forgive me. I am so sorry. I know if it had been me trying to reach you and I couldn't, I would have been frantic." Alex didn't know what else to say. He was just standing there. She wanted him to hold her. She needed everything to be okay between them.

Dimitri sighed. He wrapped his arms around her and held her tight. They just stood there in silence for a long moment. He had been so angry with her for not calling him, then he had been so worried. How could he go on if she were dead? He must have arrived here just before her. When he found out she was home and had gone up to shower without saying a word, he wanted to throttle her. Now standing here with her in his arms, he just wanted to hold her tight and never let go. He needed the comfort. He needed to feel her to know she was here and she was okay.

Alex was shocked. Dimitri was holding her with such desperation. She was so stupid. He must have been going out of his mind with worry. She knew she would have been if Dimitri was missing. She felt terrible about it. How could she make it up to him? She raised onto her tip toes and kissed him lightly. Dimitri pulled her tighter and ravished her mouth. His kiss became hard and desperate, that was the only word she could think of to describe it. He picked her up and carried her to the bed. He sat on the edge, holding her in his lap. They sat there in silence for a while. Dimitri laid his head against the side of hers while he held her tight. "Will you tell me where you were all day?" He asked as he shifted her so he could look her in the eyes. "And why you had your phone turned off," Dimitri asked clearly still annoyed.

Alex stood. So, things were still strained between them. She owed him an explanation. She climbed back on the bed and sat next to him, taking his hand in hers. "The short answer is that Marta and I went to an old cabin my family owns. We haven't been there for a while, so it needed a lot of work." She felt Dimitri stiffen. He obviously wasn't happy about her going to the cabin. She needed to talk fast. "It's far enough out of the city that you can't get cell phone reception."

"You did what?" Dimitri was angry again. He bolted straight up. He just stood there, glaring down at her. "You went out by yourself? And don't give me any nonsense about Marta being with you, she's human. She's no help against vampires or fae. You went to some deserted cabin with no way to call for help if there was trouble?"

"No," Alex interrupted. "Let me finish. Then if you want to get mad at me again, I guess you have that right. When I'm finished, you can talk."

Dimitri was still scowling at her, but he sat back down, leaned his head against the headboard and mumbled. "Fine, go ahead."

"You can't get cell phone service at the cabin but there is a working land line. If there had been trouble I could have called for help," Alex said a little defensively.

"A lot of good that would have done you. By the time anyone got there, you'd probably both be dead," Dimitri grumbled.

Dusk

"Are you going to let me finish? Or are you going to have something negative to say after every sentence? Because if you are, I'm done talking to you. I know I upset you today. I know I screwed up. If I had thought things through, I would have given you the number at the cabin just in case you needed to reach me. I've said I'm sorry. I don't know what else I can do to make it up to you!" Alex said with exasperation. She started to walk away from Dimitri. He was making her so angry. Yes, she'd worried him today, but she wasn't going to tolerate his attitude.

Dimitri grabbed her by the waist and pulled her down on the bed against him. "Okay, I'll try to control myself until you finish your explanation. Please don't go anywhere. I need to feel you close to me right now."

Alex was touched. She had really worried him. She'd never seen him like this before. She relaxed a little and continued. "So, because there was no phone service I decided to turn off my cell phone to preserve the battery. If I needed to make a call, I had the land line. I figured I'd turn it back on when we headed home. Unfortunately, Marta and I started talking about some personal stuff and lost track of time. When we realized how late it was, we panicked and rushed to get back home before dark. I completely forgot about my phone until you said you'd been trying to reach me and I hadn't called you back."

Dimitri was silent for a long time. Alex was starting to think he wasn't going to say anything when he finally asked, "Why did you go out to the cabin in the first place? You said it needed work because you haven't been there for so long. Why now?" He seemed calm again.

Alex moved so she could face him. "Are we okay, Dimitri? Before I talk to you about the cabin, I need to know we are going to be okay." She still wasn't sure how Dimitri would react when she asked him to take time off work to go on a road trip. He might get angry or annoyed with her again. She thought the timing was off but she'd promised Ariel, so she would ask for his input.

Dimitri sighed. "Yeah, we're okay. You have no idea what you put me through today. Will you please promise me you will never do anything like this again without letting me know how to find you first?"

Alex leaned over and kissed him gently. "I promise," she laid her forehead against his. "I am truly sorry for what I put you through. I feel terrible that you had to worry about me like that."

Dimitri pulled back from her. He looked at her for several seconds and then flashed her favorite grin. "I know how you can make it up to me."

In that moment everything shifted. Alex felt that the world was right again. "We did buy the Colonel for dinner, will that do it?" she asked.

"It's a start, but that wasn't what I had in mind. I think you owe me make-up sex. A lot of makeup sex!" He stood up and pulled her to her feet. "But first, I want chicken."

"Dimitri," Alex said a little hesitantly.

He quickly looked back at her. "Yeah?"

"I know I'm in no position to ask you for a favor right now, but I was wondering if you could rearrange your schedule sometime in the next couple days. I need you to come to the cabin with me. I have something I need to show you and talk to you about, but it will probably take several hours. It's really important to me." Alex hoped things were really okay between them. She didn't want Dimitri to get angry with her again.

"Sure. Tomorrow's pretty light," he said looking around the room for Alex's slippers. "I could probably reschedule a couple things and be finished by around eleven. Would that give us enough time?" He picked the slippers up and glanced over at her. He was surprised. She was looking at him so apprehensively. Almost like she was afraid - was she afraid of him? He walked over and pulled her into his arms. "Alex, what's wrong? You look like you're afraid of me?"

"I guess I am, a little," she admitted.

Dimitri pushed her shoulders back so he could look at her. "Why? You know I would never do anything to hurt you."

He sounded confused and maybe a little hurt. She wasn't doing anything right today. Well, this was as good a time as any to lay it all out there. She looked down at her feet, she couldn't look at him while she did this. "Because I'm in love with you. Do you have any idea how much that terrifies me? When I came out of that bathroom and saw you sitting there, so angry, I didn't know what to do. I thought you were angry with me, but I didn't know why. I couldn't catch my breath. It was like the earth had fallen off its axis and I didn't know how to fix it again. Then, when you just looked at me with that crooked grin of yours, I knew everything was going to be okay. Everything was right again." Now, she looked up and saw he was smiling.

"You love me?" Dimitri asked with a big grin.

"Yes," Alex answered shyly.

"Well that's convenient. Because I am so madly in love with you I'm going insane." Dimitri laughed with joy. He picked her up and hugged her tight, swinging her around. He set her down and stepped back again, "But that doesn't explain that look you had on your face," he said confused.

"I was just worried. Worried that everything was right again, and I was going to go and ruin it." She hoped she was making sense. "I was afraid that bringing up the cabin might make you mad again. That asking you to rearrange everything for me would annoy you and this time I wouldn't be able to fix it. I was afraid we were going to have another argument," she confessed.

Dimitri picked her up, laid her on the bed, then laid on top of her kissing her gently. He propped himself up with both elbows and brushed her hair away from her face with his hands. "Alex, I love you. Knowing you love me too makes me the happiest man in the world right now." He leaned down and kissed her, hard. He was still smiling. "We're going to fight sometimes and then we'll make up. That's part of life. No matter what, we can always make it right again. Please don't look at me like that ever again. It breaks my heart to think you could be afraid of me."

Alex interrupted. "That's not what I meant. I wasn't afraid of you! I was afraid of losing you! I couldn't stand it if I ever lost you." Alex's eyes were moist now.

"Well, that's convenient too. Because I feel exactly the same way about you." He sobered a little. "That's why I was so upset today. If anything had happened to you..." he broke off, unable to finish what he was about to say.

Alex leaned up and kissed him now. "Let's go get that pesky chicken out of the way. I'm in the mood for all that make-up sex I owe you," she said as she pushed lightly on his chest.

Dimitri got up laughing. He grabbed her hand and pulled her to her feet. "Actually, I'm starving. I haven't been able to eat anything all day. I've been too worried about you."

* * * *

They were laughing and joking as they reached the bottom of the stairs and saw Thomas. He was standing in the doorway to the library with a stern look on his face. "Alex, I need to talk to you for a minute." He turned and walked into the library.

Alex and Dimitri looked at each other, shrugged and then followed Thomas through the doorway. Thomas sat down at the old desk and was surprised to see Dimitri there. For the first time he saw how happy they both looked. They were almost glowing. He wasn't sure why, but that annoyed him. He looked directly at Dimitri. "This is family business. Maybe you could wait for Alex in the kitchen," Thomas requested.

"Nope," Dimitri answered. He leaned back against the wall and pulled Alex against him, wrapping his arms around her waist. "I think I'll just wait in here. You don't mind, do you Alex?" He asked as he moved aside her hair and kissed her neck.

Thomas stood up. "Look. I've tried to stay out of this," he waved his hand. "Whatever this is between the two of you because you're adults and I figure you both know what you're doing. As long as it didn't impact me, I was happy to keep my mouth shut."

He walked over to the bar and poured himself a brandy. He turned back to face them planning to continue when Dimitri cut him off.

"Thomas, I think you better sit down and drink that brandy before you say something that you'll regret later. I like you. I'd hate to have to hurt you, especially when I'm in such a good mood." Dimitri straightened, took Alex by the hand and led her to the couch. He sat down casually and crossed one leg so his ankle was resting on his knee. Then he tugged on Alex's hand until she sat down next to him. "Now, why don't you come sit over here by the fire and tell us what has you so upset."

Thomas took a deep breath. "Okay, fine. Alex, I want to know where you were all day today," he demanded.

Alex let out a little sigh. Dimitri took her hand in his. "She was unavailable," he answered for her.

Thomas glared at him. "I know she was unavailable. I just got off the phone with Bryant Jones. He said a mad man came into the store today ranting about needing to find you." He looked directly at Alex. "He claimed it was an emergency, a matter of life and death. Bryant was about to call the police when the guy finally left. He was uncomfortable about the situation and called Shawn over at Security for direction. Shawn put him at ease. He said this guy had also paid him a visit about an hour before. Shawn also told Bryant he personally knew the individual; whose name just happens to be Dimitri. Shawn assured him Dimitri is a standup guy but once Bryant got home, he started to worry. That's when he called me to make sure everything was okay with you. So being the standup guy that you are Dimitri, would you care to tell me why you were in such a panic to find Alex? Why it was a matter of life and death. And why no one seemed to be able to get a hold of her all day today?"

Dusk

"Sure Thomas," he gave Alex's hand a squeeze. "As soon as you pull the stick out of your ass and calm down."

Thomas's face went red. He was pissed. Alex knew she'd better step in. Clearly there was too much testosterone in the room. She stood up. Dimitri pulled her back down. She looked at him incredulously, but he still had a smile on his face. Dimitri was the only one in the room enjoying this little scene.

"Alex and I had a misunderstanding," Dimitri answered casually. "Long story short, I tried to call her today and couldn't reach her. As I said, she was unavailable. When I didn't hear back from her, I panicked. I went to several of her offices in an attempt to locate her. I over reacted. Unlike you, who appears to be the picture of calm and tranquility Thomas, I immediately assumed the worst. I'm sure you have never made such a mistake, but unfortunately I am merely a mortal and I jumped to the wrong conclusions. The longer it took to find her, the more convinced I became she was either in danger or she had been injured. You know, that pesky little matter of vampires and fae being at war and potentially trying to kill her and all. I'm sure you can understand my concern and I hope you can forgive my behavior. I didn't mean to cause problems with your business. I've already explained my actions to Alex and informed her she may have to do some damage control in the morning. I also suspect I won't be welcome at some of your fine establishments in the future," he paused. "Any chance I could get some of that brandy?" He flashed Thomas a casual smile. "It's kind of been a long day and if I can't get food, maybe I could at least get a little drunk."

Thomas sat there, looking at Dimitri for a long time. Then he burst out laughing. He turned to the bar and brought Dimitri a glass of brandy. Alex was astonished. Dimitri handled Thomas and his temper better than dad used to. That was probably because Thomas got his temper from dad. She looked between the two men several times. They were smiling at each other. "I guess you don't need me anymore. I'm going to the kitchen to get some dinner." she looked back at Dimitri. "Are you coming?" she asked.

"Alex," Thomas injected. "Would you mind getting him a plate? I think I have some apologizing to do."

Alex looked back at Thomas, he could see she was skeptical.

"I promise, he won't have to hurt me tonight." Thomas glanced back at Dimitri and grinned, "As if he could."

"Fine, but make it quick," she looked back at Dimitri. "I have plans for him before you two leave to hunt tonight," then she turned and walked out the door.

Dimitri looked at Thomas. He wasn't sure what they were going to discuss. Probably some protective brother talk concerning Alex.

"I know that was a load of bull you just tried to feed me. If neither of you are going to tell me where she was, will you just tell me if she was ever in any real danger?" Thomas asked soberly.

"I don't think so and it wasn't bull. She was unavailable and I did panic just like I said. I was frantic, I was sure Radek had kidnaped her or killed her and I wasn't there to protect her. I shouldn't have gone to your businesses looking for her like that. I know I've caused some problems. I wasn't in the right state of mind to be rational. When I didn't get answers I pushed harder than I should have with some of your employees. If there's anything I can do to help fix it, just let me know," Dimitri offered.

Dusk

Thomas finally sat in the chair across from Dimitri with a sigh. "Dimitri, I know it's none of my business. I've tried to stay out of this thing, whatever is going on between the two of you. But I need to know if you care for my sister, or if this is just a casual affair for you. I'm really not just being nosey. I need to be prepared to help her cope if you're not serious," Thomas stated soberly.

"I love her," Dimitri answered simply. "I understand your need to protect Alex. I also appreciate you giving us some space to figure out where we stand with each other and what we both want. I think we're still working on that last part, or more to the point I think she is. But, I love your sister with all my heart. I guess that's why I went a little crazy today. I can apologize but I will also tell you, under the same circumstances I'd probably do it again," Dimitri confessed.

"You do know she's going to drive you insane, don't you?" Thomas laughed. "She drives me insane with her stubbornness and independence and I'm just her brother. I know I'm overprotective, but Alex has had it rough with relationships in the past. I can see she's fallen for you hard. If for some reason things don't work out between the two of you, will you please try to let her down easy?" Thomas was treading lightly. This was his leader, but they were also discussing his sister's life. He had to walk a fine line here.

Dimitri interrupted. "Why do you assume if it doesn't work, I'm the one that will end things?" Dimitri was truly interested in Thomas' answer.

"Because I can see Alex is in love with you. When Alex gives away her heart, it's usually forever. Tanya is a perfect example of that. I don't believe she's ever really loved the previous men in her life. She's been too skeptical. For good reason, she typically dates scumbags. But she has let herself care about some of them and they've always let her down. They've always hurt her in some way or another. I think she is in love with you. I also believe she's hoping for a future with you. So I'm just asking that you let me know if you're not that serious about this relationship," Thomas replied.

"I am serious about this relationship, Thomas. I love your sister. I would never do anything to hurt her. Between you and me, if this relationship ends, it will be Alex that ends it. I think it's too soon to ask, but I want to spend the rest of my life with your sister. Are you okay with that prospect?" Dimitri asked soberly.

Thomas looked at Dimitri in surprise. "Seriously?"

"Seriously," Dimitri answered soberly.

Thomas smiled. "I am more than okay with that prospect. I'm ecstatic! All I want is for Alex to be happy. I think you can make her happy. I know you can keep her safe." Thomas got up and pulled Dimitri into a huge hug. "You're secrets safe with me. I hope you know what you're doing, brother." Thomas smiled a devilish smile. "Us Deveraux's can be pretty high maintenance." He thought Dimitri cared for his sister, but he had no idea he was that serious. "Oh, one more thing. Alex would probably disagree, but I would stay away from Tanya if I were you. She's bad news. For the life of me, I don't know why Alex stayed friends with her for so long. She should have kicked her ass in high school." Thomas picked his brandy back up.

"High school? Why in high school?" Dimitri was confused. She hadn't dated Adam as early as high school had she?

Dusk

"I probably shouldn't tell you this, but I'm going to. Alex was dating a guy in high school, Billie something or other. He was her first real crush, first boyfriend and all. She was gone for the guy, as much as you can be in high school anyway. She was a junior and this guy was a senior, you know the drill. Anyway, Alex was a cheerleader. She had to go to every game, but obviously she was busy the whole time. Tanya and Billie knew that. They would meet under the bleachers at most, if not all, of the games and make out. I don't know how far it went, I never really cared. Anyway, Alex saw them one night and she was completely crushed. It pissed me off that she kept dating the jerk afterwards.

I thought she would at least confront Tanya about it, but as far as I know she never did. At the time, she convinced herself it was a onetime thing. A short time later the prick dumped her. It broke her heart. I think that's why she's had such a hard time trusting men her whole life. But her and Tanya stayed friends until years later when Alex caught her in bed with Adam, another piece of work that called himself a boyfriend." Thomas drank the last of his brandy. "Anyway if Tanya knows you and Alex have something going, I guarantee she'll test the waters with you. She'll want to see how far she can get. I'm glad Tanya survived that attack, but I personally hope I never see that woman again. I have a hard time just being in the same room as her."

"Alex told me about Adam, in fact I met the weasel at the ball, but she didn't tell me about this Billie guy. Did Alex tell you what happened with Adam that night?" Dimitri asked.

"No," Thomas said in surprise. "Please tell me you broke the guy's nose at least."

Dimitri laughed. "No, but I think he probably wet himself after our little chat." Dimitri proceeded to tell Thomas about the encounter with Adam. When he was finished Thomas sat back in his chair.

"You're kidding me. The guy actually thought Alex would give him another shot after their little misunderstanding? I guess that's one way to put it," Thomas was disgusted. "I never liked that guy. I know Alex never truly trusted him, but again I have no idea why she dated him in the first place." Thomas looked into his brandy. "I really am thrilled about you and Alex. I know you will take good care of my sister. I have a lot of respect for you Dimitri. I'm glad it was you she fell for. And hey, sorry about earlier. When I heard Alex was out alone, away from her phone today, I went a little goofy. Then, when I found out you were out looking for her and you didn't call me, I guess I was a little pissed at you too. It reminded me of dad, the way he was always doing things behind my back. Thanks for not kicking my ass," he smiled. "I probably deserved a good whooping."

Dimitri laughed. "I'm glad we cleared things up. And for the record I wasn't doing things behind your back. To be honest my head wasn't on straight. The thought never crossed my mind to call you, or any of the other warriors. I just went into panic mode and started searching for Alex. I guess I'm still new at this leader thing and relying on my brothers." He slapped Thomas on the back.

"Thanks for that." Thomas was sincerely grateful he hadn't been left out on purpose.

"Oh, speaking of being the leader. I'm not going out with you guys tonight. I know that makes you a little shorthanded, but I'm sure you can handle it. I've got plans with a beautiful woman,"

Dusk

Dimitri smiled. "I think I'll take her to my house, so don't be surprised if we're not here when you get home. Also, just so you know, we're going to be unavailable tomorrow from around eleven until the early evening. If you need anything, I'll try to check my messages every once in a while. Goodnight Thomas," Dimitri said as he walked out the door.

* * * *

When Dimitri walked into the kitchen, he found Alex sitting at the table alone. She was almost finished with her dinner. He hadn't realized he'd taken so long with Thomas.

She looked up at him and motioned to the stove. "I put your plate on the warming oven. I wasn't sure how long you'd take."

Dimitri brought his dinner back to the table. "You need anything while I'm up?" he asked.

"Nope, I'm just finishing." She looked over at him as he sat down. "It's getting late, do you have to leave right after dinner, or do we have some time before you go?"

He smiled over at her. "Yes and no." He was looking at her, amused.

She knew he was paying her back for answering one of his questions that way. "Okay I'll bite," She smiled. "Would you care to explain that answer, sir?" she asked sarcastically.

"Well, I was thinking maybe you could come to my house for the night. If you're game, then we need to leave after I eat. If you're not interested then no, we have some time." He smiled over at her as he ate another bite of chicken. "Man, am I starving. Thanks for the plate."

"Are you serious? You want me to go to your house?" Alex asked. He'd never invited her over before. She'd been curious about where he lived, but figured there was a reason he hadn't taken her there yet. "Is it safe for me to be there alone until you get back from hunting? I mean you have a good security system, right."

Dimitri laughed. "I'd put my security system up against yours any day, babe! It's perfectly safe for you to be there alone. However, I'm not going out to hunt. I took the night off."

"What? Really?" she said with a huge smile.

"Really," he said. "So, does that mean you'll come home with me?"

"I'd love to," she answered.

"Do you want to follow me over in your car, or have the limo pick you up in the morning? I've got a pretty early day so I won't be able to bring you back home myself." Dimitri looked over at her.

"I'll just follow you over. I'd rather have my car." Alex couldn't wait to see his house. She'd been curious about where he lived ever since they'd met.

"It won't take me too long to finish here, why don't you go pack your bag and we'll leave as soon as I clean this up." She started to get up, but he grabbed her and kissed her before she got away. "Hurry back," he growled.

Alex followed Dimitri to a neighborhood not too far from her own. It was a nice area, pretty similar to where she and Thomas lived. He stopped at a big gate and motioned for her to pull in next to him. Once she stopped, he opened her door. "Come over here with me, I want to program you into the system." He had her put her palm on a pad then she looked into a small screen. "Okay, you're almost done. Let me just..." he was pressing buttons. "Okay. I need a voice print, so just say your name."

Alex stated her name and the gate swung open. He really did have better security than she did. "What, do you keep the hope diamond locked up inside? I haven't seen this kind of security since I visited Washington."

"No, but I like to keep my stuff secure. Now that you're in the system, you have access anytime you need it," Dimitri stated casually.

"Good to know. If I sneak over one night while you're out, will you attack me when you get home? Do I need body armor?" she teased. She was a little surprised he was giving her free access to his home.

"Probably. But body armor won't help with the kind of attack I have planned for you," he smiled. "Let's get in the house. I don't like you standing out here after dark." He ushered her back to her car. She pulled through the gate and he followed her to the front of the house. "Try the door," he pushed her to another touch pad. Alex put her hand on the pad and the small light on the door turned to green.

"That's it? No key or anything?" she asked.

"No, if you need access to the house just pull up to the front gate. The system already read the plate on your car and has a picture of you, so it can check your identity that way. Most likely, it will just open for you automatically. If not, all you need to do is pull up to the box and state your name. The system will do the rest. You shouldn't need to use the palm identifier at the gate unless the system registers something strange. Then, all you need at the door is the palm. Unless again, the system registers something strange. It might ask for a voice print. Is that clear? I know it seems sophisticated and I guess it actually is, but as far as operating the system it's pretty simple." Dimitri was smiling at her. "Now, get your skinny little butt through the door. I have plans for you tonight." He gave her backside a little push.

Alex laughed and walked through the large front door then stopped in surprise. Dimitri actually ran into her and almost knocked her over. He scrambled to hold onto her overnight bag. From the outside his house looked like a rustic old mansion. She was sure it was several hundred years old. She expected the inside to be decorated in a nice Victorian style. She was surprised at the tasteful but expensive decor. Dimitri had obviously redecorated the entire home. He had a traditional style that was classically elegant. The house was filled with antique furniture and she was sure the paintings on the walls were originals. His taste was exquisite and refined. He used antiques, marble and crystal to create a natural but classy look. She loved it!

"Uh, Alex?" Dimitri interrupted her thoughts. "You're going to have to enter the house enough for me to close the door. I promise, it won't bite."

"Oh sorry," she gave a little laugh. "The inside of your house just took me by surprise. I guess I had certain expectations from the outside and I was a little flabbergasted when I stepped inside. I didn't mean to block the doorway." She was still trying to take it all in. "Is that painting an original? They all look like originals," she said amazed.

"I'm not sure which painting you are referring to, but yes. I would say it's an original since they are all originals. What's the point in owning a fake?" He was watching her intently. So far, he couldn't tell if she liked what he had done or not.

Alex quietly walked into the library. There were so many books, a lot of them were leather bound. And was that a Picasso on the wall? Wow! Was all she could think.

Dimitri walked in behind her. He watched for a few minutes. She was adorable, and he thought she liked his place. She just wasn't saying anything. He couldn't tell if she liked the house or if she was just impressed that his paintings were originals. "Well?" he finally asked.

"Huh?" she said absently. He walked up and touched her neck. Alex jumped. "Oh sorry, I was just admiring your artwork."

"That's okay. I was just admiring yours," he smiled. "So do you like it?" he asked again.

"Like what?" she looked at him confused.

He laughed. "Do you like the house? You said you were taken by surprise. Good surprise or bad surprise?"

"No, I don't think I like it..."

Dimitri frowned.

"I love it!" She exclaimed. "Do I get a tour?"

"Sure, you want the grand tour or just the basics for now?" Dimitri was pleased.

"How about we skip the closets, but you show me around for a while and I'll tell you if I get tired and want a condensed version," she said excited.

"Well, every woman should know where the kitchen is so let's start there." Dimitri took her hand and headed down the hall.

"Very funny. Isn't this technically a bachelor pad? So are you sure you even know where the kitchen is?" she teased.

"Actually, I'm a very good cook. I guess it comes from living alone for more than four hundred years. You learn to make do," Dimitri countered.

"Sorry, I can't take your word on that. You'll have to cook for me to prove it before I believe you," Alex challenged.

"Anytime. But if I cook for you, then you have to cook for me. I need to test your culinary skills before I decide to keep you around." He stopped in a doorway and reached around to the light switch. "Here she is. I have to admit I like the way it turned out."

"What's not to like? I love the floor, is that travertine?" Alex asked.

"Yep, looks like you know your natural stone," Dimitri smiled. "The color is pretty rare. It took me a long time to find it."

"The granite counter top looks great. The colors complement each other perfectly. The granite seems to tie everything together. I'll cook in your kitchen any time," Alex was smiling. She loved everything about this house. It was elegant, but homey all at the same time. "Where's that door go?" she asked pointing to two large wooden doors.

"Oh, that's the dining area. Come see." Dimitri opened the doors and held his arm out for her to enter.

There was a big antique table in the center of the room. Over the top was a beautiful chandelier. The chairs were large and looked comfortable. She wondered how often Dimitri entertained here. She was just turning around to ask when he lifted her off her feet and set her down on the edge of the table. She was still getting over the surprise when he grabbed the edge of her t-shirt and yanked it over her head. "What do you think you're doing? We can't do this on your table!" She exclaimed.

"Umm," was Dimitri's only response. He gently pushed her shoulders back and guided her downward until she was lying flat on the table top. He was standing over her and began to undo her pants.

"Dimitri!" Alex tried again, but before she knew it she was completely naked. Not fair, he was still dressed. She started to get up, but he sat down on one of the chairs and pulled her forward. "You have to stop!" She tried again.

"Nope. I'm in the mood for dessert," he said as he leaned down and kissed her stomach, then the inside of her thigh.

Alex closed her eyes and forgot what her panic was all about. When he finished ravishing her, she opened her eyes and turned slightly to look at him. He was watching her, smiling. "You look pretty pleased with yourself," Alex observed.

"Oh I am," Dimitri said still smiling. "Next time I'm forced to have one of those awful business dinner parties, you know the ones where the guests do their best to bore you to death. I'm going to sit over there," he pointed to the chair at the head of the table, "And remember exactly how you look right now. Beautiful, relaxed and sprawled across my table naked. Then, I'll remember how you looked about two minutes ago writhing and moaning in pleasure. I think I'll put the stuffiest old bat right there where your cute little ass is. I'm pretty sure that will get me through any evening." Dimitri laughed at the incredulous look on Alex's face.

"You better come up with a good reason for the big smile on your face, Ace. If you say one word about my naked body on this table to anyone, I'll kill you." Alex climbed off the table and straddled Dimitri. While she kissed him, she started to pull off his shirt. He let her lift it over his head, then he stood up with her in his arms. "Are we going somewhere?" Alex asked hooking her arms around his neck.

"Yeah, my room. I don't think we're quite finished yet. There are still a lot of things I want to do to you tonight." Alex laughed as he carried her up the stairs.

Dimitri's bedroom was just as refined and elegant as the rest of the house. No one would have ever guessed this was a bachelor pad. There was a huge bed on a platform toward one end of the room. At the other end, there was a beautiful sitting room. It was cozy and welcoming. "So did you decorate the house all by yourself or did you have help? Or hire it done?" Alex asked.

"I did it all myself." He laid her on the bed then joined her. That promptly ended any further conversation.

Alex awoke the next morning, rolled over thinking she would cuddle with Dimitri, but he was gone. She groggily searched for the lamp and turned on the switch. She looked around, but he wasn't there. Out of the corner of her eye, she glanced a piece of paper lying on his pillow. She unfolded it and read:

"If you wake before I get back, come find me on the roof. I decided to take a swim before I head out to work."

He's taking a swim on the roof? She definitely needed the rest of the tour. She climbed out of bed and looked around for something to wear. She saw Dimitri had laid out a cream colored robe over the arm of a chair in the sitting area. Why did Dimitri have a woman's satin robe? She wasn't sure she wanted to think about that right now. She wasn't sure she wanted to think about that ever! She pulled on the robe and headed for the roof. She got lost a couple times, but finally found the door she was looking for. It was amazing. The pool was on the back side of the house. It didn't occupy the whole roof, the house had a normal slanted roof in the front, but a huge open area along the back. There were pool chairs and a BBQ area. It was like a huge party oasis.

Alex stopped and watched Dimitri swim. He wasn't wearing a suit, which was fine with her. Watching that sexy butt of his was a perfect start to any day. He must have sensed her watching because when he got to the end of the pool, he grabbed onto the edge and looked over at her. Then he smiled and swam back to the shallow end. The man was definitely not shy. He walked up the stairs and stood, naked directly in front of her. He put his hands behind her neck and pulled her into a kiss. "Morning sunshine," he said cheerfully. "Sleep good?" he asked.

"Like the dead," Alex confessed. She looked around. "This place is wonderful. I take it back. This really is a bachelor pad. I can only imagine the wild BBQ parties you've had up here." She was still looking around; there was so much to see.

"I want to sit in the hot tub for a few minutes before I get ready for work. Are you up for a relaxing jaunt in the tub?" Dimitri took her hand and started toward one corner of the large deck area.

"I don't have a suit," Alex protested.

"Neither do I." He opened the robe and slid it off her shoulders. "The robe looks nice on you. I knew it would when I bought it."

"Oh?" she teased. "I thought maybe you just kept it on hand. You know, for occasions like this when you have a naked woman in need of something to wear."

Dimitri looked over at her. He looked like her remark had hurt his feelings. "Alex, I specifically bought that robe for you," he stated.

Alex interrupted. "I'm sorry! I'm stupid. I was just trying to tease you. I didn't mean anything by it."

Dimitri took a deep breath. "I know you were teasing, but there was a hint of truth behind that comment too. I heard it in your voice." He sat down on the large bench inside the hot tub and pulled her down in front of him. She leaned back against his chest and tried to relax. The water did feel good. "I've lived a long time and I admit, I've been with a lot of women. I can't change that. But very few of them have been inside my home. This is my sanctuary and I don't bring just anyone here. In over 463 years there have been a few women I've cared about, but I've never loved any of them the way I love you. We both had lives before we met. I don't like knowing you've been with other men either, but it's something I have to accept," he paused. "I'll also tell you a secret. You are the only woman I have ever had in my bed."

Dusk

"What?" Alex was shocked. "I don't understand. If you cared about these other women, I'm sure you were intimate with them," she gave him a sly grin. "Don't tell me you've had them all on the dining room table."

Dimitri smiled too. "No, you're also the first woman I've pleasured in the dining room." He paused. "There are spare bedrooms in this house. I used them."

"Can I ask why?" Alex was sincerely perplexed by this.

"Because my bedroom is my private space. Before you, there's never been anyone I've wanted to share that with. It's always been mine. My special area. I guess it's personal and I've never wanted to share something that personal with anyone else."

Alex leaned her head back and looked up at him. "Did you know you're a sappy romantic?" She smiled at the look on his face. Then she sobered. "Thank you. Knowing that means a lot to me. Dimitri, I'm sorry I get jealous over previous women in your life. I'm just a little intimidated by them," she paused.

Dimitri was rubbing his hands over her stomach and her ribs. "You shouldn't be." He said as he kissed the back of her head. "You're the only woman I've ever loved. The only one that's ever meant this much to me. I'm sharing a lot of firsts with you, Alex. I might be more experienced in bed than you are, but I'm certainly not any more experienced when it comes to love."

"That helps. I know that sounds strange, but it does. I can't think about you with other women without going crazy. I know I'm not very experienced and I'm sure a lot of the women you've had in the past were. You are such a talented lover," she blushed. This was so hard to talk about with a man.

He brushed a finger down her cheek, then kissed her neck. "It always surprises me that after everything we've done together, you can still be shy with me." Dimitri liked that about her even if he was perplexed by it.

"That's kind of the point. Everything we've done together is usually all the wonderful, sensual things you do to me. I guess I just don't know if there's something I could or should be doing for you to make our love making better. I want it to be as good for you as it is for me." She looked away, she was shy. She felt stupid and ignorant and moronic.

Dimitri laughed. "Honey, I don't think it's possible for it to be any better for me."

She looked up at him. She had to know if he was serious. He was. How could that be?

He laughed again. "Don't look so shocked by that. First, I get pleasure from giving pleasure to you. Plus, I get pleasure from the things I do to you. I love to touch you and feel you. It makes me feel good. Then there's the simple fact that I'm a guy. We don't need all the foreplay for sex to be good. It just is. Having said that, it also gives me pleasure to see you enjoying my body. Anything you do to me, touch me, caress me, anything gives me pleasure. I especially like it when you look at me that way you sometimes do. Like you enjoy what you see. I'm only human, it's nice to have my ego fed every once in a while. I admit it."

"How could I not appreciate what I see? You're gorgeous, all big and muscular. I love to look at you. I love to caress you. Sometimes I think about doing more, trying different things with you. I haven't because I'm afraid I'll make a fool out of myself. I guess all I'm asking is that if there's something you enjoy that I haven't done, will you tell me. Maybe teach me so I can please you as much as you please me?" Alex was humiliated, but this was Dimitri. He said he loved her, don't you have to trust each other when you're in love?

Dimitri shifted to the side and then turned Alex to face him. She looked so vulnerable, like she had just bared her soul and was waiting for him to laugh at her. "Sweetheart, you could never make a fool out of yourself with me. We can try anything you like. You can try anything you like. I want you to be comfortable enough with me to try new things. When we make love, if you feel the impulse to try something, don't hold back. You'll know if I like it. Just like I know when I do something you like. You enjoy some things I do with you more than others don't you?"

"Yeah I guess," Alex admitted.

"I think that's what love is about, experimenting and exploring. Finding out about each other and learning what works best for both of you. My body is your body. Do anything you wish. But please be gentle, I'm fragile," he smiled.

"Did you know you make me feel safe and secure? I guess that's the word I'm looking for. I'm more content and at ease with you than I've ever been with anyone. I didn't know that was possible." She leaned against him again and sighed. "I wish we could stay here all day, but we both need to get out and get ready for work. We're going to be late."

Dimitri stood up and pulled two towels out of a cabinet. He wrapped one around Alex and pulled her to him. "I love you," he said as he pulled her in for a kiss. "That's all you need to remember."

Alex smiled up at him. "I love you, too."

They walked down the stairs hand in hand.

* * * *

Alex walked into the kitchen after her shower. Dimitri was just pouring two cups of coffee. He set them on the table and then walked over to the refrigerator and opened it. "I have cold cereal or fruit and yogurt. What's your pleasure?" he looked over the door at her. "Well actually, I also have bacon and eggs. But if I cook those, we'll both be late and I won't be finished by eleven."

"Fruit and yogurt for me but don't try to tell me you're a yogurt man. How is it possible you have it in your fridge?" Alex asked.

Dimitri grabbed a bowl of fruit, a container of yogurt and a gallon of milk. "Because I was hoping I could talk you into a slumber party so I went shopping yesterday." He opened the pantry and pulled out a box of Frosted Flakes.

Alex laughed. "I didn't know you were a fan of the tiger."

Dimitri looked at her and pretended shock. "Who isn't a fan of the tiger? Is there any other cereal?" he asked as he dug in. Alex laughed, maybe no man ever grew up completely.

He finished his cereal and walked his dishes to the sink. "I've gotta go. I have an eight o'clock meeting. I'm already going to be late." He turned around and was surprised to see Alex standing behind him. He backed her up against the fridge and kissed her long and hard. "You better watch out, I could get used to this." He smiled at her. "I'll be at your house as close to eleven as I can get there. You know how to lock up?"

"Yes I remember," Alex said confidently.

"Stay as long as you like." He gave her another quick kiss. "Love you," then he turned and headed for the door.

Alex stood there for a long moment. She could get used to this too. It was all so domestic and cozy. She honestly felt like they belonged together, like her and Dimitri were somehow made for each other. She felt comfortable and content. She loved this house. She loved the man even more. Wouldn't it be wonderful if they could have a long, happy life together? A couple months ago, she never would have thought that possible. Now, it was all she really wanted.

It was a little after eleven when Dimitri pulled into the driveway. Alex was waiting anxiously, so she was out the door as soon as he stopped the truck. He was driving his work truck with Montgomery Inc. written on the side. She hesitated, looked at Dimitri then back to the truck and burst out laughing.

"Care to share the joke?" he asked as he got to the bottom step of the front porch.

Alex just kept smiling. "Do you want to take that truck, or I can pull the SUV out of the garage?" she waited in silence.

"The truck's fine with me if it's okay with you." Dimitri was still waiting for her to tell him what was so funny.

She didn't. She just walked passed him and headed for the passenger side of his pickup. Dimitri got there right behind her and put his hand on the door frame. "Nu- huh, spill it."

Alex turned, he was blocking her between his body and the door. "I will, let's just get started. I'll tell you on the way," she smiled again. "I brought stuff for sandwiches for lunch. I thought you might be hungry and the cabins out of the way from any café or restaurant."

He leaned in and gave her a kiss. "I'm trusting you to share, or I'm taking that kiss back." He smiled at her. "Hello beautiful, I've missed you today." He gave her another quick kiss then opened the door and helped her inside.

Dimitri pulled through town and got onto the highway. They'd been traveling in silence for almost an hour. Alex would periodically smile and turn away. "You think it's funny to leave me in suspense, don't you?" he asked as he scowled at her smiling face.

Alex couldn't help it. She couldn't stop giggling. "I'm just a little slow, that's all. Until you pulled up in that truck, I didn't realize you were THAT Montgomery. No wonder you have such great security. You own the best security company in the nation, maybe the world. You're loaded. And it's old money," she drew out the old and started laughing again.

Dimitri smiled. "It's not nice to laugh at people," but he wasn't offended. He wondered if she'd figured it out on her own yet.

"Anyway, Calista Ainsley would die if she knew who you are! I've been hearing the rumors lately. She's outdone herself this time. You are the talk of the town! Everyone knows how you've seduced the poor, depressed rich girl to get her inheritance. I wish I could tell her the truth. I'd love to see her face when she found out who you really are. Of course, I realize she can never know. But just imagining her reaction has made my day! Thanks," she smiled over at him.

Dimitri was smiling too. He had also heard some of the rumors. He didn't care. Alex was right. He was loaded. It was easy to get rich when you'd lived as long as he had.

"So how do you do it? Hide your identity I mean. I know you don't socialize much. I've heard the rumors about the old Montgomery family. They're all recluses and fanatics. But really, you still run your business so how do you do it. I've been wondering for a long time now how dad managed it," Alex said curiously.

"I'm not sure how your dad juggled it. We never talked about that. I suspect he probably talked to Thomas though. He'd want to make sure Thomas knew how to take care of business, but not draw attention to himself. The way I do it, is by driving this truck. I hire myself as just one of the guys, one of the workers. I do installs and take orders, all the regular stuff for a while. Then I quit claiming I found a better job, or I have to move out of state. After that, I just have to stay out of sight for a while. Sometimes it's necessary to have business dinners but I avoid that as much as possible. I become the reclusive fanatic and stay out of the limelight. After about 20 years or so I usually have a complete turn over and can go back out and work again. So far, it's worked for me," Dimitri said casually.

"I can't believe I didn't put this all together sooner. Especially after Ariel insisted you were involved in security at the cabin," Alex mumbled.

Dimitri looked over at her. "Ariel? Does she know about your big secret? Was she there with you yesterday?" he asked sounding annoyed.

"Yes, Ariel does know about my plans. No, she wasn't with me yesterday. I know you're anxious to hear all about my grand plan, but I want to wait until we get there. It'll only take a few more minutes. See that speed limit sign up there?"

"Yes," Dimitri answered.

"Your turn is that road right across from it," Alex smiled. She was getting excited to show Dimitri her plan. She hoped he'd be supportive.

Dimitri turned off the highway onto a semi-gravel, mostly dirt and weed driveway. So far, he wasn't any happier about Alex coming out here all by herself yesterday. Hopefully the cabin was in better shape than the road. As he came around a bend, he saw the structure. It was actually nice. With a little work, it had potential. There were weeds growing around the porch and the windows needed to be painted but other than that, it was in good shape. "Nice," he said softly. He stopped the truck and walked around to help Alex out. "So where to now?" he asked.

"Let's go in first. I want you to see the inside. I have a lot of good memories at this cabin. I know it's not as grand as your house, but I really like it here." She unlocked the door and walked inside.

Dimitri followed her in. She was right, the inside was well furnished. It had that rustic country look. The furniture was still in great condition and the whole place was clean and fresh. "I can see you and Marta put a lot of work into cleaning this place up. It looks great." He walked over to the living area and looked out the window. "So why am I here?" he asked.

Alex put the groceries on the table. So talk first, lunch later. She opened the fridge and placed the bag of perishables inside. She grabbed a couple ice teas and walked into the living area. "Want one?" Alex asked as she held the bottle out to Dimitri.

"Sure. Thanks," he said as he took a seat on the large sofa.

"Well, I'm not sure where I should start. I don't know what order is best to tell you about my plan. Maybe we should take a walk outside so I can show you the area first."

"Okay," Dimitri said as he stood up. "Show the way."

Alex walked him around the cabin property showing him the meadow, the rock outcropping and finally the forest to the side of the property.

"It's a nice cabin. I can see why you had such a good time here as a kid. I also think I have an idea of why you brought me here. How about we go inside and you lay out your plan for me." Dimitri took her hand and led her back toward the house.

"Okay," Alex said as they entered the backdoor. She walked over and sat down on the couch. "So, I've been spending a lot of time with Ariel over the past few weeks. We've talked extensively about the fae culture, the different powers she's aware of and all that kind of stuff. I think we're all talked out. I still have no idea what powers I have, or if I even have any."

"Wait a minute. You know you're a healer," Dimitri interrupted.

"Well, everyone else seems to know I'm a healer. I have my doubts. I think that thing with Tanya was just a fluke. I had never done anything like it before and I haven't been able to do it again," Alex admitted hesitantly.

"No way, it doesn't work like that. When a fae demonstrates powers, they have those powers. They don't come and go. You can summon them at will once you get the hang of it, but you have the powers Alex. I saw it with my own eyes," Dimitri said as he sat down next to her. "How could you possibly think that was a fluke?"

Alex leaned against the back of the couch and closed her eyes. "Because I tried healing someone else and failed," she admitted.

"So? That doesn't mean anything. You're new at this. You already said you and Ariel have talked about theory, but you still don't know which powers you have. You haven't learned how to use them yet." Dimitri wondered when Alex had tried her powers and why she was so discouraged that they didn't work.

"When I healed Tanya, I was in a panic. I thought she was dying. I just kept thinking I had to help her. I had to do something. I couldn't let her die. Then all of a sudden, I was healing her. I was worried about her. I cared enough about her that I didn't want her to die, but she wasn't an important person in my life anymore. At one time she was, but when she betrayed me like that something inside me died. Something I knew we could never get back. We could never be close again. Does that make sense?" Alex asked.

Awe, Dimitri thought, she tried to heal me. "Yes, it makes sense. She wasn't just a stranger on the street, but she wasn't someone you wanted in your life anymore."

Dusk

"Exactly!" Alex exclaimed. "But then, I tried to heal you." She looked away from him. "Someone who is important to me. I was just as worried that you would die. I was desperate to help you. I was in love with you. Shouldn't those emotions have helped my powers to be stronger? If I was a healer, it seems to me I should have been able to heal you quicker," Alex said. "Instead, I failed."

"That's nonsense," Dimitri stated flatly.

She looked over at him. "Why is it nonsense?" she asked.

"For a couple reasons. First, like I said you are new at this. You don't know what the trigger was for you to heal Tanya. It could have been anything. Until you practice and figure it out, you probably won't be able to answer that question. It doesn't mean you don't have the power. Second, the fact that you couldn't heal me, means nothing. I am strong willed and I'm a warrior. Things work different with us. I'm not a good test case for a novice to practice on. I'm stubborn and in a lot of ways I've been closed off to people for centuries."

"I think you're making excuses for me," Alex accused.

"No, I'm not. Just hear me out," Dimitri paused. "I've met a lot of people like Tanya in my lifetime. I know she's your friend, but she's weak. She's the type of person that is self-serving. Her first priority is taking care of herself, damn the consequences. Basically, she's selfish and shallow," Dimitri stated like it was just a matter of fact.

Alex was shocked. She'd never heard anyone talk about Tanya like that. Well, maybe some of the girls but never a man. Men were usually fooled by Tanya's charms. They were usually so smitten they didn't see the flaws.

"I'm sorry if that offends you. Like I said, I know she's a friend of yours." Dimitri didn't want to upset her with his frankness, but he thought Alex needed to hear what he had to say.

"It doesn't offend me. I'm just surprised. I watched the two of you at the club. She turned up the charm and you and Ty seemed to be enjoying it. Men are usually flattered by her seduction act. That night, it was off the charts," Alex said quietly.

"Is that a little green I see in your eyes?" Dimitri smiled. "Did you actually think I could be interested in Tanya? You're so adorable when you're jealous." He leaned in and kissed her softly.

"Certainly that night I did. Now? No, I don't think so. You've made it pretty clear that you love me. I don't understand why, but I think I'm finally starting to get it. I can see you love me as much as I love you. I trust you Dimitri. That's new for me, but I do trust you completely. However, I don't trust Tanya. Not at all."

"I don't blame you. I hope you're not mad, but Thomas confided in me about Billie. I also told him about our encounter with Adam." He watched her for a reaction.

"I'm not mad. That actually makes it easier. I was just going to tell you about Billie and Tanya. Knowing her history, I guess you can understand why I can't trust her. In fact, I felt betrayed by her again that night at the club," Alex confessed.

"Really? Why?" he was curious now.

"I think I fell for you the first day we met. I was confused, because I thought you hated me, but I had an immediate attraction to you that I couldn't control." Alex smiled up at him. "I guess you're just irresistible," she teased.

Dusk

"I assure you the feeling's mutual," Dimitri smiled back.

"So that night at the club Tanya and I were talking. She wanted to apologize for Adam, put things in the past and pick up where we left off. I knew I couldn't do that. So, I finally told her I knew about her and Billie. She was surprised. She didn't think I knew about them. It makes me wonder how many other boyfriends she's seduced that I don't know about. Anyway, we were hashing things out when she suddenly looked your way. She asked me if I knew you guys and said something like she thought you were checking us out before, but now it seemed like you were keeping an eye on us," Alex paused.

"Maybe I was doing both," he said with a grin.

"I looked over and saw you. Apparently she saw something in my eyes because she commented about it. She realized I knew who you were and told me she could see I had the hots for the tall, dark and sexy one. That's when I left and went to the restroom. When I came back and saw her over at your table flirting with you, I knew it was over for Tanya and me. She knew I wanted you, but she went after you anyway. Well if I'm going to be honest with myself, I think that's why she went after you," Alex sighed.

"So, it wasn't my good looks and charming personality? I'm crushed," he feigned disappointment.

"I'm sure that didn't hurt. Honestly, what woman wouldn't be attracted to you? Or any of the warriors for that matter. You're all hot. Every one of you look like you stepped off the cover of Esquire," Alex smiled at him.

"I'm going to take that as a compliment. However, I'm not sure I like you looking at the other warriors. Or thinking they are hot," Dimitri frowned.

"Now is that green I see in your eyes?" she teased.

"Absolutely!" He chuckled. "I admit it. Anyway, let's get back to your powers. I know you've been struggling with how to call up your gift. Obviously, I didn't know you tried to heal me. Thanks for that by the way. It was sweet of you to try."

Alex snorted. "Don't placate me."

Dimitri smiled. "Anyway, when you healed Tanya, it was sudden and unexpected. I think you could help her because she's shallow and self-serving. She was injured and needed help. She's not strong willed, like you or I am. She's weak. That made her totally open to you. You were concentrating on her, thinking you needed to help her and she was totally open to being helped. Are you following me?" Dimitri asked.

"I think so," Alex admitted slowly. "You think that because Tanya was open, it made it easy for me to heal her. But, because you are strong willed and closed off, I couldn't get in because I'm not experienced enough?" Alex asked. She liked this theory. She'd been wondering what it meant that she couldn't heal the one man she loved with all her heart. What good was a gift if it couldn't be used to help the ones you love?

"Yes, that's my theory. You are a healer, Alex. There's no question in my mind. And, there shouldn't be any question in yours. I take it the next step of your plan, the reason you brought me here was because you want to train out here with Ariel?" he asked.

Dusk

"Do warriors have mind reading powers?" Her excitement was returning. It sounded like he was okay with what she had in mind.

"No, but I know you pretty well. Plus, it makes sense. Also, I know Ariel and she wouldn't spend any time out here unless she knew it was safe. She knows I'm the best at security, so I can see why she sent you my way. Would you have told me about this if she hadn't pushed you into it?" he asked soberly.

"Eventually," Alex admitted honestly. "I guess I wanted to impress you. I wanted to fix everything up, have all the security in place and then bring you here to show you how safe it would be. I thought if you knew you wouldn't have to worry about us, you'd be more supportive of my plan," Alex confessed.

Dimitri was silent for a long time. He was glad Ariel had talked Alex into coming to him, but he wished she had trusted him on her own.

"I can see that upsets you. I didn't realize you were associated with Montgomery Incorporated. Well, I guess you are Montgomery Incorporated. If I'd realized that, I would have come to you without Ariel's suggestion. I would have asked for your help on my own."

Dimitri looked at her. "You would have asked for my help because of my business, not because of our relationship? Do you think that makes things better?" Dimitri asked.

"Oh." Alex just realized what had gotten her into trouble. She hadn't trusted him. She hadn't gone to him like partners should so they could work out a plan together. She really was bad at this relationship thing. "Dimitri," she took his hand. He just sat there watching her. She really had hurt him. "I'm sorry. I didn't think. I guess I'm used to doing things on my own. I know that's no excuse," she paused and then tried again. "Being in a real relationship is new to me. Other than my family, I've never had anyone I could depend on or ask for help. I automatically dealt with you in the same way I deal with Thomas. I'm a little slow, but I just realized that was wrong. It was unfair to you. We are supposed to be partners and I guess I forgot that. If you can forgive me for my stupidity, I'd like your help now. Actually, I need your help now." At least he was listening and didn't look so hurt or angry.

"I have the big picture in my mind, but I don't know how to get there. I need a really good security guy. Someone who can look at this whole area and tell me what I need to make it safe. I want this cabin and surrounding area to be like Fort Knox. I can't train at the house. First, with Ariel throwing fire, the neighbors would freak. But two, there's always somebody there. I'm trying to figure out what powers I have and how to use them. I can't be in a house full of people. It makes me too self-conscious. That's why I thought of the cabin. It's secluded. I can relax, but only if I know it's absolutely safe. I trust you to help me make it safe. Not only because of your company, but because I'm important to you. You'll make sure nobody can get to me while you're not around." She gave him a pleading smile. "Please, will you be my partner? I need you."

"You're an evil woman, you know that?" he asked, narrowing his eyes at her. "You know I can't deny you anything and you use it to manipulate me."

Alex smiled. "Of course I do. But I really do want and need your help with this."

"I'll help you," Dimitri conceded. "Not because you played me though. I'll help because I think it's a good idea. You need to figure out your gifts and how to use them. Ariel can help you, but she needs to be secluded with her powers. And, because I'm the best at what I do and I wouldn't trust your safety to anybody else."

"Deal. And, I wasn't playing you. I may have been trying to manipulate you a little, but it was only because I wanted to get out of the dog house. Everything I said was absolutely true. Am I out of trouble?" she blinked her eyelashes.

"You are going to be the death of me." He pulled her close and kissed her. "You're out of trouble," he said a moment later. "But only if you make me a sandwich. I'm starved."

A few hours later, they had a rough security plan outlined for the cabin and surrounding area. Dimitri looked over at Alex. "I get the impression you want to keep this a secret from Thomas. That's a problem for me."

Alex looked up. "Why? I didn't think he would need to know until later."

"Because the warriors are a team. When Luke started hiding things from Thomas, Dante and Nicholas, it compromised the team. They split off and did their own thing. Both sides hid things from each other. I understand Luke's motivation, but I can't and won't do that. Thomas will eventually find out what's going on here. If we hide this from him, when he finds out, it will cause a rift between the two of us. I wouldn't do that anyway but I can't do that right now while things are getting so out of control with the vampires, not even for you. Can you understand that?" Dimitri asked.

"Yes, I understand. I just know Thomas is going to go into a panic. He'll want to be by my side every minute I'm here. He can't watch over me all the time. It would drive me crazy and I'd probably kill him. But, he also has things to do. He can't take care of business if he's always with me," Alex was frustrated.

"Why don't you leave the details to me? I promise you, Thomas won't follow you around or get in your way," Dimitri said confidently.

"You can't promise that. You haven't seen how Thomas gets." Alex still didn't like it.

"I can promise that. First, because Thomas will know that I'll protect you." He laughed when she shot her head up and gave him an incredulous look. "No, I'm not going to follow you around either. I'm going to install the best security money can buy at this cabin, with a few extras just as a precaution. Thomas will trust my judgment on this. He knows the reputation my company has and how much I care for you. He will also listen to me because I'm his leader. Just trust me on this. It won't be the problem you think it's going to be. Especially when he knows I'm pulling Ty in to go over the property before I agree to anything."

"Ty? Why are you pulling in Ty?" Alex was confused. "He makes video games for a living."

"Yes, he does." He looked at her seriously. "Ty has hidden talents. I'm trusting you with this because you'll find out eventually anyway. But we need to keep his talents a secret. He's an explosives expert and a demolition expert. But, in reverse, he's an anti-explosives and demolition expert. In other words, he can look at your cabin and tell me if it's sound, if it can withhold an attack by a group of vampires. He can also tell me what we need to do to improve the construction. So, I guess he's a construction expert as well. You'll understand better when you see him at work. Ty is a dangerous man and a huge asset to our side." Dimitri stood up. "It's getting late. I don't want to be out here after dark. Let's head home. We can work on this at your house."

"Are you going out to hunt tonight?" Alex asked.

"Yeah, I have to. I took last night off, but the guys can't spare me two nights in a row. Vampire activity is increasing and we all have to be out there to protect our people. Sorry, I'd love a repeat of last night but it's just not possible tonight." Dimitri took her hand and they headed for the truck.

"Well, since your house is so secure and all, would you mind if I stayed at your place? I should be safe until you get home," Alex asked sheepishly.

Dimitri opened the door and held it for her as she got in. "I'd like that. You are welcome to stay at my house anytime you want." Then he shut the door and headed around the truck.

Chapter Eight

Alex, Dimitri, Ty and Thomas were at the cabin early the next afternoon. Ty was walking around the house and the garage making notes on a pad. Dimitri was walking around the grounds explaining his plan to Thomas. Alex was sitting on the steps of the front porch watching with fascination. She enjoyed watching Dimitri work. She also enjoyed watching the warriors together. They were a cohesive group. Clearly they all had a tight bond. Dimitri had been right to insist on talking to Thomas. Surprisingly, he hadn't given her a hard time about her plan. She could tell he was asking a lot of questions, but seemed to be satisfied with Dimitri's answers.

Ty looked like he was having a ball. She wasn't always sure what he was doing, but she could tell he was good at whatever it was. He really seemed to know his stuff. He had determined the house was sound, but had a couple suggestions to help make it "vampire proof" as he put it. Now he was studying the garage. Alex knew he was going to have a lot of suggestions to fix that building. It wasn't constructed as well as the house and she knew it.

Alex looked back over to Thomas and Dimitri. It looked like they were arguing about something. She decided to go see what was going on. As she approached, she was surprised to find out they were arguing over money. "What's going on?" she asked as soon as she reached them.

"Dimitri thinks he's going to foot the bill for this project. I told him no way. He's going to have to take time off from his regular business and the materials are going to be expensive if we want to do this right, which we do. The way I see it, if we're going to fix this cabin to make it useful, we might as well make it a long term investment. What I mean by that is instead of just making it a place for you to come in the short term, let's make it a secure hide away that can be used in the future if needed. We're at war, you never know when someone is going to need a secure place to stay. If we do this right, we always have that option." Thomas looked to Alex for help.

"Dimitri, Thomas is right. You're not paying for this. Don't look at me like I've lost my mind. It's not like we're destitute and can't afford to pay our bills. We have the money, we want to pay you, why are you fighting us on this?" Alex didn't understand.

"I'm fighting you because I think it's my responsibility," Dimitri began.

"Come again?" Alex interrupted. "How could paying for a security job at a cabin that belongs to the Deveraux family possibly be your responsibility?" She was completely confused now.

"Thomas is talking about a long term investment. Using this place as a secure hide away during this war. You don't think as the leader of the warriors it's my responsibility to provide for that security? To ensure the safety of any member of the community that stays here? I'm just asking you to let me do my job," he demanded.

"That sort of makes sense. I'll give you that much," Thomas glared at her. "Just a minute Thomas, let me finish. Yes, as leader you have a responsibility to take care of your people. I understand that. I also realize that like me, you are still trying to prove yourself. We both have some pretty big shoes to fill. I think better than anyone, I understand your position. But, will you try to understand ours? There is absolutely no way either Thomas or I will allow you to lose money because you're working on our cabin. And then in addition, spend money to purchase the needed supplies. We can't do that, it's not the way we were raised. We have a responsibility to the people as well, plus it's our property. I'm their queen, don't you think it's my job to protect my people?"

Dimitri sighed. "In addition to providing for our people, I wanted to do this for you Alex. I need to do this for you. I need this place to be as safe as it possibly can be. Otherwise it will drive me crazy knowing you're out here. I plan to go overboard. It's going to be expensive. I can't let you pay for my peace of mind," he wasn't budging on this.

Alex looked at Dimitri for a long time. He wasn't going to pay for this. If it were just about her and Dimitri she might be able to find a way to live with it, but Thomas never could. "What if we try to come to a compromise?" she finally suggested.

"What kind of compromise?" Thomas asked.

Dusk

They were all silent. Each of them trying to come up with a solution they could live with. "How about this?" Dimitri finally suggested. "What if I donate my time? Hold on." He looked over to Thomas, who was about to argue. "You know as well as I do Thomas, I'm not losing anything by not going to work. It's my company. I make money whether I'm there or not. I do the jobs myself because I like to, not because I have to. It's the same as you being here today rather than at the office. How much did you lose by coming on this trip?" he challenged.

"Okay, fine. Point taken," Thomas conceded.

"So I donate the labor, my time. The two of you purchase the equipment. If there's something that I want, something that's over the top, I will bring it to you. If you don't think we need it, or you don't want to spend the money and I still want it, then I will purchase it myself. Deal?" Dimitri asked.

"I don't exactly like it, but I think I could live with it." Thomas conceded again. "Alex? You on board with this?"

Alex didn't want Dimitri to donate anything. She had wanted to pay him for what he was doing for her. But she could tell this was important to him. He did want to take care of his people. He needed to do this to demonstrate his leadership and forethought if they ever needed the place in the future. She was also sure he wanted to foot the bill because of her. As much as she loved him for that, she just couldn't let him do it all. "I can live with it," Alex finally said.

Ty approached them. "If the three of you are finished arguing, I have a couple things I'd like to talk to you about Dimitri." Ty gave a little head cock and started in the other direction.

"Is there a problem?" Dimitri said as he started to follow.

Alex looked at Thomas and they both smiled. "You're not going to be left out of this either are you, sis?" Thomas asked as he started for Ty and Dimitri.

"Nope," Alex answered as she hurried to catch up.

Hours later, they were all gathered around the Deveraux kitchen table. Marta brought out fresh pie. Pumpkin, Alex's favorite. They were going over plans again. They had changed the schematics so many times Alex was beginning to think they needed to start over with a new drawing.

"So," Ty was saying, "If we're going to make this a safe house, let's really make this a safe house." Ty looked excited.

"What exactly did you have in mind?" Thomas asked.

"Well, I know it's great to have plenty of bedrooms. Especially since we don't know how many people we may have to hide out here. But, I think we should take this room here..." he pointed to the corner room on the second floor, the room furthest away from the stairwell. "And turn it into a safe room."

Dimitri smiled, "I like it."

"What do you mean by a safe room?" Alex asked.

"Like a panic room. A room fortified with metal walls and a steel door. A room that has top notch communication and surveillance equipment. A first-rate, kick ass, don't think you could ever get in here, safe room," Ty smiled.

Dusk

Thomas was smiling too. "Yeah," he said enthusiastically. "Great idea Ty." The three of them went off on all the cool stuff they could include in the room.

Alex on the other hand, thought they were all nuts. Sure, it was a good idea to prepare for the event vampires got into the cabin. That was not probable, but definitely possible. But really, was it necessary to install a door that could withstand a rocket launcher. Alex didn't think so. "I'm getting tired and I have a couple work related things I need to take care of before I crash. I'll see you all in the morning," she sighed as she walked out the door. She didn't notice Dimitri had followed her until she was at the foot of the stairs. She turned around instantly and smiled. "Hey," she said.

"Hey yourself," he countered. "You staying home tonight or did you want to crash at my place again?" He wanted her at his house, but she looked tired and if she needed to do paperwork, he suspected it'd be better for her to stay home.

"I don't think so. I'm beat and I still have at least a couple hours of work. I assume you guys will be leaving soon?" she asked.

"Yeah, as soon as I get back to the kitchen I'm gonna make those two clean up so we can go." He was watching her, she really did look exhausted. He stepped forward and rubbed his thumb over her cheekbone. "You look so tired. Are you sure you can't just go to bed now and do the paperwork in the morning?"

"No. I've been slacking off the past few days, dealing with the cabin. I really have to catch up on a couple things. I won't stay up long. I have an early day tomorrow." She leaned in and kissed him softly. "Be careful out there, I've sort of gotten used to having you around." She smiled at him.

She was coping better with the dangers of hunting now. "Goodnight. I'm gonna miss you." Dimitri said, he really meant it. He wanted her in his bed, with him all night.

"I'm gonna miss you, too. Will I see you tomorrow?" she asked.

"Definitely. I'll come by after work. I love you, babe." He pulled her in for a longer, more passionate kiss then turned and walked back to the kitchen.

* * * *

Dimitri wasn't in a very good mood. He was already melancholy, knowing he wasn't going to see Alex when they got finished tonight. He'd gotten used to being with her, holding her all night long. Tonight, he was going to be alone. To make matters worse, they kept missing their mark. Early on, they'd come across the scent of a vampire they'd wanted to catch for weeks. Bastian was leading the way and Dimitri knew he was following the scent, but they seemed to be going around in circles. "I think we're on a wild goose chase," Dimitri finally said. "Let's pull off and regroup. We're not going to catch him tonight." He called and told the other warriors to meet him at the park pavilion.

Once they all arrived and reported, Dimitri had a bad feeling. "Something's not right. It's like the vampires are trying to keep all of us busy tonight. Preoccupied with tracking so we're out of their way. I think something big is going on and we're missing it. Not one of us has found a vampire feeding. How likely is that?"

Dusk

"I was thinking the same thing," Victor said unhappily. "Thomas and I stopped by the underground on our way here. There are rumblings the king is planning something big. No one would be specific, but I think this is just phase one of some bigger plan. I got the distinct impression he has a specific target in mind."

"I'm going home to check on Alex," Thomas said abruptly. "She's the obvious target. Maybe they're trying to keep us busy to give a group of them time to ambush the house, take her by surprise when they know none of us are around."

"I was just thinking the same thing," Dimitri put in. "I'm going with you. The rest of you guys need to start checking on high level targets. I'll call Jake to come out and help. I think we should start with warriors and retired warrior's families. That includes your own. First secure your families, then move on to previous warriors and their families. We need to check on the council members next and then move onto the general population. I know, it's going to be a long night. We have a lot of houses to check, but I still want to stay in pairs. Nobody goes anywhere alone. If any of the retired warriors are willing, have them start checking houses too. We have to warn the entire community. Anyone could be a target."

Bastian spoke up, "I know how you and Thomas feel about Alex. You both think she's only your responsibility, but you're wrong. She's the queen. That means we're all responsible for her safety, equally. I don't like you and Thomas going to the house alone. If she's the target, there may be too many vampires for the two of you to handle," Bastian argued. "I think we should all go check on Alex and then fan out from there if there's no trouble."

Dimitri thought about it for a minute. "I don't like pulling everyone in together to check on one target, it leaves the rest of the community at risk but I think Bastian is right. If they send an army to get Alex, we're going to need help. However, Bastian you are wrong about one thing. If there's trouble, nobody's going to stop Alex from fighting. That makes three, not two."

"Yeah," Ty put in. "And one of Alex is like three regular fae. She rocks!" They all laughed. Ty was certainly good PR when it came to Alex.

"Let's go. We need to hurry. I'll call Jake and have him meet at the Deveraux's." They all headed for their cars.

Alex had dealt with paperwork for almost three hours. She'd just fallen asleep when she heard what sounded like a stampede running up the stairs. She rolled over and pulled the blanket over her face just as her bedroom door flung open. Thomas stood in the doorway; Alex counted all six warriors crowded behind him.

She was shocked. "What?" She was a little annoyed but then it hit her, something must be wrong. She sat up and looked at Thomas. "What's going on?" Oh, make that seven warriors, Jake just arrived. "Why do I have eight warriors standing in my bedroom doorway at..." she glanced over at the clock, "...two o'clock in the morning?"

Dimitri pushed his way in. "We were worried about you, that's all. We wanted to make sure everything was okay here."

"Sure, everything's fine. Why wouldn't it be?" She was really worried now.

Dusk

Dimitri turned to the others. "The rest of you get started. Remember, check on your families first. Take whatever precautions you need to, then move on. The entire community needs to be warned. Thomas, you stay here with me. Once we make sure Alex is safe, we'll head out together." The warriors all hurried down the stairs.

Alex heard the front door shut. She climbed out of bed. She was sleeping in a t-shirt and underwear so she quickly pulled on a pair of sweats. "Will one of you please tell me what's going on?" she demanded. "Something has you in a panic. I need to know what it is."

Dimitri walked over and sat on the edge of Alex's bed. "It might be nothing, it might be something big. I don't know. If I'm over reacting, then all we've done is woke up a bunch of people in the middle of the night," he paused. "I don't think it's nothing though. We all went out tonight like usual. Things have really been hot lately and there have been a lot of injuries. Too many deaths. We were all prepared for another busy night, but nothing. All our groups caught a scent early on, but circled around all night with no results. It was like we were being led on a wild goose chase. Like a few vampires were trying to keep us occupied while the rest of the vamps did something else. There's also talk that the vampire king is planning something big. After we wasted most of the night chasing our tails, we regrouped. Not one of us had found a vampire feeding tonight. Again, that's extremely unusual. I know something is going on. I just have no idea what it is," Dimitri sighed. "I hope we figure it out before we're too late."

Alex sat down next to him. "There was no way you could have known something was planned for tonight, no matter what happens," she paused. "So I gather the group of you immediately assumed the vampires were after me and headed over to check?"

"Yes," Thomas answered. "You're the logical choice. Since you're okay, we have to start checking on the others. The guys went to check on their families first. Then they'll move on to retired and semi-retired warriors and their families. Then the council and their families. We have a lot of people to check on tonight."

Alex looked at Dimitri. "Call Ariel. We need to make sure she's okay and knows she needs to be on alert. Also because I'm going out with you and she'll want to come, too."

"No way!" Thomas and Dimitri said together.

"You can't stop me. So, you have two choices. I hook up with Dimitri and Ariel hooks up with Thomas. You know as soon as you call her she's going to insist on helping." Alex glared at the two of them, daring them to argue. "Or, you and Thomas tuck me in bed and run off to fight the manly fight. Then, as soon as you're out the door, I call Ariel myself and we go out together. It's your choice," Alex said with finality.

Dimitri sighed. He reached into his pocket and dialed Ariel's cell.

"Hello," Ariel answered groggily. "This better be important. It's two in the morning."

"Ariel," Dimitri began. "I know it's two in the morning. I need to know if everything is okay at your house. Have you heard anything strange or does anything seem out of place?"

Dusk

Ariel was wide awake now. "What's going on?" She sat up in bed.

"I don't have a lot of time to explain, but there's something going on with the vampires tonight. They've got something cooking, we just don't know what. It's a long story. I just wanted to make sure things are okay over there. I'll be calling your father next," Dimitri informed her.

"Don't bother. Things are quiet here. They have been all night. I had dinner with my parents. It got late, so I just crashed at their house. I'm walking down to their room right now, but we haven't heard anything. Nothing strange, the alarm is on and no disturbance there either. Hold on just a minute," Ariel paused. She knocked on her parent's door. "Mom? Dad? It's Ariel. I know it's in the middle of the night but I need to come in, is that all right?"

Her father was at the door instantly. "Ariel, what's going on?" he demanded.

"Just a minute dad. Dimitri, you still there?" she asked into the phone.

"Yeah. I'm here," he answered.

"We're fine. I just woke mom and dad up. Where can I meet you, I'm coming out to help?" She held up a hand to stop her father. "Don't argue with me, either. I'm coming. I just want to call Breena first. Make sure her and Orin are okay. Then should I meet you at Alex's house?"

"Well, it's funny you mentioned that," Dimitri said exasperated. "Alex refuses to stay home. She insists on helping.

So, she's coming with me and I'm going to pair you up with Thomas. Is that all right?" Dimitri asked.

"Sure, that's fine. Where does he want me to meet him? At his house or somewhere else?" Ariel asked.

"Thomas said sit tight. He's going to come get you. You call Breena and check on her. Then you and Thomas head over to Drake and Tianna's. I have the rest of the warriors checking on their families and then they'll start on previous warriors and their families. You and Thomas can start checking the rest of the council members and their families. If you find anything fishy, anything at all, don't try to take it on yourself. Call me immediately for backup. Promise me you won't try to be heroes," Dimitri pled.

"Not tonight. Tell Thomas I'll be ready. I'll get a list from dad and try to organize so we can catch everyone in order. You know, not drive all over back and forth. Chow." She hung up and began to explain the situation to her father.

Alex was ready to go as soon as Dimitri was off the phone. "I need to check on Marta. I know she's probably okay, but I need to check please?" she asked Dimitri.

"It's already covered. Jake and Ty were heading over there first. Once they got her to Jake's where it's safer, they were heading to Charlie's. Jake was sure he could talk Charlie into pairing with him and Ty," Dimitri sighed. "I just hope I'm not over reacting. A lot of people are going to be pissed if we wake them up for nothing."

"I support you one hundred percent on this. If you say something's up, something's up. If they're upset at you, they're going to have to be upset with me too," Alex said soberly.

Dusk

"Actually, they're going to have to be upset with all of us," Thomas interjected. "We all know something's going on. I was with Victor in the underground. Those people are always jumpy, but tonight they were off the charts. We may not find out what, but something is definitely going on tonight. Every warrior backed you on this Dimitri. If you're wrong, we all are." Thomas was half way to the door. "I'll check in with you in an hour or so unless we run into trouble. Take care of my sister. She's the only one I've got," then he was running down the stairs.

Alex and Dimitri had checked on several past warriors and their families. They were all okay and put on alert. This was one way for the community to finally meet their queen, Alex thought. Oberon had called Dimitri for more details. Once he understood what was going on, he decided to make phone calls to the rest of the council members. He promised Dimitri he'd check back in once he talked to everyone.

A short time later, Oberon called back. "I've been having trouble getting a hold of four of the council members; Elvin, Avery, Tighe and Dahl. I know Tighe and his family was going on vacation. I think he said he was going to Dublin. We should probably check his house just to make sure, but I'm fairly confident he's okay and just out of the country. I'm starting to worry about Elvin, Avery and Dahl. Of course, they could also be out of town and they notified someone else on the council. That happens, especially with Avery. He and I don't get along all that well. He doesn't usually tell me when he's not around. I did contact Alveron and Warren. They were all right and are now on alert. Ariel got a hold of Breena before she left. She and Orin decided to go to Breena's parents for the night. They'll be okay there. You know her father used to be a warrior before he took over the shop, that's one less stop you have to make."

"Good, they'll be safe there. Thomas also got to Drake and Tianna. They were going to stay at home, but remain alert. So, other than the three you couldn't locate the council is covered. I'll try to call Thomas again and see if he's had any luck with Elvin, Avery or Dahl. If not, Alex and I will head that way. Thanks for your help with this. I know we're waking up a lot of people and if it turns out to be nothing, they're not going to be happy," Dimitri sighed.

"Dimitri, you did the right thing. I don't care if it does turn out to be nothing. I'm proud of you and I'll support you one hundred percent. Be careful out there. Please let me know when you locate the rest of the council. I'm going to worry all night until I know they're okay and my daughter is back here safe. Mara's beside herself. She's been mad at Ariel since she walked out the door. Now she's decided to be mad at me too for letting Ariel go out into danger. Like I had a choice. I'll be glad when this night is over. We have a council meeting planned in two weeks. I considered cancelling it. Now, I think regardless of what happens tonight, we'll still meet to develop a strategy. Maybe by then we'll have more information to help us make some decisions. Tell Alex thanks. I know this has to be hard on her, revealing herself like this and meeting so many people for the first time. Sorry it's not the big reveal you had in mind," Oberon was silent.

"I know what you're thinking. It could backfire. I don't think so though. We've been out here for hours and things are still strange. Something is just off tonight. I'm going to let you go. I need to call Thomas for an update. Be alert. Anything could happen until the sun comes up," Dimitri hung up.

"Let me call Thomas," Alex pled. "I want to make sure he's okay. I know, I'm fretting. I can't help it. I know Marta's okay, but I'm worried about Thomas and Jake. I just need to hear Thomas' voice. That's all, then you can talk to him about business."

"Okay. Hurry though. I need to find out which direction we should head." He handed Alex the phone.

Thomas had gone to Tighe and Elvin's homes and discovered they were both on vacation. Luckily the housekeeper was staying in the house while Elvin and his family went out of town. She was a live in and didn't have anywhere else to go. Thomas told her to call if she saw or heard anything strange before morning. Tighe's stable hand was spending the night because one of the mares was about to have a colt. He planned to be around until Tighe and his family got back from Dublin. That left Avery and Dahl. Dimitri sent Thomas to check on Dahl. He and Alex headed for Avery's house.

"Check in with me as soon as you get there. So far the rest of the warriors haven't had any trouble either. Everyone they've roused has been fine. A large portion of the community is on high alert, now. I have no doubt that every person we've warned called their friends and family to warn them as well. If the vampires are up to something, at this point they're going to have a much harder time pulling it off. Unless it's already too late that is. Stay alert and tell Ariel to be careful. Her parents are worried about her. If she has a chance, she might want to call them. I think it would help if they heard directly from her that she's okay." Dimitri hung up.

"We're headed to Avery's," he said to Alex. It worries me that we can't contact two of the council members. I'm going to be so glad when this night is over. He glanced at Alex. She looked exhausted. This night was bad enough, but for her it was worse. Every house they went to either asked questions or gave her curious, skeptical glances. It was uncomfortable for him, he knew it was harder on her. They were judging her, comparing her to her mother. Yet, there was nothing to use as comparison other than she woke them up in the middle of the night and told them to be on alert because there could be trouble. What a nightmare. "The night's almost over. I'm afraid you're not going to get much sleep though. Did you get enough work done last night that you can take a couple hours to rest when we get back?" he was worried about her.

"I'm fine. Yes, I actually did get a lot done. Once I started, I got caught up. I had just barely gone to bed when you guys showed up. I think I'll be able to get a couple hours. Maybe I'll go in this afternoon." Alex laid her head back on the seat. "Dimitri, I'm not sure your plan is working. Most of these people really don't seem to like me. Okay, so I wouldn't like me either if I came pounding on my door in the middle of the night, but still. They seem curious but underneath it all, they seem skeptical and untrusting. I need to do something to change that," she sighed. "I just don't know what to do."

"Give it time. I know it seems bad tonight. We're all on edge and we're waking people up in their homes. Those aren't ideal circumstances for a first meeting. I promise, it's going to be okay. The people will like you. We're coming up on Avery's house. Let's worry about this some other time. Right now, we need to focus on our safety." Dimitri got out of the car and walked over to Alex. "Here we go. Keep your eyes and ears open."

Alex and Dimitri were just finishing up at Avery's house when Thomas called. "Dimitri, you need to get over here. We're at Dahl's house. We haven't been here long, but the house is dark. It looks like someone broke down the door and the scent of vampire is everywhere. Ariel and I are hiding in the trees. So far we haven't seen any movement or activity, but something's up here and I don't want to go in until I have backup."

"You two stay hidden. Call Nick and get him and Dante over there. Alex and I are on our way. We're just leaving Avery's. He's out of town, so if we're lucky Dahl's house is the only one that's been attacked. I'll get a hold of Victor and have him and Bastian start that way. Ty's still with Jake and Charlie. Alex can call Jake. We shouldn't take too long, so just hang tight." Dimitri hung up and called Victor. Alex was already on the phone with Jake. As they pulled up Dahl's driveway moments later, they saw that Dante and Nicholas had already arrived. Victor pulled in behind Dimitri's car. "Let's go," Dimitri said. "Standard containment. Nick and Dante, you take the front door. I'll take the northwest, Thomas you and Ariel take the southwest."

Nick and Dante went in the front door. They flipped on the light and the house erupted with vampires. They were jumping out from everywhere, doors and windows. The fight was on. Ty, Jake and Charlie pulled up and joined the fight. Dimitri stayed by Alex's side. He was still surprised at what an amazing fighter she was. He had to admit they made a good team.

Before they left the house she had asked Dimitri if she had to use a stake to kill a vampire or if a knife would work. He assured her a knife was fine. She'd gone into the library and fastened a sheath to her belt. Dimitri recognized the knife, it had been Luke's. He was glad she thought of it. It was certainly coming in handy now. It seemed fitting that Alex was using one of Luke's knifes in her first real battle. He knew Luke would be proud of her. If only he could be here to see her.

Almost at once the fighting was over. Dimitri split the men into teams of four and had them scour the surrounding area. Dahl still hadn't been found. Dimitri, Alex and Ariel went into the house to search. Dimitri had a sinking feeling they weren't going to find him. The rest of the men returned. No luck. Dahl wasn't anywhere to be found. They secured his house the best they could and headed back to the Deveraux's. It had been their meeting place for so long, it was just habit. "Do you mind if we all crash at your house tonight?" Dimitri asked Alex.

She was a little surprised at the question. "You still think there's danger?"

"Not really, I just want to be prepared," Dimitri said soberly.

"I don't mind. I think Thomas likes having you guys use our house as a sort of headquarters or meeting place. I get the impression you used to meet there with Luke and it's like carrying on a tradition," Alex admitted.

"I hadn't thought of that. I guess that would be a type of comfort to Thomas." He took a deep breath. "I need to call Oberon. He should know Dahl is missing. They weren't close, but it's still going to be a blow."

Alex was thinking about Dahl. A man she'd never met, now she was sure it was too late. Of course, they were going to search for him. They'd hope he was still alive, but chances weren't good. Most likely he'd already been drained by a bunch of vampires, his body left discarded as if it weren't important. It was so cruel. She imagined it must be an awful way to go. Tears started to form in her eyes. She was still trying to brush them away when they got to her house and Dimitri opened the door for her.

Dusk

Dimitri took one look at Alex and pulled her into his arms. "You're so tired, baby." He rubbed his hand up and down her back in comfort. "It's okay," he wished she had stayed home tonight. "I know it's hard, and you're so exhausted. Let me take you up to your room. I only need a minute with the guys and then I'll be back up."

"No," Alex pulled back and wiped away the tears. "I'm okay. I'm just so tired. I was thinking about Dahl, this man I've never met and now I probably won't get the chance. I know I shouldn't think that way. I know it's best to hope, but honestly what are the chances that he's okay? It all just made me so sad and I couldn't help it. It's just been a long night. I'm really okay. I want to be there when you talk to the guys. I need to thank them myself for everything they did tonight. Who knows how many lives were saved by your quick actions."

"I guess, but I can't help thinking about the one that's lost. The one we were too late to help." Dimitri opened the front door and guided her into the library.

* * * *

Three days after Dahl went missing Alex and Ariel were standing in the meadow at the cabin. Alex couldn't believe it. The security was amazing. Dimitri managed everything in such a short amount of time. No wonder his company was so successful. To the casual observer, nothing had changed. Alex could pick out the sensors and security cameras only because she was in on the planning. She already knew where they were located. Dimitri had even implanted cameras in the trees in the forest. Alex felt safe here. She knew she could relax and focus on training. If only she could get Dahl off her mind.

248

Dahl was still missing. Over the past three days Alex had learned he was almost fifteen hundred years old. He didn't have any family left. His wife died approximately three hundred years ago, killed by a group of vampires. They had one son, but he had been killed in battle several hundred years earlier, long before the treaty was signed. After the death of his wife, Dahl had become antisocial. He still served on the council, but that was about the only time he left the house. The fact he hadn't been located didn't look good. Everyone was still hoping for a miracle, but not really expecting one.

"So, I'm all yours for the next two hours," Alex said to Ariel. "Any idea where you want to begin?"

"Well since we have no idea what your talents are, other than being a healer, I think we should start off practicing your fighting techniques. You and I haven't fought against each other before. Thomas told me about his theory. I'd like to test it," Ariel began.

"What theory?" Alex asked.

"His theory that you can see the future," Ariel stated flatly.

"Oh that," Ariel sighed. "I think that theory is nonsense. I know you said some fae can see the future, but wouldn't I know if that was happening?" Alex asked.

"Maybe, maybe not. It depends on how it works. Plus, if you are only seeing seconds, or a fraction of a second in advance, you may not recognize it for what it is. Let's start by having you fight someone you've never practiced with before. I was thinking about having Breena come tomorrow, that way you can take both of us on at the same time. Then, we'll just see what happens." Ariel took off her jacket. "Let's get started."

Dusk

They practiced for a little more than two hours. They seemed equally matched, but Alex didn't feel like she was seeing the future or learning anything more about her gifts. Ariel was fast. Alex had to concentrate just to hold her own. "I think we got our workout for the week." Alex was bent over, hands resting on her knees, trying to catch her breath. "Before we go, would you tell me how you conjure fire and maybe give a demonstration?"

"You are demanding, aren't you?" Ariel said, a little breathless herself. "Give me a couple minutes to catch my breath, then I'll give a demonstration. I think we need to head home after that. All this expensive security won't help us if we're on the road after dark." Ariel took a deep breath.

"You're right. I know it was good to practice fighting, but I still don't feel like I'm getting any closer to identifying my powers. It's just frustrating, that's all," Alex said obviously disconcerted.

"Don't give up yet. We've only just started. I told you some fae don't come into their powers until their mid-thirties. You're kind of pushing it, trying to force them on your timetable," Ariel said sympathetically. She stood up and looked around for something safe she could use to demonstrate her gift. "I don't know where it's safe to throw fire. Do you have something that's not part of your security I can destroy?" Ariel asked.

"Oh," Alex laughed. "Let me grab a log from the forest." She came back with a short stump and placed it in the center of the meadow.

"That'll do," Ariel laughed. "Now, stand back over here by me. I'll kind of walk you through it."

Alex stood next to Ariel. "Every fae has their own technique. Some use anger to call up their gift. Some have to relax, you know get into their zone. For me, I envision what I want. First, I think about heat until I can feel it in my fingertips. Then, I visualize a spark, then a flame, then fire. In the beginning the process took a while, but now it's almost instantaneous." Ariel flicked her hand and fire flew across the meadow, landing on the stump. It instantly burst into flames.

Alex looked at Ariel in shocked silence. Then she burst out laughing. "Wow!" She finally said. "That is so cool. I wish I could do something as cool as that. I guess at this point I wish I could do something!" Alex grumbled, still amazed. "I realized you were using fire that night at Dahl's place because every once in a while I'd see flames, but I couldn't really watch you or see how you used it. I was a little busy myself. Does it kill them? The vampires? Or just injure them enough to give you an edge?" Alex asked curiously. They had started toward the house. Alex wanted to lock up and head for home too. She was still nervous about being out unprotected at night.

"Most fae need to carry a stake or knife around with them for protection. Well, they do now days. And they did in the old days. I know a lot of people got out of the habit when the treaty was in effect, but they've started up again. Of course the warriors always carried something with them. I don't have to. If I get my aim right, the fire works the same. Straight to the heart and poof, they're gone."

Alex looked up at Ariel. "Are you serious?" she questioned. "That's even more amazing!" She locked the front door to the cabin and set the alarm. "Okay, let's go. We're all locked up here."

Dusk

They were silent most of the way back into town. Finally Alex spoke. "If my only power is healing, it's not going to do us any good to practice out here. The only way I could get practice would be to try to heal someone that's been injured. Maybe I should go volunteer at the hospital or something. You know, become a candy striper," Alex was discouraged.

"Nice try," Ariel said as she stopped in front of Alex's house. "You're not going to get out of this now. It was your idea. Breena and I will be here tomorrow at three to pick you up. I have to warn you, she's good. Orin doesn't let her come out and play much. He's very protective of her, but it's going to be like taking on two of me. Only she has a different style. I think that will be more of a challenge. We're going to give you a run for your money, so rest up and be prepared. See you tomorrow."

* * * *

A week later, Alex, Breena and Ariel stood in the meadow again. They'd been practicing almost every day. Alex was getting her butt kicked. They were both so good at fighting. It was obvious the two of them had been friends for a very long time. They had a rhythm. It was sort of like watching the warriors fight together. They knew each other's moves and capitalized on that comradery. Each attack was synchronized and perfectly executed. Just when Alex thought she was catching on to their techniques, they changed. She was sore, tired and discouraged.

"Stop stalling," Breena laughed. "I haven't had this much fun for a long time. I enjoy kicking my queen when she's down." She gave Alex a little hip bump. "Awe, come on. What happened to your sense of humor? You shouldn't take it personally. Nobody can take Ariel and me in a match."

Alex smiled. "I still have my sense of humor. It's just hard to find beneath all these aches and pains. I thought we were supposed to heal immediately. What gives? I don't think I've ever been this sore before in my life. I feel like an old granny!"

"Oh that," Breena said. "You will heal. In fact, I'm amazed at how well you're still doing. Ariel's right, you are a healer."

Alex was surprised. "What do you mean?"

Ariel answered. "You've been taking major blows every day for the past week. We haven't been holding back. When you go home at night, you have to be in pain." Ariel glanced at Breena. "We've been sore and neither of us has taken the kind of blows you have. There were a couple times you really scared me. Like when Bree knocked you into that rock over there. Yet each day you come back, completely healed. No bruises or anything. We've never seen anything like it before. Most of us would be down in bed, recovering by now. Our bodies heal, but if you damage them too much without a break, healing can take days. Not with you though. Yeah, you're sore but nothing like you should be by now. It really is amazing."

Alex smiled. "So maybe I can do something cool after all?"

"I don't think you realize just how cool that is," Breena put in. "One day you will and you'll be truly grateful," she hesitated. "But for now, let's tango." She was smiling.

They had reached the middle of the meadow. They always started in the center but by the time they were finished, they had traveled across the entire area. Originally Alex thought the meadow was the perfect training ground because of its size. Over the past couple days she had often thought it was too small, especially when she hit that rock. The pain had been excruciating.

The three began their ritual. The last hour had been the same. Alex spent the entire time trying to concentrate on their next move and counter it. She found herself on her back too many times to count. This last time she'd been pushed into a tree. Her back was sore and her muscles were killing her. She stopped a minute to rest and started thinking back to that night in the alley. Those were big men. They were fast and strong. Why was she able to defend herself against three of them, but she couldn't even hold her own with these two? She remembered at first she was concentrating on each move and trying to defend herself. Then it hit her. Once the fight got going and all three were attacking her at once, she had stopped trying to anticipate what they were going to do. She had to. She'd cleared her mind and let her body react on instinct.

The same was true that night at Dahl's. The vampires were coming at her and Dimitri so fast she couldn't think, she just had to react. Was that the problem? Was she over thinking it with Breena and Ariel? She pushed herself away from the tree and decided to try a new tactic.

Ariel came at her again. Alex took a deep breath and tried to clear her mind. It was harder this time because she knew her life wasn't in danger. Ariel and Breena weren't holding back, but they also weren't trying to kill her. She took a couple more blows, but finally she was able to let it all go and stopped anticipating. Breena came at her from the right. Alex pivoted, swung around and blocked a kick from Ariel. The fight continued for several minutes.

Finally, Breena and Ariel stopped and looked at each other. They were smiling. "Wanna tell us what's been going on here for the last half hour?" Breena asked.

Alex was shocked. "Has it been that long? Really?"

"Yeah, and you were definitely in the zone," Ariel commented. "I've never seen anyone fight like that. Now I can understand why Ty is in awe of you. You were amazing. Dimitri described it best I think. He told me when you get like that, the way you were just fighting us, it's graceful and fluid like a dance rather than a fight. I thought he was just so smitten with you he was exaggerating. Not so, you are one scary woman!"

Alex looked at them for a minute and then punched her fists in the air and started to dance and whoop around the meadow. "I did it!" She exclaimed. "I finally figured it out." She danced back to Ariel and Breena and gave them both a big hug.

They were all laughing now. Alex was excited. Breena and Ariel were just amused. "So would you care to share?" Ariel finally asked. "What is it that you finally figured out?"

Alex plopped herself down on the ground. "I'm not a hundred percent convinced that Thomas is right. I don't know if I'm seeing the future or if it's something else, but I have tapped into my secret. I figured out how I do it," Alex grinned. "It's difficult to describe. I think of it as instinct. When I let my instinct control my actions rather than trying to think through it with my brain, it's almost as if I can see what's going to come next. I guess it could be seeing the future, but it's such a tiny window. It's not a few seconds, not even a partial second, it's more like a nanosecond. Such a small amount of time I couldn't ever think about it and have time to react. Like I said, I just let my instincts control my movement and I can block anything. Does that make sense?" Alex asked.

"Absolutely," Ariel said confidently. "I told you that powers work differently for each person. That's why it's so hard to find the trigger. It could be anything," she hesitated. "So, do you think it works the same for the healing?"

Alex hadn't thought that far. Was it the same with the healing? She wasn't sure. That was something she was going to have to think about. She didn't like to relive those moments in the car with Dimitri. It was too hard and emotional. She couldn't do that here with these two and she was so ecstatic about her discovery, she didn't want to try. It would only depress her and right now she wanted to celebrate. "I don't know. I'll have to think about that," Alex said honestly. "You two ready for another round? Now that I'm holding my own, I was kind of having fun," Alex admitted.

Breena laughed. "I can go again, but only a short round. I need to get home. Spending every day with you two has put me behind."

"Me too," Ariel admitted. "If you really do have this down, I think Bree and I can take a break. I'd like to bring a couple warriors out here and see how you do against them. But first, let's make sure you really can trigger this fighting thing, whatever it is, at will."

This time when they left the cabin, Alex was in a good mood. She wasn't even that sore. She still couldn't win Breena and Ariel in a fight, but she could certainly hold her own. They seemed to be in a good mood too. Maybe her enthusiasm had rubbed off on them. They laughed and talked all the way home. For the first time since leaving Italy, she felt like she truly had friends. It was surprising how much she missed that. She'd felt so lonely without Jennifer.

She knew she could never see her again, but maybe she was finally making a new start.

* * * *

Dahl was weak. He'd expected to be drained and left dead by the vampires. Now, he wished he had been. It would surprise him if he made it through another night. He'd lost count of how many days it had been since the abduction. He had no idea where he was and there was no chance of escape. Even if he had the opportunity, he was too weak to try. He'd been injured severely that first night. So many vampires had stormed his house. He knew he wouldn't be able to fight them all, but he was determined to die trying. He'd held his own for a short time, but there were just too many of them. Once they had started feeding, he was sure his life was over. Then that woman walked in, Lilith. She immediately stopped the feeding. At first he thought there was hope, but then the torture started. She was pure evil and enjoyed every minute of it. He'd lived a long time and knew he'd been lucky most of his life. Now here he was weak, near death and without hope.

He had so many cuts and bruises. The injuries he'd sustained that first night would be healed by now if he was home, if he had access to the healing tea. Without the tea, and with the nightly beatings and torture, his body wasn't recovering. He kept getting weaker and weaker. He just kept telling himself, no matter what, he would not betray his people. There was no doubt in his mind, he would be questioned again tonight. Lilith had been so pleased with herself last evening after she'd lightly brushed his cuts with lemon juice. That's probably why he was so weak tonight. He was sure she didn't realize what she was doing. She didn't know that because of her actions, he didn't have much time left.

He could hold out for just a little longer. Maybe someone would finally find him. If not, these vampires would not get anything out of him. He wasn't afraid of dying. In fact, at this point he would embrace it. The torture and pain would stop. But most of all, he would get to see his beloved Chelsea again. He missed her so much. When this was all over, he would join Chelsea in the Fade. They would be together again for eternity. She'd been gone three hundred and nineteen long years now. He wasn't ready to leave this earth, but he would embrace his destiny and look forward to joining his wife. He was also looking forward to seeing his son, Anton again. Anton had been so brave and such a great fighter. It had been hard when he died, but Dahl was proud of him. Their small family would finally be reunited after so many years. He would remember that. He would concentrate on that when the torture began. If Lilith used the lemon juice again tonight, it would be over. There was nothing he could do to warn his people, but he wouldn't aid the vampires either. He would be brave, just like his son Anton. Their queen was in danger. Alexandria couldn't know that Radek planned to have her captured again. Dahl didn't know what Radek planned to do with her, or the council for that matter. Why did they want the names of all the council members? Well, it didn't matter. He wouldn't tell them anything.

Last night Lilith promised him if he would only tell them what they wanted to know and swear his allegiance to the vampire king, he would be saved. They would protect him from the queen and her warriors. That in itself was a joke. He'd take the warriors' protection over vampires any day. Did Radek think he could capture the queen and the council, then declare himself King of the Fae? That was ridiculous. The fae community wouldn't tolerate it. No one would follow him. Lilith's final offer had been to promote him to council leader. She honestly thought the promise of power would sway him. He knew the headaches Oberon dealt with on a regular basis. You couldn't pay him enough to accept that job. Oberon continued as chair out of duty, not because he wanted the power. No, Lilith didn't understand the fae. Maybe that was a blessing. Maybe it would help the fae win this war.

The door opened and Lilith walked in. The vampire behind her was carrying a tray that held a small brush and a container of lemon juice. Dahl smiled inwardly. This would all be over soon. His only regret was those he was leaving behind. He hadn't had a chance to say goodbye.

"What do you mean he's dead?" Radek thundered. "I told you we needed answers. I need those names! That's why you questioned him instead of the young, weak vampires. You were supposed to keep him alive at least until he gave us answers. Do I have to do everything? I already had to take things out of Hector's hands. He was working too slow. I captured one of the council members and you killed him!" Radek screamed as he stomped across the room, kicked a chair and flung it into a wall. "Fix this!" He bellowed as he stomped his foot. "I want my kingdom!"

"One of the vampires brought this back from Dahl's house. We don't know how it works, but I think it's some kind of electronic device. If we can figure it out, we might be able to find something useful on it. Do you want me to ask Hector for help? See if he can figure it out?" Lilith knew she needed to try to calm Radek down. If she wasn't successful, he would completely lose it and she might end up dead. He was such a bore when he threw tantrums like this. So she killed the fairy. How was she supposed to know repeated use of lemon juice would be fatal? It was too bad, she'd been having so much fun. Finding ways to torture the weak fairy broke up the monotony.

"I don't care how you do it, just fix this and get me answers. NOW!" Radek picked up a lamp and flung it across the room. Lilith seized the opportunity and slipped out into the hallway. She needed to stay away from Radek tonight. Her life depended on it. She smiled. He'd just given her permission to visit Hector. Once there, she wouldn't leave until they had a little fun.

Chapter Nine

Dimitri was excited but nervous. Alex was on her way over. He had been so busy the past two weeks they'd barely seen each other. First, he spent all his time during the day overseeing security at the cabin. His nights were spent hunting and searching for Dahl. After two weeks Dimitri didn't think there was much hope, but he couldn't give up. Once the cabin was finished, he had to catch up on the backlog at work. Plus, Alex was spending all her time with Ariel and Breena. She was determined to find her powers, but he was worried she was working too hard. They finally had a night together and he wanted to make it special.

First, he was going to make her dinner. She still didn't believe he could cook. He'd prove her wrong. He pulled the ring out of his pocket and looked at it again. It had been his mother's. It was special to him, but would Alex like it? He took a deep breath. He was actually going to ask her to marry him tonight. His stomach did a little flip. After all this time, he finally found the woman he

Dusk

wanted to spend the rest of his life with. He really hoped she'd say yes. He knew she loved him, but this was a big step. Was she ready? He was past ready. He wanted her with him, in his house, living with him, sleeping with him. The last two weeks had been torture. He couldn't stand being away from her like this.

As fate would have it, the first night he and Alex could get together was also the night the council was meeting. They were all nervous and hoped to be done before dark, but they had a lot to talk about and some big decisions to make. One thing the council was happy about was the shift in opinion about the new queen. It seemed the people were impressed that Alex, the queen herself, was willing to spend an entire night going door to door warning the community they could be in danger. They credited her for the fact that only one fae had been lost. Of course, Alex was unhappy about that. She wanted him to get the credit. Dimitri however, was ecstatic. It was important to him that Alex was accepted and respected as the queen. He didn't care about receiving credit for his actions that night. Word was also spreading about her fighting abilities. All in all things were looking up, on that front anyway.

The doorbell rang. Dimitri turned off the stove and went to answer it. It annoyed him a little that she rang the bell. He'd made sure she knew she had access to the house because he wanted her to be comfortable here. If she couldn't make herself at home in his house, was it too soon to ask her to marry him? It didn't matter. He was going to ask anyway. He opened the door and saw her standing there. Just the sight of Alex could take his breath away. She was holding a fresh pie, which made him smile. She didn't trust his cooking skills, so she'd brought backup from Marta.

She was so beautiful standing there, smiling at him. "Hey," he said. "Come in." He stepped back to give her room.

"Hey yourself," she said with a smile, brushing passed him. "I brought dessert."

Dimitri took the pie and set it on the table in the foyer. He turned back and grabbed her, pulling her in for a kiss. He'd intended to keep it light. He had plans for tonight. He needed to stay on track. Then Alex deepened the kiss sliding her tongue into his mouth, slow and seductive. Dimitri pulled her closer and groaned. No, he told himself, he had been planning this evening for days. He couldn't do this now, it would ruin everything. He started to pull back, tried to regain control, but Alex slid her hands around his buttocks squeezing slightly. She pressed herself against him and kissed him again. How could he resist this woman? But he had to. Just as he was going to break away and lead her to the kitchen, she slid her hand between their bodies and unfastened the button on his jeans.

All his plans went out the window. They'd been apart for too long. They both needed the intimacy. No way was he going to take her in the foyer though. He wasn't that much of an animal. He quickly whisked her into his arms and headed for the library. At least he had started a fire, they'd make love on the soft throw rug in front of the fireplace, then he'd try to salvage his plans the best he could.

They were sprawled on the floor, heat from the flames danced across their bodies as they rested in silence. Alex was flat on her back, Dimitri rested on one elbow as he gently caressed her stomach. Firelight danced over her pale skin illuminating her features in the darkness. She was so beautiful. He loved every inch of her. He kept thinking they should get up, go have dinner and get the plans back on track but he couldn't pull himself away.

Dusk

"What are you thinking about?" Alex asked Dimitri. She laughed a little. "I know guys hate that question, but you look so serious. Like you're deep in thought. You're normally so relaxed after we make love. I was just wondering what was going on in that head of yours right now."

Dimitri leaned down and kissed her lightly. "I was thinking how beautiful you are." He gave her another quick kiss. "How much I love you." He gave her another kiss. "How much I've missed you," he said giving her one last gentle kiss. "Don't move an inch. I'll be right back." He got up, grabbed a thin blanket off the top of the couch and covered her. Then he pulled on his jeans and walked out of the library.

Alex was confused, but she was too satisfied right now to move. He said he'd be right back, so he would be.

Dimitri walked into the kitchen. He checked his pants pocket to make sure the ring was still there. It was. He pulled out two crystal wine glasses and a bottle of wine. He could improvise. He'd ask her while they drank wine in front of the fire. So, he wasn't following the plan. Wasn't spontaneity better anyway? He walked back into the library. Alex was still lying on the rug, she had her eyes closed and she hadn't moved an inch. She looked like an angel with the light dancing over her face.

Dimitri poured the wine. Alex slowly opened her eyes and sat up to take the glass he was holding out for her. He poured a glass for himself and sat down next to her.

"See," she said smiling. "I knew it. You are a hopeless romantic. Thanks for the wine." She leaned over and kissed him lightly.

"Here's to us," he said as he held out his glass.

"Definitely," Alex said as she touched his glass with hers. She took a sip, still watching him. She had no doubt now, Dimitri had something on his mind.

Dimitri set down his glass and took Alex's hand in his. He looked at it in silence for a long moment. Then he looked directly into her eyes. "Alex, I love you. More than I ever thought it was possible to love someone." He brushed a finger over her cheek bone. "You are the most beautiful, intriguing and special woman I have ever met," Dimitri paused. He tucked a lock of hair behind her ear.

Alex loved it when he did that. Somehow the gesture seemed so intimate, so loving. She put down her glass, she was watching him intently now.

Dimitri continued, "The last couple weeks have been torture for me."

"Me too," Alex whispered.

Dimitri leaned in and kissed her gently. At the same time, he pulled the ring from his pocket. It's now or never, he thought. He pulled back and took a deep breath. "I know this has all happened so quickly. But, I also know I love you and I want you in my life..." He stopped to correct himself, "No, I need you in my life forever." He slowly held out the ring, "Will you marry me, Alex? I promise I will love you forever. If you say yes, I will do everything in my power to make you happy for the rest of our lives."

Alex was stunned. This is what she'd dreamed of. What she hoped they were moving toward. Dimitri wanted to marry her, too!

Dusk

She flung herself at him, knocking him onto his back. She kissed him hard. Then kissed his cheeks, his neck then back to his mouth.

Dimitri started laughing. "I hope I can take this as a yes," he said.

"Yes!" Alex said enthusiastically as she propped herself up on one arm. "Yes, yes, yes, yes! Dimitri Montgomery, I would love to be your wife." She was so happy. She held out her left hand. "But first I want a closer look at that ring." She grinned while she wiggled her fingers.

Dimitri slipped it on carefully. The fit was perfect. He knew it would be. He'd sized it to the ruby ring she often wore one night after she'd fallen asleep. Then he'd taken it in for a quick alteration.

Alex sat up and studied the ring. It was perfect. She loved it! "This looks old. Is it, or was it just made to look that way?" she inquired.

"It is very old," Dimitri said a little hesitantly. "It used to be my mothers. If you don't like it we can go anywhere you want and pick out another one," Dimitri offered.

"Absolutely not!" Alex exclaimed. "I love it. It's perfect. I think it fits me, my personality I mean. I also love that it used to be your mothers. I really wish I could have met her. She must have been a very special woman."

"She was." Dimitri sat up and pulled her close. "Are you sure you like it? Really, I don't mind if you want something else."

"I absolutely love it, Dimitri. It really is perfect. It's also more special because it was your mothers. I know you loved her very

266

much, that makes it invaluable. We couldn't find a ring in the entire universe that I would love more than this one. Thank you," she finished quietly.

Dimitri pulled her with him as he leaned against the sofa. Alex settled against him, leaning her back against his chest. "I've been nervous all day," he admitted to her. "I was so scared you'd think it was too soon. Then, I was worried you wouldn't like the ring. I had almost every minute of tonight planned out to make sure it was perfect," he laughed. "Nothing has gone according to my plan, but I like it better this way. You've just made me the happiest man in the universe. I want to stand on the rooftop and tell the world." He kissed her neck.

Alex smiled. It was nice to hear how nervous Dimitri had been preparing for this. He always seemed so calm and collected, like nothing ever fazed him. Knowing he was just as vulnerable as she was when it came to their relationship was comforting somehow. "Well, plan or no plan, I'm happy about the evening so far. I don't know how it could have been more perfect." She tipped her head back and kissed him lightly. "However, if you insist on making a roof top declaration, I'll need to get dressed first. We are in New York. The neighbors might throw tomatoes or something," she laughed.

"What do you say we skip the declaration and move on to dinner?" He kissed the back of her head. "I'm starved."

"We still get dinner?" she teased. "I thought maybe you burned it and this was your way of providing a distraction so I wouldn't be disappointed. Then, you'd escape out the door to grab a burger on your way to hunt."

Dusk

He pushed her forward so he could stand up. "You're going to regret all this skepticism. Once you eat my meal, you'll be sorry. I'm not cooking for you again until you cook for me. And then only if I decide your apology for all this negativity is sufficient. Oh, and by the way, I'm not hunting tonight. Unless there's an emergency, you're all mine until morning."

"Really?" she smiled. "We really get all night?" That didn't happen very often, especially lately. There was just too much going on for anyone to get a night off.

"Really. Now, just sit tight. I need to reheat dinner. I'm sure it's cold by now. It won't take long. I'll come get you when it's ready." He turned and hurried out the door.

Alex looked around, if they were going to eat, she better get dressed. She noticed Dimitri's t-shirt lying by the couch. That would do. If she was wearing it, he couldn't. She pulled it over her head then leaned back against the couch. She was really going to marry Dimitri. She watched the firelight flicker over the brilliant diamond. All her dreams were coming true.

Tonight was the best night of her entire life! The most wonderful man in the world wanted to spend his life with her. Dimitri could have any woman. He was smart, sexy, sophisticated, but he had chosen her. She couldn't believe it. She was bubbling over with happiness and love. Nobody had more than she did right now. She had the man of her dreams and this wonderful house. What would it be like to live here with Dimitri, she wondered? She was thinking of breakfast in the kitchen, planting a garden, suddenly she realized there was a dog in her fantasy. She'd never had a dog. She laid her head on the couch and fantasized about the future.

Dimitri walked in and saw Alex sitting there asleep, her head resting on the couch wearing his shirt. He laughed, somehow she was even sexy in his oversized t-shirt. He stood there watching her for a moment. She looked so peaceful. He thought about letting her sleep but decided to be selfish. It was rare for them to have a whole night together. He didn't want to waste it. He walked over and crouched in front of her. Then, he leaned in and kissed her softly. She moaned, but didn't wake. He pressed his hands on the couch on either side of her shoulders and leaned in for a deeper kiss. He knew the moment she woke and pulled back. "Wake up sleeping beauty," he smiled.

She smiled back at him. "Sorry, is dinner ready?" She started to get up.

Dimitri stood and took her hand. "Yes, it's all ready. It's set up on the roof. I thought we could either take a swim or a dip in the hot tub after we finished. If you're up to it that is." They were headed up the stairs.

"Maybe both. I just had a little cat nap, I'm good to go for hours now." She slid him a seductive look. "The question is, are you up to it?"

He put his arm around her waist as he guided her through the rooftop doorway. "Anytime babe, anytime." He pulled out her chair and motioned for her to sit.

Alex looked around. It was like entering a magical world. The only time she'd been up here had been in the morning, when it was light outside. Sitting here at twilight, just as the sun began to set, with the small lights twinkling around them was amazing. Dimitri had created a romantic getaway. The table had a white table cloth and blazing candles situated on crystal candlesticks. There was a

Dusk

full place setting of delicate china. He'd gone all out for her tonight. She was touched. "Wow!" She reached over and took his hand. "This is nice Dimitri, thank you."

He smiled at her. "I told you, I wanted this night to be special. I deviated from my plan a little, but I think I can salvage most of it." He pulled a dish off a warming plate and handed it to her. "Sorry, I dished your plate for you. It was easier than dragging all this stuff up individually." He picked up another plate and set it on the table in front of himself.

"You cooked all this yourself?" She was truly impressed. "Is that fresh bread?" Dimitri had made steamed vegetables, broiled chicken with fettuccine and topped it off with Alfredo sauce. It smelled wonderful.

"I kept telling you I could cook. All that pessimism," he shook his head. "You would think if a woman says she loves you, she'd try to give you the benefit of the doubt. Not my woman though. My future wife is a skeptic. That's okay. I just keep thinking of all that groveling and apologizing you're going to have to do to make it up to me." Dimitri linked his fingers through hers.

"I like the future wife part," she smiled. "We'll see about groveling. I do owe you an apology though," she said as she scooped up another bite of dinner. "This is wonderful." They shared small talk throughout the meal. Afterwards, they both decided to skip the swim and relax in the hot tub. Alex felt like she was in heaven. They both settled in for a relaxing evening at home. Dimitri hoped it would be the first of many.

Alex had her head against Dimitri's shoulder as she slowly slid her hand across the water, following the rings that spread out across

270

the surface when one of them moved. "So I was wondering..." she looked up at him. "Can we get a dog?"

"What?" Dimitri laughed. "Where did that come from?"

"Well, earlier as I sat in front of the fire waiting for you to tell me dinner was ready, I was thinking about our future and suddenly there was a dog in my daydream. So, I was just wondering if we could get a dog. I always wanted one as a child, but was never allowed to have one. With so many businesses to run globally, we traveled too much. Besides, I don't think my parents thought I was responsible enough to care for it," Alex smiled. "I probably wasn't."

He leaned over and kissed her. "If you really want a dog, sure we can get a dog. However, you get to take care of it. That means you can't get one until you move in here permanently."

"Okay, I'll move in tonight. Get the truck, we'll go get my things." She smiled as she pretended to move away to stand.

"Not so fast, I have other plans for tonight." He slid a finger over her collar bone, then down to her breast.

"Can I really move in here now?" she asked. She was having a hard time concentrating. Her man had magic hands. "I don't have to wait until after we're married?"

Dimitri stopped what he was doing and looked up at her. "I might be old, but I'm not that old fashioned. You can move in here any time you want. In fact, for me, the sooner the better. I hate it when we're apart. One of my favorite things is sleeping with you." He smiled at the look on her face. "Yeah that too, but I meant just sleeping. I like to hold you all night. When I wake up in the middle of the night, I like to feel you there by my side. I especially like waking up next to you in the morning. So yeah, you can really move in here now. I'm glad you don't want to wait until after the wedding. I'd do that for you, but it would drive me crazy."

"Then it's settled. I get to move into my dream home." Alex was so excited, she couldn't wait.

"Do you mean it? I was hoping we could stay in this house, but we could move if you want to." Dimitri didn't want that. He'd just gotten the house the way he liked it. He loved this place, but he loved Alex more. "You know, pick something out together that we both like."

"I love this house. I can't think of one thing I would want to change. Maybe with time but really, I love it," Alex assured him. "Almost as much as I love the man that lives in it. I don't want to live anywhere else." She turned and caught his mouth with hers.

Dimitri slowly stood with Alex in his arms. He lifted her out of the hot tub and then stepped out after her. "Don't move," he said as he opened a cabinet and pulled out a towel. He slowly dried her off and then wrapped her in a black satin robe. Once he was dried and had the towel wrapped around his waist he took her hand and led her to the bedroom.

* * * *

The council was almost finished for the night. They wanted to get home before it got too late. Sunset had fallen a short time ago. They considered stopping before it got dark, but if they stopped, they would have to meet again in a couple days. They decided another meeting so soon would be too dangerous. They also wanted to get some of these things in place immediately. The fact that Dahl was still missing hung over them like a pink elephant in the room. Everyone was thinking about it, but nobody wanted to talk about it.

The council always sat at a round table to conduct their meetings. They liked it that way because there was no head of the table. No one person had more power than another. Avery was talking, trying to finalize a communication plan. They wanted to develop a better way to spread the word in the event of an emergency or danger in the future. Forcing the warriors to drive around and check on people was too time consuming. The council wanted an expedited system.

Suddenly, the door flew open. Radek walked in carrying Dahl over his shoulder. "Sorry we're late," he said cheerfully as he dropped Dahl's lifeless body next to the door. "Dahl here wanted to come earlier, but I couldn't leave without my friends." He looked over his shoulder and the council members saw the opening was filled with vampires.

"This is a closed meeting," Orin stated bluntly.

"Oh I know, but you see I had an invitation." He threw Dahl's Blackberry on the desk. "As you can see your friend's a little incapacitated. So I'm standing in for him," Radek countered flashing them a humorless grin. "I'm afraid good old Dahl wasn't much help after all. He preferred a beating to the sharing of information."

"So he died a hero," Orin piped in.

"I'm not sure which one of you is the head of this council, but I'm certain it's not you." He glared at Orin. "You are simply too young. I'd say it must be one of you." He looked at Avery, Oberon then Tighe. "So which one is it?" Radek mused. "You might want to control this young one. He's starting to get on my nerves."

Orin was about to make another comment, but Warren shook his head ever so slightly. Radek caught it. He studied Warren for a long time. "No, I don't think it's you either. I think you're just trying to save your friend here." Radek moved around the table eyeing each of the council members as he walked by. "You will tell me who's in charge," he demanded.

"Or what?" Warren countered. They all glanced over at Dahl. "Or we'll end up like him?" He shrugged in a nonchalant gesture trying to look like he didn't care.

Radek was furious. Did these men think they'd get away with this? He would not tolerate disrespect. They needed him! They would cooperate with him. He would have his kingdom! He kicked a chair across the room. The council members watched, still not saying a word. Radek took a deep breath. "I'm a reasonable man. Even after your people have wronged me, have stolen from me, I am still willing to resolve this situation in a peaceful manner," he paused.

Again they all looked at Dahl, then back to Radek.

"Oh never mind him," he said with the flick of a hand. "He was bullheaded and unreasonable. It couldn't be helped." Radek seemed to shrug it off, like it didn't matter.

It did matter. Everyone in the room, except for Radek apparently, knew it mattered. What did he want? What did he mean they had wronged him and stolen from him? Oberon was reminded of Radek's father Balthazar, he had been a tyrant. A mad man.

Radek seemed to be following in his footsteps. If he revealed himself as the Chair, his chance of survival wasn't very good. He would do it though. If it came down to his life or the lives of the others. He would sacrifice himself and hope the others could escape. There were so many vampires outside though. Other than Orin it had been a long time since any of them had participated in a physical fight.

"Why don't we try this instead? If you aren't willing to identify the Chair, I'll simply explain my demands." Radek cocked his head to the side. "Let me change that, I'll submit my request for the council to make things right. Once I've explained my position, you can put it up for a vote. That's what you do, right? You hear a proposal and then vote on it. Personally I don't care for such democratic nonsense. It's much quicker if one person is in charge. One person that makes all the decisions, but tonight we'll try it your way. Like I said, I'm a reasonable man," he sneered.

The council remained silent.

Radek was getting angrier by the minute. He tried to hold his temper, but it was getting more difficult. "I believe you are all aware of my lineage, but just to be clear, I am the first born son of Balthazar and Marlena. I was born six hundred years ago. Unfortunately, I only had 117 years with my great father. He was murdered in his sleep by a group of fae. I understand those members of your community have never paid for their crime, but that's something for later."

The council members glanced around the table. They all knew how and why Balthazar was killed. It wasn't in his sleep and he was not murdered. This was getting even more bizarre by the minute. Radek wasn't only a tyrant, apparently he was also delusional.

Dusk

"In that short time, my father taught me to be a great leader. Our people, the vampire community, immediately recognized me as the rightful heir to my father's kingdom. Not only was I his first born but I was his only male child, his male heir to the throne. A few months ago, my mother the Fae Queen died. I believe the official ruling was that she died of natural causes after a fairly long life. As her first born and her only male child, I am the rightful heir to her kingdom. However, through what I'm sure is a misunderstanding, I have been denied that honor. Alexandria..." Radek said with contempt. "Stole my kingdom and is trying to establish herself as your leader, your new queen. I am your King! I am Marlena's rightful heir!" Radek yelled. "I will have my kingdom. I will not tolerate this betrayal any longer." He closed his eyes and took a deep breath. "So, I am here to tell you how we are going to fix this. How you, the council, will fix this." Radek was trying to appear calm, but the council wasn't fooled. "You will immediately denounce Alexandria as queen. You will turn her over to me. As King of the Fae, I decide what happens to traitors. She is a traitor and will be dealt with appropriately. Under your direction, the fae community will embrace me as their King. Those responsible for my father's death will have to be punished of course, but all other fae will fall under my protection and my rule. Do you understand?" Radek said.

"And if we don't?" Orin asked. Oberon looked at Orin until they made eye contact. He moved his head slightly to force Orin to stop. If the kid kept it up, Radek would kill him out of annoyance. Orin took a deep breath but remained silent.

Radek had his back to the council, looking out the window. He quickly spun around and slammed his hands down on the table. The table broke in two, splitting right down the middle. Radek ignored it. "You will obey me!" He thundered. "If you don't, I will

276

be forced to take you into captivity tonight. You will be imprisoned as traitors. As such, your families will also be imprisoned. I would of course, give you time to reconsider your vote on this. I want peace in my land. Being forced to execute the entire council and their families would delay that peace temporarily. Captivity in my chambers can be very dangerous. I can't guarantee the safety of your family. I have many vampires in my legion. They must feed. You know what happens when vampires feed on fae. It's almost impossible for them to stop. No, if you want your families to be safe you must vote now. Embrace me as your king and denounce that traitor Alexandria. It's your only hope," Radek finished with a smile.

Clearly Radek thought the council would capitulate and give him what he wanted. He really was mad. The fae community would not, under any circumstance, embrace the Vampire King as their leader. Had he explained this asinine plan to Dahl? Is that why Radek claimed he was bullheaded? Oberon was at a loss what to do. They would not denounce their queen. They would not accept Radek as anything but an enemy, a narcissistic mentally unstable enemy, but an enemy just the same.

Drake spoke up. "We have heard your proposal and will discuss it. However, it is customary for the presenter to leave the room while the council debates the matter at hand. At this time we would ask you to go out into the hallway with your supporters and give us time to vote on the matter."

Radek glared at Drake for a full minute. "No, I do not believe you are the chairman of this council either. Is the chairman such a coward that he refuses to reveal himself to me, his king?"

Dusk

Oberon couldn't let this go on. The others were going to get themselves hurt in an attempt to protect his identity. He was the leader of the council. He would take the risks. He was just about to speak when Alveron beat him to it.

"I am the leader of this council," Alveron declared.

"No I am the leader," Tighe countered.

"Actually," Oberon said glaring at the other council members. "I am the council chair. If anyone is going to be taken into custody as a traitor, it will be me. The other members of this council are innocent, they were just following my orders."

"Oberon, stop trying to protect me." Avery put in as he gave Oberon his most contemptuous, condescending glare.

Radek lost it. "STOP IT!" He demanded. "You will not, I repeat, not make a mockery out of this. I demand to know immediately who is in charge here."

"I am," the eight council members said at once. Oberon was exasperated. He was trying to do his job and protect the other members. All they were doing was making things worse. They were going to end up in a fight, Radek was teetering on the edge of a psychotic trip. He was about to lose complete control. Could they possibly win with these odds? Forget win, all he wanted to do was survive. Or at the very least ensure the other council members survived.

"I will not leave the room while you vote. Isn't democracy supposed to be transparent? Therefore, give me an answer now! I am finished with this nonsense. Either you embrace me as your king, or you will be imprisoned by my soldiers," Radek demanded.

The council members looked from one member to the other. They had worked together long enough to know the decision without saying a word. It was unanimous. They were going to reject Radek and take their chances fighting. They each embraced the hand of their neighbor and made a circle of solidarity. They held for a moment of silence, then broke from the circle. Out of the corner of his eye, Oberon saw Orin slide a large knife from under his coat. The other members must have caught the same action because they too reached for their weapons.

In unison, they stood and faced Radek. He was only a few steps away from Orin and Elvin. Oberon spoke in a loud, clear voice. "Radek, we reject your request. We will not condemn our queen. We will never embrace you as our king."

Radek was shocked. Did they really think they could survive this? He would send his men out to capture their families. Every one of these men would suffer for failing to support their king! They would all pay dearly!

Orin lunged first, he tried to plunge his knife into Radek's chest. He was surprised to find Radek was wearing some kind of armor. Elvin acted quickly, he plunged his knife into Radek's right side, hoping to puncture his heart from that angle. It was clearly a serious wound, but not a lethal one. Orin was immediately on Radek's other side, stabbing him through the left ribs. Drake circled around to the back and stabbed Radek once again.

The vampires from the hallway rushed into the room. There were so many of them. Oberon had moved to the front of the line. The vampires were going to have to go through him to get to the other councilmen. Several vampires lunged for him. He was thrown into the wall. He got up and charged the group again. He took two of them out before he was thrown on top of the broken table. Part of the wooden leg lodged into his thigh. He forced himself up and charged the vampires again.

Radek was furious. How dare they attack him? Their king? His soldiers would take care of them. They were now dead men. That wasn't enough. He would order some of the vampires to track down their families and kill them, too. If they thought this had changed anything they were wrong. He would have his kingdom and he would have it tonight! Radek slowly made his way to the back of the room and out the door. He was the king, it wasn't his duty to fight. Plus, he was injured and needed to get back to the cave so Sammael could tend to his wounds.

Oberon saw Radek, the coward, sneak to the back door. As he moved, the vampires surrounded him like a shield. The warriors would have to catch up to him later. Right now, the council members had their hands full trying to survive.

Oberon realized fighting was like riding a bike. It didn't matter how long it had been since your last battle, when you were fighting for your life the maneuvers were easy to remember. The battle seemed to go on forever. Six vampires jumped on him at once. He realized the wound on his leg was bleeding pretty badly. The blood lust that wound created in the vampires made them crazy. That also made them easy targets, but he had lost too much blood and was starting to get weak. He thought he was a goner when Orin and Tighe came to his rescue. Once his attackers were killed, he realized the room was empty. There were no vampires left. The rest had either been killed or had fled.

"Thanks," Oberon croaked as he tried to sit up but failed. "We're not safe yet. Radek won't tolerate our defiance. Every one of you get home. Gather your families and go into hiding for the night." Nobody moved. Oberon was seriously injured. They all knew he needed help immediately. "What are you waiting for? Get outta here!" Oberon raised his voice. "Your families need you. There's no time to waste."

Orin spoke up, "I'll take Oberon to my house. He's right. Our families are in danger and they don't even know it. That makes them more vulnerable targets. Get home and get your wives, call your kids. Every one of them needs to go into hiding tonight. Radek and his vampires know who we are now. And he had Dahl's Blackberry. None of us can stay in our homes tonight, we may be displaced for a while. Make sure you're prepared for that."

After a slight hesitation, the rest of the council ran for the door.

* * * *

Alex and Dimitri had just fallen asleep when Dimitri's cell phone rang. They were instantly on alert. Both of them knew if someone was calling it couldn't be good. Dimitri looked at the display, then looked at Alex in confusion. "It's Breena. Sorry, I have to answer this." Dimitri sat up and answered the call. "Hello Breena, what's up?"

Breena was in a panic. "Dimitri, you have to come quick." Her voice quivered and Dimitri could tell she was on the verge of crying. "I can't get a hold of Ariel. Her father's been seriously wounded. Orin brought him back to our house, but he has so many injuries. I don't know what to do. Orin is guarding the door, he's certain we're going to come under attack any minute. He thinks Mara and Ariel are in danger too."

Dusk

"Slow down Breena," Dimitri said as he quickly threw off the covers and started searching for his clothes. Alex was off the bed in seconds. Her clothes were still down in the library. She ran out the door and down the stairs. Dimitri watched Alex go and realized his clothes were scattered throughout the house. He went to the closet and quickly pulled on some clean jeans. "Is it just you that's in danger, or are all the council members at risk?"

"All of them," Breena croaked out. She was getting more upset by the minute. Dimitri didn't have much time to get answers before she would be incomprehensible. "Alex and I are on our way. I'll contact the other warriors and let them know the council members need help. Is anyone else injured?"

"I don't think so. Not like Oberon. There was a battle at the council meeting. Radek showed up and brought Dahl's body." She inhaled a shuttering breath. "He was dead."

"Sit tight, we're on our way." He quickly pressed the button to end the call.

Dimitri and Alex were in her car by now. She was pulling out of the driveway. "Where am I going first?" she asked.

"We need to get to Orin and Breena's. Breena said she hasn't been able to reach Ariel. Do you have any idea where she could be?" Dimitri asked.

"Yes. She told me she had a date tonight and she was going to that club...what's the name of it?" Alex's mind wasn't working. What was the name of that club? She'd been there a million times when she was younger. "Oh I know, The Promenade! She was going to The Promenade."

Dimitri looked over at Alex, "Are you sure that's where she was headed?"

"Positive," Alex answered. "I used to go there all the time. We had a long conversation about the club and the type of people that go there. She's at The Promenade Dimitri, trust me."

Dimitri pulled out his phone. "Do you have your phone on you?"

"Yes," Alex answered.

"Call Thomas. Tell him what's going on. As much as we know anyway. He needs to get the warriors out there. The council and their families are first priority. We need to find somewhere safe for them to go tonight. We can move them in the morning if necessary." Dimitri was dialing a number.

Alex quickly pulled out her phone and called Thomas. They both hung up at the same time. Then, seconds later Dimitri's phone rang.

"Dimitri," Ariel yelled. "I can barely hear you. They said I needed to call you, that it was an emergency. What's going on?"

"Ariel, your father has been injured. He's with Orin and Breena. I think you and your mother are also in danger. I need you to go to your parent's house as fast as you can, gather up your mother and then get over to Breena's," Dimitri directed.

"How bad is dad?" Ariel asked soberly.

"I don't know. Alex and I are on our way. You're closer so even with picking up your mom, you'll probably beat us," Dimitri paused. "It sounds bad. Ariel, be on alert. If anything looks off at your mom's make sure you're careful. I don't have anyone I can spare. Even if I did, they're not close enough to meet up with you without delay. I'm sorry, you're on your own until you can get to Breena and Orin's." Dimitri was scared for her. There was no telling how many vampires were at Oberon's. Mara could be in real trouble.

"I'll be careful. I'm on my way to moms now. I won't keep you, I know you probably have several calls to make. Once we get there, I'm going to need to know what happened," Ariel said sounding a little panicked herself. She had a lot of disagreements with her father, but Dimitri knew how close they were. If anything happened to him, she would be devastated.

Orin stood alert on his front porch. He knew people were coming to help. He hoped they were in time, that they got here before he had to fight again. First he would need to distinguish the good guys from the bad ones. As long as the warriors came by car, he shouldn't have any trouble. Most of the vampires didn't arrive in vehicles when they were planning an attack. He figured it was because they didn't have the funds for expensive things like cars. They couldn't work during the day and most of them chose not to work at night. Suddenly there was a car flying down the driveway. It came to an abrupt stop in front of Orin's house. It was Drake. He was obviously in a panic. He flew to the passenger's side and pulled Tianna out of the car.

"Orin, you have to help her. She's seriously injured. When I got home, the vampires were already there. Our house is closest to the meeting place. I think she was probably their first target. She was trying to fight them off, but there were just too many. I got there just in time. I was able to kill them all, but she's barely conscious. I don't know what to do to help her. I tried to give her tea before we left, but I was afraid to stay at the house for long. I thought they might send more vampires just to make sure the job was complete."

"Get her inside. Breena is trying to take care of Oberon. He's in bad shape too. I can't go in. I need to guard the house in case of an attack. Dimitri's on his way. He'll know what to do and where we should go." Orin opened the door for Drake as he carried Tianna's helpless body into the house. Tonight had already been a nightmare and it was only just beginning.

The next car that arrived was Ariel's. Orin recognized it easily. Good. Ariel and Breena had been best friends for a long time, they could comfort each other. As soon as the vehicle came to a stop Ariel and Mara opened their doors simultaneously and jumped out of the car. "Where is he?" Ariel demanded. "Where's my father?"

"Inside, you two need to get in the house fast. I haven't seen any movement out here, but I don't want to take any chances." They both ran into the house in search of Oberon.

A short time later, Dimitri and Alex pulled up. Alex was driving. He assumed Dimitri had been making phone calls, rallying the troops so to speak. They too opened the door and jumped out as soon as the car came to a stop.

"Orin," Dimitri said soberly getting his first look at Orin's face. "How bad are your injuries?"

Orin was taken by surprise. In all the commotion, he hadn't even looked at his own wounds. Breena was focused on Oberon and nobody else had stayed outside long enough to mention them. "I think they're fairly superficial," Orin claimed. "I'm sure they're healing already and will be completely healed with a cup of tea and a little time."

"Tea, I can do. I won't know about time until somebody tells me what's going on," Dimitri said soberly.

Alex ran into the house to get tea for Orin. She stopped abruptly as soon as she walked in the door. "Dimitri, I think you need to get in here," Alex yelled.

Dimitri looked at Orin. "Can that tea wait a minute?"

"Yes, Oberon and Tianna are wounded pretty severely. Drake didn't know where else to go, so he brought her here. I'm not sure she's going to make it, Dimitri. Drake is holding on by a thread. All around, it's been a pretty terrible night."

Dimitri walked into the house. Orin was right, Tianna was in bad shape. So was Oberon. Tianna was lying on the couch, Drake leaning over her begging her to wake up. He was trying to force tea into her but she was clearly unconscious. Oberon was lying on the floor in the corner. Mara and Ariel were at his side. They too were slightly panicked. They were having mild success with the tea. Oberon looked so battered and bruised. Dimitri looked at Alex. She was standing so still, he thought she was in shock. "Alex," Dimitri shook her arm.

Alex looked over at Dimitri. She had been frozen, suspended in time as soon as she walked in the door. Oberon's wounds looked so much like her father's had. She had to get a grip. These people needed her help. She walked over to Oberon and leaned down to try to help him. Maybe she could use her healing powers to save him. She vaguely heard Dimitri tell Breena to get Orin a cup of tea. He needed help healing in case there was another fight.

Oberon looked up at her. He reached for her hand, but his dropped. He was obviously very weak. "I know I look bad. But really I'm going to be okay. Go help Tianna. She needs you more than I do," he whispered as he rasped then coughed.

"Dad!" Ariel exclaimed. "Alex might be able to help you."

"I know," he wheezed. "And I'll let her. After she helps Tianna, she can try to help me," Oberon insisted.

Alex looked at Ariel for guidance. "Go help Tianna. She's in worse shape than my father and dad's stubborn, he'll fight you out of principle."

Alex stood up and walked to the couch. Last time, when she healed Tanya, she had been knocked out for hours. Dimitri walked over and stood by her side. He leaned in and whispered in her ear, "Just do your best. If it works, it works. There's no pressure here. Please try not to harm yourself in the process. You scared me last time. Do you think it would help if you drank some tea before you tried to heal?"

Alex looked over at him. "Maybe. Ask Breena to bring me some, but I've been thinking about this and I have a theory. I want to try something, but I need your help."

"Anything," Dimitri answered honestly. Then he turned toward the kitchen. "Breena, I need another cup of that tea for Alex."

"Stand behind me. Put your hands on my shoulders and no matter what, don't let go. I need to feel your touch. Please try not to break contact with me," Alex warned.

Dusk

"Don't worry. I won't," Dimitri promised. "But why?"

"I'll explain later," Alex said.

She knelt down next to Tianna. "Drake, I need you to move away a little. Not too far, I just need to be able to see and reach all her injuries. I also need room for Dimitri. Maybe you could stand at the head of the couch and hold her hand," Alex suggested.

Drake hesitated, but slowly moved to the head of the couch. Alex reached out to Tianna. She had a large gash on her head. She was reminded of that night with Dimitri. She couldn't think of that right now. She had to try to help this woman. Alex put her hand on Tianna's head. She closed her eyes and tried to clear her mind. Once it was clear she focused on Tianna's wound. She tried to visualize it getting better. She'd gotten the idea from Ariel, the way she conjured fire. Maybe if she could visualize the wound sealing up, actually healing, her powers would do the rest. At first, nothing happened. She was starting to get discouraged when her hands started to feel warm. It was working!

She focused on Tianna's head wound. Her hands started to glow and Tianna's wound stopped bleeding, then the gash closed up. Alex visually searched for additional wounds. Tianna had a huge bruise on her rib cage. Alex suspected she had a couple broken ribs at least. As she completely let herself go, she could almost see the wounds as her hand brushed over each bruise or cut. The more she let herself open, the easier it was to see inside Tianna's body and know what needed to be healed. Drake's wife was bleeding internally and many of the injuries would have been life threatening without Alex there to heal them. When she couldn't find any more wounds, she stood up.

Dimitri was still there, he hadn't let go of her shoulders. He was looking at her intently. Watching to see if she was okay. They both knew what happened last time, Alex got weak and then passed out.

"I'm okay," she really was. Her theory had worked. She'd let herself go a little too much at the very end and a wave of something hit her, just for a second and made her a little dizzy. She concentrated on Dimitri's touch and it dissipated instantly. She'd waited a couple extra seconds before standing, but now she felt fine.

As Alex turned to move to Oberon she noticed Thomas standing near the doorway. Dante was at his side. She hadn't noticed them come in. Thomas's face was stern. She couldn't tell if he was angry or worried. She thought a little of both.

Dimitri realized Alex had stopped and looked over to see what she was looking at. It was Thomas. Dimitri didn't notice him come in. He and Dante must be there to report and make sure everything was okay here. He understood why Thomas looked so sober. He was concerned about Alex. Dimitri was too. Alex seemed to be okay, but he was going to watch her closely for any sign she was faking it and weaker than she was letting on. He was conflicted. Oberon desperately needed her help, but he didn't want Alex too weak to fight if they were attacked.

Alex started toward Oberon. Drake stopped her. "Tianna's still not waking up. Is she going to be okay? Can you tell me what's wrong with her?" He was still in a panic.

"Drake," Alex took his hand. "Tianna's wounds were very serious. She is terribly weak. Her body needs to shut down and focus all its energy on getting her strength back. She needs some more of that tea. The best thing you could do for her is sit right there by her side and force the tea into her. She needs a little time, but she's going to be okay. I promise." Alex let go of his hand and started toward Oberon. Drake had some injuries of his own. She would need to heal him and Orin if they were in for another fight. But Oberon needed help first.

Thomas jumped in front of her. "Alex, you can't. You're going to make yourself ill like last time. Give yourself a little break before you try again on someone new." Thomas looked at her silently pleading for cooperation.

"Thomas," Alex gave him a big bear hug. She hugged him tight, like he used to do to her. She stepped back and looked at him smiling. Thomas looked like he had calmed down a little. "Does that feel like I'm weak and in need of a break?"

"Well, no. Not really, but how?" Thomas asked, perplexed.

"I'll explain everything to you and Dimitri later. Right now I have to help this man. His injuries are serious and need immediate attention." She looked at Dimitri. "Ready?"

Dimitri sat down on the floor next to Oberon and pulled Alex onto his lap. Alex felt self-conscious and tried to move onto the floor. "Nope," Dimitri wrapped his arms around her waist. "If my touch somehow helps you do this without making yourself sick, you're staying here. I'll wrap myself around you like a cocoon if I need to."

Alex gave in. She did need to feel Dimitri's touch. Sitting here with him, his arms wrapped tightly around her, felt nice. She wouldn't forget he was there for sure. She was new at this. She would take all the precautions she could to make sure everything went okay. She really didn't want to be helpless if they needed to fight.

"Drake," Dimitri called. Drake's head shot toward them. "I need to know what is going on. Oberon's not in a position to tell me and Orin's outside with Breena guarding the house. That leaves you. I know you're upset, but I need you to tell me what happened. Give it to me in detail. Dante, Thomas and I have to know what we're up against here."

Drake paused for a moment and then began to relay the events of the evening.

Alex took Mara's hand. "Ma'am, would you mind moving over next to Ariel? It would really help me a lot if I had plenty of room to help your husband."

Alex felt a slight squeeze and then Mara let go and moved next to Ariel. She put one arm around Ariel's waist and laid her other hand on Oberon's arm. They were all connected now, a family circle.

Alex looked at Oberon. He was very weak. She needed to help him fast, but she didn't know where to start. He had so many wounds she wasn't sure which one was the most pressing. "Sir?" Alex asked to get his attention.

Oberon smiled at her. "Please, call me Oberon. Sir sounds so formal and impersonal." He was struggling to talk and his breaths were ragged.

"Okay," Alex smiled politely. "You have a lot of injuries. I was wondering if you could tell me which one was causing you the most problems. I want to heal the most serious wound first, but I don't know which one that is."

Oberon tried to inhale, but his breath came out in a wheeze. "My ribs," he finally choked out. "Lungs....hard to breathe." Oberon closed his eyes as he tried to take another breath. He was rapidly getting worse.

Alex cleared her mind and focused on Oberon's lungs. It came quicker this time. She could actually visualize the damage. Several ribs were broken and one of them had punctured his lung. He was also bleeding internally. Alex concentrated on healing his lung first, then stopped the bleeding. She then focused on his ribs. Finally the area seemed back to normal. She was going to need to pick up some of those charts of the human body to study when this was all over. She thought it would help if she actually knew what the inside should look like. It might help her heal the injuries faster.

She looked up at him. His color was a little better. "You okay?" she asked.

Oberon took a deep breath. "Much better," he confessed. "Thank you."

"We're not finished yet. What's next? Tell me where you hurt the most so I can concentrate on that area now," Alex directed.

"My leg," Oberon pointed to his right thigh. "I think you might need help with that though."

Alex removed the blanket and gasped. He had a large piece of wood protruding out of his leg.

Dimitri broke his attention away from Drake and took action immediately. "Thomas, Dante come over here now. Ariel, I need you to go get some towels. They're going to pull that object out of your father's leg. Once they do, it's going to bleed a lot. We need something to use to put pressure on it until Alex can get the bleeding to stop."

Ariel was up in an instant. Thomas and Dante were kneeling on either side of Oberon's leg. "I can't help you," Dimitri told them. "I'm not sure how this all works, but I think I'm some sort of ground for Alex. A way for her to use the energy up within the room rather than take it from inside herself."

Alex's head shot up. She tried to pivot around to look at Dimitri. "I'm not taking your energy am I? You need your strength in case we have to fight."

"No sweetheart," he said as he kissed the back of her head. "I'm fine. But I can feel the energy going through you. It's almost like an electrical current. Your theory was a good one." Ariel got back with the towels. "Okay, Thomas and Dante, you need to pull that out of his leg. Ariel, you need to be there to immediately put pressure on the wound. Alex, tell her when to move the towel so you can stop the bleeding." Dimitri snuggled in closer to Alex and whispered in her ear. "You're doing great, I think you're almost done."

Dimitri was still reeling from what Drake had told them. He was scared and angry. Radek would never get to Alex. The audacity, to think the fae would embrace a vampire as their leader. It was ludicrous. He tried to put it aside and focus on Oberon. There would be plenty of time to come up with a plan later.

Dusk

Once Oberon's leg was healed, Alex went to work on his less serious injuries. Once she was confident she'd done all she could, she pushed herself to her feet. She held out her hand to Dimitri to help him stand. "Thanks for your help. I couldn't have done that without you." She smiled at him and started toward Drake. She wanted to get him and Orin healed so they could figure out how to get out of this place. She'd only caught bits and pieces of what Drake was telling them, but she understood they were in danger here and needed to get somewhere safe.

"What are you doing?" Dimitri asked.

"I want to heal Drake and Orin. If we end up having to fight tonight, they will need to be at their best. I can't make them 100%, but I can get them pretty close," Alex smiled.

"I don't think that's a good idea. Don't push yourself Alex. You will also need to be at 100% if we end up having to fight. There's no telling how many vampires Radek will send," Dimitri was serious.

Alex turned to face Dimitri. "I know you're worried about me, but I'm fine. I don't feel like that took any of my energy at all this time. I'm still learning how to control it, but I've learned a lot tonight. I will need to learn how to do this on my own, without having to hold onto you. We both know at some point I'll need to heal someone and you won't be around."

"Do you promise it didn't take anything out of you at all?" Dimitri asked soberly.

"I promise. Let me help these guys. Once they're as good as I can get them, you can come up with a plan to get us out of here. I was thinking maybe everyone should relocate to the cabin. You know we'll be safe there," Alex offered.

"I wanted to talk to you and Thomas about that. We have three of the council members with us. That's dangerous. I was hoping you'd let us crash at the cabin until we could come up with something else. We can't split up until Oberon and Tianna are back among the living." Dimitri gave her a slight smile. "Let's go take care of Drake and Orin."

Alex healed Drake, his wounds weren't healing on their own tonight. Dimitri thought it was because he was stressed and worried about his wife. They made him drink two cups of tea and then moved on to Orin. At some point Orin and Breena had moved into the house and were standing guard at the window. Thomas and Dante were watching the windows in the back and side of the house. At first Orin refused help. He said he was good enough. Dimitri got him to change his mind after reminding Orin they might have to fight again and he needed to be in the best condition he could be.

Thomas and Dante had reported that all other council members were accounted for. They each gathered up their families and were escorted to various locations outside the city. The warriors were confident they couldn't be located tonight. They would do a more thorough evaluation in the morning once they didn't need to worry about vampire attacks.

Alex talked to Thomas and he also thought their group should move to the cabin. It was the safest place for them. They were all anxious to get out of Orin's place. They felt like they were sitting ducks. Alex and Mara took over at the windows while Dante, Thomas and Dimitri worked on developing an escape plan.

Dusk

"Dimitri?" Mara called.

Dimitri looked up. "What's wrong?"

"I think I may have seen something moving. Can you come look?" she said hesitantly.

All three warriors got up and walked to the window. At first they didn't see anything, then suddenly there was movement everywhere. "We've got company," Dante said quietly.

"Yeah," Dimitri said. "I think we've got a lot of company." He turned to the group. "Oberon?"

"Yeah?" Oberon answered.

"We might be in trouble here. I need to know how you're doing," Dimitri asked.

"Dimitri!" Ariel exclaimed. "You can't ask dad to fight in his condition."

"Not out there," Dimitri nodded toward the window. "I need to know if he's going to be okay in here, if he can protect himself and Tianna or if I need to keep a man inside."

Drake spoke up, "I won't go out there and leave my wife in here vulnerable. I can stay inside and protect Oberon and Tianna. Look at Oberon, he might be able to get one or two if they came straight at him but if more than that make it in, he's still too weak to do any good."

Dimitri studied Oberon, he did look too weak to fight. "You okay with that he asked his friend?"

"Maybe. Do you need Mara, or can she stay in here with me?" Oberon asked.

"No," Mara argued before Dimitri could say anything. "We both know Ariel's going out there to fight. You also know fighting is safer in pairs. Normally she'd be with Breena, but Breena's with Orin tonight. I'm going out there, I'll partner with Ariel. You do trust her to watch my back I assume?" she challenged her husband.

Oberon closed his eyes. How could he stand it? They wanted him to sit inside the house, wait it out in relative safety, while his wife and daughter fought for their lives.

Ariel walked over and took her father's hand. "Dad," she waited for him to look at her. "I can do this. You know I'm a good fighter," she smiled. "I was taught by the best. Mom's also a good fighter. You know that too. I know it's hard for you to stay inside while we go out there. I know you want to be there to protect mom. Let me do this for you. If you try to go out there, all you're going to do is get yourself killed."

"I don't only want to protect your mother. I can't lose either one of you," Oberon stewed.

"And we can't lose you. Anyway, you've had your fun tonight. Now it's mine and mamma's turn to kick a little ass." Ariel was grinning now. "I'm in the mood for payback!"

Oberon smiled. "You make me proud. Be careful and please take care of your mother. She's good, but she's also out of practice," Oberon sighed.

Dusk

"Okay, that's settled." Dimitri glanced out the window. There was now an army of vampires on the outskirts of the property moving in. He couldn't tell how many, but there were a lot. They were definitely going to have their hands full. "Drake, you'll stay inside with Oberon and Tianna." He turned to the rest of the room. "That leaves us with Orin, Breena, Ariel, Mara, Thomas, Dante, Alex and me. We'll stay in pairs. If you get separated, find each other. Watch each other's backs. Alex is with me." He looked at Thomas waiting for him to argue, but he didn't.

Ariel spoke up, "Mamma's with me. We know each other's moves and we're good together. Mom's got a few good tricks up her sleeve. I'm in good hands tonight." She smiled at her mother.

"Breena's with me," Orin put in.

"Thomas, that leaves you and Dante together. I need to talk to the two of you in private." Dimitri motioned to the kitchen and they left the room.

"I don't like this, but we don't have a choice. There are a lot of vampires out there. Ariel's good, so are Orin and Breena. Mara's good, but out of practice. Ariel will take care of her, but that leaves her vulnerable. We're the warriors. It's up to us to protect these guys. I don't want anyone getting inside this house. Drake's solid under normal circumstances, but he's been shaken tonight. His first priority will be his wife. Even with Drake in the house, Oberon is vulnerable. No one can get inside no matter what."

The others agreed. "Do you want us to keep an eye on Ariel and Mara?" Dante asked.

"I want to say yes, but look out there. I think we're going to have our hands full. If you see they're in trouble, yeah, go take care of them. Same with anyone else. Otherwise, let's just focus on obliterating as many of these guys as we can. Radek has to be desperate. He lost a lot of men at the council meeting. Now, he's sent all these guys here. We're gonna give his army a blow tonight. I want time, if we take out enough of these guys, they'll need time to regroup and gather more forces. You guys ready for this?" he asked.

"No," Thomas admitted bluntly. "I'll be amazed if we get out of this alive, let alone without serious injury. But let's do it." He grabbed Dimitri and pulled him into a quick hug. "By the way, congratulations. Welcome to the family and all that. I saw the ring Alex is sporting on her left finger. Not bad."

"Yeah, man. Sorry we interrupted your party tonight, but congrats." Dante put in as he slapped Dimitri on the back. "You're a lucky man. Take care of our queen. I've decided I like her."

"Yeah, me too. Let's go," Dimitri headed out the door. "Okay here's the plan, such as it is. They're coming at us from all angles. I'd prefer we all go out the front, but there's a big gathering out back. So, Thomas and Dante, I want you to head that way. Try to force them into the front yard. We're going to be safer if we can all see each other and back each other up. The rest of us will exit out the front. Orin and Ariel, both of your teams go left, Alex and I will go right. No stopping. Once you're out the door, charge hard and fast. Kill as many as you can as fast as you can. Hopefully, we'll have the element of surprise and can get a good head start. Any questions?"

He looked around the room. Nobody spoke. "Okay then, get in position and we all go on my command." Dimitri looked at Alex. "You sure you're okay?" he asked her one more time.

Dusk

"Yeah, I'm fine." She pulled her father's knife out of the sheath. "Ready," she nodded at Dimitri.

He pulled her in for a quick kiss. "Take care of yourself. I have plans for you."

"Right back at ya," she smiled at him. "Let's do this."

"Okay people, get ready we leave when I say go." Dimitri took one more look around the room and then yelled "Ready...GO!"

They burst out of the house swinging. The yard was chaos. Vampires were coming at them from all directions. Within a short time, Thomas and Dante had either killed all the vampires in the back, or had pushed them into the front yard. Alex was worried about Thomas but she also knew that out of all the pairs, Thomas and Dante were the most prepared. They did this every night.

The fight continued endlessly. There were so many vampires. Alex thought Radek must have sent all his forces to this little townhouse. She was determined to kill as many as possible. The more they took care of here, the less they'd have to deal with later. She knew Radek would have vampires trolling, turning human's into more vampires. The thought made her sick. The number of victims being torn from their homes, away from their loved ones, for Radek's selfish war was staggering. He was clearly delusional and everyone was suffering because of it.

Alex was fighting hard, but she was struggling. In order for her fighting gift to work, she had to clear her mind and rely on instinct, but she didn't want to block everything out. If someone went down, she wanted to be available to heal them so they could get back in the fight. Trying to use the conflicting gifts at the same time was proving impossible. Ultimately, she gave up and let her mind clear. There were so many vampires coming at her at the same time. She didn't have a choice. She had to operate on pure instinct. At least she could keep an eye on Dimitri. She was still amazed at what a force he was. He was so powerful and magnificent to watch. She was glad he was her partner. She had complete trust and confidence in him. They made a good team. Their intimacy allowed them to anticipate the other's movements. So far, neither one of them had been injured at all.

Mara and Ariel also worked well together. There was very little hand to hand going on between them and the vampires. Occasionally one slipped through and they'd have to take it out the hard way, but both Mara and Ariel had special gifts. Ariel, of course had fire, but Mara had ice. They stood almost back to back, neither one of them needing a stake or a knife, they had their gifts. As long as they were fast enough, they could stay a safe distance from actual danger. Ariel was fast. She swung from side to side, throwing one fire ball after another. She could only take one vampire out at a time but if one happened to slip through, she didn't mind. She fought them off by hand. Mara threw icicles, or a sort of ice dagger. With the slightest flick of her hand, she could form several icicles at once. If her aim was right, an ice dagger through the heart was as good as a stake. At first, she threw one at a time like Ariel but she was beginning to get the hang of it again. It had been a long time since she'd been on the battlefield. She was now throwing two or three at a time, taking the vampires out in groups. As Mara's confidence slowly came back, her aim also improved. She had actually relaxed a little and now she was almost having fun. As Ariel had put it, she was getting payback for what these monsters had done to her husband.

Oberon couldn't stand it. He had to know how things were going. He pulled himself up and stumbled slowly to the window.

Dusk

Looking out, he was amazed. There were so many vampires. He kept searching the yard until he finally located Mara and Ariel. His girls. They were fascinating to watch. Oberon had forgotten what a sight it was to see Mara in action. She was throwing three to four icicles at a time, groups of vampires were disappearing in an instant. Ariel was just as effective with her fire but every once in a while a vampire would get through. Ariel would take it down in hand to hand. Oberon suspected she was doing that on purpose. She would want the personal contact. She'd need to kill some of them in a fight rather than from a distance with fire. Watching her made him proud, but scared. He wished she'd be satisfied fighting at a distance, but that wasn't Ariel's style.

Drake stepped up beside him and sighed. "You know when all this started again, I was feeling a little depressed. We were at war and I was going to be sitting on the sidelines helping call the shots instead of being out there, actually fighting. I even got a little nostalgic and began to long for the fight again. After tonight, I realized I'm happy sitting on the side." He looked out at the front yard. "They are so much better at it than we are."

Oberon swung around and looked at Drake. "You don't think we were that good in our prime?" he asked.

"Oh, I think we probably were. We survived didn't we? We had to be pretty good. That scene out there used to be a frequent event," Drake sighed. "I'd hoped those days were over."

"Yeah me too," Oberon admitted. "Part of me wishes I was out there, especially since my girls are there. But I know what you mean. We held our own tonight at the council meeting, but it's a young man's game. Look at Orin, he's amazing with his sword. No one uses a sword anymore, too difficult and impractical in these

302

modern times. It's a lost talent but he makes it look so easy," he paused. "If only we could fight like the warriors. They are all so formidable. Their techniques and maneuvers put us to shame. Even on a good day, we were never that good. We're lucky to have them."

They stood there in silence watching the battle rage in front of them. Oberon finally spoke. "Have you been watching Alex?" he asked.

"Yeah, isn't she stunning?" Drake said in awe.

"Ariel told me about her. How she gets when 'she's in the zone' is the way Ariel puts it. She's so graceful but lethal all at once. Look at her move. It's like a dance, almost beautiful. Dimitri's always been a force to reckon with. The two of them together make an awesome pair." They were quiet again as they watched Alex and Dimitri. They kicked, pivoted and struck with precision. Each working on their own but also working together, taking out one vampire after another. He couldn't help but think of Dylan Montgomery, Dimitri's father and his former best friend. Oberon was proud of Dimitri and knew Dylan would be bursting with pride if he could see his son now.

"Those two would be hard to beat," Drake said as he shifted his gaze from Alex and Dimitri to Mara and Ariel. "I'd say your girls are pretty amazing as well. Mara's holding her own out there. I know it's been a long time since she's had to fight for her life, but some things you never forget. She makes it look so easy, the way she swings her arms and throws icicles all in one fluid motion. They look like daggers as they hit their mark. You have two opposing forces, fire and ice. Right now together, they are certainly holding their own. Don't worry, Oberon. Your women will be fine," Drake said confidently as he laid a reassuring hand on Oberon's forearm.

Dusk

Alex was starting to get the hang of her gifts. She had learned purely by accident that she could clear her mind for the fighting and use her gift but if she let her eyes go a little out of focus, she could see a broad picture of the whole battle field. In other words, she could clear her mind enough to fight, but still see everything going on around her. Now that she was starting to get the hang of it, it was helping her fight a lot better. She could see the vampires coming in advance.

Suddenly, off in the corner of the field, she saw Breena go down. Orin was holding the vampires off as best he could, he was magic with a sword, but Breena was definitely injured. The vampires started to swarm. At least fae blood was predictable. It always created a frenzy and the vampires attacked in hoards. Alex continued fighting, but slowly moved toward Breena. It seemed like forever, but she finally reached her. "Breena, where are you hurt?" Alex said as she helped Orin tangle with the vamps.

"One of them had a dagger. He got me in the ribs," she said in frustration. "I keep trying to suck it up and get back into the battle, but I can't stand up. There's too much pain," Breena confessed.

"Orin, can you hold them off while I try to heal her? You're going to be on your own. So if that's too much get Dimitri's attention. He can help you." Alex started to look up to try to find Dimitri, but he was already by her side.

"Alex, we're not going to be able to protect you for long. Try to heal her fast and then get back in here and help us. Do you need to hold onto my leg or something?" Dimitri asked as he swung around and killed another vampire.

Alex took a deep breath. "I'm afraid if I hold onto you, I'll hamper your ability to fight. I'll make due somehow. Breena, don't let me continue if I look like I'm getting dizzy or weak okay? If that happens, I'm going to put us all in danger."

"What if you hold onto me, use me as the ground? I don't know if that will work since you'll be focused on me and all, but it's worth a try. We need to leave Dimitri unencumbered to fight. More vampires are leaving the others and coming this way," Breena warned.

"Just do whatever you're going to do!" Orin ordered briskly. "They can smell Bree's blood from a mile away. We're getting bombarded with vampires here."

Alex quickly focused on Breena's ribs and the knife wound. As she was finishing up and scanning the area for additional damage, she realized Breena had another problem. Breena had endometriosis, the growth on her ovary was fairly large. Alex was conflicted, should she take it upon herself to heal Breena or leave it alone. As large as it was Breena had to know she was sick, but was it Alex's place to just go in and fix it? She made a snap decision and healed her. If Breena was angry at her for interfering, she'd deal with the consequences later. As Alex stood up, she felt a little off, slightly woozy, but nothing serious. She held her hand out to help Breena up then quickly rammed her knife into a vampire that had lunged for Breena's back.

Breena stood. "Thanks," she said to Alex as she quickly moved to Orin's side and picked up the fight again. The mob trying to swarm them had either dissipated once Breena's cut stopped bleeding, or Dimitri and Orin had dispatched them all while Alex was out of it.

Dusk

Dimitri was at Alex's side instantly. "Are you okay?" he asked as he whipped around and plunged his dagger into another vampire's heart. He kicked out to block another one before Alex could answer. She swung around and kicked one vampire at the same time as she plunged her knife into another one.

"Yeah a little off, but nothing serious. I'll be okay," she said as she stuck another vampire. She took a deep breath and tried to get back in her zone.

Alex was watching the battlefield. It looked like there was light at the end of the tunnel. When they started, it seemed like for every five vampires they killed ten more would join the fight. Now there were still a lot of vampires, but no additional bodies entering the front yard from the woods. She'd just finished healing Ariel. Her wound wasn't serious. She'd been fighting one vampire when another one came from behind with a machete. It caught Ariel's calf and sliced a large gash before Ariel could obliterate him. She probably would have been okay, but Alex wanted her healed just to be safe. So far, the only other injury besides Breena's was Orin. He also could have continued fighting with his wound, but Alex felt since she was there and could fix it, why leave him handicapped. Orin had been thrown into a tree and his arm was sliced by a jagged edge on one of the large branches. It wasn't serious, but the blood attracted too much attention and gave him a slight disadvantage.

She got back in her zone and conjured the battlefield in her mind. She wasn't sure how or why, but after a couple seconds Thomas' image became sharper and it was easy for her to keep track of his movement. She was startled to see how many vampires were swarming around him and Dante. Were they focused on them because they were warriors, or was there something else going on? All of a sudden she saw two vampires strike Thomas at the same time. One got him with a dagger in the stomach, the other swiped a deep gash in his left thigh. Thomas went down hard. Alex screamed Thomas' name and sprinted toward him.

She hadn't noticed Dimitri follow her but as she flung herself on the ground next to Thomas, she realized Dimitri was looming over both of them. He and Dante were in a fierce battle with the hordes of vampires surrounding them. They were shielding Alex and Thomas as best they could. Dante and Dimitri were glorious. Their strength and abilities were surreal. Ariel and Breena teased Alex about going into 'the zone' when she fought. Right now, her only thought was how much that applied to Dante and Dimitri. They were definitely in the zone on steroids. She'd never seen anything like it.

She took Thomas' hand. He was obviously weak. As she lifted his shirt, she saw how bad the stomach wound really was. This was going to take a lot of energy. She hoped she had it in her. "Don't let go of my hand, Thomas. No matter what I need you to hold me, ground me, so I can take care of this as quickly as possible. Hold on, I'm not going to lose you to these monsters." She laid her hand on his abdomen and let the power take over. Once his stomach was taken care of she quickly healed his leg. Thomas tried to stand, but he was still weak. Alex stood up and let him lean on her.

"I just need a minute and then I'll be okay," Thomas promised.

Alex moved in front of her brother. "Stand there, we'll form a circle and protect you until you're okay. Don't worry about anything Thomas, we're all here for you." Alex stepped forward to lunge into a vampire. "Did you catch that Dimitri, Dante? I've healed him, but he's still a little weak. He lost a lot of blood. He needs a minute. I thought we could form a circle around him and give him the time he needs to recuperate."

"Got it," Dante acknowledged. He had two knifes, one in each hand. He kicked one vampire as he quickly plunged each hand into two additional vampires charging his way. "If I let one of these assholes swipe me, can I take a nap too?" He flashed Thomas a quick grin. "Maybe I could just have a quick break to guzzle a brew."

Thomas laughed. "Sorry, only one man at a time, bro. Tonight, it's my turn to slack. Let me through. I want a few more minutes to pay these guys back for the discomfort I'm suffering."

Alex looked sharply at Thomas. "Didn't I get it all?" She was sure she'd healed all his injuries. "Did I miss something?" she said anxiously.

Thomas jabbed a vampire as he swung around and kicked another one into a tree. "Don't worry sis. You took good care of me. My injuries are completely healed. I'm just a little weak right now. I could use some blood. I think I'm running a little low, slight discomfort that's all." He grabbed one of the vampires and shoved him into the knife of another vamp coming at them.

"I think we're almost done here," Dimitri declared. "If we can dispose of the rest of this garbage, we can all have a beer!"

Alex took a deep breath and got back to work. In her vision of the battlefield, Thomas was still clear and bright, but a little off. She wondered if it was because he was still weak. She had a lot to learn about her gifts, but after tonight she felt like she was light years ahead of where she had been before.

The battle was finally over. Nobody knew how many vampires had been killed. Luckily, the good guys didn't lose anyone. They stood there, on their little battlefield slightly stunned. They'd killed so many vampires. It felt like eight of them against the world. Alex smiled over at Dimitri, then took a running leap and jumped into his arms. "We did it!" She shouted as Dimitri swung her around and laughed. The rest of the group gave a little whoop. Thomas and Dante did the manly handshake and then pulled each other into a hug. Mara and Ariel were holding hands and jumping around in circles laughing and yelling. Orin had pulled Breena into a big bear hug. They were just standing there holding each other quietly. Dimitri suddenly pulled Alex in for a long, hard kiss. She had her legs wrapped around him and locked behind his back. Their kiss turned deep and passionate. The group stumbled back into the house. Oberon was at the door. He immediately pulled his family into his arms. Breena and Orin were leaning against the wall, holding each other close. Tianna had awakened and Drake was sitting with her on the couch. Dimitri looked around the room.

"We got lucky tonight. Nobody has been lost yet, I'd like to keep it that way. We're going to move to a more secure location." He looked at Ariel. "We're going to the cabin."

Ariel smiled. "Good idea. We'll be safe there. It might be a little crowded, but definitely safe. I'll take mom and dad in my car. Bree knows the way. She can bring Orin, Drake and Tianna," Ariel paused.

Dimitri cut in. "We can't all go together. I don't want the vampires to be able to follow us. We'd like to keep that location a secret. Each of us will leave here and take a different route. It's what we were working on before the attack. I think we have it planned out well enough to go with it. I don't want to spend any more time here than we have to. I still don't think it's safe." He grabbed the papers off the table. "Ariel, take this map. Oberon, you look well enough to give directions. I'd like you three to leave now. Take that indirect route. Ariel once you get there, turn the alarm off on the house but make sure all the camera's and monitors are up and running. Then keep an eye on things until we get there. We all still have a few injuries, thanks to Alex they're superficial." He looked over at Alex with pride in his eyes. "Do you have enough tea at the cabin to take care of this crowd?"

"No," Alex answered immediately. "Breena, do you have ingredients we can take? I have a few but since we don't live there, I've only kept enough on hand for an injury while we were practicing. With just the three of us, we didn't need that much," Alex admitted.

"Oberon, can you get to the car okay?" Dimitri asked.

"Yes. Actually all things considered, between Alex and the tea, I feel pretty good," Oberon answered.

"Okay, the three of you need to leave. Ariel, you okay with this?" Dimitri asked.

"Yeah, I'm fine with it. I've been to the cabin a million times. I can get there just fine. I'll probably need a key though," she looked to Alex.

Thomas was at her side. "Here, use mine. If you get there and open everything up I won't need it. We think it's safe at the cabin, but we don't know what the situation is over there for sure. Be alert. If it looks like trouble drive away and call Dimitri." With that, the three of them were out the door.

"Okay, Breena have Alex help you gather up whatever you need for your tea. Do you remember how to get to the cabin?" Dimitri asked.

"Sure," she called as she was pulling things out of cupboards. "Give a map to Orin, we can get there. We can also take Drake and Tianna with us. The car's big enough to handle all four of us. The supplies can go in the trunk." She placed a box on the table.

"Can you think of anything else we might need to get us through the night? I'm not worried about tomorrow. Once it's daytime we can come back, or shop or whatever for anything else we need. I just want to get through tonight," Dimitri asked Alex.

"We might need some extra blankets or sleeping bags. We have some but with this many people we might need some additional bedding," Alex put in.

Orin ran down the hall and came back with an armload of bedding. He had two sleeping bags, several blankets and a bunch of pillows.   Dante grabbed a bunch off the top. "Lead me to your car. Let's get you guys packed. We don't have much time before you need to leave. We want things spread out, but we also don't want to wait too long between departures. The longer we stay the more danger we could be in," Dante said, following Orin to the door.

Once they got Orin and company on their way, only Alex and the warriors were left. "We better get out of here too," Dimitri warned. "I don't think I'm up to another one of those battles tonight."

"Do you want to go together or should we split up to head out?" Thomas asked.

Dusk

"Let's take both cars, leave a minute or so apart, but take the same route. We're not completely out of the woods yet. If there's trouble, I want to make sure neither one of us gets stranded out there alone. If something happens to us, you guys will have our back. If anything happens to you we'll know what route to take to find you," Dimitri decided.

"Okay you guys head out first," Dante suggested. "We'll wait about a minute, then lock up and follow."

Alex hated leaving Thomas and Dante here alone, but it was very temporary and she knew they didn't have a choice. She walked up to Thomas and put her arms around him. "Be careful big bro. You fought a good fight tonight, I don't want to have to kick your butt because you got hurt after I left," she smiled at him.

Thomas kissed her forehead. "I'll be careful, you too. Keep an eye out especially until you clear these woods. I don't trust the vampires, they could have a backup plan. I'll see you in a few at the cabin," then he pushed her toward Dimitri. "Take care of her, she's the only family I've got." Dimitri grabbed Alex's hand and they hurried to the car.

Chapter Ten

Alex was pacing the living room at the cabin. Thomas should have been here by now. She looked over at Dimitri. She could tell he was concerned too. "How long are we going to wait before we go looking for them?" she pressed. "They could be fighting for their lives out there and we're just standing around doing nothing."

Dimitri walked over and pulled her into his arms. "Dante and Thomas are good. They know how to be safe. They do this every night. Yeah, I'm a little concerned. They should have been here by now. But I'm not ready to go back out there yet. Maybe it took longer to lock up than they planned. Maybe one of them went to the bathroom first. Maybe they decided to make a quick stop for something we forgot. I'm going to give them ten more minutes, then we can go look for them. Okay?" Dimitri took her hand and led her to the chair in the corner. "Come sit over here with me. Trust me, they're not injured. I know it."

Dusk

Alex looked up at him. "You can't know that. You don't think they are but you could be wrong," she countered.

"Actually I know," he said confidently.

"How?" she questioned.

Dimitri sat down in the chair and pulled her onto his lap. He pulled her close and spoke quietly into her ear. "I know because I'm their leader. When one of my warriors gets injured, I feel it."

Alex was staring at him. "Is that true? So tonight when Thomas got hurt, you were hurting too?" she asked.

"Yes," he paused. "It's not as severe. I wasn't in the kind of pain Thomas was in. It's just a twinge, a fraction of the pain my man is feeling. Just enough for me to know when he's hurt and where he's hurt. It helps me to help my warriors," he finished. "So don't worry. None of my men are injured in any way right now. I know that for a fact. Thomas and Dante just had some kind of delay. They will be here soon."

"What if the delay takes longer than they planned? I'll be sitting here worrying the whole time. If Thomas stopped for beer, I'm going to kill him," Alex promised.

Dimitri laughed. "I doubt they stopped for beer, although I could use one about now," he paused. "I wanted to ask you something about tonight," he was watching her.

"What?" she asked.

"Well earlier, when Thomas got hurt..." Dimitri was interrupted when the door flung open and in walked Thomas and Dante. They were followed by Victor carrying a cooler.

314

Alex jumped up and ran to Thomas. She looked quickly to the cooler in Victor's hand and then back to Thomas. "You did stop for beer!" She accused. "You just got it from Victor!"

Thomas started laughing. "No, I stopped for something we needed more than beer. It's a sad day when there's something more important than beer in the cooler, isn't it?" he said glancing over at Dante.

Dante laughed. "Yeah a beer sounds pretty good right now. You don't happen to have one in the fridge do you?" He gave Alex his most charming smile.

She couldn't help it, she smiled back at him. "I think there might be a six pack in there. You'll have to share." She hugged Thomas a little longer than usual. "I was so worried about you. I was sure something bad had happened. I'd be mad at you right now, but I'm just too glad to see you," she confessed.

"Where do you want this?" Victor lifted the cooler slightly.

"Take it up to the control room. We can take turns keeping watch tonight. There are a couple beds set up in there for emergencies," Thomas directed.

Dimitri looked around the room. Nobody would even talk about going to bed until the whole group had arrived safely. Oberon and Tianna still looked beat. Breena was in the kitchen. She'd just finished pouring tea into cups and she was starting to distribute them to all the fae. She handed one to Alex. "Drink this. I think you should have at least one more before bed. You did a lot of healing tonight and even though you feel okay, you used up a lot of energy between the healing and the fighting. You need help replenishing your system."

Dusk

"Thanks," Alex took the cup. "Now that it's all over I am ready to crash. Let's figure out the sleeping arrangements so we can all get some rest." She looked at Thomas and Dimitri. "I assume someone is going to have to stay up and keep watch through those monitors in the safe room all night. Should we take shifts or how do you guys want to handle that?"

Victor spoke up. "I'll keep watch, that's why I came. You guys had a rough night tonight. Which, I wanted to talk to you about Dimitri. I think I want to lodge a formal complaint. Why is it that Thomas always gets to have all the fun? Why do you keep sending him to the hot spots and the rest of us get boring shuttle duty?" He laughed and flashed a smile at Thomas. "Next time, I'm his partner. I've been in the mood for a little action lately."

Dante laughed. "I think you get plenty of action at the club. The rest of us have to take it where we can get it."

Victor smiled a cocky grin. "Yeah, well I'm looking for a different kind of action. Too much of a good thing and all that. Three willing women or fighting hundreds of vamps? I'm not sure where the scale tips on that one. I'll have to think about it and get back to you." He turned and headed for the safe room.

Ariel was watching Victor as he left. He was hot! He was also the kind of bad boy her father would kill her for being interested in. She'd seen him once before, the night she met Alex, but she hadn't actually met him. So his name was Victor. She vaguely remembered one of the warriors getting into some big trouble awhile back. She was pretty sure it was Victor. Hadn't he been suspended for a year or something? She couldn't remember the details. She did remember it had to do with a woman though. Victor was definitely a womanizer. He was also trouble! She'd have to watch out for that one, but he was so gorgeous. He had the look of the quintessential surfer dude with a tight masculine body, bronze skin and sleek blond hair intermingled with golden highlights. Mix that with the bad boy attitude and the combination was lethal. Women must flock to him in droves. Definitely someone to avoid. So why was her heart doing cartwheels as she watched that tight body ascend the stairs?

Ariel pulled her attention away from Victor and focused on Alex. "So Queen Superstar, spill it," she demanded.

Alex was surprised and confused. "Spill what? She asked honestly baffled."

"I want to know what went on out there tonight. You told me and Bree that when you were in the zone, you had to completely clear your mind. You couldn't pay attention to anything going on around you. A meteor could fall and you wouldn't see it. Do you remember that conversation?" she demanded.

"Oh," Alex now understood where this was leading. How was she going to explain the clear picture of the battlefield she had discovered she could conjure in her head? "Yeah. I remember that conversation," she said lightly.

"So spill," Ariel demanded again. "How is it that anytime one of us got hurt, you were there in an instant to heal us? Either you weren't in the zone, which I know is a lie because I saw you fighting. Or you're hiding something," Ariel watched her intently.

Dimitri was also watching Alex. That was exactly what he'd been about to ask her before the warriors arrived.

Dusk

"Well, I'm not hiding anything. Before tonight, that was the case. I was completely oblivious to everything going on around me when I used my gift to fight. I kind of stumbled onto something else tonight accidentally. Once I practiced a little, it was pretty easy to do." Alex looked around the room. They were all looking at her, expecting her to reveal something earth shattering. She didn't think what she had to explain was that big of a deal, but she would explain so they all understood.

"And what was that?" Thomas asked.

"Well, in the beginning I was trying to do both. Get into my zone so I could fight off the vampires, but also keep track of everyone in case they needed me to heal them. It was impossible. I struggled for some time before I realized I couldn't do it. The vampires were coming so fast I just had to follow instinct and get into gear to fight," Alex paused.

"Okay," Ariel prodded.

"Every once in a while I would come out of it, the trance like state I have to go into in order to fight. I would check around and make sure nobody needed help." She paused when she saw the look Dimitri was giving her. He wasn't happy she had put herself at risk to check on everyone else. Thomas didn't look thrilled about it either. Well, things were going to get worse.

"So one time when I came out of it, one of the vamps got in a good shot to the back of my head. I thought I was going to pass out. I started to get dizzy and my eyes went out of focus. I was able to recover and pull myself together enough to start fighting again but something strange happened," she confessed.

"I remember that. It was early on and I was wondering what happened, how he'd gotten to you. I didn't realize it was because you were being reckless," Dimitri grumbled.

Alex ignored him. She didn't want to get into an argument with Dimitri over this. It was in the past and there was nothing she could do about it now. "Anyway, it's really hard to explain. You know when you watch old sitcoms and they have those really old TV sets? Usually the comedies where the picture is coming in and out so you see a flash of the picture, then you see static?"

"I think so. Where there's mostly static but every once in a while you get flashes of the show, right? Then the guy usually goes over and hits the side of the TV and the picture shows up?" Ariel asked.

"Exactly, well that was sort of what was happening to me. Things were fuzzy when I tried to see clearly. But when my eyes went out of focus for a second, before I could regain my balance, a flash of the entire battlefield popped into my mind." She paused and looked over at Orin and Breena. "Sorry that's how I thought of your front yard, as a battlefield."

"Don't worry about it. It was a battlefield earlier tonight. Hopefully from now on it will just be our front yard again," Breena said with affection.

"Anyway, finally my head cleared and I just went back to fighting but I thought maybe I would try to get the visual back. See if it was useful, you know?" she glanced at Dimitri. He didn't say anything, so she continued.

Dusk

"I remembered those pictures. You know the ones that just look like a million colored dots but if you stare at it long enough and let your eyes lose focus, a picture jumps out at you?"

Orin looked at Breena. "I love those pictures, but Breena hates them. She can never get the picture to reveal itself to her. I keep telling her it's a brain defect but she thinks it has something to do with her above normal intelligence," he smiled at her. "We decided not to debate that one."

"Well, the visions I could get sort of worked like those pictures. I can't focus on my surroundings when I'm fighting or I lose that gift so I have to kind of make it fuzzy, out of focus. Tonight when I did that, like with those pictures the battlefield suddenly jumped out at me. The picture was clear, it was subdued and grainy, almost like a bad photograph, but it was clear enough that I could see what everyone was doing. I instantly knew when someone was injured and I could hurry over to help."

Dimitri was watching Alex. "Did you know that at exactly the precise moment Thomas was injured you were calling his name?" he asked her.

Alex looked over at Dimitri. "No, but it all happened so quickly. I'm sure it probably seemed that way with everything that was going on."

"No," Thomas put in. "It was at the exact moment. At the same time I felt the pain of the knife entering my stomach, I heard you screaming my name. Then my leg was slashed," Thomas considered. He looked over at Dimitri and knew they were thinking the same thing.

Dimitri tried again. "Do you think you were seeing the battlefield, or foreseeing the future?"

Alex was about to argue, but Dimitri cut her off.

"No, just listen. I think we've already established that you, if only for the slightest fraction of a moment, can see the future when you're fighting. I think this vision thing works the same way. You see things right before they happen. It might only be a nanosecond or a millisecond, or whatever, but it's still before they happen. That's why you reacted so quickly to everyone's injuries. It's also why at the precise moment Thomas was injured, you were already reacting. It didn't just seem that way Alex. It was that way. I was standing right next to you. Remember what I told you just before Thomas got here? I know when one of my men gets injured. You reacted at the very moment Thomas was being injured, not afterwards."

Everyone in the room was silent. Alex didn't see far enough into the future to help the community, but she did see enough to help anyone in her immediate area. That fact might give them an edge in the future. It definitely didn't hurt.

Victor had returned and was sitting on the bottom step. "That's certainly an interesting development and something to ponder. We'll see how we can use it, but I think you guys need to get to bed. We have a busy day ahead of us and you all look like you could use a good night's sleep."

"Victor's right. We can discuss this further tomorrow." Dimitri looked to Thomas and Alex. "Any idea how we should divi up the rooms?"

Alex had thought about it. "I think Mara and Oberon should take the master bedroom. There's also another bedroom right next to the master. Tianna and Drake could use that one. If everyone agrees, the four of them could go up right now. Then, we'll work on dividing up the rest of the rooms between those of us that remain."

"I think you and Dimitri should have the master bedroom," Mara argued.

Dimitri answered. "No, Alex is right. You guys take the master. Go ahead and go up now. Oberon needs rest, and he needs comfort. I plan to put him to work come daylight. He's milked that injury long enough." He shot a teasing glance at Oberon.

Oberon took his wife's hand. "I'll take you up on the comfort tonight. I also plan on getting back to work tomorrow." He paused when he was standing next to Dimitri. He pulled him into a fatherly hug. "I'm so proud of you, Dimitri. I stood and watched you fight from the window tonight," tears formed in his eyes. "All I could think of was Dylan and how proud he would be if he could see you now. I think of him almost every day and wish he were still here with us."

Dimitri's eyes moistened. "Thank you," he said quietly. "Thank you for that. I hope he's proud of the man I've become. I remember what a great man he was. When in doubt I just ask myself what dad would do," he paused. "When I think of dad, I always think of you too. You were always a packaged deal. I'm thankful for the bond we share. I look up to you as much as I used to look up to my father. Thank you for always being there for me. You give me strength during these difficult times," he took a deep breath. "Now go get some rest." He smiled and put his hand on Oberon's shoulder, then gave him a little push.

Dimitri turned to Drake. "Drake, take Tianna up and get her to bed. She's doing a lot better, but she also needs all the rest she can get."

Drake stood up and put an arm around Tianna. "We'll see you in the morning," then they headed up the stairs.

"Okay," Alex said as she watched the four of them leave. "We actually have exactly enough beds, we just need to decide how to divide them up. There's one more bedroom upstairs, I was thinking Orin and Breena should take that one. Then there are two beds in the safe room, one bedroom downstairs and the couch and love seat both fold out into beds. I'm not sure the best way to divide up the rest."

"You and Dimitri should take the downstairs bedroom," Thomas decided. "That would leave me, Dante, Victor and Ariel. Two of us can stay in the safe room, the other two down here in the living room on the couch beds." He looked to the warriors and Ariel. "Any suggestions?" He was actually looking to Ariel for a solution. She was the only remaining woman in a group of men.

Victor looked to Ariel. "I'm not going to be doing much sleeping, so the two beds in the safe room are both available. Either Ariel can take one of those and you two guys can bunk down here in the living room. Or, the two of you can take the beds in the safe room and Ariel can have the living room to herself."

Dante spoke up. "Why don't we leave the living room to Ariel? Victor, Thomas and I can take the safe room. That way, we can trade off a couple times during the night. Victor can take the first shift so Thomas and I can grab some sleep. Then one of us will take over so Victor can get some sleep. We'll work out a system among ourselves."

Dusk

"We're all used to running on very little rest," Thomas agreed. "As long as we each get a few hours of shut eye, we should be okay." He looked over at Victor. "You good with that? Otherwise, you're going to be sleeping all day tomorrow when we need you to help make preparations."

"That works for me," Victor agreed. "I think we're all going to need to be alert tomorrow night. Radek might have another surprise for us once it gets dark."

Alex grabbed some bedding for Ariel. "Make yourself at home. We'll be just down the hall if you need anything." She took Dimitri's hand and everyone headed for their respective rooms.

"So," Alex asked Dimitri as they walked to their room. "I assume that was blood Victor brought in that cooler. Do you need any? Or are you okay?"

"I'm okay. I didn't get any serious wounds. My body can handle the few scrapes and bruises on its own."

* * * *

Alex and Dimitri had climbed into bed when she remembered Breena. "I'll be right back," she said to Dimitri.

He held her tighter. "Where do you think you're going now?" he asked.

"I need to talk to Breena for a minute," she admitted.

"There is nothing you could possibly have to say that can't wait until morning. I'm sure they're already in bed. They might even be celebrating our victory," he smiled. "I was just thinking we could have our own celebration."

"Dimitri!" Alex tried to sound appalled, but she was smiling. She pulled away again, but somehow Dimitri maneuvered her until she was lying underneath him.

He was staring down at her, smiling. "Yes," he said innocently.

"Oh all right," she said giving in. "I'll wait and talk to her in the morning. I just hope she doesn't get mad at me," Alex confessed.

"Why would she be mad at you?" Dimitri asked, concerned.

"I healed her without talking to her about it," Alex said.

"I know. I was there and you did talk to her about it. We were all kind of busy at the time," Dimitri said just before he pressed his mouth to hers.

Alex was still worried. It must have shown because Dimitri broke away from the kiss, rolled over and sat against the headboard. "Okay, come over here and tell me what's got you so stressed," he said with a sigh.

Alex hesitated for a minute, then sat up and turned to face him. She took a deep breath. "I feel like I violated Breena's privacy and I feel bad about it. Now I'm going to violate it again by talking to you," Alex said soberly.

"It's not a violation to talk to me. We're getting married. You're required to tell me everything," he smiled. "Come on. Let me help you," he said more seriously.

"Okay. When Breena was injured by the vampire, she did basically give me permission to help her with that wound. However once I healed her, I was looking into the immediate area trying to make sure I got everything and I saw she had another problem. She has endometriosis. Well I guess I should say I think she did and she doesn't anymore, because I decided to heal her," Alex said shamefully.

"And you think that Breena is going to be upset with you for that?" Dimitri asked baffled. "I have no idea what that disease is, but I can't imagine she'd be upset that she doesn't have it anymore."

"She probably should be. I didn't have the right to go snooping around and then just fix things. When I saw the growth, I was surprised. I'm assuming that's what she has. Obviously I'm not a doctor so I don't know for sure. I had this friend in college, Kathy. She had endometriosis and she told me a little about it. She got these growths, I guess they are basically tissue that somehow spreads throughout the body. They come from the ovaries so these lesions respond the same way a woman's menstrual cycle does. She had one on her bladder. Each month she would have internal bleeding and a lot of pain. It was almost like she had a bladder infection every month during her cycle. I felt really bad for her. I don't know about Breena, but Kathy told me she was infertile. She tried to pretend that was a good thing. She said she was grateful she wouldn't pass the disease onto a daughter. But I know she was a little sad about it, knowing she could never have children." Alex felt a little weird talking to Dimitri about women issues and menstrual cycles. He seemed okay with it though.

Dimitri was sober now. "I had no idea Breena had anything like that going on. She's not going to be mad at you, Alex. If she's been going through even part of what your friend did, she's going to be grateful to you for healing her," Dimitri paused. "I think Breena is going to be ecstatic that she no longer has to worry about that disease. Especially if she was infertile. Can you imagine how happy this is going to make not only her, but also Orin? You did a good thing tonight. Stop beating yourself up about it."

"I understand what you're saying. Really I do, but your health is personal. If she wanted me to know she had a disease, she would have told me. It was a secret. Obviously you didn't know and you guys have been friends for a very long time," Alex countered.

"True. But this is woman stuff. I can tell even you're uncomfortable talking about it with me and we couldn't be more intimate. Breena wouldn't talk to me about it, but I'd lay odds Ariel knows everything. You're in here stressing about something that may never happen. Do you really want to spend all this energy hoping Breena's not mad at you when you could be using that energy doing something more...enjoyable?" Dimitri gave her his seductive grin.

Alex couldn't help it, she laughed. She couldn't resist Dimitri, no matter how hard she tried. He was right. If Breena got mad, she got mad. Tonight they were going to celebrate! Slowly she got up and straddled his legs. "Exactly what enjoyable activity did you have in mind?"

Dimitri pulled her in close. "How about I show you?" he said as he pressed his mouth to hers.

Dusk

Alex walked into the kitchen and spotted Ariel sitting at the table drinking coffee. "Hey," she said as she walked over to pour herself a cup.

"Hey yourself," she said as she looked up. They both looked over as Breena entered the room.

"Oh, hey you guys. Any coffee left?" Breena asked.

"Sure here you go," Alex handed her the cup she'd just poured. "I'll pour me another." She got her coffee and walked over to sit at the table.

Ariel was studying her two friends. She'd known Breena long enough to know something was wrong. Alex also seemed a little off this morning. "So what's up with you two?" she asked. "Didn't get lucky last night or what? Neither did I, but I'm not gloomy like the two of you are."

"Last night wasn't the problem," Alex confessed. "This morning was."

"What's that mean?" Ariel asked.

"It means that self-righteous, over protective, ego maniac in there thinks he can tell me what I can and can't do," Alex sighed.

"Ditto," Breena added.

Ariel laughed. "You both had the same fight, or the same reaction?"

"I don't know what her fight was about, but I tried to talk to Dimitri about joining the fight. Going out with him to help sometimes. He told me... no he ordered me, to stay home. Can you believe the audacity of that man? Get this, it's his job and his duty to go out and fight every night to protect the people. It's my duty, as the queen of course, to sit home in a nice warm safe house and govern my people. I'm supposed to come up with strategies that he, of course being the mighty man, can implement. Then he just walked into the bathroom and shut me out. Like his word is final or something. Well, screw that. We're not married yet. He has no say in what I do on my time."

Ariel and Breena burst out laughing. "He actually said that?" Ariel asked. "Apparently he hit his head last night, or he has a death wish," she turned to Breena. "And you?"

"Pretty much the same thing, Orin was just a little more diplomatic about it. But same message. He's a man, therefore he can fight. I'm the helpless little woman, so I need to stay home. This conversation isn't over, not by a long shot," Breena promised. "I am going out to fight whether he likes it or not and we are married."

Alex looked over at her two friends. "So Breena, want a partner? We'll go out together, who needs them?"

Ariel took a deep breath. "You aren't going out there without me. You do know the two of you are going to get me banished from both your houses don't you? When your men find out, and rest assured they'll find out, somehow they're going to blame me. I won't be welcome in either of your homes ever again."

"You're always welcome at my house," Breena answered. "Orin wouldn't try to stop you."

"Same here," Alex put in. "Dimitri might get mad, but he won't blame you Ariel. He may be mad at you for keeping it from him though. Regardless, you won't be banished from our house."

"Okay, so the three musketeers?" Ariel asked.

"The three musketeers," Breena and Alex said at once.

They sat there in silence for a few minutes. Alex and Breena both spoke at the same time. "Can I talk to you for a minute," they laughed.

"I guess that's my cue to leave," Ariel said.

"No," Breena grabbed her hand. "I want you to stay."

"All right," Ariel said a little confused.

Alex was worried. Breena didn't seem mad, but obviously she knew she'd been healed. What did she want to say?

Breena studied Alex for a long moment. "I was wondering last night, when you healed my knife wound, did you do anything else?"

Ariel shot a look at Alex. She was curious now. Did Alex heal Breena?

Alex took a deep breath. "Yes," she said quietly and closed her eyes. "I'm sorry," she apologized.

"What? What are you sorry about?" Breena exclaimed.

"Wait!" Ariel stopped them both. "Bree, you're completely healed? All the way?"

"I think so. That's what I wanted to talk to Alex about."

"Are you mad?" Alex asked.

"No!" Breena exclaimed. "Last night I felt better than I have in months, year's maybe. Orin and I had the best sex of our lives. Why would I possibly be mad at you?"

Alex was relieved. "Well, I violated your privacy. I didn't mean to. I just healed your wound, then I was searching for anything I might have missed. You know internal bleeding or anything, and there it was. I saw the growth. I had a friend in college that had endometriosis and I assumed that's what you had, was I right?" Alex asked.

"Yes," Breena answered. "Life has been tough. Orin and I have tried to accept it. The doctor said I was infertile and the growth has caused some other problems. There are times when we can't have sex because it hurts too much. Orin's a trooper, but I know it's hard on him. Probably harder for him than it is for me. He wants to protect me, but you can't be protected from your own body. Our marriage is still strong, but our relationship has suffered because of my disease. Am I really all better? Completely better?" Breena asked.

"I think so. I can't really explain it yet but when I see something wrong, the problem looks different. Off somehow. Your ovaries, well your whole system really, was off color. That's the best way I can describe it. I could just tell it was unhealthy. I debated what to do, should I wait and ask you if you wanted my help. But then I thought, what if I got your hopes up and I couldn't help you for some reason. Wouldn't that be worse? I just made a snap decision. I was going to cure you and suffer the consequences later. I really am sorry for invading your privacy. I promise, I didn't mean to. It just happened and I reacted," Alex apologized again.

Dusk

Breena jumped up from the table and grabbed Alex into a huge hug. Then she turned to Ariel and pulled her up into a hug too. "Ariel, I'm cured. I'm really cured!" Ariel was smiling brightly.

"So I guess you really aren't upset," Alex laughed.

"Hello! The BEST sex of my life? Are you serious?" Breena said, then she heard a noise and turned to see Dimitri standing in the doorway. "Oh," she said as her face turned red. "Uh..."

Dimitri walked over and kissed Breena on the temple. "Don't be embarrassed. I'm happy for you. I told Alex you'd be ecstatic not angry," he walked over to get a cup of coffee.

"So you know about my um...problem? And that Alex fixed it?" Breena asked.

"I found out last night. Alex planned to get out of bed and talk to you immediately," he glanced at Alex. "I was able to stop her by keeping her distracted," he smiled. "From what I just heard, it's a good thing I did. It would have been a shame if you didn't get the best sex of your life. Nobody should miss out on anything that monumental," he grinned at her. "Ours was pretty good too. However, I'm not sure I can say it was the best. There was that one night when we..."

Alex interrupted. "That's enough. What Dimitri was trying to say is that with everything that was going on, I forgot to talk to you until we were all in bed. Dimitri skillfully convinced me to wait and talk to you this morning. End of conversation," she glared at Dimitri.

Dimitri looked at Ariel and Breena. "I'm sorry to interrupt, but is there any way you two could give me and Alex a minute alone?"

"Sure," Ariel said. "I want to go check on dad anyway," she got up and left the room.

Breena walked over to Alex. "I'll give you two some time, but I just want to say thank you Alex. You have no idea what you did for me. I can never repay you. I'd promise you my first born child but sorry, I want to keep it. Orin and I owe you. More than you could ever know." She gave Alex another big hug and left the room.

Dimitri looked at Alex. "I'm happy for them. What you did for her and Orin will change their lives. It will improve their lives forever. You did good," he sat his mug down on the counter. "Now. I owe you an apology," he said as he backed her up against the counter and trapped her there with his body. "I'm not really a tyrant. Yes I know, I was being 'such a man' as you put it. I over reacted," he smiled at her then kissed her nose. She was just staring at him. Her face didn't give anything away. It was completely blank.

"You're not going to make this easy for me, are you?" he asked. "That's okay. I had no right to order you to stay home. I also understand your need to participate in this war. I don't like it but I do understand," he paused as he searched her eyes. "I can also admit, to a point, I agree with you." He smiled when he saw her eyes widen. "Yes, you heard me right. I agree with you. Hiding you away would undo everything we've tried to do so far. We need to sell you to the people. You can't lock yourself up in your castle so to speak, while the community goes to war." He gave her a quick gentle kiss. "I'm sorry. It kills me to know you have to go out there.

Dusk

You have to put yourself in danger in order to prevent danger in the future. My only excuse is that I love you."

He gave her those puppy dog eyes, the ones she could never resist. "You really pissed me off, Dimitri. You can't just order me around and think I'm going to agree with whatever you say then slam the door and shut me out." Alex had already forgiven him, but he had to have limits.

"I know. But I'm forgiven, right?" He smiled at her, looking for a sign. "I'm sorry I went in the bathroom and shut you out. After I did it, I realized it was a bad idea. We're supposed to be a cohesive unit, partners. I'll try not to do that again. I know this isn't a dictatorship. It's a partnership. I also know we need to be able to talk things out. I truly am sorry." He lifted her up until she was sitting on the counter and pushed his way between her legs. "I pictured you out there fighting, then I pictured losing you and I couldn't handle it. I've never been afraid of anything I can think of, but the thought of losing you terrifies me. I didn't handle it well." He put his hands on either side of her face. "We'll find a way to compromise on this. Not today, but we'll sit down and talk about it and come up with a plan. Is that okay?" He was watching her face and saw the twinkle in her eye. "Yeah, I figured. You and the two trouble makers out there already decided to go out on your own. Didn't you?"

"Yes," Alex admitted. "Ariel was worried about upsetting you and Orin, but we decided we'd go out together. I made that decision while I was angry though. I'm not sure I could have really betrayed you like that. I think I would have at least told you what I was doing, but I still would have done it," Alex smiled. "I'm sorry too. I don't take it well when someone gives me orders, on just about anything. Just a word to the wise, you might want to avoid that in the future.

The angry monster comes out and I tend to over react myself," Alex smiled at him. Then she leaned in for a kiss. She was glad they made up. Her world just didn't feel right somehow when they were at odds.

Dimitri deepened the kiss and pulled her forward. He wanted to make love to her, but that wasn't possible. They had too many things to take care of today, he pulled back. "Are we okay now?" he asked.

"Yeah, we're okay." Alex gave him another quick kiss. "I love you." She grabbed him and pulled him in for a hug. "I love you so much. I hate it when we fight. Nothing seems right when you're mad at me."

"Me too," Dimitri admitted. He released her from the hug and gave her another long kiss. "Me too sweetheart," then he took a deep breath. "So we have a lot to do today. Victor should be getting up any time now. The warriors need to check on all the councilmen and make sure they really are safe for a while. We might need to do some shuffling. We also don't want to keep three of the councilmen together. I was thinking, if it was okay with you and Thomas, Orin and Breena could stay here for a while though."

"It's okay with me, and I'm sure Thomas won't mind. It's a perfect safe house and after that battle last night, Orin and Breena might be in the most danger from Radek," Alex said.

"I agree. I need to go talk to them about their house. I think it might be vulnerable. I thought we could move any valuables or sentimental things over here, make sure Radek doesn't destroy anything they can't replace. I'm afraid he might burn down their house or something out of anger. He's not stable," Dimitri confided.

Dusk

"Whatever they need. We also have the barn where they can store stuff. We'll take care of them. I don't want those two suffering because of what we did last night." Alex took a deep breath. "I'm going to go talk to Sam today," Alex said casually.

"Sam? Isn't that the woman at D-Tech?" Dimitri asked.

"Yeah, I had an idea. We need to separate the councilmen and keep them safe. However, who knows how long they're going to be in danger. So I was thinking, what if we set up a computer or network at each of their locations. Supply them with a computer, camera and video conferencing capabilities. The council could still conduct business without ever leaving their safe houses. Radek is probably counting on them having another meeting that he can crash. This way they don't have to meet in person, but we can still function and make decisions."

"I like it," Dimitri said. "What do you need to make it work?"

"I'm not sure. I want the best equipment possible. Top of the line stuff so the connection is clear and reliable. We'll have everything at D-Tech. That's why I want to go meet with Sam. She's a wiz and I've been out of the loop for over a year. I know whatever it takes, she can walk me through it. I'll grab all the computers and video stuff while I'm there today. Once you get the council members at their safe location, a place they can stay for a while, I'll get the computers up and running," Alex said enthusiastically. She was excited about her plan. It was going to work out perfectly, she was sure of it.

* * * *

The warriors left to check on the council members. Orin, Breena and Ariel headed over to their house to move anything important to the cabin. Drake, Tianna, Mara and Oberon all went to check on their respective houses as well. Alex headed for D-Tech. She was winding her way through the maze of the lab when she spotted just the person she was looking for. "Hey, Sam!" She called.

Sam looked her way and Alex froze. "Alex, I haven't seen you for a while. What brings you here today?" she said cheerfully.

"What happened to your face?" Alex exclaimed.

"Oh that. I'm just a klutz," Sam admitted sheepishly. "I walked into a door."

Alex didn't believe her. Sam's cheek bone was swollen and black and blue. She was still gaping. Was it possible Sam had an abusive boyfriend? Should Alex interfere, or mind her own business?

"Really, I do stuff like this all the time." Sam brushed her injuries off as insignificant. "It looks a lot worse than it really is. So, what brings you to our humble establishment today?" Sam asked.

"Why don't we go into the office? I have some things I need to run by you. There's a new project I'm working on. I have a general idea of what I want to do, but I need your help on the specifics," Alex confided.

Dusk

"Sure, I'll follow you. By the way, I've been watching John but he's behaving. I've searched everywhere for that file, but still haven't found anything. I really think Luke must have taken it home or to one of his other offices." Sam opened the door to the office and started her routine with the electronic detector.

"Thomas found a file, but it didn't have a lot in it. Either John is very careful, or dad has another file we just haven't located." They sat down and Alex explained her needs for the video conferencing.

* * * *

Radek was furious. The wounds he'd received at the council meeting were worse than he originally thought. His body was healing, but it was healing slowly. He still couldn't get out of bed. He was too weak. Hector was missing. Okay, he wasn't missing but Radek was infuriated with him anyway. Wasn't it bad enough the raid on the council members had failed? Then, those morons failed again at that poor excuse for a townhouse. He'd lost his entire army. How was that possible? Now he didn't even have Hector to order around. Lilith wasn't here to comfort him either. She was out turning vampires.

Obviously that young councilman had help. No way did a small family of fae conquer his entire army alone. Unfortunately, none of them survived to report back. Now here he was in bed, injured without an army! He let out a frustrated scream and searched for something to throw. He couldn't find anything so he slammed his leg down onto the bed, then groaned in pain. They were going to pay. Those fae had caused this pain and they were going to pay dearly!

He wanted Hector here. He needed Hector to take care of things while he was stuck in bed. Hector acted as if this was all his fault. So he deviated from the plan. Hector was taking too long. Hector had been so angry when he discovered Radek captured one of the council members and then gave him to Lilith. Maybe that had been a mistake. Lilith did kill the weakling before she obtained any information. Radek had to admit Hector would have done better. But Lilith had begged him to let her play with the creature. How could he deny her such a simple pleasure?

No, this wasn't Radek's fault. It was Hector's, he decided. If Hector had been quicker, Radek wouldn't have lost his patience and sent his entire army off to be slaughtered. Now Lilith was out trying to create a new army. That was going to take so much time, several months. Radek wanted his kingdom now. He wanted the fae to pay for his suffering. The council had signed their own death warrant the minute they attacked him. He still couldn't believe it. Those small, insignificant men thought they could take him on? They were going to suffer, but he wanted them to pay now.

How was he going to wait several months for Lilith to turn enough vampires to plan another attack? Maybe their new strategy had merit, he knew Hector was the only one that could pull it off. If he was successful... Radek's thoughts shifted. Maybe it was better to have Hector off working another angle. Radek wanted him here. He needed someone here to take care of him. But if Hector was successful, he would have the fae kingdom as well as the others. He could be patient a little longer. It was going to take several weeks of healing before he was mobile again anyway. He drifted off to sleep reveling in all that would soon be his.

Dusk

* * * *

It was early afternoon when Alex and Dimitri arrived at her house to gather some of the basics. They were going to move her other stuff into Dimitri's house later. Correction, their house. Alex was still getting used to the fact that Dimitri's wonderful house was now her home too.

They just closed the door when Thomas called to them from the Library. As Alex stepped through the doorway, she spotted Sam. Why was Sam having a meeting with Thomas? Something was up. Dimitri pushed passed her and walked to his favorite chair, Luke's chair. Alex stood there, waiting for Thomas or Sam to tell her what was going on.

"Come in and sit down Alex," Thomas called. "We have some things we need to talk about."

Alex slowly walked over to the desk and took a chair next to Sam.

"Sam hasn't been here long. I'm glad you made it back. I was just getting ready to call you and Dimitri. I think you both need to see what Sam has found," Thomas began.

Alex looked over to Sam. "Found?" she asked.

"Yes, well I guess technically you could say I stole this information from John's office. But it would probably be stupid to admit I broke into my boss's office, snooped, then stole some of his files. So I'm sticking with the story that I found them," Sam concluded.

Alex laughed. "Does this have anything to do with Corbetron and the evidence we've been searching for?" Alex asked.

"No," Thomas answered.

"But that is what I was searching for when I broke into John's office," Sam added quickly. "After you left this morning, I started thinking. You know, trying to figure out where Luke would have put any evidence he had against John. Then I started to wonder if it was possible John had gotten into Luke's office again and maybe took the evidence. Remember, I told you about the bug. John had to put it there, which means he gained access to Luke's office in the past. So why wouldn't he break in and search for any evidence against himself once Luke was dead? That's when I decided to search John's office," Sam looked over at Alex. "I know that could get me fired, but it infuriates me that John betrayed Luke and just because Luke's now dead, John acts like its business as usual. Like he never did anything wrong."

"You're not in trouble, Sam. You did take a big risk though. John's a lot bigger than you. If you had found evidence he was hiding and he caught you, who knows what a desperate man might do to keep his secret and his job," Alex warned. "I appreciate you wanting to help, but I don't want you injured in the process." She looked at Sam's face again.

"Don't worry, I could take John. He might be bigger than me but he's weak," Sam said flatly.

"Okay," Thomas interrupted. "Back to the real issue. Sam found this file in John's office." He pushed a folder toward Alex. "Dimitri, you need to come over and look at these too."

Dusk

Dimitri got up and stood behind Alex so he could view the file over her shoulder. Alex swung open the folder and gasped. On top was a picture of Luke and Thomas in an alley killing vampires. She shot a glance at Sam. "I assume you looked through this file before you brought it here?"

"Yes," Sam admitted.

"Keep going," Thomas insisted.

Alex turned to the next picture. It was a photo of Luke, Dimitri and Bastian. She wasn't familiar with the location, but again they were battling vampires. The next one was of Ty and Victor. It looked like they were at the same place, but in this photo there was an old cabin in the background. They were also fighting vampires. The next photo was of Luke, lying on the ground seriously injured. Jake was kneeling beside him, Dimitri was on his other side. Both Jake and Dimitri were also badly wounded. All three of them were covered in blood. The next photo showed Ty, Victor and Bastian. Again they were seriously wounded and covered in blood but it looked like they were on alert, watching for more vampires.

Alex couldn't stand any more. She blinked back tears. "This was the night Luke was killed, wasn't it?" she asked Dimitri.

"Yes," he said soberly. "We were outnumbered and we weren't prepared. It wasn't like the other night. For one thing, we didn't have you." He pulled up a chair and sat beside Alex. "Most of us sustained serious injuries immediately. They had the element of surprise. We walked right into a trap, an ambush. We fought them off as best we could, but Victor couldn't use his right arm. Bastian's left leg was sliced all the way to the bone. He was lucky to stand as long as he did. In addition to the temporary loss of his leg, he was also bleeding profusely. Luke was hit in the head. He

342

was hit hard. I remember watching him go down and the vampires swarm on top of him. We got them off, but he was unconscious. Jake stayed with him. He did his best to protect him, but there were so many and we were all injured. We were handicapped during the first two minutes of the battle. We think Hector trained them, prepared them and then left them to kill us all," Dimitri paused. "They came pretty close that night," he said soberly. "Somehow we all gathered our strength and worked together. We finally killed all of them, but it was pretty dicey there for a while. Luke was the only casualty that night. The rest of us eventually healed."

Sam was still sitting there, quietly. She hadn't realized this was the night Luke had died. She hadn't realized this was how Luke died. All the reports said he was attacked in an alley. After seeing these pictures, Sam had assumed Luke was attacked by vampires but she didn't know this scene was the night of his death. She was even angrier now. Those monsters had killed someone else she cared about. They had ambushed and killed a great man for no reason.

Alex looked over at Sam. She studied her for a minute. "You don't seem surprised by all of this. Why not? Do you know what's going on in these pictures?"

"Yes," Sam answered simply. "I do."

"And yet, you're not freaked out by it. You don't have questions about it?" Alex asked.

Sam took a deep breath. This family was going to have to trust her now. Trust her with their family secret. At least Luke, Thomas and Alex's fiancé Dimitri, were vampire hunters. She could trust them with her secret, couldn't she? What was it that Dimitri just said? They were at a disadvantage because Alex wasn't there? She wasn't sure what that meant, but obviously Alex was a part of this too. "My parents were killed by vampires. I've known of their existence all my life. Well as long as I can remember anyway. My mother's family was killed by vampires. Her brother and his family were killed first, then my parents and my brother, then mom's parents. I was only fifteen when I had to go live with my father's parents. More to the point, I had to hide out at my grandparents' house. Even then, I wasn't sure I was safe. For some reason, vampires seem to have a thing for my family."

They were all silent. That was unusual. Why had Sam's family been targeted by vampires? She didn't appear to have any fae in her. She seemed to be human, therefore her family would have been human. This was a strange development. One Alex was going to think about. She liked Sam a lot. If she needed protection, Alex would make sure she had it.

"Well," Alex said. "I guess that makes this a lot easier. I was worried we were going to have to do a lot of explaining to help you understand the situation. It appears you already understand, as well as we do anyway. Why do you think John had these pictures? How did he get them?" She turned to Dimitri in question.

"I would have to assume he was there that night. He must have been hiding somewhere and shot the pictures himself. We were all kind of busy and we were focused on vampires. None of us would have considered there might be a human in the area." Dimitri was clearly remembering that awful night.

"I've looked through that file," Thomas said. Just then his computer beeped. Thomas smiled at Sam. "You are a wiz. We're lucky to have you on our side."

"What were you running?" Alex asked.

"I asked Sam to do something for us that is technically illegal. So once we leave this room, it never happened." Thomas smiled as he studied the screen. "I had a theory and I think Sam just proved me right. I'm just not sure what John plans to do with these photos," Thomas added slowly, clearly perplexed.

"Well we haven't read the documents Thomas," Alex said impatiently. "I will, but in the meantime can you fill us in?"

"Sure," Thomas said. "Here's what I believe. John somehow either contacted Corbetron, or they contacted him. It doesn't really matter how that connection started, we just know it did."

"Actually we all believe it did, but we don't have proof," Alex corrected.

"We didn't have proof until I just got Sam here to hack into the phone companies files." He turned the screen around. "See that number there?" He pointed to a number about a third of the way down the page. "That number belongs to the VP of research and development at Corbetron. You can see how many times John contacted him over several months. The phone calls coincide with the start of dad's robot project."

"Why do they stop abruptly? I don't see any calls to that number after this one," Alex pointed out.

"Exactly!" Thomas declared. He pulled out another file. "Here's the file we found in dad's safe at the main office. It has Sam's memo in it detailing the suspicious activity at the lab. But look here at dad's notes, he has indicated the date Sam located the bug. The last phone call occurred the day the bug was found. Once dad found the bug and removed it, John broke contact with Corbetron."

Dusk

"That makes sense," Dimitri put in. "The bug was located so John didn't want it to be traced back to him. He broke contact and went back to business as usual, as Sam put it earlier."

"Now," Thomas pulled the first photo from the file. "Here's the part I don't understand. Two days later, John snaps this photo of me and dad in the alley fighting vamps."

"Wait," Alex interrupted. "How do you know that was two days later?"

"Because we're wearing a tux. I know exactly when dad and I got into this fight. It was on our way home from the annual charity dinner for the Sylvia Center. Two days after dad found the bug in his office." He pulled another photo from the file. It was of Luke and Jake. Again they were fighting vampires, but they were in a wooded area. "I think this was taken about one week later. Dad and Jake were checking up on another lead, trying to locate Hector. Then finally he has those photos of the ambush at the cabin where dad was killed. I don't know what he was up to though. It's pretty obvious he was following dad, but why?" Thomas asked the room in general.

Dimitri was studying the photos. "So we know John was spying for the competition. Luke finds the bug and John breaks all contact with the competitor. Then do you think he just accidentally came across the two of you fighting in the alley or do you think he deliberately followed you there?"

"Good question," Thomas considered. "I don't know the answer to that. He might have been at the charity event. I honestly don't remember. If so, he may have just happened onto us. It would be unusual for him to have a camera with him though. Especially one that expensive. It would be too big and bulky to carry around all night."

"Okay, then let's go with the theory he was deliberately following Luke. Why? What did he discover or think he knew to encourage him to follow his boss around at night?" Dimitri asked.

"I don't know for sure," Sam put in. "But I remember just before Luke died, he was spending a lot of time at D-Tech. We had the robot project going on, he was trying to find evidence on John, and he had me working on the special robot for Alex. He was in the office more frequently than normal."

"I remember that too," Thomas put in. "I just assumed it was because of the droid project."

Sam continued. "There were a couple times Luke came in with injuries. None of them were serious. It was like he was bruised or had sore muscles or something. He'd reach out to pick up a wrench or a motor and we'd all notice he was in pain, or just not as limber as usual. I specifically remember John asking him about it. He subtly quizzed Luke about how he kept getting injured. I don't know if the injuries made him suspicious enough to follow him, or if he suspected something else," Sam pondered. "Maybe John was just suspicious at first, so he started following Luke to see what he was involved in."

"Without talking to John I don't think we're going to figure out why he decided to follow dad or what he plans to do with these pictures," Thomas concluded. "Now, Sam fill them in on the rest."

Sam looked a little guilty. "Okay, but you promise I won't be in trouble?" she asked hesitantly.

Thomas laughed. "I own that company as much as Alex does. I promise we're not going to fire you."

"Okay," Sam took a deep breath. "John has been on his computer a lot lately. More than usual. I've tried to casually see what he's doing, mostly he's on the internet. Every time I go into the office he flips to his screen saver. I haven't been able to catch him through normal channels so I hacked into his computer," Sam said, looking at Alex guiltily.

Alex was amused. Sam thought she'd be in trouble for helping them. "John did that to me too. This morning after I got finished talking to you Sam, I stopped by to check in with John. He was acting funny, nervous I guess. As soon as I walked into the room he flipped the monitor to screen saver. I tried to talk to him about the lab and ongoing projects, but he really did seem nervous. He acted like he just wanted me out of his office. Now that I think about it, he also seemed a little worried or scared. I can't put my finger on it. It was all pretty strange."

Thomas flipped through the file in front of Alex looking for something. "Here," he finally said pulling out a sheet of paper. "Sam went through John's recent internet searches. She printed out a couple things of interest. Mostly he was searching for information on vampires. I assume that is in response to what he saw when he shot these photos. But the interesting thing is this," he pointed to a printout. "He was looking for private islands for sale. He also did a search for prices on accommodations in the Bahamas and Fiji. Our good friend is planning a trip. I don't remember giving him a big bonus recently. Where's the money coming from to finance an expensive getaway and a private island?"

"Would he get that kind of money if he sold his pictures to the tabloids?" Alex wondered.

"Not enough to buy an island," Dimitri answered. "Do you think he tried, or was going to try to blackmail Luke?" he asked Thomas.

"I don't think so. None of these photos make any of us look bad. In fact, just the opposite. If he went public with these, especially the ones from that last night, we'd all look like heroes. You know, the batman syndrome. The bored rich guy's out to save the world. Luke died protecting the city. You guys are all battered and bloody. This wouldn't make dad look bad. John had to know he couldn't blackmail dad with any of this," Thomas said confidently.

"Do you think he planned to blackmail you and Alex?" Sam asked Thomas. "You know, you lied to the police, the community, Luke's friends, everyone about the circumstances surrounding his death. If you want to keep it a secret, give him a private island."

"It wouldn't have worked," Alex answered. "John had to know that blackmail wouldn't work with Thomas or me any more than it would have worked with dad. I don't know what he planned to do with this, but I don't think he was going to bring it to us. Could Corbetron use it in any way?" she asked Thomas.

"I don't know how. Again, this makes us look good. Our sales would skyrocket if people thought we were out fighting monsters in the street. Like I said, it's the part I can't figure out," Thomas admitted.

Dimitri looked at his watch. "I hate to break this up, but I'm supposed to meet Ty in half an hour." He looked at Sam then looked back at Thomas and Alex. "We have to go check on that property," he said cryptically.

"Thomas, I'm going to Dimitri's." She corrected herself when Dimitri glared at her. "I'm going to grab a few basics to take over to the house. We'll be back sometime in the next few days to move the rest of my stuff out. You have the house to yourself now," she smiled.

Dimitri cleared his throat. "Thomas, can I talk to you in private for a minute?"

"Actually I need to get going," Sam put in. "I'll leave you guys here to discuss private stuff. Thanks for your time and thanks for not firing me. I know I've done a few things today that I probably shouldn't have," Sam stood. "I can find my way out. I'll let you know if I find anything else."

"Thanks again for all your help Sam but seriously, don't do anything else that might be dangerous. I don't want you getting hurt over this." Alex watched Sam leave. "I have this feeling she might be in danger. I also don't believe she walked into a door."

"I don't believe that either," Thomas admitted. "We'll keep an eye on her for the next while. I think you might be right. It makes me nervous knowing her family has been targeted so many times by vampires," Thomas looked at Dimitri. "So what did you want to talk to me about?"

"Well, Alex is moving in with me so we can start our lives together. That leaves you here alone. Most of the other warriors also live alone. I was wondering if you would consider having a few roommates for a while," Dimitri smiled at the look on Thomas' face. "I know it would be difficult, that's why I'm not ordering you to do it, I'm asking you. Next to mine, your house is the safest. Victor lives in that awful apartment, no security at all. Bastian's place isn't much better. I could go through every warrior's house and explain why it's not safe for them to stay there alone. It would just be easier and safer for everyone if you were all under one roof."

Thomas took a deep breath. "You're right, it would be safer. From your outside prospective anyway, but what if I have to kill them? What if we all kill each other? You know how we get when we spend too much time together. We're warriors. We tend to be a bit controlling and domineering," Thomas smiled.

"I'd say that's the understatement of the century!" Dimitri laughed. "You don't have to spend all your time together. Think how often you and Alex have seen each other over the past couple months. Not much, right? I just want you together at night when we're done fighting and vulnerable. Do whatever you want to during the day. Will you please just give it a try? If it doesn't work we'll figure something else out," Dimitri pled.

"Okay, but what about Marta? I won't subject her to this. That's too many men to take care of. Too many men to take advantage of her generosity."

"I'll talk to Jake," Dimitri offered. "I have no doubt he'll take care of Marta. That man is head over hills in love with that woman. If I tell him the whole clan's going to be here, he won't trust them around her. Problem solved," Dimitri said grinning.

"So you know it too?" Alex asked. "You can see how much those two love each other?"

"Of course," Dimitri said.

Dusk

"Marta doesn't see it. She doesn't think Jake feels that way about her. I told her she was being stupid but I don't think she listened," Alex confessed.

"Maybe one day they'll figure it out," Thomas added. "Okay, they can stay here. You're going to need to move Alex out soon though. We'll need all the bedrooms free."

"Thanks. I really mean it," Dimitri put a hand on Thomas' shoulder. "I owe you a big one. I know it and I won't forget it," he gave Alex a little push. "Go get your stuff, we need to leave. I can't be late to meet Ty."

Chapter Eleven

Alex was trying to situate all her stuff without invading Dimitri's space. She really wished he was here doing this with her. She wouldn't feel so intrusive if he were here. The only reason he was off the hook was because they needed to ensure the council's safety. All of them had been relocated to safe houses. Most of the warriors were centuries old. They had relatives nobody knew about. Those relatives had property. It had actually been pretty easy to find safe hideouts for all the council members that couldn't be traced back to anyone involved. Mara, Oberon, Drake and Tianna had all moved out of the cabin. Ariel decided to stay with Breena and Orin for a while. They didn't mind. Breena was thrilled and Orin was being a good sport about it too.

Alex brought a trailer load of equipment back from D-Tech this morning. It was actually going to be pretty simple to set up video conferencing in all the houses. Dimitri and Ty were going to each safe house while it was still light to check for security risks.

Dusk

They agreed to deliver computer equipment while they were there. Two birds with one stone. Alex would head out first thing in the morning and hook everything up. By the end of the day tomorrow the council could meet safely at a moment's notice.

It was starting to get late. Alex hoped Dimitri would stop by or call before the warriors met tonight to hunt. They'd gone their separate ways earlier that morning and hadn't seen much of each other all day. She was just finishing up in the bathroom when her phone rang. She quickly answered it without checking the display. She was sure it was Dimitri. "Hello?" she said anxiously.

"Is this Alex Deveraux?" The woman on the other end asked.

"It is," she said hesitantly.

"I'm calling from Secure One. You have an alarm sounding at D-Tech. Will your security personnel be responding, or do you want us to call the police?" The woman questioned.

"Um, no. I'll go check it out. Can you shut down the alarm from your location?" Alex asked.

"Yes, please call us back once everything is clear and we'll reset it. Do you have the number?" she asked.

"Yes, I have it. I'll call you once I know what's going on," Alex hung up. She glanced at her phone and called Dimitri. No answer. That was strange. Had they run into trouble? She ended that call and tried Thomas. No answer there either. Alex was now starting to worry. What should she do? She didn't dare go over by herself. It was getting dark and nobody knew what Radek was planning. He could have another attack scheduled for tonight. She picked up her phone and made another call.

"Hello," Ariel said cheerfully.

"Ariel, I'm so glad you answered. I have a problem," Alex confided. "The alarm is going off at D-Tech. I have to go over and see what's going on. We've had a lot of problems with our competitor and one of our employees. I'm worried about sabotage. I tried to call Dimitri, but he didn't answer. Neither does Thomas. Can you go with me?" Alex asked quickly. "I'm really worried about Dimitri and Thomas. It's unusual for them not to answer," she paused. "Anyway, I don't want to go out alone in case something is going on tonight but I need to secure D-Tech."

"Sure, I don't think you should be out alone tonight either. Where are you?" Ariel asked.

"I'm at Dimitri's. No correction, I'm at our house. Dimitri would smack me if he heard me say that. We decided not to wait until after the wedding to live together. I'm moving the basics in tonight. It's just so weird to refer to this as my house but I'm trying to get used to it," she said smiling.

"Your mistake is safe with me. I'll be there in fifteen. I was actually headed over to my place to pick up a few things so I'm not too far out," she confessed.

"By yourself?" Alex exclaimed.

"Don't you start too. I've already had it out with Orin and Breena," Ariel said in exasperation. "My humble home is safe. Dimitri installed the security himself. I'd know if anything had been tampered with and once inside, I'm as safe as you are now," Ariel said a little defensive. "Anyway, I'll be there in a little more than ten now and we'll head over to D-Tech."

Dusk

"I'll be waiting by the door," Alex said anxiously.

They were on their way to D-Tech. Ariel was driving. Alex was pulling up camera views on her tablet, checking different floors of D-Tech's building. "I can see five men inside. I can't tell if they are human or vampire. I think they might be vampires though. They aren't acting like a human thief. They don't look like they're trying to steal equipment or secrets." Alex took a deep breath. "What if this is a trap?"

"It might be," Ariel agreed. "If they are vamps, they're in your company for a reason. I think we still need to take care of things. Did you come prepared for vampires?"

"Yes. Once we get finished it's going to take a little longer though. I'll have to take all the security tapes and doctor them. You know, take out all the shots of us killing vampires. I don't want Shawn coming into work in the morning and seeing what my family does during their off time. Plus, there's no way I could explain you and your powers. Once I grab the discs, we'll get out of there. I can fix them at home. I don't want to be out too late in the dark. I have a bad feeling about tonight," Alex confessed.

She checked her screen one more time. "Okay, all five of them are still sticking together. Right now they're in the lab area. I've checked all the other cameras and I can't see anybody else in there. Nothing shows on the outside camera's either. I think we should still be on alert, but it looks like we only have five of them to deal with. Pull right up to the front door," Alex directed.

Ariel pulled up to the front curb and they both exited the car. The door was wide open. There was damage to the door jam, it was obviously forced. They walked in cautiously and headed for the lab. When they got to entrance of the lab area, they stopped to listen.

356

"Okay," Ariel said. "On go. We'll both go in at the same time. We need to make sure we stay together and watch each other's backs. Ready?"

"Ready," Alex nodded.

"Okay go," Ariel whispered. They rushed into the room, but nobody was there. They slowly moved around the lab, searching for intruders. There was a noise to the right. They silently moved in that direction and used a cubicle for cover as they peeked around a corner. The five vampires were standing in a group. Alex and Ariel rushed them and the fight was on. There were only five of them, so between Alex and Ariel it was over pretty quickly. Ariel saw a small device on the floor and leaned down to pick it up. It looked like something electronic. "What's this?" she asked, holding it out to Alex.

Alex took it, silently studying the device for a minute. "It's Luke's bug detector. Where'd you find it?" Alex asked.

"One of the vampires had it," Ariel supplied. "I've never seen anything like it before so I wondered what it was," she confessed.

"I'm curious to see if they brought it with them or if it was left here," Alex said deep in thought. "It's been missing ever since Luke was killed. Thomas and I have searched everywhere for it without luck. I wonder if the vampires had it all this time or if John had it," Alex looked around. "It looks like we got them all. I need to gather up the security discs and then we can head out."

"Anything I can do to help?" Ariel asked.

Dusk

"No. Just keep an eye out for more vampires and warn me if you think we have company," Alex said absently as she pulled discs from a security room.

In no time they were back in the car. "That was just weird," Alex said to Ariel. "Is there something I'm missing? They weren't trying to steal anything that I could see. They were just hanging out, like they were waiting for us to show up."

"Maybe they were waiting for you. It looked like we caught them by surprise. Maybe they thought you would go by yourself and they planned to kidnap you and take you back to Radek. They weren't new vampires. All five of them were old and experienced. Radek can't have many of those left after so many battles in such a short time," Ariel pondered. Suddenly, she slammed on her brakes. She was alert and focused on a thin roadway that led behind a strip of businesses.

"What?" Alex asked.

"There are vampires down there. I also heard voices." Ariel parked her car and tried to listen.

Suddenly Alex's cell phone rang and both of them jumped. She frantically pushed the button in an attempt to stop the ringing. "Hello?" she answered.

"Where are you?" Dimitri demanded. "I got home expecting you to be here and the house was empty. I thought we agreed you wouldn't go anywhere tonight. We don't know what Radek has planned." Dimitri was clearly angry and worried.

"Dimitri, I didn't plan to leave. I got a phone call from the security company telling me someone broke into D-Tech. I tried to call you, but you didn't answer. Thomas didn't either. Are both of you okay?"

"We're fine," Dimitri answered.

"When I couldn't get a hold of you guys, I called Ariel. She came with me to secure the building. We just finished." Alex was relieved Thomas and Dimitri were both okay.

"Where are you now?" Dimitri asked. "And what happened at D-Tech to set off the alarm?"

"We're just a little down the road from D-Tech, about four blocks west. Ariel heard something. She thinks there's vampires down the small roadway between Starbucks and that Italian Restaurant. Everything is okay at D-Tech, but a little weird. Five vampires broke in and were just hanging out in the lab. We took them by surprise. We didn't have any trouble, but it all seems strange to me. I still don't know what's going on. I pulled the security tapes. I want to go through them once I get home," Alex paused and Ariel grabbed her phone.

"Dimitri, there is definitely something going on down this roadway. I know there are vampires down there and I can hear voices. Alex and I are going to sneak down and see what's going on." Ariel handed the phone back to Alex. "Say goodbye, we need to go." She slowly opened her door and got out.

"Dimitri, I've got to go. Ariel is already headed down the road. I need to catch up," Alex started to hang up.

"No you don't!" Dimitri demanded. "Alex! I want you to wait, Victor should be close by. I'll send him your way. Wait for him to get there."

Dusk

"I can't wait. I need to help Ariel. She'll need me if there are too many vampires. Call Victor and get him over here, soon. I love you. I'll call you back when I can." She hung up the phone, opened the door and silently slid into the night leaving her cell phone on the front seat.

Alex caught up with Ariel at the end of the road. It made a T-intersection, but the connecting road was just as small as the alleyway. It looked like it was used for small deliveries. Ariel was hiding in the shadows, peeking around the corner of a building. As Alex approached, she turned and held her finger to her lips. Alex slid in beside Ariel and studied the scene before her.

John Anderson was talking to a woman. No, Alex thought, it was a vampire. He was frantically trying to reason with her. The woman had an evil grin on her face. Alex heard her tell John he was no longer useful to her and then suddenly, she grabbed his neck, twisted, then just dropped him to the ground. Alex had to hold her hand over her mouth to stop herself from making a noise. She couldn't believe what she just saw. John was dead. There was a file folder lying on the ground, pictures spread out around him. So this is what John planned to do with those photos. Was he trying to blackmail the vampires? Oh, John! How could he think he could reason with vampires after all he had seen while he was following Luke? Alex wondered who this woman was.

She watched as a large group of vampires surrounded John. Were they going to feed on him now? Alex was disgusted. She started to look away, but then out of nowhere she saw an arrow fly into one of the vampires. One after another arrows struck the feeding horde and they vanished. Alex and Ariel immediately began to search the roof tops. Alex froze. No it couldn't be, but it was. Sam was standing on the roof of a nearby building. She was dressed in black, it looked like leather and she was quickly shooting one arrow after another at the group of vampires. What did she think she was doing? She was human. She was going to get herself killed.

The woman started to scream. At first Alex thought maybe she'd been hit by one of the arrows, but then she realized she was screaming in frustration. She was throwing a tantrum. Sam kept flinging arrows. Alex had to admit, she had great aim. The woman, face distorted in anger, was hiding behind the other vampires. Typical bully, when the going got tough the coward inside always showed. The woman was giving orders for the vampires to attack Sam. Alex looked at Ariel. "I know her. I have to help her. Are you up for a fight?"

"Absolutely!" Ariel said with a smile. "Let's go in hard and fast, the same as at the cabin. Most of these vampires look like they're young, newly turned within the last month I'd guess. They're not very coordinated, but they are strong. A lot stronger than the older ones. Be careful!"

They ran into the opening and started to fight. These vampires were strong. Alex was shocked. She kicked one, then pivoted to avoid another when she was struck in the side by a third vampire. It threw her several feet across the roadway. She cleared her mind and got back into the fight. Sam was still flinging arrows. Alex hoped she kept up the good aim. The last thing she wanted to deal with was an arrow protruding from any part of her body or Ariel's. No way could Alex take time to heal anyone right now.

She ducked to avoid another blow and swung around to plunge her knife into another vampire's chest. Out of the corner of her eye, she saw the woman vampire climbing a ladder. She was almost to the rooftop. Sam was in trouble. Alex looked around her. There

Dusk

were so many vampires. What should she do? Could Ariel hold her own down here? She knew Sam couldn't survive once the woman reached her. "Ariel?" Alex yelled.

"Yeah?" Ariel answered.

"Sam's in trouble," she angled her head toward the rooftop. "Do you think you can handle things down here if I go up and help her?"

"Yeah, I've got it. Go, she needs your help." Ariel wasn't at all sure she could handle this many newly turned vampires alone, but she was certain Sam couldn't handle the woman. If Alex didn't help her she would be dead too, just like the guy lying on the ground.

Sam spotted Lilith too late. She tried to turn and shoot her with an arrow, but she missed the heart. The arrow lodged in her shoulder. Lilith screamed.

"You're going to pay for that," she yelled.

Sam held onto an arrow and charged. She'd fought vampires hand to hand before. She was going to have to do it again tonight. She just hoped she'd survive. It made her nervous to get this close to a vampire while she was so high off the ground. She could very easily get thrown off the roof and it was a long way down. Lilith blocked the arrow and pivoted. She tried to kick Sam, but missed. Sam had seen it coming and turned just in time. On her way passed, Sam shoved the arrow into Lilith's leg. Lilith screamed in agony. Suddenly, she rushed Sam and shoved her hard. Sam flew into the side of the brick fireplace and crumpled to the ground. At least she hadn't been thrown off the roof, but she hit her head on the brick pretty hard.

Sam was trying to get to her bag. She had a thermos of holy water inside. She knew it wouldn't kill the vampire, but it would burn her. It might give her enough time to get to another arrow. Sam tried to slide toward the bag, but Lilith slammed her foot down on Sam's calf. The pain was excruciating. She was certain she'd broken a bone. Sam was running out of options. How was she going to get out of this? Then, suddenly Lilith was thrown across the rooftop. She was laid out flat, sprawled on her stomach. That's when Sam noticed Alex walking toward Lilith, knife in hand. Maybe she could get to her bag. If Alex just kept Lilith busy for a couple minutes, Sam could get back into the fight and help. It was going to have to be soon though. Sam was dizzy. She was going to pass out very shortly.

Alex walked toward Lilith. She knew she hadn't thrown her hard enough to cause serious damage. Lilith was faking, waiting for Alex to get close so she could attack. That's okay, Alex was prepared. She walked right up, pretending like she didn't expect a thing. As Lilith swung her arm, Alex saw the large knife. So, this might be challenging after all. Alex pivoted and kicked Lilith in the arm. Lilith started to drop the knife, but at the last minute she was able to hold onto it. She jumped to her feet and the fight was on.

Alex was in her zone, but Lilith was good. She'd never fought a vampire as good as this one. She must be very old and skilled. She wanted to check on Sam, but all her attention had to be on the fight. Things were going so fast, she couldn't even try to use her seeing power to check on Sam and Ariel. Lilith swung around and struck Alex in the arm. The knife wound stung, but Alex could tell it instantly began to heal. She kicked out and sent Lilith flying. She had just a second to check on Ariel and see she was in trouble.

Dusk

Ariel was fighting for her life. There were so many vampires. She was just starting to get discouraged when she heard the roar of a motorcycle. Hopefully help had just arrived. She was so busy, she couldn't even look to see who it was. She kicked out and caught a vampire in the side at the same time she threw a fireball into the chest of another one. One got by and punched her in the side. She lost her balance and started to go down when two strong hands caught her.

"Need a little help?" Victor asked as he steadied Ariel until she got her footing.

Ariel threw two more fireballs, one after the other. "Thanks, I wondered who was going to win this battle. I was starting to get behind," she confessed.

Victor kicked out and a vampire flew across the road into the brick building. Ariel noticed he was holding a medieval dagger in his right hand and in his left, he had some kind of metal star with extremely sharp edges. It looked like some sort of ninja star. With the flick of his wrist two of them went flying. They struck the vampires directly in the chest and both disappeared. Ariel was impressed. She'd never seen anything like it before. Victor reached into a pouch and pulled out more stars. He was a talented fighter. She knew all the warriors were, but Victor looked like a sexy angel of death all decked out in leather and bad attitude. She marveled again at the thrill she felt just watching him work. Too bad she couldn't enjoy the show. She had to fight for her life. She threw another fireball, then swung around and kicked to block the knife coming at her from behind.

Alex saw Victor arrive. She was so relieved. Ariel would be okay now. She needed to check on Sam, but couldn't. Lilith had gotten up and was running toward her, knife flailing. Alex planted her feet and prepared for the attack. She twisted at the last minute and tried to plunge her knife into Lilith's chest. She hit metal. "So you must be one of Radek's favorites. You have body armor too," Alex prompted. She still wanted to know who this woman was, she was obviously old and close to Radek.

"I'm more than Radek's favorite. He loves me," Lilith laughed. "You think you have the upper hand, but wait until the others arrive. Right now, you're barely holding your own. When the others realize you aren't coming, they'll immediately come here and we'll capture you." Lilith was gloating.

"Oh?" Alex said absently as she blocked another swing from Lilith then swung around and kicked her in the face. "Who would that be?"

Lilith screamed in frustration. "Those vampires down there are young. They're strong, but not coordinated. We knew you'd go to that building as soon as they broke in. John told us if the alarm was set off, you'd go there yourself. You'd need to make sure your precious lab was okay. Once they get here, you're dead!" Lilith screamed.

Alex smiled. "I hate to burst your bubble," Alex ducked a punch and shoved Lilith away. "But if you're trying to hold out for those five vampires you sent to the lab, you're in for a disappointment. They're dead. Really, look around you. You only sent five guys to do the job and expected them to succeed?" Alex taunted.

"You're lying!" Lilith screamed. "You couldn't have killed them. I need them. They're the only seasoned vampires we had left to help me fight!" Lilith seemed to realize she'd just given away a secret.

"Really? I guess Radek and Hector underestimated us then. It's going to be difficult to fight a war without an army," Alex said not letting the subject drop. "Boy is he going to be pissed when he finds out you've gone and gotten his last remaining vampires killed. And the new guys are toast, too." Alex was trying to sound casual, but Lilith was out of control. She was so angry, she was a mad woman. Alex had to concentrate on her defensive moves, she didn't want Lilith to get in too many shots with that knife.

"It doesn't matter. Hector's plan will succeed. We still have a few tricks, things to experiment with. Once Hector gets back with the others, we won't need to create our own army. We won't have to wait for the new vampires to turn," Lilith had regained her composure. "Once I've captured you Radek will let me play with you, like he gave me that weakling Dahl. I'm going to have more fun with you though. I owe you for tonight!" Lilith sneered. "I'll just leave out the lemon juice. That way I'll have weeks, maybe months with you."

So, this was the one that tortured Dahl. Was she Radek's wife, girlfriend or what? "Lemon juice?" Alex questioned. "Oh, you think the lemon juice killed Dahl?" Alex forced a laugh. "Good," she tried to say it under her breath but also make sure Lilith heard her. "We were worried you knew our secret. The council will be so relieved when I tell them you think lemon juice killed Dahl," Alex prodded.

"It was the lemon juice. It had to be. What else could it have been?" Lilith sounded unsure.

"Yeah, like I'd tell you that. You're right," Alex said casually. "It was the lemon juice. You've figured it out. You're so smart. Radek will be pleased. Maybe he'll give you a treat," Alex paused.

"You're lying!" Lilith actually stomped her foot. "I'll prove it once I get to play with you."

"I doubt Radek will let you play with me as you put it. He'll want that pleasure himself," Alex said soberly.

Lilith burst out laughing. More of a cackle really. "Radek will give me anything I want. He loves me. He's the king and I'm his queen. Together we're going to rule the world."

Lilith's eyes went hard and cold. Alex realized this woman was as sadistic and crazy as Radek was. Enough of this nonsense, she needed to find a way to get to Lilith's heart. Maybe if she plunged her knife above the ribs the blade might be long enough to reach the heart that way. The problem was she didn't know anything about vampire anatomy. Were they the same as a human or did something shift when they were turned? She had to try. Alex allowed Lilith to strike her arm with the knife. As Lilith flew by, Alex plunged her knife into Lilith's side. It was a good wound, but not a lethal one.

Lilith went down just for an instant, then she pushed off from a crouch and flew at Alex. Alex planted her feet, grabbed Lilith's arms and flung her toward the wall. She landed right next to Sam. When had Sam moved over there? This wasn't good. Lilith could kill her in an instant just like John. Alex started to run toward Lilith in a panic when Sam suddenly flung a thermos of liquid at the vampire. Lilith tried to turn, but the clear liquid saturated part of her face, neck, upper chest and arm. Lilith howled in agony. Alex saw an arrow lying on the ground, the tip was covered in the liquid

Dusk

Sam had just thrown. She grabbed the arrow and shoved it into Lilith's stomach. It wouldn't be lethal, but it was clearly painful.

Lilith was up immediately. She flew down the ladder and disappeared into the night. Alex started to go after her but stopped. She looked down at Ariel and Victor. They were almost finished with the vampires below. She decided to let Lilith go. She had to be in pretty bad shape and Sam needed help. Alex crouched down to get a better look. Sam had a broken leg and three broken ribs. She had passed out again and had a big goose egg on the back of her head.

Alex moved behind Sam, securing her body beneath her arms and drug her carefully to the side of the building. The vampires were gone. Victor was tying a bandana around Ariel's arm. She must have been injured. "Hey you two," Alex called down.

They both looked up at her and smiled. "Yeah," Victor called up.

"I need some help here. Sam is unconscious. She also has a broken leg and broken ribs. I can't get her off this roof by myself."

"Grab her hands and lower her down as much as you can. Then drop her," Victor said. He laughed at the stunned look on Alex's face. "Don't worry, I'll catch her."

"Are you sure?" she asked hesitantly.

"Positive, trust me." Victor walked over to the side of the building.

Alex was nervous about it, but she couldn't think of a better plan. She turned Sam onto her stomach then slowly lowered her

368

over the side of the building. Holding Sam's hands, Alex laid down on her stomach and then lowered Sam until she was dangling above Victor's head. "Ready?" she called.

"Drop her," Victor called up.

Alex let go and Victor expertly caught Sam in his arms. He did it so smoothly, like he caught falling women every day. Alex stood to gather up Sam's things.

"Hurry up Alex. We're sitting ducks down here. We need to get you guys to the car and on your way," Victor said impatiently.

Alex ran to the ladder. She was barely able to juggle Sam's bag and weapon as she scuttled down. She hit the ground running and grabbed Ariel's hand. "Come on, let's go. I assume you're okay carrying Sam?" she asked Victor over her shoulder.

"Yeah. I got her," Victor said casually.

As they exited the alley, Alex saw Dimitri running toward them. He flew to Alex and pulled her into his arms. "Are you okay?" he said clearly worried.

"I'm okay. Really, baby I'm fine. Let's get out of here. We were going to head over to Thomas', is that okay with you?" she asked.

"Yeah, it's fine. The rest of the warriors are there and you can tell me what happened tonight. What happened to her?" he signaled to Sam.

"She got injured in the fight." Alex opened the back door of Ariel's car so Victor could lay Sam on the seat.

Dusk

Ariel got into the passenger seat. "Alex, can you drive? My arm is killing me."

Alex started to get into the car, but remembered the pictures. "I need a minute," Alex said as she turned back toward the alley.

"Why?" Victor asked impatiently.

"I need to get the file and all the pictures. We can't leave them lying around," Alex insisted.

Victor handed her the file. "Now, get home."

Dimitri leaned in through the open door. "We need to get to the house before more of these guys show up. Ariel's blood will attract every vampire around for miles. Victor will go first, you follow his bike. I'll take up the rear." He shut the door and turned to Victor. "You okay with that plan?"

"Yeah, works for me." He strolled to his Harley and pulled in front of Ariel's car. Then, they all pulled out and headed for home.

* * * *

The group sat in the library at the Deveraux mansion. Alex had healed Ariel and Sam. Sam was upstairs in one of the guest rooms. She was still unconscious, but nobody was really worried. They figured she just needed rest. Alex, Ariel and Victor had filled the rest of the group in on the night's activities. Alex and Ariel were drinking tea, the warriors were all drinking beer.

"We'll need to watch the video from the lab but I think we already have a pretty clear picture of what went on there from the conversation Alex had with Lilith," Thomas finally said. "Shawn is going to freak out when he gets to work tomorrow and all the recordings are missing. Rather than trying to alter them, I think maybe we should just keep them. We'll pretend like the guys that broke in took them when they left." He looked over at Alex. "Do you agree?"

"Yes," she said. "I'm also curious to see if the vampires had the electronic detector or if John left it there. Can you believe how stupid he was? He thought he could what? Blackmail vampires? He should have known better after everything he witnessed following dad around. I am sorry he was killed though. It was awful to witness," Alex sighed.

Dimitri pulled her closer. He was grateful she was okay. He'd been so worried about her. That frantic drive from his house to the alley was the longest, worst drive of his life. "We actually found out a lot tonight, thanks to Alex." He smiled down at her. They were sitting on the couch, Dimitri's arm resting across her shoulders, Alex resting her head on his shoulder. "Knowing their army is depleted gives us time. That doesn't mean we're in the clear, but it gives us time to plan and prepare for the inevitable attack. I was hoping we'd take out enough vampires at Orin's to give us some prep time, but we got lucky. This gives us even more time than I'd hoped for. They're going to be hurting, literally and figuratively I think, for several weeks." He looked at each of the warriors. "Everyone go home, get some rest. I think we've earned the break. They won't attack again tonight. They've lost too many vampires over the last few days."

"A little time will be nice. I know I didn't convince Lilith the lemon juice didn't kill Dahl. I thought if I could make her doubt, even if it was just a little, maybe they wouldn't be so quick to use it again. I just hope it doesn't backfire on us." Alex still wasn't sure she'd done the right thing.

They were all silent for a minute. Thomas finally spoke up. "I guess only time will tell. Whatever happens, we'll deal with it. Don't worry sis, it's not going to make things worse. It might even save someone. You have to look at it that way. They were already killing people with lemon juice. Maybe what you did will give someone more time. Time for us to help them."

Everyone else in the room agreed.

Dimitri stood and held out his hand to Alex. "We're heading home. Call me if you need anything." Alex stood and they slowly walked out the door.

* * * *

Alex spent the next day setting up computer equipment at each of the safe houses. She initially thought it would take a couple days, but she was just finishing up with the last one when Dimitri walked in.

"You about ready?" he asked. "It's getting late. I'm tired and I really want to go home," he smiled at her.

"Give me five minutes to explain how it works to Tighe and we're out of here." she smiled back. "I'm tired too. I just want to go home and put my feet up."

An hour later they walked through the front door of their home. Alex smiled. It felt so good to be here with Dimitri. To think of this as their home, the place they were going to start their lives

together.   Dimitri led Alex into the big family room and directed
her to the comfortable couch. He slid out the recliner then grabbed
the small blanket draped over the back of the sofa and covered her
with it. "You just sit there and relax. I'll be right back." He leaned
down and kissed her gently then walked out the door.

Alex was so tired. It had been a long day on the back of several
long nights. She wondered where Dimitri had gone, but she was too
tired to get back up and follow him. She flipped on the big screen
TV and settled in for a relaxing evening, just her and the tube.

Dimitri returned with a small rectangle box in one hand and a
big bowl of popcorn in the other. It smelled wonderful. He set the
bowl on the coffee table in front of the couch and walked over to the
entertainment center. "Chick flick or action?" he asked with a
grimace.

Alex could tell he was hoping she wouldn't say chick flick, too
bad. She wasn't in the mood for any more action. She wanted a
night without any fighting if that was possible. "Chick flick," she
said with a huge grin.

Dimitri sighed. "Only because I love you. Next time I get to
pick." He inserted a disc and grabbed the remote. Once he settled
in next to her, Alex reached for the bowl of popcorn. "Not yet,"
Dimitri grabbed her hand. "I have something I want to give you
first."

Alex glanced at the small box. She wondered what was in it.
It could be a bracelet, or a necklace. What was the occasion? Why
was he giving her a present? She looked at him in anticipation.

Dimitri smiled. "I was thinking about your healing. Your
theory about needing a ground was a good one. Obviously it worked

for you to hold onto me. At first I thought you needed that physical ground, but now I have a different theory. The healing comes from your head. I know it travels through your hand, but the initial trigger comes from your mind. Are you following me?"

"I think so. I have to think about wanting to heal, then the energy travels through my hand to do the actual healing," Alex supplied.

"Right. I watched you heal Tianna then Oberon and I thought you actually needed someone to ground you, physically. Then, Breena got hurt and you were able to use her as the ground. The same with Ariel and Thomas. I have a new theory. I think you just need an emotional ground. Someone you care about. Or something that helps you hold onto someone you care about," Dimitri smiled at her.

"Hum, I think I'm following you. We've already talked about Tanya. She was easy to heal because she was so open. You think I was wiped out because I didn't have an emotional attachment to her anymore," Alex asked.

"I do," Dimitri nodded. "You didn't have an emotional attachment to Tianna or Oberon either. I created that ground. But when you healed Breena you didn't need me because you do have an attachment to her. You have a closer and stronger relationship with Ariel. Thomas was the strongest. I don't think I've seen two siblings that are closer than the two of you. You didn't need any help with Thomas. His wounds were severe, but your connection is so powerful you didn't need help with him either."

Alex hadn't considered this angle, but it seemed plausible. She wasn't sure what Dimitri was leading up to. If his theory was correct, she didn't need him with her at all times. She just needed someone she cared about. Still, sometimes she had to go out alone. It didn't solve her problem.

Dimitri held out the box. "So I thought if you had something special, something that could help you think of someone you love, maybe you wouldn't need a human ground." He pulled the lid off the top. Inside was a beautiful gold locket. The outside was covered with intricate and delicate engraving.

"Dimitri, it's beautiful!" Alex exclaimed. She looked him in the eye. "So you thought if I had a beautiful locket that I could put something special in, it might be enough of a ground that I wouldn't need constant companionship?"

"Not exactly. I hope you still need my constant companionship," he said smiling at her. "I thought maybe this locket would provide you with the emotional ground you need to protect yourself while you're healing. Regardless of who is there with you." He picked the necklace up and held it out to her. "I know I already gave you my mother's wedding ring, and I promise every piece of jewelry I give you won't be a hand-me-down. Mom always loved this locket, her mother gave it to her. It was the first thing I thought of when the idea hit me. I thought it would be perfect."

Alex leaned in and kissed him. She was touched. "Thank you," she said quietly.

"Open it," Dimitri urged.

Alex took the locket from Dimitri and gently opened the clasp. Tears filled her eyes. Dimitri had placed a tiny engraved picture of her mother and father inside. It was so detailed and intricate just like the outside. She loved it. She looked up at Dimitri as one tear slid from the corner of her eye. "It's perfect," she smiled at him.

Dimitri brushed the tear away with his finger. "Maybe one day you can put a picture of our kids or something on the other side. A good friend of mine did the engraving for me. I owe him. He's usually fast, but he did this for me in just a couple days. The likeness of Luke and Marlena is amazing, isn't it?"

"It is. It looks just like them," Alex agreed. "But do you think he could do me one more favor?" Alex asked.

"I'm sure he would. What do you want?" Dimitri asked.

"Maybe someday we'll have kids that I can add to this locket but for me it would be perfect if I had an engraving of you on the other side," Alex said quietly. "It would make me feel like you are always with me. It would give me comfort at night when you have to go out and hunt."

Dimitri hugged Alex tightly. The emotion she could stir in him was staggering. That simple request touched him so deeply, he could barely breathe. "I'll call him tomorrow," Dimitri promised. His voice a little husky from emotion. He leaned in and kissed the side of her head.

Alex leaned back and placed her hands on either side of Dimitri's face. "That is the most beautiful gift anyone has ever given me. I will cherish it forever. Thank you," she leaned in and kissed him gently. "I love you," she took a deep breath. "How long do we have before you need to go out tonight?" she asked. "Do we still have time for the movie?"

"Plenty. I've implemented a new schedule," Dimitri admitted sitting back and relaxing. "We've all been so busy lately, none of us have gotten enough sleep. Even before those recent battles, we were pushing it. We've been hunting every night, chasing violent groups of vampires. I'm confident things are going to settle down for a while. For the next couple weeks at least, we are on a rotating schedule. Thomas, Dante and Nick are going out tonight, the rest of us have the night off. If they come across trouble, they can always call for backup. Tomorrow night myself, Victor, Bastian and Ty will hunt. Thomas, Dante and Nick will have the night off."

Alex jumped into Dimitri's lap. "Really? I really get every other night with you?" She was so happy. Maybe it was only for a couple weeks, but she needed down time. She needed time with Dimitri.

"Really! You're all mine for the entire evening." He brushed her hair away from her face. "So I thought we could relax with popcorn and a movie. Then if I'm still awake, maybe I'll show you just how happy I am to have the whole night alone with you." He smiled and pulled her down for a seductive kiss. "Maybe we should just skip the movie and get right to the happy part of the evening," Dimitri said as he slid his hands under her shirt to caress her back.

"Nope, I get my chick flick. I want to see if you cry at the end." She climbed off him and sat back down on the couch. She picked the locket up and clicked it shut. It was so beautiful, she started to study the design more closely. When she flipped it over, she noticed an inscription on the back. It said 'A ghrá mo chroí.' "What's this say?" she asked Dimitri? "I'm not familiar with that language."

Dusk

Dimitri rubbed his thumb over the letters. "I asked Ryan to engrave that on the back for me. It's Gaelic. A ghrá means my love. A ghrá mo chroí means love of my heart, or my hearts beloved." He locked eyes with Alex. "You are my love, my only love. You're the love of my life. You will always be my hearts beloved." He let go of the locket and watched Alex run her finger over the inscription like he had. "I thought inscribing it in Gaelic might give it a little extra power. The old legends and myths describe the Gaelic language as powerful, maybe even magical. I wanted to give you every advantage I could. It can't hurt. Or maybe I'm just a little too superstitious," Dimitri said feeling self-conscious.

Alex took Dimitri's hand in hers. "A ghrá, I like it," she smiled. "If this locket isn't enough to provide me with an emotional ground, nothing can." She gently set it on the table in front of them. As she turned around she pushed on Dimitri's chest until he was lying on his back, then she climbed on top of him and kissed him passionately. "I changed my mind," she said a little breathless as she looked down at him. "I think the movie can wait. Right now I'm going to demonstrate just how much I love and appreciate my gift and the man who gave it to me."

Dimitri laughed and pulled her back down for another kiss. "Umm," he groaned. "I like that idea." He slid his hand up her shirt and settled in for an enjoyable evening at home with the woman he loved.

THE END